"I MEAN NOTHING TO YOU . . ."

"You got that right," Jack said. "You mean nothing to me. I mean nothing to you. You understand that? You saved me when I needed you and I just felt I owed you."

"Y-you owe me nothing. . . ." Holly choked, biting her lower lip . . . pink and soft and moist.

"Don't look at me like that."

"L-like what?"

"Dammit, don't you look at me like you care. . . ."

He'd break her heart, and his own, too. He was tired of being alone, tired of being with women he bought and paid for. He needed this one stolen moment of purity.

Christ, he needed to love again . . .

SEASONS OF GOLD

STEF ANN HOLM

POCKET BOOKS

New York   London   Toronto   Sydney   Tokyo   Singapore

An *Original* Publication of POCKET BOOKS

POCKET BOOKS, a division of Simon & Schuster Inc.
1230 Avenue of the Americas, New York, NY 10020

ISBN: 0-671-74126-8

First Pocket Books printing February 1992

10 9 8 7 6 5 4 3 2 1

POCKET and colophon are registered trademarks of
Simon & Schuster Inc.

Cover art by Susan Tang

Printed in the U.S.A.

This book is dedicated with love to my grandmother, Agnes Blomquist, whose fondness of western lore led me to Deadwood, South Dakota.

Chapter One

March 1877
Deadwood Gulch
Dakota Territory

T ake them off, mister." Holly Dancer barely glanced up from the table she was intent on clearing. Her fleeting look was substantial enough to detect a gleam of silver at his hips through the open curtain of his ankle-length coat.

Continuing with her task, she shivered at the breath of bone-chilling damp air the tall stranger had brought in with him. It seeped through the thread-worn material of her skirt, and she wondered if he'd closed the front doors of the restaurant all the way. She took a quick turn over her shoulder to check.

Holly's gaze met a pair of smoky gray eyes. Their startling color shocked her down to the tips of her toes. They were cold and turbulent, like the storm clouds outside that had been unloading heavy rains all morning.

The wide brim of the man's hat dripped a smattering of raindrops on the pulled-up lapel of his single-caped ulster, the winter coat nearly reaching his ankles. Tiny droplets ran down his square jaw, as if the rain had been too much for even his sugarloaf to keep at bay. His dangerous eyes drew her attention back again. To her dismay, he stared boldly at her, not at all making a move to do as she'd requested.

1

Holly straightened her spine, the dirty dishes on her tray rattling. She did her best to disregard her apprehensions and forced herself to meet his gaze headlong. "I said, take them off, mister." For the first time since she'd been told to enforce the "no gun belt" rule in Goodnight's Restaurant, she wondered if this man would be the one to tell her to go to blazes.

He stared at her, a lazy half smile on his lips. His gaze slipped over her, coming to rest insolently on the swell of her breasts. "I thought this was a restaurant—or are you selling something else?"

His voice, a rich baritone, held a deep, mocking, and hard edge. The sound of it caused the fine reddish brown hairs at her nape to stand on end.

The implied insult hit her like a flash of lightning. The sharp sound of rain on the awnings outside suddenly became deafening in her ears. She stood to her full height and lifted her chin. "This *is* a restaurant. I was referring to your *guns*. If you want to take anything off after that, you'll have to go across the street to the Red Bird."

He gave an inconsequential perusal of the weaponry at his lean hips and holstered underneath his left arm; then he looked up at her with a scowl riveted between his black brows. "Are you serious?"

"Quite serious." Holly had no doubts he'd button up his rain-soaked ulster and leave to seek the comforts of a disreputable establishment.

To her surprise, he slipped his greatcoat off his sinewy frame and hung it on the coat tree. The corner of his mouth lifted, and he gave her another heated stare. "I'll sample the menu this side of the street first."

"Then you'd best take off those guns." Normally she would make light of the suggestive undertones from the more aggressive male patrons. However, she felt certain this man would turn her playful retorts to his own advantage.

As he unfastened the wide, plain-bar buckle of the belt that anchored his waist holster, she couldn't help noticing his long and nimble, bronzed and taut fingers. "Why are you so hell-bent on disarming me?"

2

Her eyes settled on his flashy revolver, ominous in size and far longer barreled than the revolvers that seemed so common in Deadwood. "Because the owners have had their window shot out two times in as many months and it's too costly to keep replacing the glass."

He untied the leather thong at the tight outline of his thigh. "And this is their answer?" He hung the belt by its buckle on a wall peg where several other patrons' holsters dangled, suspended for the duration of their meals.

"We can't control the bullets on the street, but we can see to it none are exchanged in the restaurant."

As he licked the rain from his lips, his mouth curved into a rough smile. His rakish grin brought an uneasy churning to the bottom of her stomach. "I'm not going to argue the logistics on the matter, I'm too damn hungry."

Rather than disengage his shoulder holster, he merely withdrew his Smith & Wesson revolver and hung it precariously by the finger grip.

"I'm light now." Removing his ivory Stetson, he slapped it against his leg to rid it of water. "Well, do I get to eat, or not?"

Holly's eyes widened. She was used to serving less than honorable patrons, but this one looked menacing and strikingly handsome at the same time. A small, razor-thin scar at the corner of his right eye ran down to the top of his ear. She fleetingly wondered how he'd gotten it. Brushing off her observation, she snatched one of the small menus she kept in the pocket of her dark gingham apron. She handed it to him, intent on seating him as quickly as possible. "This way please."

She didn't have to go far. The restaurant only had seven tables, four of which were occupied at the moment. "Do you need any more coffee, Earl?"

The miner to whom she spoke as she passed by declined with an easy smile and continued to read his morning edition of the *Black Hills Pioneer*.

Holly stopped and gestured for the stranger to take a seat. "You can have this one."

"No," he refused rigidly. "I'll take that one." Pointing to

the table along the side wall, he moved past her and settled into one of the bow-backed Windsor chairs. As he leaned against the wall, his gaze flicked to the two front windows, the entrance doors, and the revolving door that led into the kitchen.

"Would you like—"

"Coffee," he interrupted flatly, plopping his hat down and staring expectantly at her. Damp and untamed jet black hair framed his chiseled face. It waved slightly over his ears and past the wide breadth of his shoulders. He ran his fingers through the thick, inky mane, pushing the distracting locks from his temple. "Coffee," he reiterated. "Black."

His rudeness made her grit her teeth together so hard, she felt as if she'd snap her jaw in two. She suddenly had the urge to wipe the smug, self-satisfied look off his full lips. The practical importance of keeping her job quickly squashed that idea. Intending to fetch him his cup of coffee, she turned just as someone tugged the bow free of her apron string.

Holly whirled in a flash to catch Lee-Ash Malmer reaching out behind her with a sly grin on his grizzled face. She'd nearly forgotten he had been sitting at his usual table by the window.

Retying her apron, she gave her attention to Lee-Ash. As always, he made her smile when a smile was the furthest thing from her mind.

"Darlin', you goin' to give me a refill or are you goin' to make my old bones carry me over to the sideboard and fetch it m'self?"

"You're not old, Lee-Ash."

"Old enough to be your papa, darlin', but not old enough to stop tryin' to court you. You're the prettiest thing in Deadwood."

Despite herself, she felt the heat of a blush on her face. She readily retrieved the enamel coffeepot from its holder on the sideboard and refilled her friend's cup with the steaming dark brew.

"That's sweet of you, darlin'," Lee-Ash thanked her as he took a slow sip.

Holly looked down on his weathered face, a strong surge of love toward the miner warming her heart. Though he was far from old—maybe in his late fifties—the years of placer mining had taken their toll on Lee-Ash. His face classified as ruddy, his cheekbones hollow. Above his upper lip, a full mustache bore the bristles of more than a few gray hairs.

He had been her salvation after Billy's murder; he had been her only friend.

She gazed down at his miner's togs—heavy boots, corduroy pants, and flannel shirt—knowing he'd be going out to mine his claim in the abominable weather. "Maybe you should stay in town today, Lee-Ash," she pleaded softly. "The weather isn't fit for anything, and Sioux have been more aggressive since signing over the Black Hills last month."

Lee-Ash adjusted the dark blue forage cap on his whitening hair. Grasping the flat platform bill, he pulled it farther down over his brow, then brushed his fingers over the three gold stars that ornamented the front. He'd once told Holly he'd been a colonel in the Civil War, and she'd never been given any cause to doubt him. "Nope, darlin', I'm bound to hit blackjack today."

"Well, I'll be out mining with you Wednesday, for sure." She rested her hand gently on his shoulder. He gave it a little squeeze with his dirt-stained fingers.

Taking another sip of coffee, he sent her a wink over the cup's rim. "You get any more offers to sell out your claim?"

"A few."

"Maybe you should sell out, darlin'. You're workin' yourself into an early grave. It ain't right, a woman soft as you."

Holly frowned. "I can handle it. It's bound to pay off big, Lee-Ash. I know it."

"Just the same, I ain't never seen a dead man give a damn about money."

She affectionately grinned at his concern, that moment more glad than ever of their friendship. Their claims adjoined, and he stubbornly guarded hers against jumpers while she worked for Mrs. Goodnight. On her days off, he

5

would come for her, and they'd ride out of town together to work on their respective claims. They'd share lunch and talk over their ideas on mining and anything else. It had been that way . . . ever since Billy . . .

But she didn't want to think about Billy now. Yet even as she was trying to dust the cobwebs from her mind, she felt the gunslinger's smoky eyes on her. He only served as a reminder that Billy had been gunshot in the back, robbed for his small poke of gold dust. To this day, the sheriff had not been able to identify the person who had killed her husband.

It seemed so long ago, longer than seven months. She'd changed so much. Deadwood had changed. She no longer viewed the town through innocent eyes; no longer did the wild streets kindle her girlish imagination. Now she had a woman's mind. And Billy . . . well, he'd changed her; he'd done things. Things still too painful for her to sort out.

Holly felt a jerking on her apron tail again, and she smiled thinking it was Lee-Ash trying to pull her out of her reverie. But the wayward gesture had come from behind. She returned to the present with an uncontrollable thud of her heart.

Turning, she saw the giver of the playful tug was the newcomer, his mouth shaped in a tight line. "That got the old-timer a cup of coffee. I figured that's what a man had to do around here to get one."

A thousand icy retorts formed in Holly's head, but for the life of her, she couldn't spit one out.

"Son," Lee-Ash called, as the tables sat close enough that the miner's voice needn't be raised to converse with the stranger, "that right is reserved for me only." Though Lee-Ash spoke the warning in a light tone, it was a warning just the same.

Rather than have the two men bicker, Holly quickly grabbed a cup from the sideboard. She practically slammed the mug down on the table and filled it. Squaring her shoulders, she took out her ordering pad. "Have you made up your mind what you'd like to eat?"

"What do I have to do to get it?" His smooth voice carried an underlying insinuation. To her chagrin, she found her gaze drawn to his lips again—full and sensuously shaped—and for a scant second, she wondered about their softness.

"J-just what the blazes do you mean by that?" she sputtered.

"It took a pull on your apron to get a cup of coffee. Just wondering what it takes to get a plate of food."

His eyes raked over her lithe body outlined in a navy serge dress as if searching for more bows to pull. Thankfully, there were none. Only an army of tiny buttons marching down the front in the small valley of her breasts.

Vexed by his blatant examination, Holly threatened him without thinking of the consequences. "You do that again, mister, and you'll find yourself at the Red Bird with an empty stomach."

Lee-Ash leaned over on the heels of his chair and added, "Only a fool riles a skunk, a mule, or a cook, son. You'd best hobble your lip . . . and your eyes."

Frowning down on his menu, the man didn't appear challenged by the wisdom in Lee-Ash's words. "Then I guess I'll order a steak and three scrambled eggs. You have Saratoga chips?" he queried, lifting his dark brows in expectation.

"They're a dinner item."

"I haven't eaten since yesterday's lunch, so it feels like dinner to me." He stretched out the dog-eared menu for her to take, his knuckles inadvertently brushing over her wrist. The heated contact sent her pulse to an erratic rhythm. "Charge me whatever you want for them."

Holly stared at the dark straps of his black suspenders, which contrasted against the pristine whiteness of his wool shirt. She couldn't argue with a request like that. "All right, I will. But I can assure you we're not cheap."

The deep rumble of his laughter couldn't have caught her more off guard. "You've made that quite clear, baby."

"Yes, well . . ." She was so nonplussed over his change in character, she fumbled for a reply. "Yes, well, remember that." She turned to go when his resonant voice stopped her short. Keeping her back toward him, she refused to face him again.

"I like my steak rare."

7

Holly didn't acknowledge she'd heard him when she moved on. She silently refilled other coffee cups, then disappeared through the revolving door to the kitchen.

Once inside the cozy cooking area, she slammed the near-empty enamel pot onto the butcher's island. Her actions startled the two women, mother and daughter, at the zinc-lined dry sink; they looked up with expressions of curiosity in their hazel eyes while Holly rattled off a peculiar mix of Polish and Czechoslovakian under her breath.

"I am sorry, Mrs. Goodnight, Carrie," Holly apologized, suddenly flustered over her outburst.

"It's all right, Mrs. Dancer," Mrs. Josephine Goodnight assured in an easy tone. "I've taken on that old pot myself more than a time or two. Bad customer?"

"I'm not sure."

Holly pressed the pads of her hands against the worn grain of the block and tried to collect herself. She ran her fingertips across her wrist as if to wipe the man's touch from her skin. What had gotten into her? Usually she could jest with the customers, even those making more suggestive comments. She'd never been downright rude. Why had this . . . this gunslinger gotten the best of her?

Inhaling deeply, Holly gave Carrie his order.

"Can you start it, Mrs. Dancer? I'm almost finished with these pies." Carrie expertly whisked the wooden roller over buttery dough.

"Of course." Holly scanned the disorderly area for the large frying pan.

The kitchen was made up of a hodgepodge of appliances. The painted red dough box and cherrywood preserves cupboard gave the room its color. The tin-paneled pie safe sparkled in the corner. Across from them, the wall cupboard housed dishes and utensils arranged in neat rows like soldiers ready to march. Cluttering the stove, banned to the far wall, were the wooden bowls, paddles, and spoons.

Holly found a freshly washed pan by the cast-iron stove, wrinkling her nose at the charred odor coming from underneath the metal plates. She glanced at Carrie, who confirmed her suspicions.

"Blackened again," the honey-haired girl said as she pinched the edges of an apple pie together.

"I've almost given up on the new one getting here. Did you send that inquiry wire like I asked you?" the girl's mother asked, dumping a handful of onions into the hash grinder.

A guilty red flushed Carrie's face. "I forgot."

"Landsakes, girl, I don't know how you can when the stove stares at you every day as a reminder. You must have other things on your mind." Then Josephine's face creased in a smile. "Perhaps Mr. Conrath La Fors."

"Mother," the girl groaned, but her eyes sparkled brightly.

Holly shook the stove's damper and checked the fire underneath the plate. "I'll go to the telegraph office this week and wire Cheyenne for you."

"Thank you, Mrs. Dancer. I'd appreciate that," Josephine Goodnight said, cranking the handle of the grinder.

Holly deposited a thick slab of beef into the hot skillet. Brushing back a few stray strands of hair from her temple, she crossed the room and pushed open the revolving door a fraction.

Her lips turned down in a frown. She thought that maybe the gunman by some chance decided to go to the Red Bird after all. No such luck.

He occupied the same chair she'd left him in.

His booted feet stretched out in front of him, and his arms folded across his chest, Jack Steele surveyed the sidewalk outside the window. He missed nothing, no one. He noticed every hat, every face that went with it, and every gun not concealed underneath the protection of a coat—going as far as to define the caliber of those distinguishable by an outline. From there he inspected the boggy, rutted road that served as the major thoroughfare into Deadwood.

The icy rain had done little to slow down the noisy traffic of freight wagons and bullwhackers on Main Street. Teams of oxen labored in the cold air, their panting breaths creating large, misty gray clouds. Solitary riders trudged through the congested maze, angling for premium spots at the hitch rails.

A muscle quivered in Steele's jaw and he turned sharply toward the kitchen entry just as the door's edge revolved back into place and the pair of sky blue eyes disappeared. His hand had automatically gone down into the side of his right boot; he halted upon seeing who peeked at him. He should have been used to being glared at by now.

A fleeting twinge of remorse ran through him that perhaps he'd been too hard on her, but it snapped before it took hold. He wasn't in the business of making friends. Christ, but if he were, he'd sure try to make more than "friends" with this woman. She was the best-looking female he'd seen in a long time. Not like the town whores he sometimes associated with for business and—hell, if he was being honest with himself—pleasure. Painted and powdered, they offered cheap imitations of what a real lady should be. This one, though, possessed genuine quality.

He'd had the chance to freely appraise her while she'd been pouring coffee for the other customers after taking down his order.

Some would say she was too thin, but he wasn't overly fond of women with a healthy amount of flesh on their bodies. He hadn't been able to call her pretty, it being too common a word for her. She was striking in an exotic way. Her rose-hued cheekbones were high, almost too distinguished, but they went with her slender torso; her well-shaped nose tilted slightly.

Recalling her mouth, a rich shade of pink, now made him hold in a short laugh thinking how she'd compressed it while putting up with his demands. He had the feeling she didn't know just how enticing those lips were, full and lush.

Jack inhaled deeply and let his breath out slowly, drumming his fingertips on the tabletop. Her stunning face—no matter how soft and tempting—didn't stand a chance against cold reason; he'd come here to do a job. How long had it been since a respectable woman had given him the time of day? Weeks, months . . . ? He groaned at the thought, but it could very well have been years. Years without roots, years without a home. But he'd had all that and given it up. He'd sacrificed it all to become a man without a past.

"I swear, I ain't never seen jewelry like that, son." The old-timer's words broke through the miserable turn Jack's recollections had taken, and he turned his head. The miner gawked admiringly at his expensive shoulder holster. "Fine piece of leather goods."

Jack nodded once, reluctant to give the old man any kind of verbal encouragement. He was rewarded for his reticence by another question.

"You don't talk much, do you?" Lee-Ash's graying brows raised in amused contempt. " 'Less it's to fang a little venom in someone. You're about as sassy as a brace of rattle-snakes."

"No one asked you." Jack brushed off the comment, and yet deep inside him, the barb had pierced like a rusty nail in the pit of his soul. It was rare—if ever—someone dared to insult him.

"Damn right," Lee-Ash snorted, tugging on the bill of his hat. "But where Holly's concerned, I speak m'peace. Son, we may not have very many respectable women in Dead-wood, but the ones we do have, we durn well take care of."

Jack licked his lips and clenched his teeth into a taut smile. "I'll remember that."

Glancing toward the kitchen door once more, Jack heard his stomach rumble in empty protest. Where the hell was she with his breakfast? Hunger gnawed his tolerance to the nub. He'd ridden hard all night battling the wintry rains, and his patience had dwindled to a short fuse, just itching to be set off by one match. And that match was in the kitchen peeping at him when she should have been rustling up some food.

"Never seen a gun like that one there."

Jack followed the old man's line of vision to the diamond-engraved revolver that hung up on the peg in its waist-belt holster.

"Buntline," Jack mumbled. "There's only six like it."

"Buntline what?"

"Ned Buntline—he modified it. It's a Colt's single-action .45."

"Mind if I take a quick look?" Lee-Ash righted to his feet, not giving Jack a chance to deny him. "Durn, the girls catch me with this and I'll get the broom for sure." Pulling the twelve-inch-barreled gun from its worn holster, Lee-Ash weighed it in his hand. "Heavy piece of iron. How the blazes you—"

Jack saw the woman—Holly—approach Lee-Ash with a none-to-happy look on her face. Her azure eyes signaled storm clouds on the horizon. The frame of spiky dark lashes narrowed in unleashed ire. He thought to warn the miner he'd be caught, then decided against it. He wasn't in the good Samaritan business. At least she'd finally brought his food.

She didn't give Jack a second look as she crashed the steaming plate down on the table in front of him, some of the Saratoga potato chips hopping off the side and onto the table.

"Lee-Ash, just what do you think you're doing with *that?*"

Lee-Ash nearly jumped out of his boots. "Now, darlin', don't go gettin' yourself in a ruckus! I was only lookin' at it. I'm not settin' out to shoot up the place."

Jack took up the salt shaker and gave his steak a liberal dose. "You best put it back, old man. The hammer's down on empty. One slip and it'll blow the lady's heart out." He cut into the beef as if what he'd said were nothing more than a mere observation of the weather.

His fork abruptly clattered to the plate, the speared piece of steak still on it. "What the hell is this? I said rare, not *raw!*"

Holly snapped her head toward him, feeling her face warm. "We're having stove trouble." The idea of serving him a barely cooked slice of meat had begun out of spite over his flagrant undertones, but following the plan through hadn't given her the satisfaction she'd thought it would. Embarrassment stole through her.

"For Christ's sake, I can't eat it this way."

She tried her best to ignore his exasperation, recalling the anger she felt toward him. Though she was more than a little scared of him, the prospect of the restaurant being shot up

12

made her forget about her shame. "I thought I told you to keep that gun on the wall, mister." Her head jerked to the miner. "Lee-Ash! Aim that thing at the floor!"

Jack poked around at his eggs, looking for any kind of hidden objects. "I did. Look to your friend here. He keeps holding it like that and it's going to go off for sure. Look at the trigger."

Two pairs of eyes did just that. The trigger, held back by a piece of rawhide, squeezed against the finger grip.

"All you do is thumb that hammer, old man, and the fancy window is shot to hell."

"Well, put it down, Lee-Ash!"

Lee-Ash hesitated and examined the ingenuity of the gun. "I ain't never seen the likes of this before. This one of them quick-draw gimmicks?"

Having found no booby traps in his eggs, Jack grew more than mildly entertained by Holly's outburst. She made a damn enlivening sight, her eyes all glittery with fire, her small, upturned breasts swelling against the blue of her dress at her indignant huffs.

"The gun goes back on the wall, mister." Her accent, more pronounced, gave him a moment to consider its origin. He couldn't quite distinguish it. "If you want to eat—"

Her next words became cut off as a tall, lean man sporting a drooping mustache noisily pushed open the doors of the restaurant. All eyes moved to the newcomer, Jack's included. Holly briefly noticed his fingers tightening on his fork, the veins becoming prominent on top of his hand.

From the front of the man's woolen overcoat, the gleam of a badge winked.

Holly spoke first. "Sheriff, what's wrong?"

Sheriff Seth Bullock's keen eyes, rimmed with red, looked as if he hadn't slept all night. His voice came swift, yet he spoke distinctly, like the educated man he was. "I just rode in from Gold Run and down around Lead. There was a stage holdup last midnight." His tone lowered. "Johnny Slaughter has been shot and killed by road agents."

"Oh, no . . ." Holly breathed softly with disbelief. Johnny Slaughter drove the Sidney and Black Hills Stage Coach. He'd been the first person she and Billy had met upon leaving New York who'd actually seen the streets of Deadwood.

He'd driven their Concord coach from the Nebraska plains, giving them their first glimpse of the Black Hills. She'd noticed the creek that ran parallel to the stage road, shocked to see the water a vivid scarlet. Johnny had told them the Sioux must have been out for blood the night before. She'd felt needles down her spine and shuddered until Johnny jokingly laughed and said Whitewood Creek ran red because of the many mine tailings being washed down the stream.

At the time, she could have cuffed the man for scaring her. Billy had laughed it off, but then, Billy usually laughed at any joke. Especially the ones that made her look foolish. She'd seen Johnny several times since then, and he'd gone out of his way to be extra nice to her, as if he'd felt bad about frightening her so.

"Poor Johnny . . ." Hot tears blinded her vision, and Holly fought to keep them under control.

Seth removed the heavy gloves from his fingers with a quick tug. "I've got a posse organized, and I'd be beholden if you could fetch us up some hot coffee."

"Anything at all."

"Need any extra men?" Lee-Ash didn't hesitate to ask.

"No, Colonel." Seth's look was solemn. "If it's any comfort to you, Mrs. Dancer, he didn't suffer any. He was shot in the heart and died quickly." The sheriff blew his breath on his hands and rubbed them together, a puzzled expression coming over his face. "Strange, though. The chest wound left twelve buck shot in a perfect circle. I've never seen anything like it in all my days as a lawman. It appears he was hit by a professional."

Holly felt the color drain from her face. Frozen with terror, it took all of her strength to turn a slow glance to the powerfully tall man behind her. Her heart beat so frantically, she felt it right down to her fingertips, pulsating and pumping wildly.

Lee-Ash still held the Colt's Buntline Special in his hand, and he gingerly, as if handling a thin glass bottle of nitroglycerin, set it down on the table in front of Jack. "Son, I believe this is yours."

Chapter Two

*H*olly questioned the stranger with her eyes, hoping he would vehemently deny her silent accusation. His face could have been carved in granite. It revealed nothing. She tried to keep her fragile control from faltering, but her mind ran away with the image of Johnny Slaughter's slumped-over body, his heart shot out. Only moments ago, this man had warned Lee-Ash his awesome revolver could take out hers.

She wanted to scream to Seth that a suspect could very well be right under his nose! As she thought of a way to sneak the sheriff off so she could tell him, he addressed the gunslinger himself.

"Jackson Ledgeway Steele, if my memory serves me right. I recognize you from your tintype." Seth stuffed his rawhide gloves in the pocket of his coat.

Holly involuntarily moved away from the table. Jackson Ledgeway Steele. His name fit him, ominous as the gun he strapped to his thigh.

"I don't believe I know you." Jack's low and smooth voice edged an iron command.

"I know you. I've got a warrant for your arrest down at my office. Damn shame it's invalid now."

"Damn shame," Jack mocked, his gaze unwavering.

Seth Bullock laughed with a sharp bite. "Funny how all those witnesses in Texas just disappeared."

"Funny."

"Where were you last night, Steele?" Seth leaned over to straddle his arms on the tabletop, his fingers curling under the edge.

Holly could barely breathe anticipating Steele's answer. She tossed a quick look to the sideboard for the fresh coffeepot. If a ruckus broke out, she'd lump his head with it.

"Am I being accused of something, Sheriff?" Jack's dry tone bore the brittleness of a fall leaf.

Seth pulled back. "That all depends. You're lucky we've got a lead that Sam Bass's gang was responsible. From what I've heard, you're not a man to ride with a pack of outlaws. You're your own enemy."

Jack gave vent to a caustic laugh. "You figure all that out from one tintype and a stale warrant?"

"You bet, Steele. I'm the best." He aimed a loaded forefinger at Jack. "Remember that on your way out of Deadwood."

Pressing his shoulders into the semicurved chairback, Jack crossed his arms over his chest. "I'm not planning on leaving Deadwood. I thought I'd stay and play the saloons. Do a little scratching for Black Hills gold."

The drollness of his intention caused Holly to wonder what he meant by it. Since the sheriff apparently had matters in hand, she discarded the idea of the coffeepot, perturbed at herself for having thought of it in the first place.

Holly left the group, slipping into the kitchen. She returned a short time later with the other two women and a wicker basket covered by a coarsely woven cloth to keep the cold out. Handing it to Seth, she told him, "We packed some biscuits and ham slices, too."

"Obliged, ladies." He accepted the offering and gave Jack a final counseling. "I'll be watching you, Steele. I catch you with anything but house cards in your fingers, these fetters—" he patted the shining silver ring of a handcuff that stuck out of his coat pocket "—will be on your wrists while the cards are still in your hands."

"I'll keep that in mind."

17

"You'd be smart to." Turning, the sheriff strode from the restaurant. Frosty fingers of air pervaded the wake of his path. They swirled around the flannel drawers and petticoats underneath Holly's dress. Her skin chilled, but this time it had nothing to do with the cold.

Lee-Ash eyed Jack cautiously, then returned to his seat.

With solemn faces, Carrie and Josephine returned to the kitchen. Holly felt gooseflesh skittering to attention on every inch of her body. "I'll add up your bill, ah, Mr. Steele. I'm sure you're anxious to be on your way."

"I haven't finished my meal." Jack gave his plate a once-over. "What there is of it that's edible."

"We really are having stove trouble." She said it more to convince herself his bloody steak really could have been the fault of the cooking appliance. Since he seemed set on staying until his hunger was appeased, Holly hastened to add, "I'll bring you some flapjacks."

He flared his nostrils and glowered at her. "You think I killed your friend?"

Swallowing hard, Holly looked to Lee-Ash, then back at Jack. "I . . ." She certainly wasn't going to admit he scared her to death—not to his face. "If Seth had thought you'd killed Johnny, he would have arrested you."

"Goes to show you how a person's character can be misjudged, wouldn't you say?" Jack stretched his tapered, Levi's-clad legs out in front of him and kicked off a clump of mud from his splotched Wellington boots.

She backed away, her pulse spinning a faint thread of hysteria through her. Was he baiting her again? "I'll get those pancakes. . . ." The silvery gleam of his .45 caught her eye as she turned away. *"That—"* she pointed to the Buntline "—is going back where it belongs."

As if picking up a dead mouse by its tail, she pinched hold of the revolver's barrel and carried it to Steele's gun belt and slipped it safely inside the holster.

She reappeared several minutes later with a new plate for him. Scurrying about the restaurant, she tried not to dwell on Jack while he ate. As soon as she saw him finish the last bite, she calculated his bill and handed it to him. "I didn't charge you for the steak."

"Honorable of you. I'm sure—" His words abruptly cut short, as if he'd taken a single-edged bowie to them. The next thing Holly knew, he was lunging at her.

She screamed in horror as his sinewy arm curled roughly around her waist and brought her crashing to the floor. Her bearings completely in a jumble, she blindly saw Jack reach down into the side of his boot. He withdrew a small-caliber Frontier revolver just as the thunder of horse's hooves clattered over the boardwalk in front of the restaurant. She barely caught a flashing glimpse of the rider's head and shoulders. He wore a hat slung low over his forehead, and a blue bandanna covered his nose and mouth.

A bullet exploded into the room, and the sharp sound of breaking glass echoed in her ears.

Disorientated and frightened, Holly shrieked at the top of her lungs. Jack put his hand savagely over her mouth, his fingers clamped against her tender skin. "Shut up!" he hissed between gritted teeth.

Then the roaring of rapid gunfire dazed her hearing as Jack squeezed off a succession of bullets. After each piercing report, glass shattered down to the floor.

With Jack's full weight above her, Holly wasn't able to see anything. His well-muscled legs wrapped around her thighs like a vise.

She heard him curse under his breath once the hoofbeats left the boardwalk, dimming as they pounded down the street. He removed his hand from her mouth and slid it over the slope of her neck, locking his fingers on her shoulder. With his face only a fraction of an inch from hers, she stared into the dark depths of his eyes.

For a timeless minute, she was consciously aware of him. She'd never had such intimate contact with a man except Billy, and his lean body had been nothing to compare to the solid contours of Steele's. She felt every button of his shirt brand her through the bodice of her dress.

Her chest heaved with the effort to breathe. She gasped breathlessly, her voice hoarse and low. "I—I thought you said you weren't armed."

"I lied."

Holly quaked at the cool way he admitted it.

Jack thrust his body upward, his heavy weight upon her gone. He extended his arm and pulled Holly to her feet. No sweat marred his hand, the tendons deathly strong and subdued with warmth and calluses.

"Durn blazes to Hades!" Lee-Ash shook the dangerous rubble from his forage cap. He'd been underneath his table and now stood up. "Son, somebody doesn't like you."

"Whoever it was is on his way out of Deadwood by now. Damn fast. You all right?" Jack asked Holly.

She nodded and snatched her hand out of his.

"The shooter was a sorry marksman," Jack said as he assessed the street that moments ago composed a sea of activity. It was now barren as a prairie; anyone with half a brain had run indoors. "Missed you by a long shot."

"M-me? Me?" she repeated, feeling one of the tortoise-shell side-combs slip from her hair and land with a patter on the floor. "I think you've got that wrong, mister." *Ping*, a hairpin joined the comb. Who would possibly want to shoot at her?

"I'm never wrong," he retorted. "You holding together, old man?"

Lee-Ash came protectively to Holly's side and gruffly patted her shoulder. "Hell, yes. If this don't beat all, darlin'. There ain't never been any durn blatant shots in here. Usually just the stray ones."

Several long strands of Holly's mahogany hair framed her pale face in a wild disarray. Her lower lip quivered and she sought to steady it between her teeth.

"Guess your gun enforcement is a waste of time," Jack observed with a bite Holly wanted to bark at.

Straightening her spine, she retaliated. "There wouldn't have been any shots fired if you hadn't been here!"

His brow arched arrogantly. "I wouldn't make a wager on that."

Outside, a small crowd gathered to peer inside the restaurant, satisfying their curiosity and seeing if anyone needed a trip to the funeral parlor.

The kitchen door revolved open with the creak of a dry wagon wheel. Josephine Goodnight wedged her round face through the inch-wide crack. Upon viewing the disaster, she swung the door open full force. "Landsakes! What in heaven's name happened? We heard the shots. . . . Mrs. Dancer! Are you all right?"

Holly mutely nodded as the woman came over to her. Together, they walked to the piles of jagged shards littering the floor to survey the damage.

The left window, where the gunman had taken a triangular wedge from the pane, held intact. Spidery cracks fanned out from it, but it wouldn't be too costly to replace. Jack's damage, on the other hand, would mean replacing the entire bottom sash of the left window, both door insets, and the top two panes of the right window. "Did you have to go and bust them *all* out?" Holly finally asked.

"Sorry for the inconvenience, ladies. I suppose I should have opened them first." The sarcasm in his apology was more heavily barbed than a wire fence. "Better yet, opened the doors and given him a full target."

Jack strode heavily on his booted heels toward the wall peg. He grabbed his waist-holster and buckled it on without a word.

"Where are you going?" Holly's composure came back.

"I prefer my meals cooked, and without lead in them. Guess now you've got more than stove trouble."

"You'll have to wait a minute, *Mr. Steele,*" Holly called to him. "I need to recalculate your bill."

"Get on out of there, Dewdrop!" Holly clutched the narrow handrailing and whipped her reticule over her head by its strings. She would have tossed the lightweight purse at the nanny goat if it would have done any good. But nothing ever did.

She stood on the outside steps of Goodnight's Restaurant that led to her living quarters above the kitchen. She inclined her head at the pecan-colored animal who grazed in the tiny plot she called a garden. Her face grew grim as she watched Dewdrop nibble away at the few precious green shoots. Growing anything but gold in Deadwood could be heralded as a miracle, and she'd managed to breathe a little life into a few seeds that would have been carrots, turnips, rhubarb, and, she'd hoped, lettuce. With nearly all fruits and vegetables coming from a can, it would have been nice to have something fresh.

"Durn goat." Holly left the stairs and shooed the nanny with a wave of her hand. It only sent the animal toward her looking for food in her gloved palm. "Get on, Dew. I don't have anything for you. Go back to the Gem."

Holly pushed down the fur-trimmed hood of her woolen pelisse and tilted her face to the sky. Snow weather, she thought, as she watched the gunmetal clouds above her swirling and clustering into odd-shaped formations. They took away what precious little sun the deep gully of Deadwood ever received. Most times, the winter mornings stayed dark until a high sun leaped fully blown from White Rocks.

No sun, no vegetables.

"Come on, Dew," she sighed, and returned her gaze to the goat. "I can't fight the clouds and a goat today."

The nanny shook her stubby horns and twitched her tail as Holly crossed over to the small, screen-enclosed porch at the side of the restaurant. She took up a short piece of rope and tied it around Dewdrop's neck. "Let's go."

Holly moved through the narrow alleyway wedging Goodnight's Restaurant and Bent and Deetkin's Drugstore to the hubbub of activity that beckoned ahead.

One word could easily describe Deadwood's Main Street: mud.

Mud covered everything. Horses were coated with it, vehicles were painted with it, sidewalks were sunk inches deep in it. Between the slippery mud and garbage, combined with the manure from horses, mules, and oxen, Main Street could be called nothing short of a first-class sewer bog.

Getting from one side of it to another left the traveler with an experience he'd never forget. Several crossing spots had thick timber planks laid over the muck, but they were so slick, one could barely stay on them; every person's step threw up a shower of mud as if from some huge atomizer. But for all the good intentions the planks served, they created large mill ponds, damming up what little drainage the street afforded.

Onto this quagmire, Holly and Dewdrop skittered and elbowed their way through a jostling crowd.

Holly decided to go to the Black Hills Telegraph Office first, then take Dew to the Gem so she wouldn't have to backtrack.

The voices of roistering miners, untutored tenderfoots, and noisy bullwhackers echoed across the congested street. The mooing of tired and panting cattle, the loud braying of mules, and the incessant rasping of numerous saws and the resounding blows of many hammers comprised the sound of Deadwood. With real estate an immense commodity, new buildings began framing daily as others completed the final shingles of a roof. The fleeting smell of pine never got quite strong enough to overcome the foulness of the road, and the passerby often wondered if he'd really smelled something good at all.

Amidst the pandemonium, a woman with a goat in tow didn't give the rowdy men who occasioned the streets cause to laugh. In fact, just viewing a woman in skirts—ugly or beautiful—was enough to send every hat in Deadwood to tip politely toward her, almost creating a fine breeze in her wake from the subtle gestures.

Though with the town matrons, it was a different story. They didn't approve of Holly doing man's work without a man by her side. Their greetings came to her in the form of pursed lips and shaking chins.

As usual, Holly gave a courteous nod of her head. Nothing more; nothing less. Her face bore the perfect image of dignity and respectability. After Billy had been killed, she'd been so overrun by suitors, she'd fairly taken to locking herself in her room. But once word had gotten around that the widow Dancer had no intentions of any upcoming nuptials, the young bucks had backed down—a little. There were always those whose persistence kept at her like an uninvited wasp on a picnic outing. Namely, Devlin Breedlove.

At the thought of Breedlove, she frowned and tugged on Dewdrop's rope. Turning down Lee Street, she entered the telegraph office. Mud already covered the floor from previous visitors' shoes; her side-buttoned ones were no exception. She needn't bother lifting her skirt. She wore her hems several inches shorter than the current fashions for hygienic reasons due to the bad street conditions.

"Mrs. Dancer," James Halley greeted with a bob of his visored head. He looked beyond her to Dewdrop, who had trouble maintaining her footing over the planked floor.

Holly pretended not to notice his inquiring stare and got on with business as if it were completely normal for her to be in the company of a nanny goat. "I'd like to send a wire to Cheyenne, please. Are the lines up today?"

"Last I checked," he said, still eyeing Dewdrop skeptically. Shaking his head as if to clear it, he shuffled through the disorganized clutter of papers and wires on his desk. He found a clean pad and pulled the pencil from its resting angle atop his ear. "What'll it be?" he asked, swiping his tongue over the lead point, then poising the implement over his pad.

She recited the message just as Mrs. Goodnight had instructed, addressed to the Dakota Freight Company in regard to the new range purchased from Perry and Co. Stove Works over two months ago. She paid Halley two pinches of gold dust and left him to stare at the white patch on Dewdrop's rump as they exited.

"Come on, Dew." She took them on the course toward lower Main, crossing through the section of town called the Badlands. It housed an infinite number of "cribs"—small, one-story dingy white houses with only room for a door and a tiny window. With increasing frequency the reputable establishments were thinning out, taken over by the numerous saloons and theaters. The Melodeon, Wide West Saloon, Nuttall and Mann's No. Ten, and Bella Union belched out song and merriment that flowed into the street.

Snuggling one gloved hand deeper into the folds of her pelisse, Holly wondered if Jack Steele played in one of the saloons she passed by. The thought of him still being in town both frightened and intrigued her. Much as she'd like to, she couldn't discount the fact that he was the most masculine and attractive man she'd ever seen. Though he was more than physically appealing; he had saved her life from random gunfire, and she put value on that.

Intuitively she felt Jack had an integrity that common sense should have told her wasn't there. Quite possibly he was a killer . . . a ruthless desperado without scruples or regrets. It didn't make sense, and she wasn't sure she wanted to try and figure him out. Maybe she had built his image up in her mind the past three days since he'd shot up the windows. Maybe he wasn't particularly attractive at all. He'd been so steel-edged, it made him appealing in a dangerous sort of way.

He'd given her two double-eagles. More than enough to compensate for the damage he'd done, and a generous tip for herself. She'd felt a consuming guilt about ruining his steak, but words of apology never formed on her lips.

She'd tried to put the incident out of her mind, thinking Jackson Ledgeway Steele had taken Sheriff Bullock's advice and left town.

The rattle of chips and whir of the roulette ball came filtering down on the street from the gaping doors of the Gem Theater.

Dewdrop stopped in her tracks, her cloven feet nearly skidded out from underneath her. She shook her head and bleated obnoxiously. Holly yanked on the rope, but the nanny refused to cooperate.

"Come on, you," she coaxed, and jerked a little harder. The goat only cried in protest. "We're here."

Holly adjusted her hold to grip the rope with both hands, then she gave a stiff pull, putting all her strength behind it. A tug that should have hauled the devil from Hades landed Holly flat on her bottom, her muddy feet swinging right out from under her.

She let out a string of incomprehensible words as Dewdrop nudged her with squat horns. A low laugh sounded from the doorway of the theater as Adley Seeks came up to lean against the frame.

"Miss Holly, what the hell are you doing down there?"

Holly's gaze met his mocking eyes. "Bringing back this starving critter of yours." She stayed put on the boardwalk, even though a small gathering of patrons had filled the doorway as well.

"Dew?" He called to the goat. "Come here, sugar." When

the nanny didn't readily come, Adley called over his shoulder in an unintelligible voice that soon saw his hands filled with a basin of foaming Gold Nugget beer. Dewdrop practically came at it in a run as Adley handed off the bowl to someone inside. The goat traipsed contentedly into the lighted interior of the Gem to seek her reward. "This goat is never out of my sight."

"You're a liar, Adley Seeks," she disputed. "You keep that goat out of my garden."

Adley crossed his arms over his vested chest and talked around the lump of chaw in his mouth. "Why don't you come inside and I'll buy *you* a glass of beer? We can talk about it."

"You're not going to get me in one of your boxes."

Adley was the "box herder" for the Gem, and Holly had no desire to be inside—or even outside, for that matter—with him. He'd been trying to entice her for months to take on a position entertaining men behind the curtained boxes of the saloon.

"I catch that goat on my property one more time and I'm talking to the sheriff."

"I'm sure he'll put it on his list of priorities, right there next to killings and the like." Adley's facetious tone made Holly all the madder knowing what he said rang true. Seth Bullock had more important things to do.

Holly made the move to struggle to her knees, her gloved hands digging deeper into the murky boardwalk. She shuddered and tried to push herself up. Behind her, a grip as strong as forged iron slipped around her waist. She screamed and swung her elbows, thinking Adley was trying to force her inside.

Looking back, she instantly stopped struggling, overwhelmed by the cold glint of gray eyes that penetrated her very soul.

Chapter Three

*H*olly's heartbeat drummed wildly in her ears as Jack Steele's hands tightened around her waist. He lifted her easily into the circle of his arms, her back coming in contact with the hardness of his chest. Her every nerve ending centered on him and she twisted in his embrace to see his face again. A sliver of amusement flickered in the eyes that met hers. One corner of his mouth pulled into a crooked smile.

At that moment she perceived that no false sense of romantic notions had overcome her sensibilities. He was everything she'd remembered.

"You having some new trouble today, Holly Dancer?"

His deep voice jolted her back to reality. She moved out of his hold and clapped the mud from her gloved hands. "Nothing I can't handle."

Garbed in a double-breasted gray shirt that mirrored the color of his eyes, Jack wore no coat. She quickly came to the conclusion he must have come from inside the Gem Theater.

"I expect you do have your own way of handling things." Jack pushed back the brim of his hat.

Adley snickered and ran his fingers through his oiled hair. "You got that right, Steele. She's a crazy one. I've seen her

27

dressed in Billy Dancer's old clothes going off to pick at that worthless claim of hers. Anyone else would have sold out and—"

"Seeks," Jack interrupted, "you don't have anything between your ears and above your neck."

It took a moment for Adley to figure out the riddle, then realization dawned on his slick face. "You didn't think so a minute ago when we were playing faro."

"What makes you think I didn't?"

Adley's face colored like a ripe tomato, his fists balling at his sides. "Why don't you come back inside and give me a chance to beat the tail off you, then?"

Jack reached around the edge of the open door. He retrieved his long black ulster and donned it with ease. "I've got an appointment with someone."

Adley snorted. "If you're thinking to go off with her"— he gave Holly a sharp stare—"you're setting your sights way off. She's like an ice cube in lemonade."

Holly felt a hot blush travel across her cheeks. Adley's dart hit home. The meaning drew exactly on what Billy had always told her.

Jack snatched Adley's collar in his hand and bunched up the material in a choking knot. He slammed him against the planked wall with the force of a bull and rammed his knee between the bouncer's legs. The impact intentionally fell short of the target, and profuse beads of sweat lined Adley's upper lip. "You son of a bitch," Jack snarled. "You ever say anything like that in front of the lady again and I'll have to teach you a lesson in manners."

The corner of Adley's left eye twitched uncontrollably. For a tense few seconds Jack held on to him; then, with disgust, he freed Adley with a shove.

Adley Seeks collected his cut-upon dignity and swiped off the splinters from his shirt-sleeves. "I didn't mean anything by it. Forget it and I'll buy you a drink."

"No."

Grunting, Adley straightened the starched collar of his expensive shirt. "Have it your way, then. Don't say that I didn't offer." He disappeared into the boisterous commotion of the Gem.

Holly had watched the entire spectacle with bewilderment. Before she could decipher the motivation behind Jack's actions, he walked away.

"W-wait! Wait for me!" she sputtered, and took off after him.

He'd thrust his hands into his coat pockets. His ragged breath billowed behind him in a white haze as he stalked toward Wall Street. She stared at him, not at all able to read him. The angle of his ivory hat made him look menacing. A deep scowl marked his forehead, and his full lips pressed together in a brooding line. After what had just transpired, she should have still been afraid of him. But she wasn't.

"What do you want?" Jack never lost the momentum of his strong steps.

"I—I . . ." Why was he so mad all of a sudden? "I wanted to thank you for standing up to Adley for me."

Jack stopped so abruptly at the corners of Wall and Main Streets that she nearly collided with him. "I'm heading across the street. This is where we part company."

Holly had planned on going to Adams Bros. Banner Grocery, but now that Jack claimed the same direction, she hesitated. Would he think she was following him? She quickly put that thought to rest. It was a public street. No sense in doing without the supplies Mrs. Goodnight needed.

"I have to cross the street, too," she finally said.

"I guess any respectable man would halt traffic and lay down his coat for you." Holly's eyes widened. "But I'm not respectable," he finished, cutting short her thoughts of chivalry. "No reason to ruin a good ulster."

"No, of course not."

"Hell, you're already covered with mud."

"Yes I am." Without as much as a backward glance, she ventured out on the precariously placed planks that sunk to below an ankle in places.

Without warning, Jack reached around behind her cloaked bottom and scooped her into his muscular arms. He held her tightly to his hard chest and stepped onto the thoroughfare.

"This isn't necessary!"

He ignored her proclamation as she tried to squirm loose. "Stop it or I'll drop you," he commanded, pulling her more securely into his grasp.

Breathless, Holly held in her outrage. "Put me down unless you want your coat full of mud."

"It'll wash off."

Furious, she tried to hold herself away from his chest. She refused to put her arm around his neck. Her gloved hand grazed his lapel; she wasn't able to discern the coarse fabric. The unique, rugged smell of him pulled her to him, but she leaned as far away as possible without falling out of his arms. However, the movement of his walk pushed her into his chest, defeating her with his every step.

Jack's footing held sure as he crossed through the throng of animal congestion; then he dodged a wide, sunken shaft at the side of the road. A miner's claim. Any piece of land in Deadwood marketed as fair game, even if that plot centered in the avenue of Main Street.

Reaching his goal, he stepped up on the unrefined boardwalk and stomped the mud from his Wellingtons.

Jack's face came very close to hers. His hardened edge vanished. Had she not been so confused by the moment, she would have seen the questioning unrest in his eyes changing his character; his face lit with a deep, troubled frown. Unaware of his quandary, she thought only that the man was not as rough as he pretended.

He curved his unyielding fingers tighter around her thighs, drawing her possessively toward him. His full mouth tipped only a whisper away. Afraid, she pulled back from him.

Jack's attitude brusquely changed. She heard him swear an oath, loosen his hold, and deposit her unsteadily on the sidewalk. She backed away on unsure feet, clutching the top of her hat with a shaky hand. Her cheeks blazed warm as any furnace, and probably just as red. What had just happened between them? It was so intangible, she couldn't begin to grasp an explanation.

"I've got an appointment." Jack finally spoke.

"Yes, so do I," she returned almost too quickly.

Jack made no effort to leave, and in that instant a female

voice cooed Jack's name. Holly's chin snapped up, and for the first time, she realized they stood in front of the Melodeon.

"Jackson Steele, I swan, this little ol' gal's been waiting scads of minutes for you!" A silvery blond woman with skin as white as magnolia petals draped herself at the entry doors of the Melodeon. She'd dressed scantily in a diaphanous gold wrapper, a tightly cinched satin corset and a red, short-ruffled petticoat billowing underneath. An assortment of cosmetics made up her cherubic face, serving to enhance her plain features. "Jack, honey lamb, it's damn cold out here." Her rouged lips pouted lushly.

"Wait inside." Jack's voice returned to its resolute tone. He looked to Holly without a single apology in his gray eyes.

The woman didn't give Holly a second glance as she flounced inside the musical interior, her golden robe fluttering behind her.

Jack dispassionately faced Holly and clenched his jaw tight. He offered no explanation, and at the moment, she didn't want one. She wasn't owed one. His actions only served to renew her distrust in him. She'd actually thought he possessed some fine thread of morality after he'd stood up to Adley Seeks for her. How wrong she'd been.

Without saying good-bye, Steele disappeared into the parlor house with the sounds of its antiquated piano and twanging banjo.

Her cheek felt as if she'd been slapped. She wasn't sure whether she was more disgusted or disappointed.

The Melodeon wasn't as grand as the Gem or Bella Union. In fact, it boasted nothing more than a makeshift stage at the end of the long gambling room. Lobster Lou sang ribald songs, and Dickie Brown played the banjo to create a sort of minstrel show.

Jack allowed Amaryllis to take up his hand and guide them around the lively gaming tables to a corridor at the rear of the building. "I swan, Jack, I didn't know for true if you were *eeeevver* coming." Her backside swished with more gusto than a horse's tail flicking flies. The pointed heels of her dainty slippers staccatoed over the rough floor as she dragged him to a narrow door at the end of the hall. "I was about to freeze my little bum-bum off, for waiting for you, I was." She exited through the back way that led to the cramped alley. "But you said you'd come back, so I . . ."

Jack heard Amaryllis's incessant chatter, but he wasn't listening. All of his thoughts were focused on Holly Dancer. The look of revulsion he'd seen on her face jabbed at his gut like a hot poker. He didn't like the feeling.

Having her in his arms had played havoc on his mind and his body. It was out of character for him to succumb to a woman. Gestures of valor didn't belong with a man like him. Not anymore.

It had rankled him to lose his temper in front of her; he could get enraged enough to kill a man. He didn't want Holly seeing that. He only wanted her to see what he was willing to show.

Prior to entering the restaurant three mornings ago, he'd already known a little about her. He hadn't been prepared to face such a self-assured, determined woman. He admired her resolve to make a go of it in Deadwood when any other woman would have left the day her husband's casket had been lowered. He commended her vitality, her headstrong, no-nonsense demeanor. Rarely, if ever, had he come across a lady with those attributes.

He'd deliberately pushed her to the limit that rainy day to see what she was made of.

Seeing her today had struck him more than he cared to admit. She was more stunningly beautiful than he'd remembered. He'd looked into her eyes and saw azure like a clear, cloudless summer sky. Her sweet mouth had tempted and been there for the taking. Had he not possessed an iron-clad will, he would have ground his lips on hers right there on the boardwalk. But he wasn't being paid to kiss her; at least not so soon anyway. If he had to fit it into his plans, he'd be more than willing to. More than willing.

The past several days he'd tried to find out who'd taken a shot at her. He had a suspicion it wasn't a random incident. He'd offhandedly asked around in the saloons if they'd ever witnessed that sort of trigger-happy event prior to

Goodnight's. A smart rider with an objective wouldn't go gunning into a crowded restaurant. He'd wait until he could single his man out and make no mistakes about plugging his mark through. Whoever had ridden that morning was not a professional, and sloppy at best. Jack hoped his insinuation would flush up a culprit, make the guilty shooter mad enough to speak out against his commentary. But no one said anything, nor was anyone concerned enough to follow up on the incident.

At least his barroom questions had garnered him one vital piece of information: Billy Dancer was a regular customer at the Melodeon with a harlot named Amaryllis, who could gossip up a blue streak.

"... I called to Dickie ..." Amaryllis's chatter broke through Jack's thoughts. "I said, 'Dickie, was that big, tall Jack Steele looking for me when I was with another buck—er, gentleman caller?'" The soles of Amaryllis's satin slippers were crusted and caked with dried, and now fresh, mud, as she made this alley crossing more than a dozen times a day. "And he says to me, 'No, Amaryllis, sugar, there ain't been that handsome Jack Steele here today.' Oh, dammit!" Her dressing shoe stuck like glue in the squashy earth, and her foot slid out. "Jack, would you be a darling and get that for me?"

Amaryllis tried to balance herself on one foot while she waited. "I swan, but I'll never get used to all this damn mud." She looked up to Jack, who hadn't made a move for the shoe. The unamused expression that greeted her made her reconsider her request. She bent down to retrieve the recalcitrant slipper herself. "Never mind, honey lamb. This little ol' gal can get it herself." She leaned onto the outside of the building and sunk her fingers into the black sludge. Shivering, she withdrew the ruined shoe. "We're here, anyway."

The red feather in her white hair bounced as she hopped up the short steps of a small, whitewashed cabin and opened the door.

She fumbled a moment for the kerosene lamp, then turned up the flat wick to give off a sparse light.

"There we are, sugar."

Jack closed the door behind him and rested his back against the jamb. He noticed the overpowering smell first. Stale perfume; stale liquor; stale lovemaking. It instantly repulsed him, but he forced his expression to go blank. The cramped room only afforded space for one bed, a lamp and washstand, and a common clothing chest.

His gaze returned to the bed that had been hastily made up since its last customer, the violet satin coverlet rumpled in disorderly waves, the few throw pillows precariously placed.

Jack felt his chest tighten to the point of pain. He'd been in this situation more times than he could count, and it had never bothered him. But now, after the look Holly Dancer had given him, he felt as if he'd sunk to the lowest pits of the earth.

"Excuse the clutter. I swan, I sometimes loan this room out to another girl, and she's a damn slovenly thing." Amaryllis went to the washstand and rinsed the dirt from her fingers. She bent down to unroll the garter off her fishnet, then removed and deposited the soiled stocking on the floor. She lifted her creamy white leg to the basin and scrubbed off the mud between her toes; she repeated the process on her other foot. "There now," she declared, finishing with her towel. "I feel like my ol' self. Come on, honey lamb, you come here and tell this little ol' gal just what you like. Damn shame I was busy when you first came by asking for me." She patted the coverlet with an inviting hand.

His stomach clenched with her words and he slowly came to her. He sat down, his weight causing the bed ropes to creak and moan. Beads of uncharacteristic sweat broke out on his forehead. Christ, but for the first time in three years he didn't think he could go through with it.

Amaryllis gave a tinkly laugh and teased his coat sleeve with her fingertips. "Can't have this on, sugar." She tried to tug his arms from the ulster. "I wouldn't have figured you for the shy type."

"No," he bellowed. "Leave it on."

Amaryllis's large green eyes filled with surprise. "Why . . . sure. We can take things slow." She backed away and brought her legs up on the bed to sit Indian style. The full layers of red ruffles on her petticoat hid her legs from view. "I know what you need, handsome. A little ol' swallow of Century." She reached under the bed and pulled out a crock of distilled whiskey. The cork came free with a pop, and she giggled.

Jack wiped the rim with his coat sleeve and took a liberal dose. The alcohol burned a track of fire down to the pit of his belly, and he welcomed the slapping jolt. He took one more good swallow before handing it back to Amaryllis.

"No, thanks, sugar. This little ol' gal prefers something more substantial." She grabbed for the brown box on the small lampstand and lifted the lid. "Chocolates. You want one?"

Jack declined with a slight shake of his head. He watched as Amaryllis popped one sweetmeat after another into her rosebud mouth and chewed with pure relish. He decided to question her and get it over with as soon as possible.

"A fine-looking woman like yourself must keep busy."

She licked a smudge of candy from her fingertip. "I do my share. But I could become *rreeeal* slow if you wanted to make an arrangement." Her red lips lifted prospectively.

"You do that often? Make arrangements?"

"Well, not since one particular buck—er, caller."

A muscle in Jack's jaw tensed. "What happened to him?"

"The rascal got himself killed, he did." She pouted unbecomingly. "It was the best damn arrangement I ever had. Paid me good not to give it to anybody but him. Said his wife was a real dead fish under the testers." She tittered as if recollecting. "He was a wild one, he was. I miss my Billy."

Jack's face showed not a single emotion as he asked his next question. "You know why he got killed?"

"Wweeell." Amaryllis leaned forward, a great valley of cleavage on display for Jack. "Nobody ever asked me that before. I think"—she paused dramatically—"his wife did the deed."

Jack wished he hadn't given Amaryllis back the Century jug. He could have used another blinding swig. Instead, he cracked his knuckles and waited for Amaryllis to elaborate.

"From what Billy told me, she was greedy. They had a gold claim together that Billy figured was to hit pay grub real big. Billy said he'd leave her and we were going to share it. I think she must have found out what he was planning and she put a slug in him. She still owns it, you know. Any other woman would have sold out. Not her. She prospects it herself."

Amaryllis picked up a chocolate, bit into it, and made a face. She put it back in the box. "I've never seen her. Her kind and mine don't mix socially, but I can tell you, she's real plain. Nothing to hold a torch to me, Billy said." Amaryllis selected a truffle, dropped it into her mouth, and smacked her lips. "I miss my Billy, but I could forget him quicker if you were to say you wanted to strike up an arrangement."

"We'll see if I think you're worth it." The delighted look on Amaryllis's face made the muscles across Jack's abdomen go tight.

"All right, sugar. Now you're talking. I know just about everything there is to know on how to pleasure a man." Her hand rested intimately on his leg and she slid it up over the contours of his thigh. "Let's get down to business then, shall we? It'll be ten dollars—in gold dust."

Jack glanced to the worn gold scale and blower on the lampstand. The prattling girl was serious when it came to compensation. He looked at the blower again—a shallow receptacle made of tin where the gold dust was weighed. By shaking and gently blowing breath upon it, sand and other worthless sediments would separate from the dust, and the weigher would get nothing but pure gold for his pay. He returned his line of vision to Amaryllis. "I don't have ten dollars."

Her painted eyebrows darted up in a grim arch. "Oh . . . *wweeell,* for you I'll give it to you for five dollars."

"I don't have five dollars." He was being blatantly obvious, and she didn't realize it.

"Now, listen here, honey lamb, as much as I think you're

a handsome rascal, this little ol' gal doesn't do business for free."

"I don't know. Dickie Brown said you did favors."

"What?!" Her lips pursed like a persimmon. "Why, that no-good, dirty-dealing dog of a banjo player. Just because I sometimes—oh, pooh, never mind. I may be cheap, but I'm not for free! Now, get out!"

Jack was already on his feet with that very intention.

Holly found herself unable to concentrate on Samuel Richardson's *Pamela*. The virtuous young maid wasn't holding her attention tonight.

She set the book down on the soft feather tick of her bed and snuggled deep under the warm comforter.

Staring up at the ceiling, she looked at the flickering patterns the iron parlor stove gave off. Why did half of every day have to be in darkness? At least during the daylight, she would keep busy in the restaurant or her claim—or even her garden. Nights, she was trapped in her room with only her worries and fears for company. It was hard being alone.

Even harder to admit she was lonely.

Not for the first time, she wished she and Billy had had a baby. Not necessarily a part of Billy to live on, but a person who would love her just the way she was. A person with whom she could share her life.

She tried to blot out thoughts about her husband. She avoided thinking of him whenever possible, but sometimes it was as if he were standing over her shoulder, laughing at her, teasing her. He'd abused her mentally, in ways that no one would ever guess on the surface. She knew she would rather die than marry again. She couldn't face the humiliation a second time.

A series of scampering thuds echoed on the stairs leading to her entry door. Holly froze, becoming alert to every sound. Jack's assumption that someone meant her harm flooded through her mind, and she feared he may have been telling her the truth. Only when she heard a low meow and fighting hiss did she breathe.

Cats.

Of course. No one would want to shoot her.

Holly's musings interrupted, they took a path toward Jackson Steele. The man with a shoddy past, the manners of a scoundrel, and a heart surely blacker than any stove.

Yesterday afternoon had pulled the illusory daydreams of him from her mind like a rolled window shade gone awry. He was a man who consorted with Badland girls. Why that should come as a surprise, she didn't know. It was clear he took claim to the type of man who preferred to buy his women.

She wondered what it would have been like to kiss Jack. What had made him stop? It was most likely for the best. If he had turned away as Billy had, the pain would have been unbearable. She was a woman with no experience, a woman who wasn't pleasing. How many times had Billy told her that? He'd grated it into her over and over until she thought she wasn't normal. That surely there was something wrong with her.

Carrie often hinted Holly should accept a man's invitation to go to dinner or the theater. She'd kept on about it so long, Holly finally had to confide in the girl that she just wasn't interested in men.

Though only seventeen, three years younger than Holly, Carrie seemed to know more about delicate matters than Holly did. She assured Holly the right man would come along. After all, he had for her. Carrie, as she put it, was "awfully in love with Conrath La Fors." Conrath worked a freight-hauling business and was away from Deadwood for long periods of time, but when he was in town, Carrie's cheeks were always flushed a pretty pink. She'd said it was due to Conrath's kisses. Holly wished that once in her life, her cheeks would flush from a man's kiss. Or better yet, she could make a man's cheeks flush with a kiss of her own.

Rolling onto her side, Holly stared at the close wall. She felt safe and protected from the world in her bed. The sharp pitch of the roof cut into the room, lowering the expanse of wall next to her bed. It didn't allow her to sit up straight on one side of it.

The room may have been cramped, but she welcomed its offering of comfort and its center-of-town location, where she didn't feel isolated. She'd moved here shortly after she'd become a widow. This new home was very different from the split-log cabin she and Billy lived in on the outskirts of Deadwood. It had been from that house she'd been summoned to identify Billy's bloody body.

Visions of that afternoon had tormented her terribly. She could not remain in the cabin, where she felt Billy's spirit touching her. She'd thought to escape her nightmares, but even in the safety of these new walls, they still crept through her dreams. Often she woke up with tremors raking her body from reliving the experience in her sleep. A day didn't go by without her wondering who murdered her husband.

She closed her eyes, leaving the round wick up on the kerosene lamp to softly illuminate the room; lately, that was the only way she could go to sleep. The darkness bothered her. It made her feel lost.

She lay there for a long time, listening to the muffled sounds of the street traffic below that didn't let up, even at night—horses, wagons, miners, sometimes the late stage.

But more often than anything else, gunshots exploded. The gunshots never slept.

"Twenty-one in the red and around goes the little ball again. Get your bets down, gentlemen."

Jack tossed down several house tokens and massaged the back of his neck. The corded muscles felt as if they'd been stretched out on a rack. As the hours had circled off the clock, the tendons had stiffened a fraction more. The injustice of it all was that during the five hours he'd been in the saloon, he hadn't learned a damn thing.

He focused his tired eyes on the trophy heads secured to the far wall, the numerous suggestive paintings, and the back of the bar where shelves sparkled with crystal glasses all lined up in a row. For a moment he had to remind himself he was in Deadwood's Red Bird.

"I'm due, you lily white ball! I'm due!"

Jack pressed his fingers to the bridge of his nose and looked over his hand at the disorderly stripling standing across from him. The youth's hair, nearly white from the sun, contrasted with a face baked a golden brown. He wore a large, bleached frontier hat so new, Jack could smell the freshly tanned leather even through the smoke-filled air.

"What you looking at, Steele?" Tom Deerhorn buckled his blond brows down and added his own tokens to the table.

"I'm just playing the wheel, Deerhorn."

"I don't like the way you keep looking at me. Something wrong, *friend?*"

Jack bit back the urge to laugh. The kid couldn't be any more than twenty, eleven years younger than Jack, and he talked to him with more nerve than he ought to. "Like I said, *friend,* just playing the wheel."

"Well, keep your nose to it then." Deerhorn took out a crooked cigarette and put it to his lips. "Hey, Angel," he called to a reed-thin girl who walked by holding an empty tray. "Bring me a pitcher of Gold Nugget beer. And another shot glass of whiskey fer the doc here." Tom reached out his elbow and nudged it into the ribs of the older man standing next to him.

Doc Timmish gave an exaggerated cough at the poke to his side, then his reddened face cracked with a bent smile. "Right neighborly of you, son," he slurred.

Jack watched the scene with irritation. Deerhorn had plainly set out to get the old man drunk an hour ago, and it had worked. Any information Jack might have gotten from the aged coot vanished like the bottom of an empty glass. He'd tried to get Doc Timmish to talk about his practice, his part in doctoring the two miners who hadn't died instantly. Looking at the ruddy-faced, gray-haired man now, Jack almost felt sorry for the men who had had to submit any kind of hope to the good doctor. He could hardly hold on to the circumference of his glass.

"Black, thirty-five," the dealer called out.

Deerhorn let out a snort of disgust. "Damn thing is house-rigged, I tell you! Nobody can lose this much!"

Jack leaned his elbows on the table. "Don't be a sore loser, Deerhorn. You've done all right from the doc here."

Tom clenched the misshapen cigarette in his straight

white teeth and leaned over the table. "And just what the deuce you mean by that, Steele?"

"You got him foxed and took a damn healthy amount of his gold."

Dr. Timmish, though far gone in his cups, straightened himself and adjusted the ruffled black ribbon tie at his throat. "Son, 'sat true? You trying to bushwhack me?"

Deerhorn ignored the question. His coffee brown eyes narrowed annoyingly on Jack. "Listen hyar, I—"

"I don't want any trouble, gentlemen," the dealer intervened.

Jack pulled back and stood to his full height. Without a word, he reached around to the hook on the wall and grabbed his ulster. Slipping it on, he made his way through the rear of the crowded saloon while buttoning the greatcoat closed.

The frigid air outside cleansed his lungs, a pure welcome to the stale barroom. Jack inhaled generous amounts. Turning down the alley, he decided to head for his room above the Gem and call it a night. Deerhorn had hampered any chance he'd had getting Doc Timmish to talk.

Jack's Wellingtons crunched over the half-frozen, muddy ground as he made his way down the narrow passage. Only a faint moon guided his steps while he headed toward the main street.

"Hold it right there."

Instantly Jack's hand gripped his Buntline and he swiveled, the powerful revolver raised at a deadly angle. His thumb eased the hammer back until he heard the slow click, then realized he faced Tom Deerhorn.

Jack relaxed his tense arm and put back the Buntline. "Christ," he muttered with agitation. The young buck had gotten his heartbeat up for nothing. "What do you want?"

"I want justice." Deerhorn stood in the mellow light, both his arms arced over the carved ivory handles of his gleaming Colt .45 Civilian models. Through the front separation of his winter coat, Tom's gun belt rode so low at his hips, Jack thought if the whelp took in a deep breath, the holster would fall to the ground.

"What the hell you think you're going to do? Shoot me because I called your scheme?" Jack nearly laughed now at the absurdity of the situation. *"Friend,* you most likely have never fired those things."

"A lot you know, Steele. Road agent's spin."

"What?"

"Border shift. The roll. I know 'em all, fella."

"Christ," Jack breathed again. "You're nothing but a snot-nosed kid. Get out of my way."

"Yeah?" Deerhorn shook his head, his new hat white as his hair under the light of the moon. "Yeah?" he repeated in a louder tone. With that, he removed both guns. "I'll show you I can do a road agent's spin."

For a brief instant Jack's hand went for the Buntline, then he stopped himself midmotion. What was he defending himself against? The kid couldn't wipe his own nose, much less do a spin.

Tom Deerhorn's face took on a heavy mask of concentration. He even went as far as to chew on his lower lip as he faced both revolvers, upside-down, toward Jack. "Yeah, well, watch this. I can double-hand 'em." He jerked his wrists, and the Colts' barrels, spun upward.

A loud explosion boomed, then a look of pure horror widened Tom's eyes, the whites a ghostly contrast against his face.

"Dammit!" Jack cursed, and automatically grabbed for his upper arm. "You stupid idiot!"

"Hangnation! Steele! Are you hit?"

"Hell, yes!" Reaching into his coat, he seized a bandanna and stuffed it inside his sleeve to stop the blood from flowing.

"Damn! Ding bust it! I guess my left hand needs a little more practice." Deerhorn had dropped his Colts back into his holster and came over to where Jack leaned against the timbered wall of the Red Bird. "You hurt much?"

"Hell, yes!" Jack yelled. His arm felt as if a squad of red ants had invaded it. "You fool kid."

"Well, damn. Cripes." Deerhorn removed his hat and ruffled his blond hair with shaking hands. "Damn. Golblast it all. Damn. I didn't mean . . . mean I was just . . . I mean . . . damn."

"Shut up!" Jack had to think.

"I'll . . . I'll get Doc Timmish!" Deerhorn slapped on his frontier hat with a wide grin over his face, as if he'd just thought of the ultimate solution to the situation.

"No you won't!" With his good arm, Jack latched on to Tom's collar to stop him from leaving. Fire shot through his wounded arm at the sudden movement he made, and he stumbled. Jack's unsure steps staggered them both toward Main Street.

Leaning against an awning post, Jack scanned his surroundings. Where could he go? He needed medical attention, but he'd rather chance it alone than let old Timmish take a look at him.

"I, ah, Steele . . ." Deerhorn started talking. "Ah, you know this weren't no planned thing. . . . Ah, I, that is, the sheriff doesn't have to—"

Jack had the urge to belt the pup right in the mouth. "Shut up." He squeezed his eyes closed, and when he opened them, a light in a window across the street caught his attention. Though faint, it shone enough to tell him Holly Dancer was still up. Without considering what implications his visit would have, Jack nudged Deerhorn with his knee.

"Take me over there."

Whether Holly had dozed off or not, she wasn't sure. She felt as if she were in some kind of transition, not really asleep, not really awake, when she heard the reverberating sound.

An insistent knocking pounded the door.

Holly pushed herself upright and grabbed for the pocket watch she kept hanging on one of the iron bed headposts. In the semidarkness, she saw the time was nearly three.

The loud knock came again.

She scrambled out of bed. She didn't think to snatch up a robe as she slept in a long flannel gown, one of Billy's old red plaid shirts, and heavy woolen stockings. Padding swiftly to her linen chest, she lifted the lid and dug between the folds

43

of a blanket. She pulled out a scratched single-action, small-caliber revolver.

"Who is it?" she called through the closed door, the firearm unsteady in her inexperienced hands.

"It's Jack. Open the door."

Holly's pulse instantly awoke. Jack Steele? Her fingers tightened around the trigger.

"Dammit, open the door"—his words were garbled—"before someone sees me."

She ran her moist left palm down the side of her nightgown, contemplating the reasons for his being there. "What do you want?"

"Open the damn door," he enunciated more clearly and in a resonant voice. Holly inhaled deeply, afraid if she didn't let him in, he'd alert her neighbors, who already thought she courted trouble by living alone in town. After a long moment, she did as Steele asked.

Unbolting the lock, she kept the revolver pointed at Jack's chest; he didn't seem to notice—or even care—that she had a gun on him.

His tall stature filled the frame. The merry red glow from her three-legged parlor stove gave him a reddish hue, and her low-glowing lantern allowed her to make out his features. Downy snowflakes clung to the brim of his sugarloaf and the long black hair that rested on his shoulders. His hawkish nose was a little red from the cold; his warm breath puffed around him in the nippy air.

He stumbled into the room, one arm crossed over his chest, and his fingers gripping his biceps. At first she thought him drunk. But he didn't smell strongly of liquor. He smelled familiar, though not in the way she'd associate a scent with him.

"What t-took you so long, baby? I damn near froze to death waiting for you." He surveyed the dim room intently, as if looking for something he'd lost. "I n-need a place to sit down."

"I don't think you should stay long enough to sit down. What do you want?" Her insides trembled with his forbidding presence.

Ignoring her question, he brushed passed her. She felt the cold from his ulster as it rubbed against her sleeve. He swayed, and she thought him intoxicated again. Then it dawned on her maybe he'd been smoking opium at one of the dens in Chinatown.

He coughed. "You planning to hold me up with that cap-and-ball piece? 'Cause if you are, I can save you the trouble. . . . Just lost it all gambling. . . ."

Holly looked down at the gun in her hand, then at Jack Steele. "What do you want?" she repeated, a little more frantically. As if to prove she meant business, she cocked the gun's hammer back. It submitted with the stiffness of an arthritic joint. The chamber popped out like a kernel of corn and landed to the floor, six bullets rolling in as many directions.

"Oh, hell," Jack mumbled at her inept maneuver. "Got to oil the thing once in a while." He moved in a circle, appearing to not really see anything at all. "Need to f-find a chair . . ."

Not knowing how to put the revolver back together, she silently chided her own stupidity and Billy's neglect of the weapon. Seeing Jack so intent on finding a place to sit down, she kicked the bullets out of her way and retrieved the only chair she had. A small-framed one that went with her cherrywood desk. Just as she offered it to him, Jack deposited himself on the bed. He moaned while trying to struggle out of his greatcoat.

"You've got to h-help me do this."

She took a step toward him, noticing the ashen color on his chiseled face. A damp shock of black hair hung over his brow, and he tossed his hat to the floor.

"Get it off!" he growled impatiently.

She started with a gasp at the demanding order. For a moment she was reluctant to move closer. He slumped his shoulders, as if giving in to whatever ailed him. The defeated action made her legs carry her forward.

Holly shrugged him out of his right sleeve. She reached around and began tugging on the other cuff. "I'll help you with this, but then—"

45

He groaned and clenched his teeth at the movement that at last freed him of his coat.

The peculiar smell assailed her nose once again. A memory flashed through her mind. He smelled like Billy.

He smelled like Billy the day he died.

Chapter Four

*H*olly inched away from the bed with leaden steps. Below his left shoulder and encompassing his upper arm, a deep crimson stained Jack's once pristine white shirt. A soaked bandanna lay in his lap.

Her mouth went dry and her heartbeat rose to a nearly uncontrollable level as she dragged her gaze up to meet his dark eyes. "What happened to you?" she choked in a tight whisper.

"I didn't take a greenhorn seriously." His hooded lids slipped closed and he fell back onto the coverlet with a husky groan.

Holly fought back the urge to bolt to the door. She pressed her knuckles to her mouth to keep her fingers from trembling. *Think.* Her mind dredged up the commands. React. Do something to help him.

Holly stumbled to the bed and sat; Jack lay with his legs still planted firmly on the floor. Her nightgown tangled up her calf, and his weather-chilled pants leg jolted a coldness next to her bare skin. "Mr. Steele?"

She swept her hand across his forehead and flinched at the intense heat of his damp skin. The melting snow on the ends of his hair had left a raw earthy scent to mingle with the distinct sweet-sharp smell of his blood. The scent tripped alarm in her brain, and she found she had trouble breathing.

"Oh, please . . . Mr. Steele. Can you hear me?"

Her heartbeat hammered in her ears. Slowly he opened his eyes, peering at her through the thickness of his black lashes. His gray eyes shone like two pieces of obsidian. Pain creased the edges of his mouth, and he licked his lips.

"Get the preacher out of your voice," he warned hoarsely. "I'm not going to die. I just hurt like hell."

"You need a doctor. I'm going to get one."

"No." As he reached for her wrist, his strength caught her off guard. "That damn drunk, Timmish, would end up finishing me off."

Her pulse tripped and staggered where Jack applied pressure with his thumb. She stared down at him. The effort at holding her cost him dearly. He'd paled considerably. He wasn't going to release her until she relented. "All right," she murmured. "I won't get him."

Jack let her go with an audible breath and sunk further into the bedclothes.

"If you don't want me to get a doctor, who's going to take care of your arm?"

She waited. A lone bead of sweat trailed its way to his cheek, but she refused to break the nerve-shattering tension.

He turned his head toward her. "You."

Damn him. Why was he doing this to her? Billy's lifeless face rose up in her mind. She forced herself to blot out the image.

Holly glared at the pool of red seeping across the sleeve of Jack's shirt and smearing her sheets. "I should kill you myself," she said in a high-strung tone that fed off her sheer terror. She leaned over him and stuck her fingers into the breast strap buckle of his shoulder holster. The supple leather gave way easily, allowing her to slip the heavy ensemble from him. She dumped it on the floor.

"I'll have to sit up to get my shirts off," Jack supplied.

Holly slipped her arm behind the broad expanse of his back and did her best to help him, though Jack did most of the work. He grimaced and hunched forward, trying to stifle his stiff breaths.

Raising his right hand to the top button at the collar of his shirt, Jack tried to slip one out of its hole. He fumbled with the pearl button, unable to free it from the slit.

Holly angled closer, nudged his fingers away, and gently took over. "I'll do them."

Jack kept his chin straight as her hands contacted with the warm flesh of her neck. She bent her head, feeling a few strands of her hair catching in the beard roughing his chin. She didn't free them; neither did Jack. An odd thought struck her: She'd never once taken Billy's shirt off for him. "I thought you were so handy with a gun, Mr. Steele. What happened?"

"Any horse's tail can catch cockleburs."

There was the faintest bit of sarcasm to Jack's words. Holly smiled inwardly, his confession lifting some of her anxiety and diverting her. "Maybe so, but I figured you for the type to keep your tail clear."

Holly reached the waistband of his denims and tugged the tails free. Once the shirtfront parted, she guided his good arm out first.

Her brave mood was quickly snuffed out as she was forced to contend with the wet sleeve of his wounded area. Her stomach swirled with panic, pushing at the top of her ribs. She bit hard on the inside of her lip, tasting her own blood as she peeled the sodden fabric from his undershirt. An uncontrollable shiver raced across her skin.

It was plainly obvious now how he'd gotten the wound. A burnt odor permeated from his shirt as she tossed it to the floorboards. She wondered why she hadn't recognized it before. "You've been shot." Holly spoke her conclusion aloud.

"I've been inconvenienced," he grumbled with annoyance.

Looking down at the small band at the neck of his undergarment, she knew she couldn't slip it off the way she had his shirt. Jack stared at her with trust in his smoky eyes. She condemned him again. "Hold still."

"I'm not going anywhere."

Holly grasped the worn hem of the ribbed material in her hands and gave a strong tug. It split with an ear-shattering tear, and she ripped it up to his collar.

"Damn!" Jack croaked, and balled his right fist into a hard knot on his thigh. "You should have warned me!"

"I told you to hold still."

"Damn," he ground out, catching hold of his ragged breath. Then a small fire kindled in his piercing eyes as he captured her gaze. "You do that to me again when I can enjoy it."

Panic assaulted her anew, only this time of a different kind. He was toying with her, she knew it. He couldn't possibly mean what he was saying. He spoke in delirium. She didn't dignify the barb with an answer. Instead, Holly worked quickly to remove his undershirt. She'd rather be scared senseless of his blood than his suggestive words.

The exposed wound gaped at her like a demon. Holly sputtered a dry cough as the air choked out of her lungs. She balled her hands into fists, driving her nails into her palms. He depended on her, so she willed herself to stop acting petrified for his sake.

The bullet had grazed the edge of his bronzed skin. It seemed as if there was blood everywhere. Down his biceps, his forearm. Smudged against the line of his ribs. Everywhere. How could she not have seen it on his coat? Down the side of his arm, a fresh trail ran past what had begun to cake over.

Holly felt dizzy. She forced her eyes open in spite of the light-headed tornado whirling to sweep her up into its funnel. For a timeless moment she stared at the wall, uncertain of her surroundings.

Then a gunshot resounded somewhere down on Main Street and she snapped her chin up, her teeth rattling in the process. She shook her head and rapidly blinked her eyes, trying to clear the cotton out.

Holly sneaked a look at Jack, who gawked at his wound. He hadn't noticed she'd nearly fainted. Maybe because he appeared to be on the verge of doing just that himself. "I think you'd better lie down, Mr. Steele." Holly's voice cracked as she got her bearings back. "You're as pale as buttermilk."

"Hell if I am." But Holly saw that he'd broken out in a

sweat again. Droplets ran down his temple and over his square jaw.

Snatching up a clean towel, Holly pressed it over the flow of blood. Jack tucked the ends under the pit of his arm.

His tongue darted out to moisten his dry lips as he looked up. "You have anything to drink?" he asked in a gravelly inflection.

"Water in—"

"No. I meant something to get me drunk."

Holly left the bed and fetched a small bottle of apricot brandy from her desk drawer. She handed it to him.

Jack squinted at her. "Never figured you the type to have anything. Glad you are." He opened the stopper with his teeth and took a liberal dose of the alcohol.

Holly watched Jack as he swilled the amber liquid with a slow tilt of his head. His Adam's apple bobbed smoothly with each gulp. When he'd downed nearly the entire contents, he replaced the cork.

"Use some on my arm," he exhaled shakily.

"All right, but I really think you should lie down. You look as if you're going to—"

"Hell if I am." Then he narrowed his eyes to wedges. Swaying back, his upper body plunged to the mussed sheets. The bed ropes protested the sudden dead weight, creaking sharply. The brandy bottle tumbled from his fingers to the floor with a dull thud.

The room suddenly grew very quiet. And very still. Holly was on her own now.

She thanked God she'd been blessed with a mind that generally worked on common sense. Whenever she'd had a cut from the kitchen, she'd cleaned it with alcohol or vinegar, put liniment on it if need be, and a bandage if it was bad enough. That's what she'd do for Jack. And fast.

Holly moved quickly, wanting to tend Jack before he came to. She snatched up the basin on her washstand, poured a generous amount of water in it, and sloshed a fresh cloth around. Squeezing some of the excess water, she sat down next to him. Without hesitating, she gently pressed the cloth to his injury.

Jack jerked sideways out from under her touch with an incoherent growl. Holly reassuringly settled her hand over his chest to placate him. His racing heartbeat barreled under her palm.

Holly's breath caught in her lungs and she waited a long moment, then continued. When she saw the taut cords spanning his chest slacken and felt the speeding heartbeats slow down, she exhaled and moved the cloth over him once more. This time, his reaction wasn't so violent. He cursed in a muffled moan.

She continued with diligence and efficiency, rinsing the cloth often. Soon the basin water was stained a dark reddish brown. Once she was finished wiping the area clean, sticky blood oozed from it all over again. She fumbled for the brandy bottle and popped the cork off.

The heady bouquet of the liquor was an inviting assault, and she took a stiff taste. She shuddered as the sweet-fiery alcohol streaked down her throat, leaving her gasping. The lone drink was just enough to pacify her strained nerves, and she placed a fresh towel under Jack's upper arm. A searing knot formed in her stomach, so afraid was she of what his reaction would be as she let the remainder of the amber liquid trickle over him.

She'd known Jack was a powerful man, but at that moment, she hadn't realized just how potently strong he was. Even in delirium, he overwhelmed her. Eyes shut, he shot his right shoulder forward and reached for her across his chest. His good hand grabbed her wrist, capturing her in a bruising vise. His gray eyes opened for just a flash, venting daggers at her.

"Damn you," he swore at her through gritted white teeth.

Though he was staring at her, Holly knew he wasn't really seeing her. A cloud of pain pinpointed his irises. He released her as quickly as he'd taken her, his lids slamming shut.

Panting, Holly tried to collect herself, tossing her long hair over her trembling shoulder. He didn't know what he was doing, she reasoned. She patted dry his arm and the surrounding area. Then she wrapped the wound tight, but not too tight, with some strips of old sheeting she'd retrieved from her chest.

She made quick work of cleaning up the rest of his skin and the stain of blood on his right hand. His swarthy face remained passive. Somber shadows had settled under the closed fringes of his lashes. As she stroked the caked blood away, every fiber of her being centered on the raw strength of his bare chest. His muscles were tight and well pronounced. In the subtle valley of his chest nestled an inky wedge of coarse hair.

Holly felt a prickling sensation of excitement kindle to life inside her. She stamped the spark, rejecting any understanding of the complex meaning. She looked away, her labors finished.

Raising the back of her wrist to her forehead, Holly swiped at the cold moisture on her brow. She bent down and lifted one of Jack's heavily booted feet and tugged on the heel of his muddied Wellington. With a fierce pull, the boot came off. She did the same for his other foot, her fingers coming in contact with a small-caliber gun hidden inside. The man was an arsenal: three guns. From what she'd seen, he didn't hold the law in high regard, and she guessed he voiced his disdain with molded metal.

Holly swung his legs up onto the bed and yanked the soiled bedclothes out of her way so his head could rest on the softness of her pillow.

Her job complete, she should have turned away and rinsed out the basin. But she didn't. Jack's slumbering face commanded her attention. The prominent, chiseled features she'd clashed with that day in the restaurant were now unguarded. He didn't look so intimidating. So dangerous. He looked almost . . . placid.

And undeniably handsome.

His full lips were wide and slightly parted as he breathed through his mouth. The sardonic edge to his visage was gone, and she freely observed the line of his nose, the angle of his jaw, and the faint hairline scar just below his right eye. Vertical marks of a scowl marred the distance between his dark brows. It made her think that he genuinely was a brooding man since the impression remained even in his sleep.

Holly had the unexpected urge to reach out and smooth

back a thick lock of black hair from his temple. Her heart hammered against her rib cage and she was excruciatingly aware of his masculinity. She focused on the flatness of his abdomen and the dark line of hair that disappeared into his waistband. Her eyes strayed to the contours of his wide shoulders and solid chest, realizing that she'd just touched those compact, stony areas, but without really touching him at all. She'd done so as a doctor would a patient, not as a woman would a man. Modesty rose in her and she was glad she hadn't thought of it sooner.

A red-hot piece of coal hissed in the parlor stove, an announcement to Holly that she should add more fuel to keep the room warm enough for Jack. As it was, she mentally reprimanded herself for not having had the insight to cover him sooner.

Guiltily Holly unfastened his waist holster, which sheltered his Buntline. She maneuvered the belt from around his lean middle and put it next to his other one on the floor.

She pulled up the blankets to cover his naked chest. Then, as if that weren't good enough, she tucked them higher under his jaw. But even with only his face for her view, she still felt drawn to him. Impulsively she reached out and combed back the hair from his forehead with her fingers. The strands were silky, not like she thought they would be. Not coarse and rough like Steele.

She cast her eyes down and, for the briefest of moments, felt sorry for herself. Felt sorry for her lack of desirability to a man like Jack Steele. But as quickly as the pity came, it retreated.

She moved from the bed without a backward glance.

A sluggish *tick . . . tick . . . tick . . . tick* intruded on his black fog. The relentless rhythm roused Jack just enough to rankle him, to make him cognizant of the fact that he hurt like blue blazes. His upper arm felt as if someone had sledged it with a hunk of wood, ramming a thousand hot, pinpointed splinters into his muscles. His nerve endings pulsated and throbbed from his neck and shoulder, right down to his fingertips.

He tried to ignore the blasted ticking, but it tugged at his consciousness, hauling him further away from the onyx pit he'd stumbled into.

Maybe if he rolled over, the infernal noise would go away. Too late Jack realized the error of his line of thinking. His poor judgment cost him a jab in his arm akin to that of an ice pick, and with it, a shower of needlelike, fiery pain. Sweat instantaneously broke out on his forehead.

He couldn't seem to open his eyes. His lids were heavier than irons. As a substitute for what he couldn't see, his sense of smell heightened. He filled his nostrils with the distinct scent of a woman.

It was . . . damn . . . Without the distraction of his sight, he swore it to be orange blossoms. It flitted all around him from the pillow. The fact that he could distinguish it made his heart trip. It was sweet and pure. Not two-bit.

The subtle fragrance toyed with him, an alluring strength. All at once he knew where he was . . . who he was with. It was Holly. He smelled Holly Dancer.

Slowly his eyes opened and he willed himself to lift his head a fraction. Her name whispered off his lips.

"I'm here."

She came to him, from where, he didn't know. He'd dropped his head back into the softness of the pillow. Orange blossoms billowed around him and he breathed it in his lungs, savoring the intoxicating perfume.

"Mr. Steele?"

Jack's vision was filled by Holly's face as she stood over him. Christ, she was beautiful. She'd twisted her burnished hair on top of her head and left wisps framing her delicate face. Concern reflected in her azure eyes, as well as the exhaustion he was sure came from a lack of sleep. She dug her straight teeth into the pink flesh of her full lower lip.

"Thank goodness, you're awake."

He heard her breathe a sigh of relief. "I'm awake." He stifled the strange gnawing in his belly. "How long have I been out?"

"A few hours. It's nearly six."

He computed the loss of time, then his mouth dipped into a deep frown. "What did you do to me? I keep hearing a damn ticking in my head."

55

Holly offered him an apologetic smile and leaned toward the wrought-iron headboard. He heard her fumble with something, then she showed him a gold filigree pocket watch on a chain.

"Then I haven't lost my sanity."

"No," she answered solemnly. "Just a lot of blood."

Going over the sequence of events, he didn't remember much. Pieces here and there. He felt like an idiot for passing out on her. "Was it bad?"

"I don't know of a good gunshot wound." She looked at him from underneath her long, spiky lashes. "Does it hurt terribly?"

He saw no reason to lie to her. She'd seen him at his worst. "Yeah. It burns. You have any more brandy?"

"No, but I have medicine." Holly crossed the room to her cherrywood desk. He turned his head and followed her with his gaze. For the first time, he realized she was dressed like a man. Corduroy pants outlined her slender legs and calves, the hems tucked into heavy work boots. Her shoulders were enveloped by a pale blue flannel shirt that fit her loosely.

"I have"—her voice interfered with his perusal, and he was obliged to stop and listen to her as she faced him and read the label on a thick crystal bottle—"the Great English Remedy. It cures noises in the head, dimness of vision . . . oh . . . and aversion to society." Holly raised her head and gave him a nervous laugh.

He wasn't immune to her quip and cracked a slight smile even though his arm was burning like a rebellious forest fire. "A least it's nearly full. Does it work worth a damn?"

The amusement from her voice faded. "Well, not as good as brandy for my—" She stopped herself short.

"Don't you know dollar elixirs won't even get a flea drunk? I never figured you the type to nip, Mrs. Dancer."

Her blue eyes grew defensive. "You already said that. I only drink it once a month." Her jaw snapped closed as if she'd said too much.

He let the obvious meaning slide by. "Do you have anything else that works like brandy?"

"All I have is Hood's Sarsaparilla."

"Give me some."

She grew flustered. A rose blush mingled over her porcelain complexion up to the wealth of her mahogany hair. "It's a—a female remedy."

"Oh, hell," Jack snorted. "Then give me the English one till you can get me some whiskey."

The sound of her boots was muffled as she crossed the throw rug.

"Do you need any help?" she asked.

For a minute he wasn't sure what she was talking about. Then he remembered he couldn't sit up without his arm blazing him to death. "Yeah. Prop me up a little."

Holly reached behind him and adjusted an extra pillow to rest on the headboard. When her fingers came in contact with his bare skin, he repressed a jolt that shook his gut. The intimate feel of her hand over his shoulder maddened him in more ways than he cared to admit. The fact that he could be affected by her when he was shot up with pain made him feel unscrupulous.

Her hand slid across his shoulders, and he clenched his stomach. She could cause him to catch fire in a place that wasn't even hurting if she didn't leave him alone. "That's good. I can do it," he grumbled unkindly, instantly regretting his tone.

With a slightly wounded look on her face, she handed him the bottle. He refused to make an issue over an apology, conceding it was the damn pain making him uncivil.

Jack popped the cork and lifted the tonic to his lips. The elixir, a bittersweet concoction, had a strong alcohol base. He gagged down several swigs, then handed it back to her.

Jack's fingers met with hers briefly; she snatched them away and hugged the bottle to her breasts—what he could see of them. "Why are you dressed like that?"

Her reply was cut short as a hollow knock came at the door.

Jack instinctively threw the bedding from his chest and,

with quick-fire reflex, reached for the Buntline at his hips.

He came up empty.

"Where the hell's my gun?!" His voice tightened to a constricted whisper, and hard as he tried not to, he could only think of one thing:

She'd called the law on him.

Chapter Five

*H*olly took a quick jump back, stunned by the force of his words. "It's—it's under the bed." She kept her voice as low as Jack's.

"Get it," he ground out through clenched teeth as the knocking sounded again.

Holly teetered between obeying him and not; she'd thought she'd known who was at the door and didn't see any reason to aim a gun at it. "Wait a minute! I'm expecting—"

"I know who you're expecting," Jack growled, his face twisted with pain; only, the pain she encountered didn't seem to come from anything physical, rather an emotional ache. "Damn me for trusting betraying women."

She was utterly confused by his response. A hot prickle of uneasiness worked its way up her spine, her pulse escalating as she tried to explain. "I'd never betray you. I didn't get the doc—" But he cut her off.

"I can't reach my gun!"

The desperation in his voice made her nervous. Maybe it wasn't Lee-Ash at the door, after all. Maybe whoever had shot Jack had come looking for him, and somewhere in his alcohol-drugged haze, he was at odds over his capabilities.

"Don't just stand there. Get my gun!" The blatant urgency in Jack's tone startled Holly to awareness, and she dropped to her knees. He seemed so blindly insistent, she'd better appease him. She feared he'd hurt his arm if she didn't do as he asked.

Stretching out her hand, she fumbled over the cold floorboards under the bed. Her fingernails scraped across the finely tanned holster leather, and she passed it by for the icy butt of the revolver. Clutching the heavy piece of iron, she yanked it out and labored to lift it to Jack.

He seized the Buntline from her hand and slapped the chamber open. "You left it loaded."

Holly nodded, realizing he'd expected her to take the bullets out. The honest truth was, she'd forgotten. He'd looked so harmless against the crisp whiteness of her sheets, she hadn't thought of it.

With a flick of his wrist, Jack closed the single-action cylinder. He trained the .45 directly on the upper center of the door just as a flat fist attacked it.

"I really think I should ask who it is. . . ." But the cautioning glare in Jack's eyes made her voice trail off. Perspiration gathered on his upper lip and forehead as he fought to keep his revolver steady. Clearly he struggled with his fading consciousness.

"Darlin'?" came the drawl on the other side of the door.

The endearment immediately registered within Holly. Like a spring sun melting winter snow, her joints thawed into a river of relief. *Lee-Ash,* she sighed to herself. Lee-Ash—just as she'd suspected.

She turned toward Jack, lifted her chin, and gave him a look that should have cowered a herd of buffalo. "Don't you *ever* scare me like that again," she choked over her own heartbeat. "Put that gun down."

Jack struggled to sit up higher, the twelve-inch-barreled Buntline still clamped in his large hand. He appeared confused and cocked his head toward the door with a frown. "The old man . . . ?"

He lowered his weapon-holding hand, but she wasn't sure he was aware of its slack, for he kept the web of his thumb resting over the hammer.

"Darlin', you in there?" Lee-Ash questioned.

She answered without any consideration of Jack's approval. "Yes. Yes, I'm here, Lee-Ash."

"Tarnation, you had me worried." His muffled voice came through the door. "You ready to go? It's durn cold out here."

"Y-yes. I'll just get my things," she called out, meeting Jack's dark look.

"I told you I thought I knew who it was," she reprimanded him, much as if he were a little boy. "You worked yourself up for nothing, Mr. Steele. I think you'd better explain yourself. Who did you think I was expecting?"

"I figured you'd called the sheriff on me."

"Now, why would I do that?"

"Because I'm trouble."

"I think the only one you're trouble to is yourself . . . and whoever shot you. What did you do to get that hole in your arm?"

He looked up at her through heavy eyes filled with confusion. He worried her. She'd thought to leave him for a few hours, but now she wasn't sure. Maybe he was going into some kind of shock. Why did he keep looking at her like that? Like she was some kind of ghost or demonic apparition.

"I didn't do anything. A stupid kid used me for target practice."

"Then he should be reported to the sheriff."

"Like hell," Steele growled. "He doesn't have the brains to stick around, and if he does, I'll take care of him in my own way."

"I just bet you will." Holly stood motionless, the steady measure of her watch ringing through the room. "I have to go," she whispered, making up her mind. "Will you be all right?"

He didn't answer; he stared at her with an intense scowl that left her weak, though confident with her decision. She forced herself to turn away. Moving to her clothes cupboard, she pulled out her pea jacket and slipped it on. "If I don't go, he'll wonder what's wrong."

"Go where?"

The calmness that had returned to his voice lessened her sense of guilt for abandoning him. "I'm going to work my claim, Mr. Steele." Holly grabbed an india rubber poncho from a hook on the wall by the door. After shrugging it over her head, she fetched a battered hat from the remaining hook and dropped it on her hair.

He apparently recovered enough to blurt out, "You're going out there—like that?"

Jack's assessing gaze traveled the length of her, and she suddenly felt bared to the soul: plain and unfeminine. Heat suffused her face as she looked down at her miner's trappings. She'd always worn Billy's old clothes to work; it wasn't practical for her to wear a dress. There had been numerous stares and remarks, but none had ever stung her as Jack's had. For some reason, his comment smarted far worse than all the snide comments Adley Seeks had ever doled out.

"Yes. I am," she finally said, feeling every bit as worn out as she was. She disregarded his obvious disapproval with a bitter swallow and forced her shoulders back. She couldn't change now, not that she would have. "I'll be back around noon to change your bandage and bring you something to eat." She put on first one heavy rawhide glove, then another.

Holly took up a canvas pack that rested next to the doorframe. The urge to hurt him back was strong, but all she could think of was an ultimatum. "When I come back, you greet me with the barrel of that gun, you're liable to have your lunch on the floor."

Then she slipped out of the room on an icy curl of March air.

The clock on Herrmann & Treber Liquor Dealers storefront read a quarter past one. She was late. She hoped Jack's appetite would be slow in returning as well.

Holly stood on the muddy boardwalk; the rumbling sound of dilapidated wagons and the brassy clink of horse tack cluttered the air of Main Street. She slung her knapsack across her back, mindful of the two bottles she'd just put inside. Early Times whiskey for Jack; apricot brandy for herself.

She hadn't had time to make it to Chinatown, where she usually bought her brandy, so she'd been forced to buy the liquor at a store in town that catered to men. Glad for her unintentional disguise, she'd entered the establishment with a little less apprehension. Covered with grime from head to toe, J. Treber took her for a miner and filled her order without question.

There'd been no questions from Treber, but Lee-Ash had asked plenty earlier that afternoon. Guilt flushed her all over again. As much as she shared her innermost secrets and dreams with Lee-Ash, she couldn't explain Jack Steele's presence in her room without it sounding indecent.

Since the truth was out of the question, she'd had to concoct a plausible excuse to leave work midday, one that Lee-Ash could have no argument with, no further inquiries. She told him she was coming down with her monthly.

That had buttoned him up tighter than an overcoat, and he obligingly rode back to Deadwood with her, adding all the more to her remorse. Lee-Ash would never let her make the trip alone. There were too many Sioux marauding about in the Black Hills. So he'd seen her safely back into town and deposited her at the livery. Then he turned his horse around and headed straight back the way they'd come to finish out the day at his claim.

Holly pushed down the lump of shame thickening her throat and stepped off the boardwalk, trying to reassure herself she'd done the right thing. She'd never lied to Lee-Ash; she didn't like the dishonorable feel of it. It made her stomach upset, and it was Jack Steele's fault.

The storm clouds that had hung low early in the morning when she'd left had all but disappeared. In their place domed the clear expanse of blinding blue sky and a biting chill that seeped through her well-worn garb, despite the coat she wore. The heavy snow had sunk and melted under the high glare of the sun and now lay in patches, like linen spread to bleach.

She crossed the street, with its heavy flow of traffic: a mixture of horses, mules, wagons, and even a small party of mongrel cats and a lone Bantam rooster. A bullwhacker with his team of eight oxen pressed over the new layer of droppings, flourishing a long whip with skillful skyward sweeps. The sharp crack echoed behind her as she sprinted out of its way and hopped onto the populated sidewalk.

No hat tipping saluted her today. Today she blended in with the scenery, unnoticed and unappreciated, lost among the hundreds of other miners who flocked into town.

Disappearing down a narrow alley, she rounded the corner and pulled open the rear entrance of Goodnight's Restaurant and entered the warm kitchen. The pleasant waft of sweet baked goods and fried meats instantly made her mouth water, a sore reminder she'd left her lunch with Lee-Ash.

Carrie Goodnight looked up with a start; her slender fingers ceased working in a large bowl of flour and lard. "Hey, mister, you came in the wrong door. Service is out front."

"Carrie, it's me."

The girl's pale face colored a shade and she blew a strand of honey blond hair away from her forehead. "Why, Mrs. Dancer, I'm sorry! You've never come in here in your work clothes."

She'd never been in too much of a hurry to get to her room. "I must look a sight." Holly glanced down at the candle wax drippings on the toes of her boots.

"You darn near put a scare in me." Carrie moved to the dry sink to rinse off her hands. "What are you doing back in town so early?"

"I felt a cold coming on." Then, for emphasis, Holly sniffed.

Two lies for Jack.

"No doubt," Carrie admonished. "If you don't mind my saying, I think you're plumb crazy to be out there with the rest of them, my father included."

Maybe so, she admitted to herself reluctantly. She was driven to it for motivations she wasn't prepared to explain. She needed to prove to herself she could make it on her own. "I have to." It was all she would admit, a poor excuse with neither a reason nor rhyme.

"That's what Conrath says about freight hauling. I can hardly think about it every time he leaves town on a job, knowing he's out there with all those hostiles—especially after what happened to Johnny Slaughter. It just about sends me into a fit if I dwell on it." Then the young girl's heart-shaped mouth curved into a smile. "But it sure is sweet when he comes back to me. He got in this morning."

Holly only listened with half an ear as it dawned on her that Jack Steele lay precisely above the very spot in which she stood. If Mrs. Goodnight got wind of it, she'd evict her for sure. The very idea made her shift her feet and cast her gaze upward.

"He brought us red apples from Sidney," Carrie went on. "Real apples you don't have to make cider out of! They aren't frozen. He kept them in a burlap sack stuffed with straw. I think that's the most awfully considerate thing, don't you? I made some into a pie."

Holly was vaguely aware of the buttery-spice smell coming from the oven and forced out an appreciative "Mmm." Then she flicked her glance toward the ceiling again.

The revolving door flapped open and Josephine Goodnight bustled into the room, her hands laden with a tray of dirty dishes. It took a minute for Holly's appearance to register in the woman's eyes, then recognition came with a twinkle. "My lands, Mrs. Dancer, you put my heart to work." She deposited the tray on the butcher's island and took a small tablet from her apron pocket. Flipping through it, she read off several orders to her daughter. "I'll need one roast pork, turnips, and applesauce. Two fried chicken and potatoes."

"Yes, Mother." Carrie inclined her head in compliance and set out to work.

"Enjoy your day off, Mrs. Dancer. Help yourself to lunch." Mrs. Goodnight scurried from the galley as quickly as she had entered it.

"Go ahead, Holly," Carrie said, dishing up a plate of mashed potatoes. "Take some of that roast turkey. It's good for what ails you. And there's bread pudding in the warming oven."

"Thank you." Holly hastily picked up a plate from the wall cupboard and began filling it with slices of white meat. She took a modest helping, afraid that any more might peek the girl's curiosity.

"As soon as that pie's finished, I'll bring you up a slice. That ought to—"

"No!" Holly protested too swiftly. Seeing the disconcerted look on Carrie's face, Holly blurted out, "I—I'm going to take a nap right after lunch. I'll be sleeping, so there's no need to bring it up. I can come down later for a piece." To drive home her meaning, she forced out a sneeze.

"Oh." Carrie's light brows tilted up. "Well, I hope it's nothing serious. I'd better take these plates out to Mother so they don't get cold. Feel better, Mrs. Dancer."

"Yes . . . thank you." Holly coerced another small sniffle.

As soon as Carrie left the room, Holly spooned a generous helping of bread pudding next to the meat. Looking over her shoulder, she added a turkey leg, feeling every bit the thief as she was doing so. Even though she'd been given permission, she'd never have taken so much for herself. Not pondering over a reason, she impulsively grabbed a handful of potato chips out of the canister. She covered up the overloaded plate with a napkin.

Pushing open the door with the heel of her boot, she backed out onto the screened-in porch. She took up a bucket from the utility bench and filled it with water from the cistern. She'd have to clean up in her washbasin. She wished more than anything to be able to fill her half-tub and take a hot bath. But since Jack would be her audience, that was out of the question. There was the bathhouse on lower Main, except it was another one of Deadwood's male-dominated commodities. Regretfully she loaded her arms with the plate and nearly full bucket.

As she trudged up the outside stairs to her room, a sudden attack of butterflies invaded her empty stomach. The prospect of finding Jack waiting for her played havoc with her routine life. If he'd thought her attire offensive when she was clean, what would he think of her now? She was covered with mud and grime from head to toe.

She almost went back down to clean up on the porch. Almost. Let him coolly look down his nose on her; she wasn't concerned about his approval, nor anyone else's. Her independence had freed her from reprimands.

Holly juggled her load and groped for the small doorknob. A slow turn saw the solid wood give way inwardly. She hoped he'd taken her warning about his gun seriously, but just in case, she wanted to make sure he knew it was her at the latch.

"Mr. Steele?" she called out. Despite her best efforts, her voice was faintly breathless. "It's Holly Dancer."

When there was no answer, she conjured a whole slew of fearful images in her head that he'd induced himself to bleeding again—or worse, died. Without preamble, she stepped inside, her eyesight adapting to the veiled darkness of the drawn curtains. In the low light of the lantern she'd left on, she immediately focused her attention on the bed.

Jack was sprawled out on the rumpled covers, one leg dangling over the side of the mattress. She strained her vision to see his chest was indeed moving, albeit lazily. She allowed herself a breath of relief, then tipped the corner of her mouth to a tight smile. For a man who apparently prided himself on being audaciously alert, he certainly was dead to the world asleep. His forearm crossed over his wide chest; the long-barreled revolver kept guard in his lean fingers, his hand nestled in the thick wedge of black hair at his breastbone.

The very sight of him sleeping in her bed did funny things to her insides. She was never more painfully aware of being a woman, and these new feelings were too pleasant to be true. They contradicted everything she knew about sex, going against the grain of her brief experience.

She wanted to touch the bare expanse of his chest; to comb back the dark strands of hair from his brow. The memory of his silken hair came back to her in a teasing reminder, and she was sorry she'd ever touched him at all.

Restlessly she set the plate and bucket on the edge of her washstand and slipped off her canvas pack. She set the knapsack down without care to being quiet, hoping he would wake up and she wouldn't be left alone with her disconnected thoughts.

He made no motion. It annoyed her.

She moved to stand over him. Holly found two empty bottles on the mussed sheets that twisted over his flat abdomen and exposed thigh. The Great English Remedy and—her eyes widened a fraction—her Hood's Sarsaparilla. Jack must have been in desperate pain.

She watched him a moment; watched how some random dream played across his ruggedly handsome face. There was no denying she'd never seen a more striking display of inherent strength. It commanded the arch of his black brows, the strong line of his nose, and the firmness of his mouth. The shadow of his beard only added to his masculine appeal.

She denied the cascade of flesh-raising tingles raining through her and blamed them on the coolness in the room. She decided for now to pull a blanket over him, then check the parlor stove. When she reached for the spread, her fingers bumped the cold spine of a leather-bound book. Pulling it free, she saw that it was the second volume to *Pamela*.

Her mouth curved into a smile. She would have liked to see the expression on his face when he'd started reading the romance novel, with its sentimentality of the feminine mind. Holly set it back on the bed just as Jack shifted his weight. His movement sent the book plummeting to the floor with a sharp slap.

Jack leveled the Buntline to a deadly angle before his charcoal eyes flitted open.

Holly cried out her protest and jumped clear of his accurately pointed revolver. "It's me! It's Holly!"

A faint, disorientated expression glazed Jack's eyes as he focused in on Holly's face. As he came completely around, he apparently recognized who he was contending with. "Dammit." He choked the sleep from his deep voice. "What the hell are you trying to do to me?"

"N-nothing." Holly tried to get hold of her slipping composure. His aim was a dangerous reminder that he was a man used to holding guns on people.

Jack winced as he settled the revolver into the folds of the blanket. His chest rose and fell with pronunciation as he got his bearings back. "Damn . . . What time is it?"

"One-thirty," she replied in a clipped tone, averting her eyes from the well-muscled span of his naked chest. She told herself she didn't care if he was so offhanded about nearly blowing her head off.

"Thought you said you'd be back by noon." He turned his head to face her, then his curved brows came crashing down to a sharp point. "What happened to you?"

Holly turned, slipped off her soiled rubber poncho and pea coat, and hung them on the wall hook. She knew it had been coming, so why was she so upset that he'd make a point of her disheveled appearance?

She was mad at herself for feeling less than whole in his eyes. By the time she faced him again, she was so infuriated by her humiliation, she sharpened her gaze on his face, hoping her expression wasn't as muddied as she felt. "I mine in the dirt, Mr. Steele. I get dirty," she stated in a no-nonsense voice. Then she looked down and smoothed a dried piece of mud from her pants—as if it made any difference.

The knees to her trousers were crusted with the dark, claylike soil, her boots covered with taper wax and dirt. The only thing halfway clean was her shirt, and that had only been saved since she'd worn her coat in the mine. Her hands were grimy where the dirt had sifted past her gloves. No doubt her face was just as smudged. She looked up to see Jack getting an eyeful.

The appreciation in his gaze as he skimmed over her muddied trousers muddled all her scathing thoughts. He countered his own attack by battling her with a slow, seductive rake. She was baffled by the turn of events, and even more perplexed by her own body's response—the strange aching in her limbs that made her knees tremble.

She tried her best to ignore his hard stare, but she could have sworn she saw a flicker of admiration mixed with his study. There was a brief moment when she thought he might be admiring her as a woman, then quickly quelled it as unlikely.

Holly resolved to put an end to the game he was playing with her, working her teeth over her lip and trying to ignore his review. "How are you feeling?"

He gave up his perusal, but not without a small fight in his gray eyes; then he gritted his teeth. "Like I've been struck by a freight wagon. How can you tolerate these blasphemous tonics? The aftertaste is enough to make you wish you rode out the long haul on your own." Raising his good arm, he rubbed his fingers across his stubbled jaw.

"You're not supposed to take them both at the same time, nor are you supposed to drink the entire contents at one sitting." She furrowed her brows. "Just how did you get the Hood's? It was on my desk."

He gave her a deep grimace. "It was crucial that I get up."

Holly was sure her cheeks colored the shade of a ripe raspberry over his obvious meaning. She didn't make matters worse by dwelling on the subject, though felt inclined to ask, "How did you manage on your feet?"

"I nearly knocked myself out," he countered, with a fine edge of disgust in his resonant voice.

Holly had the feeling the admission of deficiency was as painful to him as his wound. "Then you'd better stay in bed until you're up to it."

She went to the single window, wondering how long that would be while parting the muslin drapes. She wasn't sure she could outlast him.

A warming splash of sunlight swelled across the small room, momentarily distracting her.

Deadwood, being in such a deep gulch, was never privy to a golden-pink-swept sunrise or a purple twilight. A high sun appeared a little before noon from White Rocks, the limestone peaks in the east, and several hours later, instantly vanished beyond the heavily timbered Forest Hill to the west. Holly rarely frequented her room at this time to observe nature's cheating game; she hardly ever saw the direct sun play across her planked walls.

"Why do you work a claim?" Jack asked, startling her by his question. "It's a lot of work for a man, much less a woman."

She stared out the window, not quite knowing the answer herself. At one time there'd been too many reasons to count, and now they'd melted down to one which she couldn't explain or even hope that he would understand. It had to do with accomplishment, of proving her worth to no one but herself. It was a compensation she needed in her life. "My late husband owned the claim, and I can't part with it" was all she told him.

Tossing her hat off, she tilted her face to the bright rays, letting the heat rain down on her cheeks, her nose, and her chin.

"How did he die?"

Holly froze, the sun seemingly burning over her while a coldness knotted in her stomach. "He was murdered," she finally replied. "Shot in the back for the small poke of gold he carried."

"I'm sorry."

Holly felt his sincerity. "Thank you."

"You have any ideas who did it?"

Surprised by his direct question, she said slowly, "No. Should I?"

"Just thought you might be interested. He was your husband."

"Of course I'm interested," she returned, more than a little indignant.

"Sorry I asked." Jack's tone was flat.

Why had he gone out of his way to rile her? Or had she only imagined it? One could never be sure in Deadwood when a stranger asked questions. She had no reason to think Jack's probe was anything more than innocent, but just the same, she cut off any further inquiries by turning away from the window. "I brought you something to eat, and I'll change your bandage as soon as I've cleaned up."

She extinguished the lantern and poured some of the water into her basin.

Once at the washstand, she saw Jack's reflection in the mirror, assessing her from his position in the bed. He stared at her through half-open eyes that she willed to turn away, but they did not.

She suddenly wished she had cleaned up on the porch, free of his interest in her personal care. The simple task of washing her face and hands turned into something wickedly intimate, and not even in marriage had she had a man's attention over her grooming.

It both aggravated her and stimulated her as she rolled up

her soiled sleeves. She told herself to ignore him, to go on about her business as if he weren't there. But when she was barely able to hold the soap between her fingers, she couldn't help turning to face him. With difficulty she asked, "I . . . would you please look somewhere else?"

He made things more trying by his counter. "Why? You planning on showing me something I shouldn't see?"

"No," she breathed sharply. "It's just that I'm not used to . . . that is, I never . . . Just close your eyes."

He gave a short laugh, raked her over once with his lazy gaze, then averted his attention to the ceiling. She felt stark naked in front of him, and it angered her that he could strip her down with a mere look in his coercing eyes. She vented her frustration as she vigorously worked the cake into pale suds and scrubbed her hands and arms.

She thought to tell him something to keep him occupied. "I got you some whiskey."

Holly felt him looking at her and forced the heat from her skin, swishing the cold water over her burning flesh, shivering from the bite of it. She'd almost forgotten what she'd told him, then remembered while dipping her elbows in the basin to rinse off her arms. "It wasn't easy getting it."

She was talking, but she didn't really know what she was talking about. She knew she was acting flighty and nonsensical, but she couldn't help herself. Anything to divert her awareness of him.

She snatched up the soap again and ran it across her cheeks. She talked while soaping the rest of her face. "Treber thought I was a man."

"Treber must be in need of a pair of pince-nez glasses."

"What?" Holly froze and chanced a glance at Jack. The mere look in his eyes indolently appraising her was more than she could stand. She was shocked by her overwhelming feel of . . . arousal. Her breasts felt heavy, and the core of her being melted like hot candle wax.

Jack licked his full lips. "I said, Treber must be blind. It's more than apparent you're no man."

"Oh . . ." She turned back to the washstand, the hairs on the back of her neck prickling under his irreverent gaze. "Well, for your sake, you should be glad he did." Though she spoke the words, she didn't hear herself actually saying them; she was caught in a cloud that had her senses pitted against Jack Steele.

Closing her eyes, she doused her face with fresh water and grabbed for the towel from the bar on the washstand. She dried herself, then stared at him. Now that she no longer was occupied with what she assumed Steele found provocative, she dared him to look away with disinterest, the way Billy often did.

A muscle in Jack's jaw tensed, as if he read the challenge in her stance. Despite herself, an ache pressed down in the bottom of her stomach as her gaze swept over his chin, then moved upward toward his mouth. Was it really as hard as it looked? Or soft like her own? Would it be moist against hers if he kissed her? Her pulse veered down a hazardous road.

Instead of confronting the fascination and explosive currents he evoked in her, she deliberately shut them out, refusing to believe them true. She couldn't bare a man's rejection again. But ignoring Jack was like ignoring a man in a ladies' fashion shop, especially since she still had to change her clothes.

Since he'd disregarded her request to keep his eyes averted when she'd washed, how on earth was she going to keep him from watching her strip out of her dirty clothes?

"Mr. Steele, you'll have to turn away so I can . . . finish up." She anticipated trouble from him, and when it didn't come with his one-word answer, she was relieved.

"Sure," Jack's voice cracked, laden with huskiness as he leaned his head deeper into the pillow and closed his eyelids.

Holly dashed to her clothes cupboard behind the bed's headboard and practically flung one of the doors open. She rummaged for a dress and shoes, heedless to which she selected. Yanking a paisley concoction from a hanger, she draped it over the rail board and deftly unfastened the buttons on her flannel shirt. In record time she kicked off her boots, shucked free her trousers, and stood in her chemise.

Grabbing a heavy petticoat from a dowel in the cupboard, she shimmied into it and disregarded any notion of the endless act of lacing up a corset. The dress glided over her head and, in a frantic nimbleness of her fingers, was fastened posthaste.

Collecting herself with a hand to her racing heartbeat, she stepped clear of the corner and out into the room.

"Damn fast change," Jack drawled.

"Yes, well . . ." She patted down the folds in her dress.

"You always take your clothes off so fast with a man around?"

"Yes! No! I mean," she choked in defense, "I never have a man around."

"Damn shame." Jack's inspection traveled down the close-fitting front of her cotton dress. "No one to appreciate your pretty feet."

"My feet?" Holly looked down. She'd been so reckless getting dressed, she hadn't paid attention to the cold bareness of her feet. Her toes curled over the floorboards, and she attempted to push down the hem of her dress.

She managed what she hoped was a casual walk to the corner where she'd left her shoes. "Anybody else would have had the sense not to mention that."

"I'm not anybody else."

No, you're not, Holly thought. You're toying with me like I'm a ball of yarn and you're a cat. Well, it won't work, Mr. Steele.

It only took a second to pull on her stockings and glide her feet into her kid slippers.

Holly moved to the washstand, poured fresh water into the pitcher, and dumped her dirty water into the now empty bucket.

Crossing to the bed, Holly deposited the necessary items to change his bandage on the edge of the mattress. She looked at Jack's expectant face, trying not to dwell on the misery she was going to put him through, but at the same time, thinking it oddly fair he suffer as much as he was making her suffer. Did he know what he was doing to her? "Do you want the whiskey?"

"Why not? My stomach was killed off hours ago."

Holly passed him the Early Times, and he popped the cork and lifted it to his lips. She watched as he effortlessly downed a generous portion of the pale brass-colored liquor. "How does your arm feel?"

"Like a firecracker," he conceded grim-faced. "But watching you the past half hour has made me think of something else."

She flushed in what felt like a royal fashion, knowing he had been thinking the exact same things as she had. "I guess misery deserves company."

"What does that mean?"

"I don't feel that well myself."

Jack handed her back the bottle. "Do me now then," he commanded evenly.

Do me? She wouldn't have known what to do with him in a million years. She glanced at his face and realized he was talking about his bandage. Her face flamed at the traitorous thoughts her mind played on her. She inhaled shakily and set out to work. She bit down on her lower lip and looked once at Jack. He'd shut his eyes and clenched his teeth tighter than a closed trap.

"What did you think of *Pamela?*" she asked offhandedly, rinsing the cloth out.

"Who the hell is Pamela?" He kept his lids down, his nostrils flared against the pain.

"The girl in the book you were reading."

"Oh, *her,*" he muttered. "How can you read that stuff? It's nothing but romantic bullsh—" He cut himself off and rephrased his comment. "Idealism."

At that, Holly cleansed his arm with a little more pressure than the first time, causing him to let out a gnashed yelp. She knew he was right about the book. It was purely fictitious. No man could ever want a woman so much, he'd give anything to have her.

He peered at her through his inky lashes. "No argument?"

"Unfortunately, no. It is a lot of nonsense. I don't know of a man, especially one in Mr. B.'s position, who would go to such lengths to have Pamela."

"Then you don't know the right kind of men. Some would kill to possess a woman."

Her heart tripped over a beat. The look in his eyes said

that he was that sort of man. What sort of woman would he be after? Preoccupied with that thought, she trickled some of the whiskey over his upper arm without warning.

"Dammit!" he ground out with a jolt.

"Sorry," she mumbled, and quickly dabbed at his wound with a towel. "Have . . . have you ever killed a man over a woman?"

He stared up at her, his gray eyes piercing. "I've never found a woman I wanted bad enough."

"Oh," she breathed jaggedly.

"Why do you ask?"

"I . . . No reason."

"I think you're reading the wrong kind of books, Holly Dancer. You should be concentrating on dime novels. There's plenty of action in them. Damn good chance some are about me."

"Modest, aren't you?" Holly retorted, sure he was making fun of her. She rewrapped his arm with fresh bandages and was tying them off when Jack skimmed his hand across her forearm to gently caress her wrist. The sudden tender gesture made her breath catch and her hands still.

"I do that to you?" he asked in a low rumble, rubbing over the bruise on her wrist.

Holly looked down on the blemish that had turned a purplish yellow overnight. So caught up was she in his touch, she was barely able to think about an answer. His fingertips were strong. Imagine. just those small appendages so deathly powerful, yet so coaxingly sweet. Jack Steele was a man with many discrepancies. He was confusing her more by the minute. "Yes," she finally managed. "You didn't know what you were doing."

Jack's callused hand drifted down. His fingers meshed with her own and he stroked her palm with the ball of his thumb. He moved in a circular motion, all around the pad of her hand, massaging the joints where her fingers began. She couldn't believe the innocence of his gesture sent her pulse racing out of control. She wasn't sure what to do . . . what to say.

Holly lifted her gaze to Jack's. He was staring at her as no other man ever had—with desire, as if she were the most beautiful woman he'd ever seen. It made her feel faint and breathless. If he did kiss her, it would be passionate and all-consuming. Two of the things she wasn't.

Not wanting to disappoint him, Holly pulled her hand free. "Your . . ." Her voice was heavy with glazed emotion. "Your lunch is getting cold."

She pushed off the bed to fetch the plate she'd left on the washstand. She felt herself breaking out in a sweat. Swaying, she leaned her fingers over the stand's top, taking a moment to calm her nerves; she kept her back toward him. Things were happening here that were unexplainable and went against her every practical sense.

She wavered, her mind reeling. "Mr. Steele, why did you come to me for help?"

His reply was long in coming, and she was about to turn around when she heard him say, " 'Cause I wanted to see if you slept barefoot to your ears."

The very implication of it set off a catastrophic reaction within her that made her surrender to her heart and hope. Hope that there was a chance, yet knowing he was lawless and she was order. He was fire and she was ice. Yet despite all of the obvious, he'd given her a feeling she'd treasure long after he'd ridden out of the Black Hills and taken his dark allure with him.

He'd made her feel desirable.

Jack stared at the shadows on the wall, then turned his head to the pallet on the floor below him. Holly lay stretched out in front of the parlor stove, her back toward him. She'd been asleep for hours, yet that state had overlooked him. He assumed she was able to sleep because she was bone-tired. He, on the other hand, had done nothing but get drunk on poisonous tonics and Early Times. A combination that addled his brain and left him with a headache, not the sleep he needed. But what relief would he get in slumber? What little sleep he'd had that day was clouded by Holly Dancer's face. Christ, she was a perplexity.

It had been one thing to trifle with her and know she'd reject him, but quite another to see a glimmer of surrender in her azure eyes. Her chin held a position of indecision, then defiance. Her lips worried with self-doubt and hesitation. But in the end, he knew he'd won. She'd have him.

It had been a long time since a woman on the right side of the parlor had even come close to succumbing to him. He'd started something, and it was he who'd been caught in the trap. He never intended to feel anything for her. He'd thought to put his heart-rending days long behind his spurs. And yet, when she'd stared at him with confused desire, he wanted to enfold her in his arms, and rather than ravish her mouth, he wanted to tenderly touch his lips to hers and kiss away her apprehension.

He slipped the mouth of the Early Times bottle to his lips and poured into his throat another drink of numbness. Though all the liquor he'd consumed had done nothing to ease the ache within him. It settled in his chest and spread to his loins, making the pain in his arm seem like a womanish prick of a sewing needle.

He wanted her.

Bastard that he was, he wanted her for his own personal reasons.

She mewed from her makeshift bed and stirred, lazing over onto her back. He shifted, feeling himself grow tight and heated as he hungrily appreciated the outline of her breasts and the flatness of her belly beneath the blankets strewn over her.

Her long mahogany hair was plaited down her head and streamed next to her in a thick, glossy rope. Only hours ago, he'd watched her arrange the rich strands. It had fascinated him the way she could glide her fingertips, weaving her hair into a perfect braid. Amazingly, he'd never once seen a woman fix her hair. Usually he was on the other end—the woman was taking it down.

He recollected their late lunch and the conversation—what few words he'd spoken. She'd carried the dialogue, informing him on everything from the current weather to the latest gold prices, after handing him his plate. He'd been surprised to see she'd tossed on some potato chips and wondered what made her do it. He'd eaten in silence, listening to her go on; he'd sensed her talk was being fueled by nerves.

Dusk set in soon after they were finished. He'd watched her make an early bed on the floor and wearily lie down on it without even bothering to light a lantern after closing the drapes. It seemed as if she'd drifted off to sleep effortlessly.

Jack forced his gaze away from her now. He had to have been out of his mind when he'd told Deerhorn to bring him here. What had he hoped to accomplish by coming to Holly Dancer? An answer to her husband's murder? Hardly. She seemed more than unwilling to talk about it. Did that mean she was still in love with the man? For some reason, that thought made him clench his fingers into tight fists.

It was easier to think that despite what she said about being interested in the identity of her husband's killer, she didn't give a damn Billy Dancer was dead—the latter hardly an appeasing alternative.

Steele closed his eyes and willed himself to sleep. A feat only made harder because he was commanding himself to do so. He kept thinking about his throbbing arm. Damn that Deerhorn. The young whelp better have ridden out of Deadwood if he knew what was good for him.

Sometime later Jack realized he must have dozed off. When he opened his eyes, a faint slash of light filtered into the room. He groaned and lifted himself onto his good side, resting the bulk of his upper body's weight on his elbow. It was then he noticed Holly's absence.

How had she gotten out of the room without his hearing her? Twice she'd eluded him; first coming, now going. Two times more than his pride could take. He'd always dignified himself as being one of the most alert men he'd ever known—even in the dregs of a good drunk.

Her pallet had been made up and cleared away, the blankets folded on top of her trunk. He could only assume she was working at the restaurant since today was Thursday, having picked up at least that much out of their conversation the previous night. Her days were mapped out like the territory, the same no matter how you read it week after week.

Jack pushed himself to sitting with a heavy complaint. He slumped over the headboard and gritted his teeth against the pain. It wasn't too much from his arm now, but his head was splitting wide as a jagged valley from getting filled to the ears on bug juice. Rubbing his eyes, he focused on the washstand in the corner and the basin that was hopefully full of stone-sobering ice-cold water.

Standing, he pushed his bare feet over the chilly floorboards as he took his first step, his heel hitting the empty bottle of whiskey. He muttered a curse under his breath as the glass rolled out from under him. Stumbling in the curtained light of the room, he moved to the window first and looped open the drapes. Resting his forehead against the frosty panes, he looked discreetly down on Main Street.

It must be midmorning by the loaded freight wagons traveling each direction, though the sun wasn't over the mountains yet. Jack studied the goings-on a minute, recognizing the bleached frontier hat tilted over Tom Deerhorn's white hair. He lazed against the awning post of the Red Bird across the street, brandishing a low whistle at the few ladies who passed by. They rightfully snubbed him, and he had the denseness to laugh at the scoff.

The blood pounded over Jack's temples at the sight of the no-account cow pie who had incapacitated him for two days.

Tom fit his holsters, adjusting them over his narrow hips and making a big play of the procedure. He'd reached down to pinwheel the rowel at his boot heel with his thumbnail, watching it glint in slow revolutions. When he lifted his chin up, he caught sight of Jack at Holly's window and gave him a mile-wide smile. He'd apparently thought things between them had been smoothed over; his show of teeth instantly faded as he saw the rage come to light on Jack's face.

Forgetting to be inconspicuous, Steele fumbled with the latch on top of the sash to open it. Viewing that, Deerhorn's brown eyes bugged and he made a quick leap to the corner and kicked up mud down Lee Street.

"Dammit to hell!" Jack yelled through the eight-paned glass window as it remained stuck in position. Pounding his fist on the frame, he sorely felt the need to handle the strength of his gun, if only to imagine what it would feel like to nail Deerhorn to the wall. But when Jack reached down for the Buntline, he was once again reminded he was bereft of that piece of iron. Where the devil had Holly gone and put it now?

The pitcher of water took second place to finding his Colt .45. He felt buck naked and downright uneven without the secure weight of the weapon next to his right thigh.

He veered his direction to the desk and a tin box with small holes decoratively punched in its top. There were two bullets next to it.

They weren't his.

It came back to him that she'd pulled a gun on him the night he'd come. If he'd been someone she needed to protect herself against, she would have been left up to the mercy of her intruder over the inadequacy of that firearm she owned.

Curious, he flipped the box's lid open with his index finger, wondering if he'd find his Buntline inside.

It was not.

He should have gone on with his business; instead he was drawn to the contents. Poking around the oddly shaped pieces of her fallen-apart gun, he brushed aside the chamber, walnut hand grip, and more bullets. He stopped when he came in contact with a plain gold band. No doubt her wedding ring. Touching the sacred symbol made him break out in a cold sweat, and it conjured a few of his own devils. He shut them out, much as he always did when they decided to open his door of humanity.

Forcing himself to indifference, he continued on with his examination of the box, knowing that he was a blackguard for doing so. This was Holly's personal place. A place he had no right to be in. But the possessions were a piece of her that he could not see from the woman herself. Here she was vulnerable to him.

Inside were odds and ends, mementos of things past. Theater ticket stubs, a single pearl, two coins, a lone hair comb with one of its teeth missing, and a pair of ornamental Chinese earrings.

He picked up the intricate jade earbobs and fingered them, imagining for a moment . . . He damned himself. He couldn't get involved. Not with her, not with anyone.

Jack slammed the tin lid down and looked at the bullets next to the box. He stared at them for a long time; so long, his eyes grew dry. Blinking, he flicked the lid open again, pulling out the pieces of the gun. He scattered them on the desk and rearranged them in their proper order.

It was a seven-shot Smith & Wesson .22 revolver made in the early 1860s; its barrel tipped upward when you broke it to reload. It had been ahead of its time back then, being the first to use metallic cartridges. Now it was outdated and had been improved by the Colt manufacturing company.

It was still an accurate piece, though. Accurate enough for even the best arms men to count on it.

Jack rolled the three-inch barrel and examined it. There was no telling how recently it had been fired. Picking up a bullet, he held it up to the light to discern the end stamp and calculate how much power it held.

One thing was obvious. It was small-caliber—the same type bullet Billy Dancer had been killed with.

He told the voice inside him to shut up, and constricted the sickness that rose from his belly. Steele wanted to deny what stared him in the face; he wanted to brush it off as coincidence. But it was a link.

It was the only one he had, and damn him, he had connected it to Holly Dancer.

Chapter Six

Jack lingered at the desk to reassemble the Smith & Wesson; he reasoned the small exercise would force the stiffness from his arm. His well-intended motives goaded him each time a block of pain sanded his nerve endings. He disregarded the cool sheen of moisture on his brow as he oiled the weapon with some ancient gun oil he'd found in a rusted can at the back of one of her cubbies. Wiping the iron parts with a clean cloth first, he expertly fit them back together; they coupled like a puzzle. A deadly puzzle.

Now he leaned his weight back on the chair's rail and rolled the freshly lubricated cylinder with the tip of his forefinger. Listening to the smooth whir it made while turning full rotations, Jack detected no rough spots. The weapon had been set right. Right enough to slug a miner in a dark alley and make off with his poke—if it had ever been used for that.

He hated being cynical, but over the years cynicism had taken over optimism and he'd grown accustomed to trusting no one but himself and his instincts. But as he thought over his beliefs, a contradicting voice gave him a lecture in a mocking tone; he'd trusted Holly and she'd kept his whereabouts a secret, and so, he suspected, had that lack-brain Deerhorn.

Jack compressed the cold trigger, the easy click snapping in his ears. He felt his pulse ticking at the back of his neck, surging down his arm, as he fought the impulse to trust her. Trust and honor—these virtues had failed him in the past. Facts—those, he could count on. Solid and tangible.

Irritated, he returned the gun into its shiny box and flipped the top down. He shoved a shock of annoying hair from his eyes and picked up a goose-quill pen and a snowy leaf of parchment.

He made a list of places to investigate, people to talk to. All the while, he reasoned he was headed in the right direction. Though as the list grew, he slowed the pen. Abruptly he made a long line down the center bottom half of the sheet. The left column took the heading "guilty"; the right column, "innocent." He made what he considered a reasonable list of explanations in Holly's favor, the most meaningful—from what he'd seen—that Holly Dancer couldn't use a gun. That fact left room for instinct; instinct was the reason he'd left a law practice. Hunches could save a man's life; though where Holly was concerned, his hunches had been botched the day he'd set eyes on her.

Staring down at his notations, he scratched several out and added others in their place. Someone had taken a shot at her—she had that in her favor. But then again, could be she'd been working with a partner . . . or a lover . . . and crossed him bad enough for him to want her dead.

Frustrated, he blew a strand of hair from his nose and grabbed up another sheet, pausing to sink the angled point into the inkwell again.

Absently he let the quill hover over the fresh piece of stationery; a single black drop fell and marred the page. He should compose her a note, but he had never been any good at words of thanks, much less writing them down. Were he to leave her a letter of gratitude, it may mislead her to thinking there was more to it than that. He had to keep things noncommittal. When at last he decided this, the ink drop had turned into a confusion of scratches and doodles he paid no attention to, finally stabling the pen.

He picked up his original list, tested the ink for dryness,

then folded it. Standing, he put the paper in his pants pocket.

Jack searched the room, finding his holsters and Buntline under the bed once again. As he knelt to retrieve them, his equilibrium faltered and he fought against the idea of lying back down.

He couldn't.

He had to get out of Holly's room—get to where he wouldn't be subjected to the smell of orange blossoms and the clean scent of castile soap that clung to the air.

He needed to be rid of the complications of her domain; her impractical book *Pamela;* her ridiculous tonics; and God help him, her beguiling face.

Jack gathered up his Wellingtons and sat on the mattress's edge. He needed the use of two hands to put them on. The cords of his left arm muscles strained as he grabbed hold of the boot's side to slip his foot in, the searing pain so intense, it left him panting—and damning himself for it. Impatiently he threw the boot. It landed with a whack on the floor. He stood, seized it, maneuvered his toes through the opening while hopping about, and stomped his heel down hard into it without the aid of his hands.

He hadn't been able to find his shirt and undershirt, and refused to use what must have been one of Billy Dancer's hanging from a hook by the door.

Rigging a makeshift sling for his arm out of several strips Holly had set aside for bandages, he attempted to tie it on; he cursed again, his haste to be out of the room hindering his fingers and making them work against him. Finally he calmed enough to get the job done, and he eased into his coat bare-chested. The strain on his shoulder muscles made him grit his teeth.

Jack grabbed his hat from the headboard and fit the crown low on his forehead. As he opened the latch, frosty winter air instantly seeped through his long coat and met with his shirtless chest, causing his skin to prickle and bump. He took one quick survey of the alley below and deemed it clear of unwanted attention.

Heedless of the cold, he closed the door behind him; his intentions and thoughts were on one person:

Edward McIntyre, leader of the league of miners in Deadwood Gulch.

The man who had hired him.

Holly was working at the butcher's island gathering flour from the granary bin when she heard three sharp, heavy clomps above her head. She dropped the full scoop she held, powdering the hem of her brown broadcloth dress, the tips of her shoes, and the kitchen floor.

She glanced desperately at Mrs. Goodnight, who rinsed potatoes in a colander at the dry sink. Apparently she'd been too engrossed to hear the ruckus coming from Holly's room.

Another clomp. Holly quickly snatched up a chicken roaster and smashed the lid over the pan like a cymbal. Josephine turned and gave her a curious stare, which Holly countered with feigned innocence and a slight upturn at the corner of her mouth.

Holly held in her breath, waiting to see if the noise would come again; it didn't. She didn't know whether to be relieved or worried to death. What was going on up there?

Fearful images began to build in her mind. What if Steele fell out of bed and couldn't get up? What if he was lying there, his arm bleeding again? She felt momentary panic as her imagination ran on. What if the boy who shot Jack had found him and they were battling it out?

She chewed on her lower lip and cast her gaze toward the ceiling. She had to force herself to remain calm, to not fly out the door to see for herself what was going on. If she did that, it certainly would arouse Mrs. Goodnight's suspicion.

Holly bent to clean up the flour, her head tilted to catch any further noises aloft.

Silence. Not even the remotest hint of a scuffle.

She rinsed out her rag in the wash bucket and tried to quell the uneasiness in her stomach.

It wasn't until nearly a quarter hour later she was able to slip out and dash up the stairs to her room to check on Jack.

By the time she'd shoved the door inward, she'd formed a dozen different scenes in her head.

Emptiness wasn't one of them.

She squinted, peering around the room, expecting to see him sprawled in a corner somewhere. Nothing. There were no signs of a struggle; no disruptions of any kind marked the apartment—except for the rumpled bed, which she always made up prior to going to work.

Her shoulders fell forward in disbelief, her heartbeat slowing to normal. Stepping inside, she tried to find signs of foul play.

She could see none.

Holly slumped onto the untidy bedclothes and rested her cheek against the cool wrought iron of the footrail. He was gone, pure and simple, and of his own accord. Why that should even remotely disturb her was a mystery. She should have been breathing easier over his departure.

Then why did she suddenly feel so abandoned . . . so betrayed? What had she expected? Accolades of praise and undying thanks?

She smoothed the sheets; they smelled like Jack. The masculine scent of him that was uniquely his own: a little bit like the leather from his holsters; a slight hint of Early Times; and—she shuddered—blood.

She absently touched the coverlet where she'd scrubbed at the bloodstain he'd made the night he'd come. It had left a dull brown mark she'd have to have cleaned at the Chinese laundry. Then all visible traces of Jack Steele would be gone. It would be as if he'd never come.

Holly pressed her hand to the mussed-up feather pillow, following the low valley it made where Jack had rested his head. Her cheeks burned in remembrance of his watchful stare, and she quickly smashed her fist into the indentation.

Quietly standing, she assured herself his absence was for the better. Her resolve revitalized her, and she leveled her chin with a weak smile.

Sunlight glared off the empty whiskey bottle on the floor next to her writing desk. As she walked to pick it up, she noticed Jack had opened her curtains before he'd left. Bending, she picked up the Early Times and set it on her cherrywood desktop. She noticed her inkpot had been moved.

Her attention now focused on the single piece of stationery covered with hen tracks and . . . an eye. Holly sat down
and studied the parchment. Most of what was on it was
mindless scribble; what caught her interest was the eye. It
had been formed around a heavy droplet of ink, which had
become the iris and pupil. The eyelid was shadowed by
diagonal lines and the single brow, dark and defined. Below
it was written "We Never Sleep."

Who never slept?

The three words had been gone over numerous times; so
much, the paper thinned and the ink had bled through to the
plain sheets below it.

Holly exhausted all interpretations of the bizarre note,
deciding it was nothing more than an eye with a silly little
paradoxical saying. Even so, she couldn't bring herself to
destroy it. Instead, she creased it in quarters and stuck it in
her tin box.

Then she saw her revolver had been pieced together. As
she picked it up, the nutty odor of oil came to her nose. The
eight-ounce Smith & Wesson felt light in her hands compared to Jack's heavy Colt. She gripped the butt and curled
her finger over the trigger.

The ominous power of a firing piece—even a .22—came
back to her in a rushing vision. She closed her eyes and saw
Billy's prostrate form and the blood saturating the back of
his shirt; the deathly chalkiness of his face and skin; the cold
table he'd been put on at the undertaker's.

Holly's lids flew open and she dropped the Smith &
Wesson with a strangled cry. Tears stung her throat, and she
scraped the chair away from the desk. Blindly she moved to
her kerosene container at the shelf of her washstand and
lifted it. Relief swept through her, seeing it full enough to
fuel her lamp tonight.

There was no comfort in the darkness now that Jack was
gone.

She condemned him for ever coming to her—for ever
making her feel the slightest bit safe from her nightmares;
for making her feel like a beautiful rose. Now the petals had
fallen, leaving only an ugly stem, and it was so much easier

to be angry with him than face the acute sense of loss at his departure.

Suddenly she felt very plain, very stupid, and oh, so very alone.

No moon gilded the land, the solitary dark night the only company. Jack swore at the heavy blackness around him, with only the faintest of light coming from the thin sprinkling of stars in the jet expanse of sky. From his seat in the saddle, he could barely make out the spiny boughs of blue spruce and rock that littered the sides of the gorge he was entering.

He should have been here two nights ago. He held on to hope Edward McIntyre had kept returning each midnight thereafter to wait for him when he hadn't shown.

As he'd been instructed by McIntyre's communication, he was to leave his horse tethered at a copse of scrub brush, then follow the ravine's edge until it came to an abandoned shaft. He should enter the mine and follow the left drift until he came upon McIntyre in the winze. It seemed overly cautious to Jack, but he'd rather be alive to wonder about it than dead knowing he'd been too careless.

Jack found the mouth of the deserted claim, but to descend into the bowels of the earth through a dark hole he knew nothing about required a lot of fool courage. Even he wasn't above admitting the blasted pit scourged his male ego. He nudged the brim of his hat up to afford him a better view, then swung his full weight onto the rotten ladder which hadn't been used in years; it moaned in a sleepy stretch.

His left arm, painfully weak and still smarting like the devil, hindered his decline. Slow and steady, his right hand gripped the rungs.

The distance to the bottom was undeterminable, making Jack all the more wary. Pieces of igneous rock loosened and rolled to the bottom; their scratching noise as they fell to the unknown below him made his stomach tighten. At least their descent gauged the depth, and he guessed it to be some thirty feet.

Damp and slippery, the ladder had missing rounds, leaving his footing unbalanced and a sweat to moisten his underarm. At last his Wellingtons touched bottom. His relief was short-lived as he wondered what sort of snakes and nocturnal creatures he'd be stirring up. He had the strongest impulse to strike a match and see for himself, but McIntyre had forbidden him any type of light. The letter was clear on following the unlit drift until he came upon the meeting area.

Jack's fingers worked across the thawing walls of the mine; the incessant drips made his heartbeat build to an irregular speed. Christ, but he'd give McIntyre a thing or two when he came upon him; there damn sure would be a better place next time. The hollow crunch of his boot heels made him wonder if he was only stepping on rock or God knew what else.

Nearly a hundred feet ahead of him, the sparse glow of a taper outlined a brawny man in a full-length coat, high-crowned Buckeye hat, and rubber boots.

"Steele?" the man inquired in a raspy deepness that echoed off the low ceiling.

"Who the hell else would be fool crazy enough to be down here?" Jack stepped into the illuminated clearing and for the first time came face-to-face with Edward McIntyre.

The scant light profiled most of the man's face in shadow. All Jack could see was the vague contours of his beefy features under the edge of his hat: his overly large nose, fat red walrus mustache, and ruddy cheeks. "So you finally made it. The boys and I were beginning to wonder if you'd ever show up, man. You made a blessed spectacle of yourself arriving in Deadwood with that shooting at Goodnight's, then disappearing into the night. No one's seen you since."

"I misjudged the depth of a green cow clod and dirtied my boots, but I'm here now." Jack extended his hand toward McIntyre, who firmly gripped it. "Why the meeting here?"

"Not many places are safe. As it is, we're taking a risk."

The gravity in Edward's voice made Jack impatient to start on the case; his senses came to life, keenly aware and filled with anticipation over the chase. He had the capacity to solve this man's problems and bring some outlaw to justice; Jack had no doubts he could do it—he had scores of times in the past.

"What do you have?" Jack asked him.

"What have you already found out?" Edward countered.

"Not a hell of a lot. I stopped by Doc Timmish's office this afternoon. The good doctor's recount of things is about as blurred as the bottom of a saloon glass. And I talked to one of the girls at the Melodeon who knew Dancer, but Miss Amaryllis's testimony can hardly be counted as evidence."

A glitter sprung to life in Edward's eyes at the mention of Amaryllis, but he didn't pursue her name. McIntyre dug into the deep folds of his winter coat and produced a folded piece of paper. "Here then. It's the names of the men who've been killed, their claims, and the numbers."

Jack took the list and tucked it inside his ulster without opening it. "Who's working these claims now?"

"No one except the wife of one of the men."

Jack's lips tightened, but he controlled any flicker in his eyes.

"There was only one other," McIntyre continued, "that reverted back to a family member who lives in the East somewhere; but they've yet to declare it as property."

"That's all you've got."

"Aye. That's all."

"Not much to go on."

"No, it's not."

Jack exhaled, his breath coming in a puff of mist before him. "Dancer got it with a bullet; how did the other four go?"

"Apparent accidents and a suicide; sloppy at that. It's a foul game, and the player is getting greedy by outright uncovered murder. What I can't understand is, the claims aren't even high-yield productions."

"Maybe somebody just doesn't like miners."

"Then Deadwood's the wrong place for him."

"Have you thought about it being the Sioux?"

"Sioux wouldn't have been so careless." McIntyre flattened the mustache that drooped on either side of his smooth-shaven chin. "They'd have taken a scalp and been done with it. The red devils take pride in what they do and don't go covering up their evil deeds."

Jack tucked his mending arm to his chest, shoving his good, gloved hand into his coat pocket. He rocked on his heels. "What about Bullock? Can he be trusted?"

"Sheriff's a good man, but good men don't get the job done."

Jack laughed tightly. "Yeah, it takes a bastard to catch a bastard. Right?"

"It was a compliment, Steele. Take it as such."

"Sure."

"William's a good friend of mine and never would've recommended you for the job had your reputation for getting the job done not been what it is. We don't give a bean if the perpetrator is caught dead or alive; we want him stopped. Our women and kinfolk aren't here to be stranded alone."

Jack needn't have been reminded. Holly Dancer swiftly came to mind, and he wondered if she'd been stranded by her own doing. Hell, it was a cheap shot, and he was a son of a bitch for even thinking it. Whatever the circumstances surrounding Billy Dancer's death, he was sure she hadn't the guts to clip them all down.

"What'll you do now?" McIntyre asked.

Crossing his arms across his chest, Jack inhaled sharply. "Guess I'll have to take up mining and pan myself out as some crowbait."

"You know anything about mining?"

"Nope. I suppose I'll have to learn fast. You got any tips?"

"Venture out on your own and learn from your mistakes. There isn't a miner alive in Deadwood who'll take you under their wing; not even me. We're a distrustful lot when it comes to gold."

Jack shrugged with a small smile. "I may know someone who might."

The eerie plops of water that had steadily fallen during their exchange formed a tiny river at Jack's feet, dampening the soles of his leather boots. "Now, if we're finished in here,

I'm getting the hell out." He turned with a halt, then called over his shoulder, "Hey, McIntyre."

"Aye?"

"This is the last time I'll ever go down in a hole I don't know anything about."

"Durn blasted nitwit!" Lee-Ash yelled to Wes Travis as he rode an untamed bronco wildly up and down Wall Street, kicking up big clods of mud. Some of the muck sprayed Holly, who stood next to Lee-Ash; she jumped back and flicked the grime from her poncho with a gloved hand.

"Durn nitwit." Holly echoed Lee-Ash's sentiments as Wes made another pass. Whooping and hooting, he waved his hat in the air at anyone who cared to look. And quite a few did.

It was Wes's trick; Holly had seen him do it a hundred times. He'd ride hell-bent for leather up and down the streets, circle back to the livery he and his brother Charles owned, then dismount and say he'd accidentally gotten onto an unbroken horse. Such a demonstration caused so much attention, it wasn't long until every greenhorn in Deadwood came hording down to the livery to meet the man who'd held on for his life. And once there, the new arrivals were sucked into buying up a little of Deadwood's prime horse-flesh.

"The brass of him still doin' the hooraw." Lee-Ash checked the cinch and latigo straps on his bay, then smoothed his hand over the glossy hair of the animal's shoulder. "You'd think the Travis boys would have sobered up after what happened last night with them Sioux raiding their place."

Holly turned to view the Travises' stock corral where the roughly hewn logs had been knocked down in the middle of the night. A makeshift wall of new lumber had been hastily rope-tied in its place. It frightened Holly to the core to think the Sioux had crept into Deadwood unnoticed. First a few horses stolen . . . What was next? A few citizens? she wondered, staring at the uniformed military staffing the street.

"You all set, darlin'?" Lee-Ash asked.

Holly had loaded up her horse with her mining gear, water, and provisions to last a full day. It would be at least sundown by the time she and Lee-Ash returned to town. The newest offense by the Indians ensured it would be a long day; every second, she'd be looking over her shoulder. It was almost enough to make her wonder if the gold was worth it.

Almost.

Like all the other miners, she had caught their fever—their passion that drove them to the ore. Each time she rode out with Lee-Ash, she dreamed of finding something that would prove to the local denizens of Deadwood she wasn't crazy. She knew they talked about her behind her back. No matter how much she told herself it didn't bother her, the sad truth was it did.

Holly lifted her booted foot up into the stirrup of her mare, Jubilee, and swung her leg over the saddle. Lee-Ash mounted, too, and was about to flick the reins when he let out a low whistle. "I'll be a durned mudhole to a hog. . . . Lookie yonder at who's headin' dead aim for us."

Through the host of horse riders, one man stood out above the rest; Jack Steele guided a magnificent gray straight toward them.

Holly's heartbeat began a disloyal quickening, defying the vow she had taken to be utterly impassive where Jack Steele was concerned. She caught herself smiling at him. He returned the gesture easily, and something inside her snapped. Sensibility returned with the clarity of a brook, and just as cool. The smile on her lips faded, replaced by a thin line of indifference.

Now, if only she could will herself to be blind.

The early morning haze shrouded Jack in opacity, making him appear enigmatic. At the sight of him outfitted in black and astride the impressive mount, nearly every woman's favor—respectable and not—was caught. Though she fought it, her own body responded to him. A tightening spread through her, and her palms grew moist.

Jack's hat slung low over his eyes, the brim affording her no view of his gaze, but she felt it on her. Everywhere. Burning her, dueling with the crisp air that settled over her clothes. Her pulse picked up again as he neared, and she told herself that he was not worthy of her time, she wouldn't linger while he came toward them. But even she knew the weakness of her shallow threat.

She'd wait, as much of a nitwit as Wes Travis.

Dragging her stare from him, she concentrated for a moment on the gelding he rode. He'd loaded it down with enough new tin and metal to start a cannery. Pans, picks, shovels, canteens, spring points, and even a brand-spanking-new frying pan. The gleam around him was so brilliant, he resembled a medieval knight.

Holly caught the wide crack of Lee-Ash's full grin as Jack reined in his horse, the gear rattling and clanking together as it swayed to a halt.

"Son, you settlin' into the tinker business?" Lee-Ash guffawed, sweeping off his forage cap for a better look.

"I'm taking up the mining business." He looked directly at Holly, not even flicking a glance to Lee-Ash. Despite herself, a blush flamed like a danger signal on her cheeks. She proudly disclaimed the treasonous color and met his gray eyes full on.

"Afternoon, Mrs. Dancer," he greeted sweet as pie, and as nonchalant as a preacher making a Sunday call.

"Good afternoon, Mr. Steele," she addressed with formality, biting back the sharp edge to her voice. If she hadn't known he'd been gunshot four days ago, she never would have suspected there was anything wrong with him. Either she was a good doctor and he a fast healer, or he hid his pain well.

"Son, you take up mining today and you ain't apt to see the light of tomorrow. All that tack's likely to alert the entire Sioux nation when you traverse the woods, you crazy idiot." Lee-Ash crossed his arms over the horn on his saddle. "You may know how to swivel the holler end of a pistol, son, but when it comes to diggin's, you ain't got a grain of sand in your crop."

"Old man, you're lucky I like you."

"Durned near don't know why," Lee-Ash spat. "I'm not quite sure if I like you or not. Any man who could've been responsible for Slaughter's demise don't sit right in my craw."

Holly felt herself blanch at the mention of Johnny Slaughter. Just that morning, she'd walked by the stage office to see Johnny's bloodstained vest nailed to the door as a reminder to the local citizens—and those just passing through Deadwood Gulch—they didn't take a killing lightly.

"I thought you left town, Mr. Steele." She tried very hard to keep the tartness from her words. She wouldn't give him the satisfaction of knowing he'd upset her.

"Now, why would I do that?" He'd sidled his horse close enough to where she could clearly make out the scar that ran down past the corner of his eye to disappear in the thick black hair below his temple.

She faltered under his penetrating gaze. "It's just that . . . well—" she cleared her throat "—the last time I saw you . . . I'd gotten the impression you weren't staying."

"Last time you saw me, I wasn't fit for riding, much less anything else." The double meaning to his statement made her skin prickle and heat up like a cinder.

"What in tarnation you two talkin' about?" Lee-Ash queried, forcing down the bill of his hat across his whitening hair.

"N-nothing," Holly stammered, nearly forgetting that Lee-Ash was there at all. She struggled to compose herself, to block out the chaos Jack brewed in her. "Are you really taking up mining, Mr. Steele?"

"Why not?"

"For one thing, whoever sold you all that gear is probably having himself a good laugh at your expense this very moment."

Jack grew visibly irritated; a muscle faintly ticked at his jaw. "What do you mean by that?"

Lee-Ash chuckled. "Polishin' your pants on saddle leather don't make you a rider, son. You'd a been better off with an old, beat-up pan, one that can hold the gold dust in the groves. This here one you got ain't good for nothin' till it gets roughed up."

"Then why do they sell new ones?"

"'Cause there's durn blamed loons like you who'll buy 'em!"

"Shi—" Jack stopped the apparent curse on his lips and

looked up to Holly with a scowl on his dark face. She couldn't help smiling, thinking it oddly amusing that some-one had pulled something over on the invincible Jack Steele. "I guess I've been had."

"I guess so," Holly agreed, her lips upturned softly. "What are you going to do?"

"I'm coming with you."

He'd said it so matter-of-factly, Holly was completely thrown off guard. When he'd proclaimed himself setting out to mine, she'd just assumed it was off on his own. Coming with *her*? Hadn't he made it plainly clear he was not a man to be with anyone? The only reason he'd come to her in the first place was out of necessity, and when he'd gotten what he'd needed, he'd left.

And without a good-bye.

"I really don't think you should come with me, Mr. Steele. I like to work alone."

"So do I," Jack said, straightening his legs and lifting up a bit in his saddle to draw his inordinate height to the fullest. The stretching sound of leather mingled with his next words. "But sometimes being alone doesn't get the job done."

"And what does—"

Holly wasn't able to finish her sentence.

Lee-Ash butted in. "You know, darlin', he might have hisself a good idea."

"What?" Holly blurted.

"Now, hear me out. I don't take too kindly to the notion of you blackjackin' alone—you've always known that, even though our claims adjoin—'cept now with the Sioux hotter than a griddle, I ain't so sure you ought to go out no more."

"Really, Lee-Ash." Holly's voice rose an octave. She didn't like being chided, much less in front of Jack. "I can handle myself. I've got a gun on me—"

"You don't even know how to use the damn thing," Jack interrupted.

She gave him a warning glare. For him to go further would uncover just how he came to know her abilities with the Smith & Wesson. "I do, too, know how to use it." She dared him to dispute her.

Despite her threat, he snorted, "Sure."

His one word made her so mad, she nearly shook. She had the urge to whip out the .22 and squeeze off a round for his benefit, but even as she was imagining it, she knew Jack had good reason to debate her abilities. When he'd seen her with the gun, she had been painfully inept with it. Could she help it if Billy had never shown her how to oil it?

"Darlin', I really think he ought to fall in with us. Just for today. I know I'd feel a heap more safe knowin' there's a gunslick guardin' my back."

"How do you know he won't be the one to pierce it?" Holly instantly regretted the insult; it was childish at best—a shoddy retort—but it had rolled off her tongue before she could stop it.

"Oh, you don't have to worry none about that, *Mrs. Dancer,*" Jack drawled. "Unlike some, I do all my shooting from the front."

Without a word, Holly kneed Jubilee to the right and headed down Lee Street toward Main; if she stayed one more minute, she'd be sorry for it. She didn't think she'd ever been angrier in her life.

A matter of seconds later, she heard Lee-Ash lope up beside her, and the rattling of Jack's absurd equipment as he followed suit.

Holly kept her eyes straight ahead as they left the congestion of Deadwood behind them.

Keeping her gaze on the road ahead, Holly declared, "Understand this, Mr. Steele. I can't tell you where you can or can't go, but if you've got the notion to settle in alongside of us, you'd better get rid of all that garbage you're toting. Namely that pan that sounds like a kettledrum every time it smacks the side of your stirrup."

"How am I supposed to pan for gold without it, Mrs. Dancer?"

She gave him a glance over her shoulder. "I don't pan for gold, I dig for it."

Holly could have sworn she saw his mouth tighten. "Dig?" he repeated.

"I've got a shaft that goes back nearly five hundred feet."

"Oh, hell," Jack muttered. "You work underground?"

"I do."

The look of blatant astonishment mixed with a little horror on his face was enough to make her hold on to an amused smile that lasted for a long time.

Jack reined back while he followed Holly and Lee-Ash out of Deadwood and over Whitewood Creek. Without stopping, he unlooped the pans and half his gear from his saddle horn and whang ties, then dumped them on the slushy ground below him. The hell with it, even though the asinine stuff had cost him a lot of dimes; he wasn't about to be attacked by Indians, or Holly Dancer again, for that matter. It was a stupid thing for him to get tricked into, and it burned him hotter than a prairie fire.

Curse that no-account Tom Deerhorn, for it was that peabrain who'd set him up. Jack had happened on him earlier that morning inside the Big Horn Store. Once spotted, Deerhorn had taken a run for the back door, but Jack bunched up his coat collar and halted him dead in his steps. Deerhorn had fumbled for an apology, saying it was the liquor that had made him careless with his guns. The pitiful look on the kid's face had made Jack let him go in disgust. And when Tom had pleaded to make it up to Jack, Jack grudgingly allowed the man to put in his two bits on what was essential equipment for mining, since Tom was aiming to do some gold hunting himself.

Jack had been bamboozled. Either Deerhorn was plain witless, or he'd known exactly what he was doing. Regardless, Jack wasn't going to let the ball ride on the wheel again. One way or another, Deerhorn was going to be branding a horse of a different color.

No sooner had Jack disengaged his shiny pan, it became snatched up by two Chinese boys in black satin caps and tunics. Their round faces beamed and they quickly scurried out of sight across the lots of Shine Street.

Jack pressed his heels to his horse and made up the distance between himself and Holly. He didn't ride up next to her, the view from behind far more interesting at the moment.

She made no disguise of the fact she was a woman. A

Columbia Stetson topped her head, her shining braid trailing down her back. The loose-fitting dull slicker that covered her bunched up on the cantle of her saddle, allowing her legs to show. At least the shape of her upper calves had been spared the injustice of her costume.

She rode effortlessly, her posture erect, her shoulders swaying softly with the horse's motion. He wondered, not for the first time, what possessed her to keep Billy Dancer's claim. Deadwood was no place for a widow lady, much less one who insisted on placing herself in the men's territory.

"You comin' or ain't you, Steele?" Lee-Ash called over his shoulder.

Jack nodded. "Just keeping a watch out on the rear of things."

Holly turned her head and flashed him a look. Jack couldn't help but give her a corrupt grin and skim his gaze blatantly over her bottom. She jerked her line of vision straight again.

His mouth flattened.

He felt every bit the criminal she accused him of being with her sky blue eyes. In the past, parodying a renowned gunman had been an amusing part of the job; now he wished to Christ he'd never invented that part of himself. Around Holly Dancer, he had trouble keeping a rein on his artificial identity; Jackson Ledgeway Steele defied everything *he* was about. It was no wonder she disdained him—or who she thought he was. In hard reality, her hostility aimed on a caricature of his own imagination.

And rightfully so.

Jack had never been one to get emotionally involved with a woman while on an assignment. Nor had he been inclined to entangle himself while between cases. It had been a long time since he felt his emotions slipping from control. He'd thought to get a clear head by leaving her; instead, it had been cluttered by her memory. Somehow, he'd gotten caught up in Holly, and he'd be damned if he'd let his guard slip. In his line of business, mistakes were costly. He was violating his own laws, and the penalty was a sure calling card to the bone orchard.

He had to keep reminding himself, until he could prove otherwise, he had no one else to shadow. McIntyre had said only one claim was being actively mined: Billy Dancer's. There had to be a reason why.

"You ever cross lots through these woods afore, Steele?" Lee-Ash asked him.

"No." He'd entered into Deadwood from the southeast, through Sidney, Nebraska.

"Then you keep in with us and keep your eyes skinned for anything that don't look true. Sioux are on a renegade, and they don't cotton to white folk in their backyard."

The statement made Jack reckless with unleashed anger. Then dammit, what was Holly doing here? Was the gold so important to her that she'd risk her life for it . . . maybe even take someone's for it?

They left the outskirts of town, the crude cabins and tents replaced by an occasional jerry-built shanty. The hillsides, tangled with the weather-grayed trunks of decaying trees, made Jack think the town had been aptly named.

Cutting through a densely wooded area, they crossed over several streams bordered by melting snow. Bare aspen and birch remained softly mantled with white on the windward sides of their trunks. Here and there, willow sticks had been set up by the boundary of the narrow trail to mark it in the heavy snows. The ponderosas soon thinned out, interspersed with gulches and slopes of spruce. A hint of warmth penetrated the dismal sky as the sun fought its way over the majestic granite summits to their right.

Jack took stock of their trail, criticizing himself for his inattention. It was his habit to observe a trail. A man never knew when the shape of a hoofprint became a valuable clue.

Lee-Ash's bay had recently been shod; the shoe covered the entire hoof, leaving the heel protected. The nails had been countersunk and left no mark in the ground. Jack's gaze moved to the tracks Holly's chestnut left over the half-frozen patches of icy slush. One hind hoof dug up the earth in a peculiar fashion, showing the hoof to be crooked.

Jack mentally recorded the imprints as they passed a group of men huddled together on the banks of a poorly draining creek. Ankle-deep in the frigid water, one hunkered over a scarred pan and swilled the sedimentary contents over the edge; two others at the edge of the tributary manned a sluice box and rocker.

Lee-Ash raised his hand up in the air as a silent greeting, not lingering on the miners or what they were doing.

As soon as they'd left the placers behind, Lee-Ash swiveled around in his saddle. "A word to the wise, Steele. I didn't know them diggers, and I don't reckon they want to know me. Minin' is an unsavory business when it comes to trust. There ain't any."

"I'll remember that." Jack waited for Holly to turn toward him, too. When she didn't, he almost rode up next to her to see her face. He held himself in check, looking at her with fleeting regret, which he forced himself to let go of.

They forded a rapidly flowing stream where several men shoveled dirt into the box-shaped receptacles. Jack observed the miners as they added water from a large dipper made of a kerosene can attached to a handle.

As before, Lee-Ash did not slow their pace, nor did he let his gaze loiter on the workings around him. He pushed them onward to a hilly area littered with dead timber.

A quarter hour later, Lee-Ash pulled up and angled his horse toward Jack. "This is where we split up. M'claim is just a fraction up yonder." He pointed to a clearing that had recently been felled of its surrounding trees. "Holly, mind yourself and give me the signal if you need any help." Lee-Ash looked directly at Jack, as if giving him a silent warning.

"I will," Holly promised.

"Son, I'm goin' against the rules of the trade. I'm trustin' you with Holly's welfare." He pointed his finger at Jack. "But sure as there's a heaven and hell, you don't see fit to hold to your end of it, I'll come after you, make no bones about it."

"I'll keep that in mind, old man," Jack returned dryly.

Lee-Ash gave Holly one last look, then nudged his horse forward, leaving them alone.

Holly hesitated slightly in her saddle, squared her shoulders, then dismounted. Jack watched her, wondering if she'd talk to him anymore.

He swung his leg over his pommel and jumped down to his feet. Holding on to his horse's reins, he walked toward her, noticing the sign stuck in the ground at her feet.

DANCER'S DESTINY

We the undersigned claim 300 feet below this notice for discovery and 900 feet or three claims above this notice for mining purposes.

William Lyle Dancer
Holly Paulina Dancer

"Dancer's destiny," Jack remarked as he stamped over the mulch of soft yellow leaves beneath his boot heels. "Your husband's idea?"

"It was."

"Some destiny."

Holly gave him a biting stare. He waited for her to say something more, and when she didn't, he was disappointed. He'd wanted her to get mad, spout off at him, maybe give him a clue as to her feelings on her husband's death. Instead, she held herself back.

"Come on if you're coming." Holly had tethered her mare on the low branch of a naked tree and removed some equipment from her packs.

Jack hobbled his own horse next to hers and followed her toward a pile of oversize white rocks. Moving some pieces of dried brush, she revealed a hole in the ground the diameter of a wagon wheel. Without waiting for him, she backed into the pit and quickly disappeared.

A flicker of cool apprehension coursed through him. "Hell," he blurted, then took the three steps toward the shaft. He jerked a sharp breath from his lungs and swung his weight onto the rope ladder, glad to find it constructed of fresh hemp and seemingly steady.

Slowly Jack descended into the veiled blackness. The trip to the bottom made short work, and he was startled by the warm body waiting for him. Holly's gloved fingers worked over the material of his greatcoat, slipping around his right arm. He felt her against his back, and he turned to face her.

In the dim light, he bent his head forward enough to feel her breath on his cheek; the sweetness nearly crushed him, his arousal threatening to undo even his strongest resolve. He couldn't read the expression in her azure eyes, the sunlight from above not bright enough.

"I wanted to make sure your arm was all right on the way down," she finally said, backing away.

"Did you?" Jack didn't want her to pull away, not yet. The fleeting smell of orange blossoms mingled with the mineral scent of the earth around them. He damned himself for doing it, but he breathed in deeply and held it inside his lungs.

"Yes, of course. I didn't want all of my hard work to go for nothing."

The wound, Jack thought. Which pained him more? Her words or his arm?

Holly stepped back far enough that she disappeared from his view. For a brief moment Jack panicked from disorientation until he heard the scratch of a match. A wavering golden glow sprung to life as Holly replaced a thin taper in its iron holder hammered into the gallery.

For the first time, Jack got a sense of where he was. The unknown with Edward McIntyre suddenly became a reality. Candlelight bounced off the ancient rock, silts, and iron-bearing mud that surrounded them. They stood in the beginning of a narrow passageway lined with several rows of timber and supported by heavy cross timbers that upheld the roof.

"You do all this?" Jack stared at the overhead, wondering how the hell the wood stayed up there . . . and more important, how long it would.

"No." Holly lit another candle and handed it to Jack. "Billy and Lee-Ash did."

"It stays up there?"

"It should."

"Does it ever come down?"

"Sometimes."

Jack nudged the crown of his hat higher. "You're damn casual about the whole thing. Don't you ever worry about getting stuck under here?"

She faced him, her delicate features softened by the hazy light. "Yes," she whispered. "It scares me to death, but I can't think about it."

Jack silently stared at her, surprised by her candid admission.

Her apparent weak moment of openness closed shut like a spring-hinged door. She occupied herself by fishing out two miner's candles from her pack. Sticking their black wicks up to the already burning taper in the holder, she lit them. After handing one to Jack, she picked up the knapsack she'd brought with her and slung it over her shoulders. Without a word, she trudged forward, leaving him to come after her.

He did, his hearing tuned to all the sounds around him. There were far-off, indistinct echoes, the slow respirations of the rocks, drinking air and oozing moisture through their sluggish pores as they swelled and pushed against their straining bonds of timber. And there was cold, a frigid, penetrating cold air that seeped into his lungs, nearly smothering him.

Drips and trickles moistened the sides of the gallows frames, the candle rays shining and fading off the columned avenue Holly led him down.

Damn, was Holly's breath as labored as his own? The very idea that he was below the light of day, with a bunch of barkless tree trunks and sheer guts to keep a ton of rock from falling on his head, made him go clammy. He felt suffocated and stifled, but there was no way he'd let Holly know how affected he was. If she could take it, so could he.

The bulky square pieces of wood suddenly stopped, leaving the rough walls exposed. Jack told himself if he was schooled on the reason why, he'd have a lot less to fear. "How come there aren't any more supports?"

Holly's voice came to him on an echo. "I only just cleared this way last week."

"How did you do that?"

105

"Black powder. And only when Lee-Ash helps. I never use dynamite."

Jack's chest constricted and his mouth quirked into an uneven smile. What sorts of conversational topics she'd bring to a ladies' tea. No wonder he'd heard she'd been ostracized by the townswomen.

Jack wiped at his brow with the back of his hand, hunching forward to duck under a low spot in the ceiling.

"We're almost there. Just a few more yards. Are you all right?"

"Fine," he answered. "Damn fine."

Holly stuck her candle into the wall above her head. She slumped off her pack, took Jack's miner's candle from him, and secured it opposite hers. "You should have stayed in town, Mr. Steele."

"And miss all this fun?"

"This isn't a game, and quit acting like it is or just go back up and leave me alone."

Jack leaned against the side of the drift and fought the urge to slide down and catch his breath. "I can't do that."

"Can't or won't?"

"I promised the old-timer I'd keep my eye on you."

"Tarnation, I don't need an eye on me any more than I need your handicapped body to be the one that it belongs to. You can't protect me."

The stab hit hard as a lance, right through his mending arm. It was enough to make him forget all thoughts of sitting down, and to bolt upright. In two angry strides, he faced her. "You may think the devil of me, and I sure as hell have given you cause to, but I could protect you with both arms shot to hell."

He dug his fingers into the soft flesh of her upper arms, the movement causing a dull ache to throb through his shoulder. He jerked her roughly to him, her head snapping back as she looked up into his face. He saw a fine thread of fright woven through her eyes; good, she should be scared of him. He was scared of her.

Holly fought to pull away from him, but couldn't. An invisible bond joined them together, and she didn't have the strength to back out of his hold. His arms held her like vises, even the one that had been shot. She wondered if he was indifferent to pain, that it came effortlessly to him to ignore it. For surely his grip on her was killing him. It killed her to be this close to him.

She'd never thought to feel desire in a man's arms, and now she struggled against the weakness in her knees and the lightness in her head. Her only weapon was her anger. Anger at him that he'd left her; anger at him that he'd goaded her all morning until she'd broken.

"I knew you had no manners, but I never thought you were a coward," Holly gasped, her moist breath mingling with that of his as Jack's face pressed closer to hers.

"I've never backed down from a fight in my life."

"You ran away from me," she said so softly, she could barely hear the words.

The pressure of Jack's fingers dug deeper into her shoulders, and she could see the familiar scowl on his face falter. "I thought you wanted me gone from your room."

"I did. You never should have come to me in the first place."

"Then why are you so mad that I left?"

He was deliberately harassing her, hounding her to admit more. Well, she wouldn't. She wouldn't tell him that she'd been devastated to find him gone. Devastated to realize that she'd depended on his presence in her room. That his very nearness made her feel things she'd never felt, that she never could hope to feel with anyone else. Something between them had sparked, and she wasn't sure how to put out the fire without getting burned.

"I'm not mad that you left . . ." Holly was unable to meet his dark gaze. "I think it would have been nice if you'd written me a decent note, letting me know you were all right." She lifted her lashes. "But I should have known you wouldn't. You're not a man to say good-bye . . . or thank you."

"Is that what you want?" he shot back with a huff. "A proper thank you?"

She suddenly grew afraid of his tone.

"I can thank you just fine, but not in words."

Before Holly grasped what Jack's intentions were, he kissed her. The surprise contact brought a cry from her lips. As she struggled to quell the gasp, his mouth sealed hers, the protest blending to a moan. Only when she stopped fighting did she become aware of the sharp awakening inside her that radiated from the bottom of her stomach.

She felt weak and dizzy, and had Jack not clung to her, she would have stumbled down to the floor. Confusion darted in golden flashes, and she blindly wondered where the coldness had gone that Billy had accused her of; Jack's touch melted her into a river of heat. She fervently wished her gloves were off, for she may never have another chance to feel the silkiness of his hair, the coarseness of the beard at his jawline. Her hands slipped up over the rough material of his ulster, pressing him closer to her.

She could feel his immediate response. He plied her lips open with his tongue and sought entrance to her mouth. Holly was shocked. Not by what he did, but by the fact she wasn't repulsed by it. Billy had attempted this once, and it made her feel humiliated. But Jack was so much more skilled.

He coaxed, running his tongue over the smoothness of her teeth, then the edge of her lower lip. He nipped at her sensitive flesh, inviting her to do the same to him. She did, and without restraint. Never had she been so brazen; it seemed as if her inhibitions had dissolved, her insecurities fled.

When Jack deepened the kiss once again, she felt him pressing her further into the frozen wall, backing her to it until her heated body collided with the cold bank in a shattering meeting of two varying degrees. The bulk of his weight on her made her breasts ache, made the intimate place between her legs grow heavy and moist. How could this be happening to her? To them?

It was lunacy.

The cold shock of their intimacy came when Jack's hand slipped up under her slicker and managed to part the buttons of her coat. She felt his hand cup her breast over the material of Billy's old shirt; he caressed her, teased her, tormented her. The sweet agony of the contact was enough to draw her out of her false illusions. This was wrong.

She couldn't.

"J-Jack." She moaned for him to stop. He apparently misread the plea as submission and grazed his thumb over her nipple. Despite the coarse material of the winter shirt that covered her, the bud responded and tightened. "Jack . . . please." She moved her head away, tilting her mouth from his. "Stop it," she murmured against the roughness of his cheek.

"Christ," Jack grated, resting his right arm on the wall behind her. This did little to alleviate his weight from her; it actually was worse. Every time his chest rose and fell, it grazed against her own trembling breasts.

"We can't do this . . . I . . . can't." That was all she could say.

"Can't or won't?" He came back at her with words of her own, words that she had spoken to him not minutes before.

Holly tried to push out of his arms, but he would not relent. She was trapped by his sinewy body whether she liked it or not. "There are things you don't know about me," she whispered, not believing that she'd actually said what she had. To tell him about her and Billy's marital relationship would be the heart of all embarrassments. She could never confess to anyone, much less a man of Jack's virility, what a nothing she was when it came to . . . intimate relations.

Jack righted the brim of her hat, then discarded it. Holly watched the battered felt Columbia float to the floor. "Like what things?" He ran his callused finger down the contours of her cheek, making her shiver; then he brushed back a loose tendril of hair that had escaped from her braid.

Holly wished he wouldn't touch her, and at the same time, wished he wouldn't stop. "Things that are best left alone."

She felt him tense. "Like maybe something to do with your husband?"

He had read her mind. Merciful heaven, was it so painfully noticeable that she was inept, that she was not pleasurable? The shame of it burned her cheeks until she was sure she flamed profusely.

"What about him?" Jack prodded her. "What about Billy Dancer? Is there something about him that you want to tell me?"

"I . . . no . . ." She couldn't.

Jack suddenly grew very angry. Was it because his hunch had been right? she wondered. That she wasn't woman enough for him, and he wanted to know if Billy had thought the same thing? That at least he wasn't alone in his displeasure of her? Why then had he kissed her so long? Had tortured her so?

The hard truth made her bitter, made her want to lash out at him for making her open old wounds. "Yes!" she shouted in the frosty air. "It has everything to do with my husband! I hated him, and I hate you for making me remember why."

"And you're glad he's dead, aren't you?" The words were spoken between lips that had hardened into a thin line; just moments before, they were softly, deliciously pressed against her own.

"Yes." That simple word tore him away. As much as she'd wanted him gone from her, she sorely felt the loss of his strength, his warmth.

Jack leaned against the damp wall across from her and slumped down until his knees were bent in front of him. He combed his fingers through his long ebony hair. Despite his menacing edge, to Holly, he looked like a little boy lost. It looked as if he fought an internal conflict within himself.

"I'm sorry if my lack of remorse over my husband's death offended you." The apology was weak, to say the least; and unnecessary, though it had sprung from her lips without any premeditated thought. It was none of Jack Steele's business how she mourned, or didn't mourn, Billy Dancer.

"I'm not offended. I've never been remorseful—"

A distant echo snagged Holly's attention. What had Jack

said? She had no chance to return to the thought when the heavy thud rang again. Quartz? she wondered, sifting down from the walls? She dismissed the notion until it came again, stronger and heavier than just rock.

Twisting toward Jack, Holly whispered, "There's someone in the tunnel."

CHAPTER SEVEN

Harry told her, grim. Once she worked, she drew

from the bullet and reinserts the bullet until it slots

Shadow toward Jack. Holly glanced at Harry, then

out of the pistol.

Chapter Seven

Jack shoved himself to his feet. Automatically his right hand had crossed over the breadth of his chest. Now she understood why his holster was strapped under his left arm—for a border draw of apt swiftness. He reached for the revolver's butt, whipping the Buntline out with accurate smoothness. Grasping it in both hands, he aimed down the darkness of the drift with a deadly steadiness.

Holly blinked, comprehension slow in dawning that he'd done all of this so quickly. His stance froze in taut readiness, though his chest rose and fell sharply from the exertion.

Holly had known he carried a reputation for a gun arm, but it never really seemed to fit him, despite what had happened at Goodnight's Restaurant. Now she was certain it was all true. Seeing him poised and ready to blast the ancient rock walls down, she knew him to be as dangerous as Sheriff Bullock had said.

But as much as he frightened her, she'd never felt more protected in her entire life. She had automatically relied on Jack; it had come naturally to her and without any warning. The fact that she had, distressed her. She was a woman on her own; she should have gone for the small .22 tucked into her pants pocket, or at least one of the shovels and picks at her feet.

"You think it's the old-timer?" Jack's gravelly voice was tight.

"No," Holly whispered. "Lee-Ash wouldn't be coming for us nearly this early."

"You have any ideas who it might be before I go down there and see for myself?" He arched sarcastic dark brows, and Holly knew he was referring back to her lecturing him for nearly shooting up Lee-Ash at her door.

"No. I don't." Defensiveness answered him. "It could be anyone. But anyone with any sense wouldn't come down here looking for certain trouble." Then her throat went dry. "It's the Sioux come to kill us!" She shivered.

"Nobody's doing any killing but me." Absolutely emotionless, his voice chilled her to the bone.

"What should we do?"

"Go after them." Jack picked up his hat, then took a step forward.

"Wait!" Holly blurted. She tried to hold on to her control, but it was fast becoming as fragile as thin ice. Without thinking, she went to him and pressed her fingers around his rigid shoulder. Jack briefly looked down at her hand, then lifted his gray eyes to meet hers.

Holly wasn't sure why the river of apprehension had charted its way through her. Certainly he was a man who could take care of himself. Still, the thought of something happening to him made her dizzy with fear. "I'll go with you."

Jack lowered his head closer toward hers, and she inhaled sharply. She thought he was going to kiss her again.

"Good idea," he agreed, his lips very close to hers.

"W-what?" She shattered.

"You come with me."

"With you . . ."

"Yeah. I don't know how to get out of here in the dark."

"The dark? But we've got candles."

"Not anymore." Jack backed her to the wall and promptly snuffed out the taper in the wrought holder just above her head. His long, powerful fingers grazed the sleeve of her poncho when he brought his arm down.

The tunnel took on an eerie incandescence under the sparse light of the remaining candle. Holly stood perfectly still, trying to read Steele's face for any clues of weakening emotion through the mask of intensity he wore.

But there was nothing; only the hard, ever-present edge of his scowl.

Jack licked his lips, his teeth gleaming white in the darkness. "No candles. They can't see us before we see them."

The solitary golden flame behind Jack wavered on a nippy current of air that swept through the mine. Then, with a last breath, it sputtered and died under Jack's fingers as he put it out.

Holly was glad Jack remained next to her in the pitch blackness. Only one other time had she been in this cave in complete darkness. Billy had played a trick on her, blowing out all the candles and refusing to light them until she was crying helplessly. She shuddered in remembrance, impulsively wanting to throw herself in Jack's arms and feel his strength envelop her.

Jack must have sensed her disquiet, because for an instant, he held on to her gloved hand, then quickly let it go, snatching away the safe feeling. "Christ, but it's dark as a gun barrel in here without any light. Can you find the way out?"

The question sliced through her like a blunt blade, carving out any false illusions of his chivalry. She reprimanded herself for allowing the situation to get the better of her and vowed it would not happen again. "Of course I can find the way out," she replied, her resolve brandishing sparks of indignation. She pushed at his brawny chest. "Move away from me so I can."

Immediately she heard him step back. Without a word she stretched her gloved hand along the uneven wall to guide her toward the exit.

Jack latched on to the hem of her slicker. "Be quiet when you walk."

His solicitous tone made her want to yell and shuffle her

feet to the extreme. What the blazes did he take her for? A complete ninny? She, more than he, knew the jeopardy of their predicament. No one—*no one*—went into a mine uninvited unless he meant to get shot at.

Holly forced the heaviness from her limbs and continued, telling herself that they would have the advantage were they to be walking into a trap. But no matter how wide she opened her eyes, she couldn't see anything but pitch in front of her. She tried to concentrate on where she was going, and at the same time keep her footfall silent. The intense pressure nearly buckled her knees.

As she came to a separation in the drift, her hand lost hold of the timbered wall and she tripped, falling forward with a lurch. The slicker, clenched in Jack's hand, kept her from sprawling to the hard ground. Gripping the waterproof material, he pulled her back against the solid contours of his chest.

"I'll walk ahead from here," he whispered into her ear, his lips touching her skin and sending a tingle throughout her that made her shoulders quake. She forced the riotous shudder from her, willed it to leave her be.

After Jack pulled away, she nodded in agreement even though he couldn't see the acknowledgment. His hand smacked hers as he attempted to pull it into his grip. She refused, instead grabbing hold of the single cape on Jack's ulster.

Jack didn't comment on her action, and she was grateful he pressed on. Though he didn't know where he was going except the direction she'd pointed him in, he walked faster than she did. She fought to keep hold of him and watch her step at the same time. Were the material of his coat not sewn so well, she would have ripped the cape right off. She pulled, tugged, and yanked, working against him. Her heart hammered in her ears as her footing fumbled, her ankles twisting over the loose debris below the soles of her boots.

When Holly thought she could abide the strain and darkness no more, hazy rays of sunlight filtered down through the opening just ahead. Dried particles of mud and sand sifted down in motes, a sign of recent occupation at the top of the shaft hole.

A cold knot formed in Holly's stomach.

"Stay here until I come back," Jack commanded in a tone that brooked no argument.

She didn't give him one.

Stepping into the circle of light, he seized hold of the base of the rope ladder. He made his way up, and within seconds, he'd disappeared from her view.

She strained her ears to listen, but she could only hear the rush of blood pounding throughout her body. No voices conversed above her, no gunshots, no shouts, just desolate silence.

She waited an eternity for him to return; he didn't come back. Tense foreboding flooded her, making her want to cry and shout at the same time. The tight knot within her begged for release. Her eyes stung with dreadful tears as she realized something must have happened to him.

Shaking, she withdrew the small Smith & Wesson from her pocket and cocked the hammer back. Silently she prayed she wouldn't have to use it. Grasping the rungs of the ladder, she ascended toward the light with her heart caught in her throat.

She squinted trying to adjust to the brightness of day. Her grip on the gun loosened, made worse by the rawhide gloves she wore.

Once within reach of the top rung, she slowly peered over the edge of the rooted rim.

Nothing out of the ordinary greeted her. Both Jubilee and Jack's gray horse stood tethered where they'd left them, swishing their tails.

As she lifted a foot for the next rung, she felt an iron grip on her arm, yanking her upward and out of the hole.

Spontaneously she squeezed the trigger of her Smith & Wesson. The sound of the bullet cracked open the motionless air.

Whoever had her, shoved her, pushing her to the ground face-forward. Sharp rocks bit through her heavy clothing, bruising her hips and knees. The .22 was roughly snatched from her fingers and she winced, cutting her lip with her teeth. She tasted her blood, then the dirt as her assailant pinned her hands behind her back. Her ragged breathing made her think she'd choke on her own fright.

"Don't move!" her attacker growled. Startled, she realized the man she'd been tumbling with was Jackson Steele.

"W-what are you doing?" she screamed in between frantic gasps.

He sat on top of her, his weight on her buttocks, his knees straddling her hips. Leaning forward, his body crushed the small of her back and shoulder blades. His mouth brushed hotly against the hollow of her cheek when he threatened, "Don't you ever pull a gun on me again."

"I—I didn't pull it on you! I was only—"

"Save it."

His lack of belief inflamed her, and the injustice of her situation hit her full force. He'd thought she tried to kill him! Infuriated, she attempted to buck him off her, but her efforts were no match for his evenly distributed weight. In a blind frenzy, she kicked at him; her heels barely connected with his back, and she ended up doing more injury to her toes as they bashed into the ground.

Jack finally relented and rolled off her. She coughed and wheezed for air, pulling large drafts into her lungs. It took a minute to catch her wind, blowing a wisp of hair from her eyes. When she was able, she staggered to her feet. As she faced him, her anger catapulted and she swung, missing him by a mile, and hearing nothing but the whooshing air for all her effort. "What's the matter with you?!"

He'd easily jumped out of her way. "There was no one up here," he ground out, an accusation accenting his words.

"What do you mean?" Furious, Holly stared at him with consuming rage.

"It means I came up here and there was no one in sight. Never was."

Holly took a quick turn around her, not believing him at all. She'd heard someone; she was positive. "I know what I heard, and I *heard* a strange noise."

Jack whacked the dirt from his denims and combed his fingers through the long black hair wildly framing his chiseled face. His gray eyes had darkened to prisms of steel,

117

just as lethal, just as cold. "You're reckless with a gun. Why didn't you stay put?"

"What?" Uncontrollable fury made her numb with shock. "I thought something had happened to you."

"Something would have if I hadn't knocked that cap-and-ball piece away from you."

Her anger ran recklessly beyond her control. Unable to stop herself, she charged him.

Holly's fists butted into the flatness of his belly through the open fold of his greatcoat. The muffled smack satisfied her as Steele let out a loud "Oof!" and doubled over, his face grimaced with surprise.

"Goddammit, lady!" He teetered on his boot heels, and she thought she'd brought him down. But before she knew it, he'd seized her by the waist and jerked her to him. Her neck nearly snapped from the jolt. Once pressed against him, she was powerless to free herself from his mighty hold.

"You are as crazy as they say," he said in an even tone as if holding a raw emotion back.

Something inside Holly cracked; her anger broke free, replaced by an emotion far stronger—disgrace at being ridiculed by Jack Steele. The thin ice finally gave way and she could feel her throat constrict, the backs of her eyelids moisten with hot tears. For some unaccountable reason, she'd thought better of him than to stab her with words of gossip.

Her vision blurred and she shoved at him, weakly and not with much effort. Lowering her chin to her chest, she swore he would not see her cry, and she pushed at his chest again. To her relief, he let her go.

For a long moment she couldn't think of what to do, then as if she'd been kicked, she moved into motion and began clapping the brown leaves from her cuffs and slapping them off her thighs and slicker.

"Holly, I . . ."

She ignored Jack's feeble attempt at an excuse; she would not give him the satisfaction of an apology to ease his conscience, if indeed it turned out he had one. Let him rot in his own misjudgment of her. She'd not let him appease himself at her expense.

Sniffing, she walked over to her gun where it lay in a clump of dead, brown meadow grass and retrieved it. Brushing off the bits of mud, she deposited the warm Smith & Wesson back in her pocket.

"Ho, there in the clearin', it's Lee-Ash Malmer," came Lee-Ash's distinctive voice as he emerged from a grove of pine. He gripped his army revolver evenly in his weathered hand. Scanning the surrounding area with a hawkish glare, he lowered his weapon. "What in durn tarnation is goin' on here? I heard gunfire."

Holly remained quiet. She'd let Jack do all the talking since he seemed to want to say something. When he didn't speak up, she spared him a glance to see him hunting for an explanation and coming up empty.

"Nothing, old man," Jack gruffly answered, adjusting the brim of his hat, smoothing the edge with his fingertips.

"Nothin' but trouble," Lee-Ash assessed as he stared coldly at Jack. "What in the devil happened?"

Jack looked to Holly and she quickly looked away, feigning interest in the candle wax drippings on the toes of her work boots.

"Well, somebody knows somethin', and they durn well better be chipper about it and ante up."

The rush of a slight wind whispered through the boughs of the surrounding cedar; it was the only answer Lee-Ash got.

"Holly, talk to me," Lee-Ash pleaded.

Lifting her chin, she murmured, "My gun went off accidentally."

"Accidentally?" Lee-Ash holstered his army Colt. "Darlin', didn't I teach you better than to do that in Sioux country?"

"Yes, I'm sorry, Lee-Ash." Holly knew she surely flushed to the roots of her hairline and, Jack's hot gaze on her wasn't helping matters. "The fault was all mine."

"Tarnation, you durn well put the skeer to me. Af'er them Sioux raidin' the Travis boys, I thought . . . well, I thought the worst." Lee-Ash made a loud sniff, then rather embarrassingly took out a large blue gingham neckerchief and blew his nose. He stuffed the cloth into his back pants

119

pocket, the tail hanging out, and scratched at a shock of white hair on his temple.

Jack could have kicked himself in the butt from here to Sidney for the look of hurt on Holly's face. Damn him to hell and back, but he was a short-fused cuss, and it had come right around and hurt the one person he wanted most not to. Seeing her standing there, her back straight, her lips trembling, he knew she was on the verge of falling, and he was the one who had pulled the floor from underneath her.

It was just as well the old man had come when he did, for when it came to apologies, Steele was no good.

Jack shoved his fists into the side pockets of his coat, gritting his teeth. He'd felt the bandages around his upper arm grow sticky after his tumble with Holly, and knew he'd caused himself to bleed again. No doubt penance for his behavior.

"Old man, consider my day finished. I'm leaving her in your hands."

Holly swung her face around, and for the first time, met his stare. Her sky blue eyes were clear as summer and, dammit all, filled with relief. He suddenly wanted to stay and change her mind about him, to lighten her distress and make her trust him again. But as he thought it, his mind's voice mockingly laughed at him. He couldn't demand her trust when he had none to give.

Jack strode to his horse and made a pretense of checking his saddlebags. He felt both Holly's and the old man's eyes on his back. "This isn't my idea of fun. If you two want to scare yourselves senseless watching every fly that buzzes in the breeze, be my guest. Unearthing gold isn't worth it to me when the ground I'm turning over could be my own grave." Jack swung around.

"But like you said, Steele, nothin' happened." Lee-Ash ran his fingers over the three gold stars on his forage cap. "You promised you'd keep a watch out on Holly."

"I think Mrs. Dancer can take care of herself." Jack watched as Holly settled alongside Lee-Ash, her mouth set and pretending not to understand his meaning. "You have any worries about it, you stay with her."

"I'll do that," Lee-Ash spat. "Don't know why I ever counted on you in the first place."

"And I don't know why you're willing to risk your life and hers for a speck of metal you have no guarantees about."

"That I can answer you: It's too rich to quit and too poor to pay; and if that makes me a sorry dreamer, then that I am, son."

"Then we've finished our business," Jack countered sharply. He sunk his foot into his stirrup and mounted his horse's back, the saddle leather protesting under his weight. Taking up the ribbons, he wove them through his fingers and nodded curtly to Holly and Lee-Ash before setting off at a gait.

Not a minute after leaving their view, a tuft of red suspended from a tree slowed him down. He reined his horse to a stop and lifted himself in his saddle to get a better assessment.

Stuck in a thinning limb, the feathered butt of an arrow sunk its head in the rough bark. Jack stretched his arm out and snapped the shaft out between his thumb and forefinger. The arrow had been hastily put together, the workmanship poor. He was no expert on Indian weaponry, but he'd bet his life this implement was not made by any Sioux. If not, by whom?

And more important, why?

It had been placed at a strategic spot, one where Holly could not possibly miss it when she rode back into town. Jack instinctively looked down, but saw no fresh markings in the trail. He made a quick search of the area from his horse, rounding several trees until he found a heavy branch of ponderosa and a bevy of hoofprints. One horse; one switch to rub out the tracks. Jack bit down on a groan . . . Christ, Holly had been telling the truth.

The Sioux would never have left a calling card; they would have come in straightaway and done them in. Somebody had gone to a lot of trouble to scare Holly. Just like that day at the restaurant. Somebody wanted her out of town—in or out of a casket. He could only wonder who had been behind this latest attempt. He hadn't seen her with anyone suspicious, namely a man who could have been jilted.

He almost turned around and went back, but decided against it. There was no sense in riling her and the old man. Whoever had left the arrow meant it as a warning—this time.

Jack nudged his horse to a single-foot and headed back toward Deadwood.

Maybe he'd misjudged her after all, but at the time he'd argued with himself . . . strange noises, guns going off . . . It was too reminiscent of a dime novel, and he'd read enough of them to know that any clue was meaningful. Now that he had a minute to calm down and think about it, he couldn't envision her really trying to gun him down. What would be the point to it? Unless she'd go to any lengths to protect her gold and he'd gotten too close to it.

Hell, he didn't know anything anymore. There used to be a time when everything he thought was right, with no room for doubt. But now, reservations were taking their toll on him. He had to get some tangible proof, some undeniable evidence against or for Holly Dancer. And that came around to his original plan.

He had to stay close to her.

But this time, he'd keep his distance.

Holly lingered for a brief moment in front of the office's glass window, assessing her reflection. Rarely, if ever, did she indulge herself in fine clothing. There was only one outing she performed important enough not to wear kitchen clothes:

Her weekly trip to Devlin Breedlove's assay post.

She tilted her head constructively, then frowned. Who was she trying to fool? Wearing a fine dress wouldn't bring her luck, it only made her feel better when Breedlove's findings were less than enthusiastic. Still, she couldn't help thinking she looked like a mature businesswoman in her blue-gray dress with its brown stripes and tight-fitting basque. The sleeves had slashings of brown silk and puffed slightly at the shoulders.

Holly took in a breath, then let it out, painfully constricted in the corset she wore. She hadn't worn one all day, and now it felt as if she were shackled in iron. The heavy horsehair cushion that formed the bustle made the small of her back ache more than it already did from bending over a shovel all afternoon.

She disregarded her carefully groomed likeness and pushed in the door to Devlin Breedlove's office. An overwhelming collection of strange smells immediately struck her. Potash, borax, saltpeter, alum, and a number of other odors she couldn't quite place wafted through the closed curtain that led to the laboratory.

The small front waiting room boasted nothing but sparseness. Three leather barstools lined up to a single crude counter. Since it was so late in the day, no one occupied any of them.

Closing out the chill, Holly swung the door back into place and made her way to the partition. She nudged it aside and peered into the helter-skelter room.

Devlin huddled over a bubbling vat and ladled out a mixture that appeared to be tea. He poured it in a pan and sloshed it over small formations of rock. So engrossed was he in what he was doing, he apparently hadn't heard her enter.

Holly hesitated at the threshold of the laboratory, fascinated by the workings surrounding her. The bottles of chemicals had the power to give her her dream. Months of disappointment were suddenly forgotten, as they were each time she visited the assay office. Today could be the day Devlin Breedlove would tell her what she held so preciously in the leather pouch was blackjack. Filled with hope, she stepped inside.

Holly cleared her throat to make her presence known, and Breedlove looked up. Had he been an unattractive man, the deep lines of concentration on his face would have made his appearance haggard. Instead, she could say Devlin was a pleasantly handsome young man with waving brown hair, deep brown eyes, and a softly manicured mustache. The lines vanished upon gazing at her, and he lost all interest in what he was doing.

"Mrs. Dancer," he addressed in a wilting accent left over from his native England. "It's always a pleasure to see you."

"I hope I'm not interrupting anything . . . it's just that you didn't hear me come in."

"I'm working on a new extraction." He ran his hands down the front of his scarred leather apron. The corners of his eyes were animated, and for a scant moment Holly thought there to be an intense, undefinable gleam to them.

Holly looked down at his worktable. A hodgepodge of equipment cluttered it: delicate glass-cased scales, syphoning tubes, pans, levels, glass pipes, and at least a hundred bottles of chemicals. How he kept track of anything was beyond her.

"What are you making?" Holly inquired with true interest as she moved into the lab.

"Sagebrush tea."

She hadn't the faintest idea how sagebrush tea could extract gold from rock, but she was willing to try anything. And Devlin Breedlove had the reputation as a man who would try anything to extract gold from ore.

"How does it work?" she further asked.

"If you give me a sample, I'll test it."

She wondered if she imagined his lack of willingness in discussing his new product. Whether she had or not, she'd give him her samples.

"I won't be able to get to it until later this evening," Devlin muttered, abruptly engrossed with his pan of sagebrush tea when she didn't readily hand over her pouch. "Could you leave it?"

Holly hesitated. She was anxious to find out what quality she had brought him this time. Always in the past, he'd told her it was nothing of great value, and the color only marginal.

She wasn't sure she should go to another assayer. Billy had trusted Devlin Breedlove and no other, so she acquiesced. "Very well. When can I come back?"

Devlin knit his brows down in a strong frown, and she was afraid she'd angered him, though why, she wasn't sure. He must have sensed her distress, because his features immediately softened. He dipped his fingers into a bucket of clean water and wiped them off on a soiled towel. "I'm afraid I must apologize for my manners, Mrs. Dancer."

124

Devlin moved toward her and braced her elbow in his stained fingers. He'd touched her one other time, and it had upset her, as it did now. But she suffered it, thinking he meant to make amends.

"I'm sure you are very busy. I didn't mean to rush you, it's just that I'm so anxious to see if—"

"Yes, yes." Breedlove patted her forearm. "I know how hard it must be for you after your husband's death." He gazed down at her, and she swallowed, not quite sure why she'd suddenly grown so apprehensive.

"Yes . . . yes, it has been difficult." Holly eased herself free and deposited her samples on the counter.

"We should dine together one evening, Mrs. Dancer. I know how lonely you must be."

For a man who was a passing acquaintance, he seemed to "know" a lot about her. "I keep myself busy. Between the restaurant and the mine, I hardly have time to think about anything else." She inched her way toward the curtain. "If I could come back tomorrow morning . . ."

"Very good." Devlin's courteous visage had evaporated and he turned away, once again immersed in his work. "I'll get to it as soon as I can."

"Thank you." Holly wasn't sure he heard her, and she didn't really care at the moment. She was glad to be leaving. Something about Devlin unnerved her, and thinking back, she tried to remember if he'd always been so preoccupied or if she'd only imagined it.

It was nearly dark when Holly finished her errands after leaving the assay office. The reputable businesses that would remain open for another hour had lit their coal oil lamps and lowered their window shades.

Hearty aromas of mining town dinners wafted out to the streets from various restaurants—juicy meats from the Palace next to Langrishe's Variety Theatre, fine spices from Delmonico's, and even the Crumbs of Comfort Along the Crack in the Wall served up plates full of liver and onions to any passerby inclined to order it.

The succulent smells reminded Holly of her own hunger, though she was in no hurry to get home to Goodnight's

Restaurant. She clutched several parcels wrapped in brown paper, necessities she'd purchased: hair soap, more garden seeds, and a jug of kerosene, which had just gone up to three dollars a gallon.

Like always, twilight was both a blessing and a curse to her. She loved the hazy canopy of blue-gray sky and the way the stars seemed to light up all at once. She loved the sounds of the saloons and their pianos and singers as they geared up to play until the wee hours of dawn. Traffic on Main Street grew heavier as the miners came in from a laborious day to seek solace in their cups and discuss the day's events; talk was cheap, and many a man boasted of riches, though none to compare to the Homestake Mine Company, which had sprung up around Lead several miles to the south.

The price she paid to view the scene at dusk was her own impending hours of solitude during the long night ahead. She shrugged off the thought, concentrating instead on everything around her.

The air, though still tinged with the sourness of poor sewage, offered a refreshing change compared to the confines of musky dirt and the iron scent of a pick and shovel.

Holly walked slowly, smiling inwardly to herself. She occasionally stopped and peered at a shop's window display. George Stokes advertised a Ball's coiled-wire-spring elastic section corset . . . warranted to retain its perfect elasticity until the corset wore out. The dry goods featured a scarlet and yellow parlor shawl, floral tilting water basin, and bolts of moiré, gingham, and nankeen.

"Buy you dinner?"

Holly snapped her head up from her musings and swung in the direction the masculine invitation came from.

Jack Steele lounged under the doorframe of Jim Persate's Wide West Saloon. His black hair fell absently across his forehead, still damp from a recent washing. Pushed back to the extreme, the brim of his ivory Stetson complemented his dark locks and left his face free of any shadows. He'd changed his clothes since earlier in the morning. A fresh pale blue chambray shirt lay flat against his chest while denims tightly encased his long legs. As always, he'd donned his long black coat, the front parted, the lapels turned down. When

126

he shifted his weight, she noticed he wore the same black suspenders she'd first seen him in.

"Said, buy you dinner?" he repeated.

So surprised was she by the offer, not to mention his sudden appearance, she was momentarily at a loss. "Dinner?"

"Yeah, dinner." He said it with a lazy drawl that made her heart jolt.

She felt an unwelcome wave of heat swell through her body. His nearness kindled feelings in her she'd tried bravely to put to an end. She'd been halfway successful, not having any thoughts of him at all since leaving Breedlove's office. Now she could see her imminent doom. His charismatic storm gray eyes penetrated through her, leaving her both disarmed and defenseless.

She wanted to run away from him, but she could not. Despite self-conscious doubt and the injury he'd inflicted on her that morning, she was not a coward. She would stand and face him, dare him to cast any more insults at her.

"You want to buy me dinner?" Holly returned crisply. "I hardly think after you expressed your eloquent opinion on my sanity, we should be dining with one another. I may take up my cutlery and turn it against you."

Jack gave her a faint, one-sided smile. "I deserved that." To her dismay, he pushed away from the Wide West's doorjamb and crossed over the boardwalk to her. She was reminded once again of how tall a man he was, how wide in the shoulders as they swayed easily, confidently; how muscular in composition, his lean legs, taut belly, under the tight outline of his clothing. Swallowing, she didn't back down when he closed in much too close for her comfort. She tilted her chin up to view his face, her heartbeat racing helplessly beyond her control. In her time of need, she found her senses had deserted her.

"If I were you," he said, angling his head rakishly, "I'd have said a lot worse to me just now." Jack braced his hands on her shoulders, the kerosene jug in her grasp suddenly feeling like a canister of heavy black powder under his subtle pressure. She knew she should tell him to go to blazes and take his hands off her—that people would stare and it

127

wasn't in line with propriety—but she liked him touching her, even if it occurred on a public street. Her heart had put out the white flag, and she'd traitorously accepted it.

Steele smiled at her again. "Since it appears you're willing to let me, I'd like to apologize."

"You want to what?"

"Apologize." He loosened his hold, but not by much. "I realize the list of my gross injustices is long." As he stroked each of his thumb pads over the material at her collarbone, her skin prickled pleasurably beneath the intimate gesture. "I rode back to town, had a few drinks, and came to the conclusion you weren't trying to gun me down."

"Of course I wasn't," she returned quickly, fighting against swaying toward him. Her mind felt as if she'd inhaled a draft of expensive perfume: woozy, drugged, and languishing in the wicked waltz it danced throughout her body.

"You were trying to, ah, protect the situation the best you knew how. And we saw how good that was. You're a lousy shot."

"I didn't mean to fire any shots," she murmured, trying to think of something—look at something—other than the light dusting of black hair that curled at his shirt's collar.

"Could've fooled me." As he leaned his face in closer toward hers, she shifted her gaze to his mouth; big mistake. "Twice you've taken a gun to me and slipped on the trigger. What else was I to think?"

"That I was coming to your rescue?"

He threw back his head, laughter rumbling from his chest. His voice mesmerized her, sweeping her off her feet; she'd nearly succumbed to him when his rhetorical humor rang clearly through her. *He was making fun of her.*

Holly shrugged out of his slandering hands. "If you're finished apologizing, I'll be on my way."

"You haven't said you'd have dinner with me."

"I didn't and I won't."

"Why not?"

"Because . . . I can't." Holly turned away, not giving him the opportunity to change her mind. Fickle as she was where

128

he was concerned, she would rebel against herself given the chance.

She'd barely taken a few steps down the knothole-infested plankway when he drew up by her side. Without a word, he snatched the kerosene container from her hold.

She allowed him; she was helpless not to.

"Maybe I shouldn't have been apologizing, maybe I should have been saying thanks instead."

"For what?" she asked, keeping her line of vision on the pedestrians ahead of her.

"For whatever you want."

There was something in his husky tone that made her immediately think of the kiss they'd shared. If he dared try and thank her for it, she'd turn her Smith & Wesson on him, and this time he'd make no mistakes over her intent.

"You stitched up my coat." Jack pointed to the barely visible seam in the shoulder.

"But I had to destroy your shirts."

"I wondered what happened to them."

"I burned them."

He arched his dark brows, but said nothing more.

They passed Nye's Opera House, the Buffalo Saloon, and Shoudy's Meat Market in silence. No longer was Holly given the liberty to window-browse; conscious of every move she made, she took care to appear at ease in Jack's presence. Though convincing her erratic pulse of that fact was not so simple. It sped on a breakneck coarse, zeroing in on her willpower. She almost forgot to cross the street at the Red Bird Saloon, then stopped short a step.

Reaching for the kerosene from Jack, she waited expectantly for him to give it to her.

He didn't.

"I have to go now." She had to inform him of the obvious, and his reply was not at all what she had in mind.

"I'll walk over with you."

She flustered. "That's not necessary."

"Necessary or not, I am." His mellow baritone intoned no compromise.

Jack had barely fit his hand on the small of her back to

guide her when a sultry voice beckoned him, its harmony so hot and humid, Holly quickly formed her own image of the woman without turning around.

"Hallo, Jackson. Haven't seen you in here for days. Where you been, honey?"

Holly took in the woman who'd addressed Jack. The impression she'd made in her mind of a southern belle lounging on the porch of a magnolia-scented plantation jagged right off the map. The sultry voice belonged to a joy-girl from the Red Bird; thin as a rail, her torso swam in a bulky man's lambskin coat that could have weighed more than she did. Her sable hair was twisted into a doughnut at the top of her head, her hollow cheeks stained a vivid red from the cold.

"Quiet, Angel," Jack returned casually.

Angel folded her arms across her flat chest and cuddled deeper into her hip-length coat; her lanky legs were exposed, covered only by a pair of heavily knitted navy stockings. She peeked around Jack to get a glimpse at Holly. "Sorry, honey. I didn't realize you already had company."

"I'll catch you some other time."

"You do that." Angel smiled solicitously.

Way down deep inside Holly grew a gnawing little tremor. She tried hard to fight it, but it spread and blossomed into a fiery red ball that could only be called one thing: jealousy.

Never in her life had she ever felt such a consuming intolerance of rivalry. Never had she wanted to compete with a woman of Angel's indisputable status for a man like Jack Steele. Never had she wanted to vie for a man's attention regardless of who she'd be up against.

The admission of jealousy had been dredged up from a place that had neither logic nor reason, but she could find no intelligible ground to deny it.

She was attracted to Jack Steele.

She wanted Jack Steele.

She could not have Jack Steele without paying the ultimate price: her surrender to a cold truth she hadn't the power to change.

With that, she did the most rational thing she could think of. Before Jack could stop her, she snatched the jug of fuel from his hand, hightailed it across the street, bounded up the steps to her apartment, keyed open the door, and flung it closed upon entering. She dumped her parcels on the bed and ran across the room and nudged the edge of the curtain aside in a breathless stroke.

Jack remained affixed in front of the Red Bird, glaring at her window, while Angel stood behind him curiously doing the same. Holly sucked in her breath and drew back, afraid of being seen. She counted to ten, then eased her gaze out the glass again.

She watched Jack a long moment; he laughed at something Angel said while lifting his head up to observe her window. This time she remained, assured he could not detect her gaze on him.

It wasn't long after that he turned and went inside the Red Bird with Angel. Holly told herself she was glad he'd gone with the slim woman; it was much better this way.

Dropping the curtain, Holly leaned against the wall. Maybe she was a coward after all. Had she not been so deathly afraid of Jack's rejection, she would have stayed and fought for him.

But too many of Billy's badgering words haunted her to take the chance.

A kiss was one thing. . . . To get involved with anything more . . . She would die of shame if Jack knew of her incapacity to feel fulfillment while being intimate.

Yes, it was much better this way, she told herself as she brushed her knuckle over a tear that had snuck down her cheek.

A darkly garbed figure stood hidden in the shadows of a spired ponderosa. With only a crescent moon barely brightening the expanse of marked-off land in front of him, he was out of view from the small campfire not several yards in front of him.

Two men huddled at the warming blaze, sitting back on their heels and heartily eating their evening meal. One swiped a piece of bread at the bottom of his tin pan to sop up the bean juice; the other bit into a spit-roasted rabbit's leg. They didn't talk for a lengthy period. Finally one spoke up, and the cloaked man who had been observing them quietly stepped out from his hiding spot.

With the two miners in conversation, he made his move. Taking care where he placed his footing, he followed the edge of the clearing as far as a new opening in the ground. A narrow and fairly shallow depression, it descended no more than eight feet. The two miners had evidently struck granite and had to reroute their original shaft.

The lone figure stripped off his gloves, then reached into a long leather sack at his waist and untied the string with his teeth. He checked the men at the fire, their backs toward him, then took a step to clear the edge of the hole. Shoving his hand into the bag, he pulled out a fistful of what appeared to be dirt. Handful after handful, he sifted down into the fresh mine. It caught on the quarter ray of the moon, glittering and shimmering like magic dust as it settled into the just-begun shaft.

The job finished, he slipped into a silhouette of trees. A small smile of satisfaction lit his mustached upper lip as he noiselessly made the long walk back to his horse.

Jack Steele gulped down the last of his bourbon and headed toward the double doors of the Gem Theater—away from Adley Seeks's cocky voice and the wild game of faro he'd been carrying on all evening with any lame idiot who cared to while away the time. Though a poor excuse for a residence, the Gem was in the heart of the Badlands and a central vantage point to all of the disreputable saloons. From his room at the end of the second floor, he could look down on lower Main Street and part of Wall Street.

The sharp evening air penetrated his lungs as he stepped outside to clear his head. He lazed a moment on the boardwalk to pull out a cheroot and place it against his lips. Striking a match against the wall behind him, he touched it to the end, then waved it out.

Steele circled his fingers over the awning rail, meeting with the three-inch span honed to smoothness. The heels of Adley's boots had sanded the wood in that area to a fine grain from all the lounging he did outside, his feet propped up on it.

Leaning over the canopy of the angled awning, Jack took an impression of the jet sky and low-illuminated one-fourth moon. Midnight called the hour. Time to go to work.

Buttoning up his ulster to the collar, Jack drifted down Main Street. Most of the saloons had closed their doors against the cold, but the twangy pianos and brass-nail girls' giggles could be heard trickling out onto the mucky thoroughfare. He paused in front of the Melodeon and wondered if a second visit with Amaryllis would prove worthwhile. Doubt answered him.

Jack continued on at a faster pace, noting the shops locked in darkness. Langrishe's Variety Theatre was open, the show in its last act. Jack didn't stop long enough to listen to the music. Crossing Gold Street, he stepped onto the curb and walked with his hands dug into the warmth of his pockets. Once across from Goodnight's Restaurant, he paused.

A faint glow came from Holly's room, as if a single lantern had been left with a low wick. He tried to dismiss her from his thoughts, though the decree was not an easy one. He'd wanted to go after her today, but knew she was running away not only from him, but from herself as well. Something deeply troubled her, and he needed to find out what it was. He sensed it had to do with Billy Dancer. That was why this evening was so important. He needed evidence to prove her innocent of any crimes. He felt she was, but in the past, margin had always built room for doubt.

Jack flicked his cheroot into the street; it sizzled in a puddle framing one side of an animal trough. Striding a few more yards, he went around the clapboarded side of the Red Bird Saloon. For a fleeting moment he scanned the narrow passage, his arm suddenly paining him as he thought of Tom Deerhorn. He took a minute to curse the stripling, then snuck up the side steps to the city recorder's office of the Lost Mining District.

Once at the top of the landing, he did his best to listen for anybody inside above the ribald songs of the Red Bird. Jack had put the clerk, Henry Chapman, under his surveillance during the week. He closed the office at precisely seven o'clock each evening, then moseyed on over to the Red Bird for exactly two pints of beer. After that, he went upstairs for one hour with Angel. Then it was home to bed. Angel told Jack of her and Henry's pillow talk; Jack found out Chapman took sleeping powders and never returned to the office until the next morning.

True to Chapman's habit, the doors were locked for the night. No lights brightened the inside, nor did a guard dog watch the building. Canines were something he'd come up against in the past. A cheap, efficient way of monitoring a business without putting an irresponsible man on the payroll. There had been a time or two when he'd spent his card winnings on half-pound hunks of meat as deterrents.

Jack jiggled the lock and found it held fast. He pulled out a hairpin he had in the vest pocket of his coat and stuck it in the keyhole. For several minutes he jimmied and poked at the tumbler, with no luck. His patience spent, he pulled out his .38 from his shoulder holster. Waiting for a noise from the saloon next door to cover him, he held it poised over the bottom pane of glass in the door. When the expected ruckus broke out at the Red Bird, he rammed the revolver's butt into the glass.

The crunching of glass breaking mingled with the loud, drunken voices next door. Jack waited tensely and looked down over the rickety railing to the narrow alley. Nothing moved.

He knocked several pieces of protruding glass from the doorframe and reached inside to turn the knob. Easing into the room, he wasted no time pulling out a match. After striking it, he headed directly to the files. He'd been able to familiarize himself with the city recorder's office several days ago; he'd asked Chapman a few questions on how he'd go about filing a claim. All the while, he'd been sizing up the way the room had been organized. Now it was a matter of finding the right files.

Jack stalked to the wall of cabinets and began opening drawers. The match burned low, and he struck another. He couldn't take the actual documents. Breaking and entering was an offense that in emergencies, he reasoned, came with the job. Stealing was another matter entirely—besides, if you were caught, it held more weight. So he quickly pulled the claim files he was interested in, scanned the contents, and put them back. The process was complete in a matter of minutes and two matches. Once finished, he quickly turned to leave.

He took no time to digest what he read; it was not what he wanted to see, and he wasn't sure how he could turn the stark facts to Holly's favor. Her name appeared on two of the documents, binding and legal—and, in his mind, potentially lethal.

Small shards of glass ground under his boot heels as he closed the door behind him. As he was about to take the exit steps two at a time, a low and educated voice halted him in midmotion.

A sick comprehension doused Jack, sobering him to the turn of events. He damned his luck as he looked down the persuasive barrel of a Springfield revolver trained dead center on his chest.

"Good evening, Mr. Steele," Seth Bullock greeted hospitably. The star on the sheriff's lapel winked under the natural luster of the moon—a silver image of justice. "I expect your bed at the Gem's going to be quite cold tonight since you'll be sleeping in a cell down at my jail."

Chapter Eight

"Make yourself light, Steele. Slow and easy. Keep your hands where I can see them." Bullock stood unyielding at the base of the stairs. His soft white Stetson kept nearly all of his face in shadow, except for his most distinguishing feature—a drooping mustache that covered his entire upper lip.

Jack considered his options. From what he'd heard, the sheriff was a man who abhorred bloodshed. He strongly doubted if Bullock would gun him down if he disobeyed the order; he'd put up with the chase first.

"Don't even think it, Steele. I can read you like a newspaper." The revolver in Seth's hand didn't waver an inch.

"Yeah? I heard you're not the kind of man who likes inking up his hands."

"You got that right, but it doesn't mean I won't put you to the presses if I have to. You can either shoot or put up your gun. I'd suggest coming peaceably so we don't have to get things dirty."

Jack smiled blandly, realizing with a sense of doom that he'd be locked up for the night. During times like these, he wanted to waive his cover and let the sheriff know they were on the same level; but he didn't have enough information on the case to go around making confessions, even if they were to the local long arm. At least his stay at the jail would be a short one—just until daybreak, when Chapman returned to the office. Once the clerk told the sheriff nothing had been stolen, there could be no action taken against him other than a fine for destroying property.

"I don't suppose you keep the heater lit in your jail at night?" Jack asked caustically as he made a show of unbuckling his waist holster and the thong tied around his thigh.

Bullock chuckled. "Now, why would we go and give you boys all the comforts of home?"

"Didn't think so."

"Come on down here so I can take that piece, and that other one resting under your arm."

Jack slowly descended the landing and came to a halt at Bullock's level. He passed over the holster housing his Smith & Wesson, then slipped his Buntline free of his shoulder harness. He thought a moment to keep the small pistol in his boot, then decided against it. The sheriff would find it anyway.

Jack was about to reach down and fish it out when he heard a familiar high-pitched twang behind him.

"Hot damn, this hyar pardner's got you covered, Steele!"

Jack swung around as Tom Deerhorn swaggered confidently down the alley between the Red Bird and the city recorder's office, the rowels of his spurs jingling like a pocketful of newly minted coins. Poised in his hands, his twin Civilian Colts caught the low gleam of night.

The sheriff immediately turned, trained his Springfield on Deerhorn, then rapidly pivoted back to Jack, as if he wasn't sure who posed the most threat.

Jack combed his gaze over Tom Deerhorn long enough to realize Deerhorn was deadly serious. Cocked at a confident angle, his bleached frontier hat smashed his slicked-down-for-a-fight, sunny white hair.

"Deerhorn, what the *hell* are you doing?" Jack asked, his voice threatening to raise beyond the measure of normal octaves.

"I'm a-coming to your aid, friend."

"Goddammit, put those shooters away," Jack ordered. "I can handle this."

"Ho, tell, my friend. This hyar appendage of the law was over you like a buzzard circling fresh meat. He's aiming to calaboose you in the hoosegow."

"I know that, idiot."

"What the deuce is going on here?" Bullock charged, momentarily switching his gun back on Deerhorn. "Drop them, cowboy."

"Do it, you fool kid," Jack seconded.

"Ding bust it if I will. I'm helping you, Steele, whether you want it or not. I owe you." Deerhorn faced off against the sheriff. "You ever see a road agent's spin, tin star?"

"Don't you do it!" Jack barked to the kid, the nagging pain in his arm still a fresh reminder of how clumsy Deerhorn's road agent's spin was. "Put the guns down!" Jack yelled above the shouts inside the Red Bird, not caring if he did draw an audience. Easing himself in a crouch, he made ready to slide his hand into his Wellington and put a plug in Deerhorn's gun arm if he had to. He'd be damned if he'd be involved in the accidental shooting of a lawman.

"I know what you're thinking, Steele." Tom waved the silver pistol in his grasp. "I'll admit I was a mite sloppy befer, but now I've got it whittled down better than any stick. I can pull it off slicker than bear grease. Faster than a hookshop with a line out the door."

It was Deerhorn's presumptuous boasting and lack of serious regard for the situation that made Jack not think twice about pulling out his Frontier. In less than one second the small-caliber piece was directed at young Tom's groin. "Put them back, Deerhorn, or I'll blow you in two."

Bullock, having been caught unawares, struggled with his predicament, trying to keep his own revolver on both the men, finally selecting Steele.

The three of them stood there for what seemed a full minute: Jack aimed at Deerhorn, Deerhorn pointed at Bullock, Bullock trained on Jack.

Sheriff Bullock growled authoritatively, "I don't know what you two have worked out, but now you'll both be sharing a cell. Steele, you drop it or you've got a slug in you sure as sunshine. And you, cowboy, you make the slightest move to scratch yourself and you won't be itching for a long time. Drop them."

Deerhorn's coffee brown eyes narrowed in on Jack. "We can shoot up a lot of dust and disappear befer this hyar lawman has a chance to sneeze."

"Hand me your irons, you belligerent son of a bitch." Jack stretched out his arm.

"Golblast, I was only trying—"

"I don't care what you were trying to do. You don't hand me those Colts right now, I'm going to bust your jaw!"

Deerhorn gave a little tremor of terror, his eyes bugging; then he lowered his guns. "Awright, Steele. If that's what you want." He passed over his weapons, and Jack doubled-handed them.

"And now it's your turn," the sheriff told Jack.

Jack lowered his Frontier and delivered it to Bullock along with Deerhorn's Colt .45s.

Seth had to juggle the weapons in his arms. "Since I can't rightly keep a hold on you boys, I want you to slap on the fetters." He fumbled in his coat pocket and tossed a pair of handcuffs to Jack.

Jack raised his hand and caught the shining rings and chain in midair.

"Your right wrist, Steele. His left."

Jack dangled the iron circles from his fingers, the links between them ringing together. He gritted his teeth, balking. "You cuff me to this kid and the next charge you slap on me will be murder, Sheriff."

"It doesn't make any never mind to me what charges I bring up against you. You slip them on, nice and snug."

Jack balled his hands into tight fists, then unclenched them long enough to roughly grab hold of Deerhorn's wrist and snake the cuff tightly around his skin without a word.

Deerhorn looked up, his face beaming with a broad smile. "This hyar is my first incarceration, and I'm damn proud to be sharing it with the likes of someone as infamous as you, Jack Steele."

"Shut up before I shut you up." Jack circled his own wrist with disgust.

"Let's be on our way, boys," Sheriff Bullock said as he motioned them out the alley and onto the main street.

Bullock trailed behind Jack and Tom, his revolver raised despite the load of guns he carried. They crossed over to Lee and Sherman streets, down toward Washington and Monroe, where the jail had been established.

The slight trek left Jack's feet cold by the time he reached the sheriff's office. He forced himself to stop thinking of a warm bed, a tumbler of bourbon . . . and Holly Dancer. By the time he'd reached the prison, his mood had darkened from anger to misery. He stomped off the near-frozen mud that caked the soles of his boots.

The small, jerry-built jail had chinks between the logs barely adequate to keep out the winter frost and snow. No shingles nailed down the roof, just planks fit together that had been so hastily put up, their lengths still remained uneven and waiting for the carpenters to line them up; no awning protected the entrance door, nor any kind of step up. A single, narrow window had been cut out to the left of the door, and Jack wondered if it worked.

Bullock lifted a ring of keys from his coat pocket and opened the wooden entry. Stepping back, he nudged Steele and Tom inside. A cold glass lantern hung on a nail at the side of the wall; the sheriff took off the chimney, turned up the wick, and lit it.

Jack viewed his accommodations for the night with little encouragement. As Bullock forewarned, the comforts of even a shoddy saloon like the Gem looked good in comparison. The potbellied stove slumbered to one side of the room. No scent of coal smoke cut out the smell of forged metal that clung to the jail's one and only newly constructed cell. Bullock's half-open rolltop desk resided in the far corner. Wanted posters papered the wall, their clutter enlivened by a lone color flyer for Langrishe's Theatre.

Bullock spun the combination to a Smith Brothers safe next to his desk, opened it, and tossed in the arms he'd collected from his prisoners. He fit his hand into a pigeonhole at his desk and retrieved a small hoop with a solitary key. Opening the iron-grated prison door, he stood back. "I find any bulges and bumps on you not accounted for by the average human anatomy, there's going to be hell to pay." Seth inclined his head. "Lift up your arms."

Jack complied with a curse while the sheriff ran his palms up and down the insides of Jack's legs. He made Steele unbutton his ulster and frisked the sides of his ribs and under his arms. Seth did likewise on Deerhorn, who snorted with disgust and made an off-color remark about being inspected.

Satisfied, Bullock ordered them inside the small cubical. "Make yourselves comfortable," he said with heavy sarcasm.

Jack didn't move, instead raised his wrist, taking Deerhorn's arm with it. "Aren't you forgetting something, Bullock?"

"That's right." Folding his arms over his chest, Seth frowned. "You know what? Those cuffs weren't mine. I borrowed them from Deputy Whalen. Damned if I know where Mike has taken himself off to. Until I find him, I reckon you boys are stuck with each other." He gave Deerhorn a scoot, sent both men into the cell, then closed the door with a click that reverberated permanency as he turned the skeleton key.

Jack swung around and grabbed hold of the frame. "I don't know what kind of game you're playing, Bullock, but it's a sick one." He spat out the words contemptuously. "Find that goddamn key."

"I'll do that. I'll look for Whalen first chance I get. He might even mosey on in here. He's the night deputy, but business has been a little slow."

Deerhorn's fingers wrapped around the iron on the door and he wiggled it; the hinges creaked like an old, rusty bedstead. "You law fellas think you own the towns, but I've got news fer you, pardner: We do. You won't get the cottonwood over on us. We'll come gunning after you first thing we're free of this stink hole or my name ain't Thomas Gray Deerhorn!"

Jack shot Deerhorn a glare, narrowing his eyes to glacial slits. "I warned you to shut up!"

Bullock laughed at Tom's threat. "I'll be watching for you with eyes on my behind." Walking away with amusement, he sat himself comfortably at his work-strewn desk. Taking out a packet of papers, he began filling them out with an ink pen.

"I believe that man just insulted me." Deerhorn's mouth gaped open stupidly. Pursing his lips, he yanked off his hat and tossed it to the floor.

Jack ignored Deerhorn's remark. Like Deerhorn, this, too, was his first incarceration. He already felt like a penned animal, helplessly trapped beyond the boundaries of freedom. Were he honest with himself, he'd admit he had it coming.

Steele felt the day-old beard roughening his jaw while surveying their surroundings, noting the splatterings of blood on the floor and the two hard benches that lined the confinement. He wondered if the smeared marks of crimson were leftovers of barroom nosebleeds and haphazard gunshots, or if Bullock had landed one of the bloodying blows himself; the latter seemed hardly likely from what he'd seen of the man. He strictly followed the book.

Seth Bullock rose from his desk and nestled deeper into the woolen coat he hadn't removed. He headed to the gun case at the front wall—void of any guns on its racks—and took out two army blankets from a bottom drawer. Handing them through the bars, he gave them to Jack. "I'll be seeing you boys in the morning."

The sheriff left and locked the entry door behind him.

Deerhorn spat and noticed the stains on the floor for the first time. He lifted his stupefied gaze up at Jack and swallowed hard enough to bob his Adam's apple. "Well, how do you propose we break out?"

Jack's nostrils flared and he snorted in disgust. Kids like Deerhorn had a few things to learn about law and life. Stupid threats weren't the way to handle a lawman, and stupid suggestions didn't get a man out of trouble. "Too bad we don't have any of that mining gear you bilked me into. We could dig our way out."

The loaded mockery flew clear over Deerhorn's head. "Right damn shame we don't, ain't it? But it would've taken all night to tunnel out."

"You lack-brain," Jack mumbled, and jerked on the cuff at Tom's wrist.

"Ow!" Tom winced. "What did you go and do that fer?"

"I wanted to see if there was anybody inside that fool head of yours or if you were sleeping on your feet. In all my days, I've never seen a more addled man than you."

"I may have to take offense at that, Steele." He ruffled his pale brows and frowned dejectedly. "I come to your aid, friend, and you've done nothing but tell me to shut up. Might be I had good reason to shoot you in the arm after all." His face drained to the color of fresh milk the minute he spoke the words. "I . . . I didn't mean that."

A lethal calmness glinted Jack's eyes as he sucked in his breath. "Listen, I've got an idea."

"Yeah?" Deerhorn let out a sigh of relief, apparently thinking Jack let the belittling comment slide.

"Yeah." Jack took an abrupt step toward him, and Tom jumped. "You see that bench?"

"Absolutely."

"You push it over next to that one." Jack motioned to the narrow, makeshift cot nudged up to the side of the cell.

Deerhorn eagerly scraped it across the floor, Jack having no choice but to go along with him. Tom huffed and shoved it to where Jack pointed. Turning around, he waited with bright expectation on his face for Jack's next words. "Now what?"

"Now this." Jack loaded his fist with enough power to punch out a bronco, landing the square of his knuckles dead center on Tom's jaw; his whitened chin snapped up, quickly coloring to shades of red. His eyes rolled into the sockets, then his lids shuttered closed. Lanky legs buckled under, landing him smack in the middle of the bench he'd just moved. Jack braced his legs apart so he wouldn't follow Tom down since they were cuffed together.

Once Deerhorn was sprawled across the narrow board, Jack shook out his throbbing fingers, damning himself for having to go to such lengths. It was either that or strangulation.

The position of the other bench allowed Steele to lie down

without tangling himself in Deerhorn's prostrate form. He stuffed the scratchy blanket under his head for a pillow and tried to keep his mind clear of Tom Deerhorn for a little while, instead concentrating on what he'd found out in the recorder's office.

He'd expected to find Holly's name on one of the documents; he hadn't expected to see it more than once. She owned two mines. Billy Dancer's and another man's who'd been murdered. The evidence didn't reflect on her favorably, and he couldn't come up with the reasons for her dual ownership. There was another name in the files, too. One that he couldn't figure. As soon as he got out of jail, he'd begin investigating his new suspect. He hoped this new name would in some way alleviate his misgivings about Holly.

Wanting to see her innocent had turned into an obsession; just once, he'd like to be wrong about something, about his suspicions. In Holly Dancer's case, she'd baffled him at every turn, leaving him riddled with questions.

The only one who could answer them was the woman herself. He couldn't give her time to come to terms with whatever was bothering her. He had to pursue her.

Relentlessly.

He thought of his Chicago law practice. His departure had been legislated by discontentment and skepticism of the court's legal procedures. Having to pick up the pieces after the criminal disasters had helped constitute his ever-growing frustration at the system; by the time he'd been brought in, he'd had to believe in his own judgment of character to see a trial to its end. Though never in the past had he been wrong; the penalty fit the remedy. He realized now with chilling clarity, there could be exceptions.

For the first time, he regretted his decision to work for William—though at the time, he had been anxious to leave Chicago and its hellish memories. He'd always lived his life by one rule: Don't play games with the law. He was fast beginning to realize the seriousness of playing games with the heart. He couldn't afford to feel anything for Holly Dancer; but the practical warning came too late. He'd already placed everything he had on her.

Wishing he had a shot of bourbon to warm himself, Steele closed his eyes, knowing the sun wouldn't break through soon enough to suit him.

Holly dished up two plates of sunny-side-up eggs and buttermilk biscuits, with two cups of black coffee on the side. Her dampened mood made her set the meals on a wooden tray none too gently. Her trip to Devlin Breedlove's office this morning had once again been discouraging. The samples she'd left him were worthless.

Holly covered the tray with a heavy linen napkin just as Carrie Goodnight came through the revolving door and into the restaurant's kitchen.

"Did the sheriff tell you to fix up two plates today, Mrs. Dancer?" Carrie asked.

She nodded, moving on to the stove and keeping watch on a thick slab of ham she browned.

"I'll bet he didn't tell you *who* they were for." Walking around the butcher's island, Carrie sidled up to the cupboard. Her elbows thumped down on the counter, and she looked up at Holly with knowing hazel eyes.

Holly saw her friend brimming with the need to disclose the names. Though Holly doubted it would matter to her. The men locked up in the jail were usually stray wranglers, penny thieves, or claim jumpers. The restaurants took rotations supplying their meals, and it so happened Goodnight's turn had come around this morning. "Well, who?" Holly finally inquired when Carrie didn't supply the names; then she worried her lower lip at the sudden thought popping to mind. "Did Sheriff Bullock find who killed Johnny Slaughter?"

"No," Carrie replied sullenly, as if that would have been a better prospect than who actually had been incarcerated. "No, but somebody infamous."

"Pray tell, who?" Holly took the griddle off the stove and put her hands akimbo on her aproned hips.

"Somebody named Thomas Deerhorn and . . . Jackson Steele."

Holly knew her face blanched; she could feel the blood seeping down into her neck, and she grew hot all over. *Jack?*

In jail? What had he done? She wasn't sure she wanted to know the answer, but had to hear it regardless. "Did the sheriff say why he was arrested?" She forced herself not to tremble.

"Something to do with"—Carrie pursed her lips as if recollecting—"breaking and entering."

Holly brought her quivering fingertips to her lips and pressed them on her mouth. No matter what she'd thought Jack capable of, she couldn't believe he'd actually go and do something like that. She couldn't quell the urge to see him, to make sure he was all right. His arm had only just begun to mend, and now he'd had to sleep the night in the jail. . . . Thoughts of him in the comfort of her bed came to mind, and she couldn't lay to rest the intimacy they'd shared; hard as she might try, she felt a bond with him like no other in her life. She had to go see him. She needed to see him.

"If you don't mind, I'll take the tray down to the jail this morning." Holly stripped off her dark gingham apron, removing any margin for argument. "I won't be long, and it would save you the trip."

Carrie pushed away from the sideboard, took up a knife, and cut several slices of the ham. "It's fine with me. I'd rather stay here anyway; it's too cold outside. Besides, I don't mind telling you, after what happened in here with Mr. Steele the last time, I'm a little afraid of him."

Holly lifted her pelisse off a hook by the door and fit it over her shoulders, surprising herself by saying, "I'm a little afraid of him, too."

But it was a fear of her feelings where Jack was concerned more than anything else.

"Get up, Steele."

Jack slipped open his eyes, unaware he'd dozed off until the sheriff called him. He heard the clink of keys in the cell lock, then the door squeaked open.

"I found Whalen."

Jack struggled to sit up, his injured shoulder stiff from having been in an awkward position during the night. Once sitting, he massaged his dark brows, smoothing them outward; he looked down at Deerhorn, who snored noisily, still sprawled out on his back in the exact position he'd landed.

"Looks like your friend got himself in the way of a fist," Seth commented as he unlocked the handcuffs from Jack's wrist, then Tom's limp one.

"Yeah." Freed from the circlet, Jack rubbed his tender wrist, then gazed at the dark bruise spread across Deerhorn's jaw; yesterday it looked like a strawberry, today, a yellowed blueberry. "Yeah, he did."

Seth Bullock straightened and slipped the tiny key into his vest pocket. "I talked to Henry Chapman this morning, and he said far as he could tell, nothing was taken from the office."

Jack stood up and stretched out his rigid joints, ignoring the sheriff's comment.

Leaning against the frame, Bullock waited. "You care to tell me what you were doing in there?"

"I needed to file a claim," Jack flippantly replied, knowing he pressed for more trouble.

"You know—" Bullock put his arms over his chest "—you're on thin ground with me, Steele. You're in my town now, and smart-mouthed gunslicks like you don't sit well with me. Best thing you can do is ride out of Deadwood when you're finished with your stay here."

"I am finished," Jack reminded him. "You can't hold anything on me. I'll pay whatever fine there is."

"Not from the way I look at it." Seth slouched, hooking his fingers in his belt loops. "Breaking and entering, conspiracy to overtake an officer of the law, threatening an officer of the law—just to name a few."

"We both know this young pup had his own ideas. I was going along peaceably with you."

"Maybe, maybe not." Bullock pushed away from the frame. "I need to review the situation."

Jack sunk down on the bench, straddling it with his long legs. Clearly Bullock had made up his mind. "How long?"

"How long what, Steele?" Crookedly, Bullock smiled.

"How long you aim to keep me in here?"

"That's a right fair question, one deserving a fair answer."

His full brown mustache ruffled above his upper lip, and he smoothed the wiry hair. "Till someone meets your bail. Since I can't rightly think of a soul in Deadwood fixing to do that, I think it's safe to say you'll be staying for breakfast."

Seth hinged the door securely behind him and headed for the stove. Opening the cast-iron door, he peered inside to see it stuffed full of fuel, then struck a match with his thumbnail and set it to blaze. From there, he took up residence at his desk and examined a new batch of federal posters he'd carried in with him that morning.

Jack brought his forearms down on his knees and stared at the tips of his boots. The hem of his greatcoat grazed the floor, and he bunched it up, tucking it between his legs. Without moving, he raised his gaze to the sheriff and gave him his most menacing, furious glare, though it was completely wasted on the preoccupied lawman.

He felt penned up and constricted; furious and helpless. He needed to get word to Edward McIntyre to post his bail, but he had to do it discreetly.

While he was sorting through several possibilities on doing just that, the planked door to the jail swung inward with a burst of cold air. On the chilling current came the smothering fragrance of too much spicy perfume. Scandalously clad, Amaryllis appeared, her face partially hidden from view by the flimsy hood sheltering her springy platinum curls. Her thin, nearly see-through gold wrapper billowed about her bare ankles and curled up over the short hem of her brightly sequined red dress.

She slammed the rickety door shut and let out an "Oo!" as it blew in again and smacked her hind end. Bracing the knob, she gave it a strong shove into the doorjamb.

Amaryllis sniffed and collected herself, smoothing down the ruby ostrich-feathered trim that encased her made-up face. "I swan, that nasty old wind does ruffle this little ol' gal's feathers." As she peeked a glance upward, her rosebud lips lushly melted into a full line. "Mornin', Sheriff. I came to pay a call on one of your lock-and-keys."

Seth Bullock leaned back in his chair, his weight causing the wooden joints to creak and moan as he settled in and crossed his legs at the knees.

"And now, who might you be?" he asked in an official tone that held more than a hint of curiosity.

Amaryllis flounced to the center of the room. "Why, I'm Amaryllis from the Melodeon, and I've come to see Jack Steele. Actually, I've come to stake his bail."

Seth rolled the chair forward, fitting it closer to his work-filled desk. "Have you now?"

"I certainly have," Amaryllis assured him with indignation. She stuck her kid-gloved hand into the receptacle of her purse and yanked out a crumpled wad of bills. She paraded them in front of the sheriff's nose.

Seth made a choking noise from deep within his chest, and short of waving his hand in the air to clear the pungent scent of perfume, he wheezed, "How did you know he was in here?"

"This little ol' gal knows scads of things. Most likely some your mammy never taught you." She tittered with laughter, then sobered as if realizing what she'd just suggested to a man of the law. "Well, never you mind. I just knew, that's all."

Bullock sat up and assessed Amaryllis with a keen eye. "Where did you get the money?"

"Now, now, Sheriff, you don't have call to go and ask me that. Why, it's just the same as asking a lady her age, and I can tell you for true, I'd never divulge that sort of information. I have the money, it's mine, and I'm giving it to you. All you have to do is give me that ol' sugar, Jack Steele."

"Steele," Seth called out to Jack, who'd kept his eyes propped on Amaryllis since she'd entered, "you know this woman?"

Jack's grin flashed briefly. "Yeah, I know her." Then his mouth slipped into a seductive curl. "What took you so long, baby?"

Amaryllis's made-up face whitened even more under the layer of powder dusted across it. "W-why, I just had scads of things to do this morning. I couldn't get on down here until now."

Seth Bullock took the money from Amaryllis. He counted it, then gave her back a single bill. "He's not worth all that."

"Oh, I declare." Her red lips converged into a perfect pout.

"Looks like you're going to be getting out of here, Steele." Bullock grabbed a special-looking form with heavy black letters adorning the top and took up his pen. "Much as I hate to say it, you're free." He looked up to Amaryllis, who hovered over his desk; biting back a cough, he said, "I have to fill out his release papers before you can take him. Sit tight a minute, Miss Amaryllis."

"Oh, I sit real tight, sugar." She bit her rouged lip and forced a demure smile on her mouth. "Can I converse with the prisoner whilst you're taking care of that officious business?"

"If you don't get too close to him. I haven't searched you for weapons, but judging by your attire, I'd say it's safe to say the only weapon you're carrying is your perfume."

"Why, thank you, Sheriff. You aren't nearly as unprincipled as I thought you'd be." She promenaded away from the desk, his obvious insult sailing completely over her head.

Jack stood and moved to the front of the cell, gripping the cold iron grates in his fists. He never thought he'd be glad to see Amaryllis, and here she was coming to his rescue. He could only imagine what had prompted her to come, and even worse, what he'd be forced to do to make it up to her.

Amaryllis reached him, glanced over her shoulder to see if Seth was watching, then pouted as if truly dejected over his incarceration.

"Why, Jack Steele, I swan I ain't *neeever* been so blue as when I found out you'd been taken to the coop. This little ol' gal pretty near boo-hooed her eyes out, she did."

Jack leaned forward, his face only inches from hers and separated from it by his confinement. "Is that right?" He studied Amaryllis for a moment, coming to the conclusion her cherubic face may look sweet as cherry pie, but underneath all the honey, aggravation burned hotly. Should he top her with brandy, she'd light up like a Roman candle.

"Course it is, sugar." Peeking over her shoulder again, she saw the sheriff busy with his papers. She turned back to Jack and lowered her voice. "Now, listen up quick. I never would have come here if it weren't for the good pay I was getting. I don't take kindly to being brushed off after I go and set aside prime working time. Not to mention that crack about Dickie Brown was more false than a pair of wooden teeth. And I had the black eye to prove it!" She frowned at her own rise in voice level, quickly softening it again. "That's the last time I'll ever go accusing someone until I have the damn truth."

Tom Deerhorn roused with a moan and flapped open his eyes. His nose wrinkled and twitched, sniffing at the air in noisy puffs, then a doltish smile dazed his mouth and he boosted himself up to a sitting position. Upon seeing Amaryllis in her frothy attire, he blinked his brown eyes once and his gaze traveled the length of her. Utterly captivated, he snorkeled up another deep draft of air and sighed. "Ma'am, you're the purtiest-smellin' whore I ever did set my nose to."

The plume in Amaryllis's hair tipped with her head to one side, as if she was noticing Tom for the first time. "Who the dickens are you?"

"Thomas G. Deerhorn, ma'am. And I think I'm in love with you."

Amaryllis batted her kohled eyelashes and poked her nose in the air with incredible surprise. "Why, I declare!"

"Deerhorn, close up your mouth." Jack's gaze bored down on Amaryllis, and he whispered between clenched teeth, "Who sent you here?"

"Big Eddie McIntyre waylaid me," she replied, as she stared brightly at Tom. "What are you in for, sugar?"

Grinning from ear to ear, Deerhorn puffed out his chest with great pride. "Aiding a criminal against an officer of the law. Resisting arrest."

"Why, I swan! What an act of humanity."

"How do you know Edward?" Jack gritted, his patience slowly being worn away.

"He's a customer of mine, if you must know. Came in this morning, woke me up, dammit all, and gave me a handful of greenbacks. Said to get myself on over here and I'd get to make a tidy profit for my efforts." Her green eyes sparkled as she looked at Tom. "Now, lamb, how long you aim to be in this here coop?"

"Dang burn if I know hell from high water." His jaw swollen, Tom rubbed his knuckles across it and moved it back and forth with his index finger. "You come to hock me out, too, sweetheart of my everlasting life?"

Amaryllis giggled. "Oo! I swan, but you've got the words of a poet!"

"Hot damn, she likes me, Steele!"

Jack grated his fingertips over his eyelids, unable to view the pathetic scene. He pressed the pad of his thumb over the bridge of his nose, trying to squeeze out the images. Christ, but Edward McIntyre took a chance by involving Amaryllis; he could only hope her density would keep her curiosity at bay. The woman couldn't keep her mouth shut if it were gagged.

Seth scraped his chair back and knelt in front of his safe. The combination lock twirled under the guidance of his hand, then he swung the door open and took out Jack's guns. "All right, Steele." He made his way to the cell. "Don't think I won't be watching your every damn move. Were I the devil side of the law, I'd run your butt out of my town with the end of my revolver. Damn if I'm not tempted."

"I guess I'm supposed to be grateful for that, Bullock?"

"I don't need a man like you beholden to me." Seth Bullock slipped the key into the cylinder. The gate swung open to freedom, and Jack stepped clear of the prison. Deerhorn forlornly looked on as the sheriff returned the bars to their confining place.

"Goddamn, what about me?"

"I don't see anybody circulating your bail, Deerhorn," Seth reminded him.

Amaryllis knit her painted brows together as if she wanted to say something, but kept quiet with the sheriff so close. Instead, she concentrated on Jack; she threw herself in his arms.

As Steele reflexively caught her in his embrace, her rouged lips locked down on his. The kiss left him cold. It ended as abruptly as it began. Amaryllis looked up into his face and fanned her curled lashes. "I sorely missed that, Jack, honey. I'm damn glad to have you out of this nasty ol' place."

Jack knew she was putting on a show for the sheriff's sake,

but somehow he felt as if she were showing him a thing or two at the same time. A slightly indignant gleam showed in her heavily lashed eyes that said she was still put off by his refusal to bed her.

Easing her out of his embrace, he set her back on her feet at arm's length. As he did, he caught sight of Holly Dancer standing in the open doorway holding a cloth-covered tray. Jack stepped forward, but she didn't move; she did nothing to hide the contempt in her azure eyes.

He knew then, she'd witnessed the entire scene.

"Mrs. Dancer." Seth warmly smiled, and Holly forced herself to return the pleasant gesture. She felt light-headed and wasn't even sure she could move. The shock of seeing Jack in the arms of another woman—the woman she distinctly remembered from the Melodeon—had been her undoing.

She hadn't been sure what to expect when she volunteered to bring Jack his meal, but certainly finding him kissing and embracing a company girl wasn't it. She'd envisioned him being miserable behind the guard of a prison door; she'd hoped he would be glad to see her.

By the look of things, she'd been wrong on both accounts.

Holly took short steps and placed the tray on the desktop, then moved back. She hoped against all odds that her cheeks weren't flaming like red begonias in June. Trying her best to keep her voice level, she said, "Good morning, Sheriff. I brought the breakfast tray." She kept her eyes averted from Jack Steele.

"I forgot it was Goodnight's turn to supply the meals." Seth cocked his head toward Deerhorn. "You're lucky, cowboy. You could've been eating grub from the Common Cattle Company."

Holly looked away from the wall of hanging papers and slipped a glance at Jack; he stared directly at her, and with an assessment that made her insides churn. She blinked once, noting the woman with the white hair and feathers gaped at her, too. She couldn't help noticing the woman's lush red lips, and try as she might to put an end to it, she couldn't help envisioning Jack's mouth touching the pouting display. Holly wanted to slap her. Or him. Or maybe both.

Shocked by her own temper, Holly tried to reason with herself. She had no claim to Jack Steele. But even as she told herself that, shame burned in her stomach. He'd kissed her in the mine in much the same way she'd seen him kissing this woman.

"Good morning, Mrs. Dancer." Jack's drawl came easily to her ears, and she swallowed down her rage, obliged to answer him, with so many sets of eyes staring at her.

"Mr. Steele." She folded her hands together in front of her, fearing she may lash out at him yet for his callous behavior. Any sympathy she'd had for him vanished. "I see you spent the night indisposed."

Jack gave her a crooked tilt of his mouth, and she squelched an impulse to swipe the grin from his face. "Not every bed I sleep in can smell of orange blossoms."

Holly jerked her chin up. How dare he mention her bed in mixed company, though surely no one knew what he was talking about! Holly glanced self-consciously at the colorful woman and retracted the thought. Surely she knew. A mischievous sulk marred her powdered face.

"Am I missing something here, sugar lamb?" Amaryllis sidled up next to Jack and looped her arm around his waist. But as tall as he was, and as short as she was, the gesture ended up being even more lewd as her fingers came to rest on the tight outline of his hips under the parting of his coat front.

Jack didn't push her hand away, a fact that stung Holly all the more. How could she have been so blind to think that he was interested in her? She should have known from the start that a man like Jack needed women like the one he was with now. Someone with experience . . . and no thoughts of romance clouding her judgment.

"Why, I swan!" Amaryllis's velvety outburst caught Holly's attention. "'Mrs. Dancer,' huh? You're that fancy wife of Billy's!"

At the mention of Billy's name, Holly's heart went still. The room became a soft blur, and she swayed ever so slightly on her feet. Why would this woman know Billy? Though their marriage had been less than desirable, the thought had never occurred to her that Billy would have visited the girls of the saloons. Her mouth dry, she barely heard herself ask, "How did you know my husband?"

"Wweeell, you could say—"

Amaryllis was cut off with an "oof" as Jack roped his arms about her and clutched her to him in a tight embrace. She gasped and looked up at Jack in wonder. "Why . . . Jack, sugar . . ."

"The prettier the mouth, the better it looks shut."

"Steele." Bullock, who had stood back and silently watched the exchange, frowned hard and shoved Jack's guns into his hands. "This isn't a social palace. You're free. Get on out. I might take the lock to you again."

Jack holstered his Smith & Wesson, Buntline, and the small revolver he kept in his boot, then smoothed down the crown of his hat, securing it on his forehead. "Obliged, Sheriff."

"Hey, Jack, what about me?" Deerhorn hung on to the cell's grates with an abandoned look on his suntanned face. "And you, sweet pet, I'm in love with you."

"Well, you hold on to that feeling, lamb, and you come visit me soon as you're liberated. I'm down at the Melodeon —don't you forget it."

Amaryllis snuggled in next to Jack with a satisfied lift to her mouth. Holly quickly looked away when Jack's gaze came down on her; there was something in his eyes that said he wanted to speak with her, but whatever it was, she didn't want to hear it. She felt a sickening tightness in her stomach and longed to run free of the room, which, despite its coolness, stifled her.

Holly bid the sheriff a hasty good-day and made it to the doorknob without faltering. She pushed her way past Jack and Amaryllis, who were at the jamb. She bumped arms with Jack and flinched away, skittering around him.

Stepping out onto the boardwalk, she was glad for the brisk wind slapping at her face. She needed a jolt to snap her out of her shame. Shame that she'd believed Jack needed her; shame that burned deep within at the realization that Billy had no doubt been unfaithful to her.

Behind her, Holly could hear Amaryllis's churlish laughter. It floated on the breeze and followed her.

But she wouldn't run away from it.

She wished to put her hands over her ears to cover that laugh. The pitch, the inflection, the mirth at her expense. It reminded her so of Billy's that it nearly made her sob with chilling remembrance.

It was as if Billy had come back to haunt her.

Holly wrapped her wet hair up in a towel and stripped out of her navy serge dress. She quickly washed herself in the basin, then donned a clean nightdress. Over that, she slipped into a red flannel shirt, buttoning it up tight; on her feet, she wore heavily knitted socks.

The kerosene lamp cast a hazy light in the room as she sat down next to the parlor stove to rub her hair dry.

Loud voices and the thump of boots on the boardwalks filtered up from the street. It was Saturday night, and the miners had come into town to do their weekly carousing.

Holly ran a brush through her mahogany hair, untangling the strands until they reached her waist in a fine wave.

The red coals hissed and popped, and in spite of herself, she jumped at the sudden natural noises.

Never had she been more aware of stray gunshots than she had since Jack Steele rode into town.

Jack . . . She reproached herself for even thinking his name. She'd come to the decision to void him from all her thoughts. There was no sense in tormenting herself. He'd made his feelings perfectly clear this morning, and it was all for the better that she go on with her life.

Her hair still damp, she absently skimmed the bristles over it, thinking of her unfinished book, but lacking the interest to pick it up tonight.

A knock sounded at the door, and she started.

She froze. A second knock came. It scared her into motion; she dropped the brush and stood up, quickly crossing over to her desk and reaching for the .22 inside her tin box.

Her hands shook as she gripped the cold butt and made a steady walk toward the door. She had no chance to ask who it was. Halfway there, she heard Steele's deep voice creep through the wood and beckon her.

"It's Jack. Let me in, Holly, or so help me, I'll break the door down."

Chapter Nine

Go away," Holly told Jack, the portal remaining firmly closed in front of his face.

Jack leaned into the door, grabbed hold of the knob, and twisted. Locked. He slumped his shoulder against the edge and, for a moment, thought of busting it in. "Holly, unlock it and let me in. I won't go away." For emphasis, he struck his fist dead center into the wood. It resounded with sharp clarity that broke through the freezing night, causing a dog some shops down to take up a throaty bark.

Jack waited; when his patience could take no more, he lifted his palm again. He was about to let go when the lock gave way and the door opened.

He remained at the threshold, the warmth from inside slipping out to him and curling around his shirted chest and legs. He'd left his coat unbuttoned; why, he wasn't sure— maybe to keep his senses sharp knowing where he was going and why. Now that he was here, he was momentarily dumbstruck.

In all his days, he'd never seen a more beautiful woman.

Jack instantly panned his gaze over her, taking in the soft folds of her nightrail, the plaid shirt that sagged off her gently sloping shoulders . . . and the fall of her wealth of burnished hair. It cascaded nearly down to her hips in soft waves of reddish brown, which, in the dim light from behind her, almost appeared golden red. Holly lowered her hand, and it was then he saw the three-inch Smith & Wesson wrapped in her fingers.

"Come in, if you're going to," she said. "You're letting cold air in."

She turned away and padded silently to stand at the wrought-iron end post of her bed. Gripping the ornate design, she discarded her gun to the downy comforter.

Slipping the door closed, Jack reclined against it a minute. It was too easy to get lost in the way she looked, but he couldn't help himself. Only when his breathing settled down to a more even beat did he move past her to the headboard of her bed. It seemed to be the designated divider between them, though a most unsuitable one. All he could think of was tumbling down on it with her.

Jack dispensed with his hat, tossing it to the bed. It landed smack in the middle of the mattress. Jerking at the cuffs of his ulster, he took it off and doubled it over the back of her writing chair.

Feeling more apprehensive than he was comfortable with, he licked his lips and tried to summon the clearly rehearsed speech he'd been practicing since leaving the Gem. Not a single word came to mind that made any sense. Never once in his life had he wanted to explain himself to a female.

"What do you want?" Holly finally spoke up, crossing her arms over her breasts. He couldn't help noticing she wore no undergarments, and knowing her curving flesh was unconfined brought a surge of heat through his loins. He damned his lack of control, though didn't raise his gaze for a long moment.

Eventually he cleared his throat, feeling much like a youth by the crack in his voice. "I need to talk to you."

"I don't think we have anything to say." She didn't flinch.

"We do." Jack combed his fingers through the thickness of his hair, smoothing it away from his forehead. "I think we need to get a few things cleared up." He shifted his weight to one leg, stuffing his hands in his denim pockets. "What you saw at the jail wasn't what you thought."

Holly broke away from his gaze and crossed to the parlor stove. She snatched up her brush and drove it through her damp hair. The strokes were long and hard. "I think it was fairly plain what I saw. And there's no reason for you to have to explain anything to me."

Jack closed in on her and stood only a breath from her back. He couldn't stop himself from fitting his hands over her shoulders and spinning her around to face him. She clutched the brush as if it were her only weapon against him. Her summer blue eyes glittered, and he could see she was hurting. Their sparkling depths made him curse his own weakness. Were he any kind of man at all, he'd damn his professional ethics and tell her everything; he'd tell Jack Steele to go to hell. But even as he was thinking it, he knew he could not. To give his alias away would leave him vulnerable and without protection. Damn him, he could not; not yet.

"This is all Deerhorn's fault!" he yelled. The need to blame the situation on someone pulled at his insides. "That kid you saw me behind bars with—that's the one who shot me! If he hadn't pulled a gun on Bullock, I'd never have been locked up."

The total confusion of his state of mind made his anger run wild. Unknowingly he took it out on Holly. He loosened the fingers that had bit into the supple flesh at the shoulders of her gown and shirt. "I don't like this any more than you do. I shouldn't have to explain anything to you. What I do is my own business." The tears that seeped past her eyes only inflamed his disgust at himself, and he shook her, drawing her closer to him. "But for some unknown reason, it's important to me that you know at least one truth about me. Amaryllis is not a 'friend' of mine in the sense you're thinking. She bailed me out of jail—nothing more."

He could feel her trembling, and a moan caught in his throat, but he didn't loosen his hold.

"You don't have to say anything to me," she whispered. "I mean nothing to you. . . ."

The chord struck home, for suddenly he knew she meant everything to him. It was his own lack of belief that kept him at arm's length. Even though he knew he'd already become too involved with her, he had to constrain the feelings to

160

succumb totally. Knowing that, he was forced to lash out, "You got that right. You mean nothing to me. I mean nothing to you. You understand that? I only wanted to set you straight."

She tried to nod, but he could see she was breaking in two. "I . . . I understand."

Tormented and wanting nothing more than to kiss her tears away, Jack pressed on, down a road with blinders hindering his emotions. "You saved me when I needed you, and I just felt I owed you."

"Y-you owe me nothing. . . ." she choked, biting her lower lip . . . pink and soft and moist.

"Don't look at me like that."

"L-like what?"

"Like you're going to break apart." His head only inches from hers, he breathed in her familiar blossom scent. It killed him a thousand times. "Dammit, don't you look at me like you care. . . ."

"I—" Her full mouth quivered, and she blinked the tears wetting her spiky lashes.

"Christ . . ." he breathed, and lowered his lips to the crystal droplets. He kissed them away, nuzzling the softness of her cheek, pressing his mouth over her warm skin. She melded next to him, and he wrapped her in his arms. She was so sweet; too sweet for a hardened man like him. He'd break her heart, and his own, too. But he couldn't stop. Not to save himself . . . or her. He was tired of being alone; tired of being with women he bought and paid for. He needed this one stolen moment of purity.

Christ, he needed to love again.

Tilting her chin up, he murmured, "Look at me." He said it so softly, so unlike his normal gruff tone, it seemed as if someone else had spoken it. He was glad to hear that he had an iota of tenderness left within himself.

Holly obeyed, her lids fluttering open. The intensity in Jack's gaze was staggering. It was as if she were seeing him for the very first time. Gone was the rough-edged exterior; gone were the scowling lines. In their place, gentle desire, something that made her want to cling to him.

"Look at me when I kiss you," he crooned in a voice that sent delightful shivers through her.

She did as he asked, marveling in the passionate energy of his gray eyes; their irises were reflective pieces of finely cut gems, penetrating her very soul.

He lowered his face, and she drew in her breath, swaying deeper into his embrace. She brought her hands to the soft curves of his shoulders, bringing him closer. Working her fingers through his thick black hair, she faintly smiled at the glossy locks, having wanted to do this very thing for a long, long time.

At first Jack's lips were soft, hesitant, as if even he himself wasn't sure what response it would bring. But as the kiss lengthened, the strength of it grew powerful, and it was undeniably the most sensual thing she'd ever experienced. She wanted to be this way forever, never leaving the circle of his arms, nor relinquishing the touch of his lips against her own.

It drugged her into a dance of the senses, magically leading her to an enchanted promenade.

She suddenly knew why Carrie flushed when she spoke of Conrath La Fors. If this was what she'd been lacking in her marriage, then she'd never been married at all. She was untouched, Jack the first to unearth in her what desire truly was.

Her heartbeat raced and she fought to keep standing. She could not stop stroking his hair, the corded muscles in his neck, the twill of his winter shirt where it covered his sinewy back which swayed down to the curve of his buttocks. Still, she needed more. She wanted his shirt off him. She shuddered. What had become of her to turn so greedy that his kiss was not enough? She wondered if it was this way for Jack, too. Or if she was so unseasoned, she easily fell off her feet.

Jack lifted her into his arms without breaking his kiss. He hugged her body close to his chest, and she pressed her lips into his, softly, slowly, then dramatically with fervor. She didn't care where he was taking her.

She felt them go down on the bed, the springs protesting under their burden. Jack cushioned her back into the mattress, the effort causing him to break the kiss; his breath rasped against her cheek, hot and moist.

All her sensibilities were gone. She didn't want to tell him to leave, she wanted him to stay. Just this once, she would take a chance. The hard strength of his body was like a jolt of heat surging through her veins. She felt the rigid contours of his gun belt and the butt of his revolver digging into her waist and thigh; she wiggled to adjust her body away from the pressure. Her movement caused him to groan, and she wondered if she'd done something wrong. She stared blankly at him as he raised himself upward and frantically fumbled with his shining buckle. His black hair fell over his brow and tumbled into his thick lashes. While he yanked at his belt, she reached out and stroked his hair back. Turning his face, he pressed his mouth into her palm. The contact made a river of heat seep throughout her being and center between her thighs.

Jack hurtled his gun over the side of the bed, cradled her face between his callused hands, and kissed her again; hard. She returned it with equal measure as his hand traveled the length of her body, sampling every intimate curve. He traced the outline of her hips, upward to the swell of her breast. She inhaled sharply, and as she did so, Jack's tongue delved into the recess of her mouth. He captured her and teased her, much as he had done that day in the mine. This new art of kissing was strangely foreign and erotic. It made her feel wicked, and at the same time, transported her to an exotic cloud of heaven.

He combed through her long hair, twirling it around his fingers and releasing it. His hand skimmed over her collarbone, then to her breast. Languishing in the softness of his touch, her breasts felt heavy, the core between her legs damp and hot. These new feelings made her dizzy and confused. She wasn't supposed to feel like this, was she? Billy had said she was cold . . . unarousable. . . .

But Billy had never touched her like Jack.

Burying his face in her neck, Jack breathed a tender kiss there. As he circled the crest of her breast with his lean fingers, the nipple sprung into a tight pebble, responding to the coaxing caress. As wonderful as the feeling was, Holly wanted more. She wanted to feel Jack's warm body against hers. She knew that she'd lost her mind, because that was not how you made love. Billy never took her nightgown off. Then why did she want Jack to? Why did she want more with Jack than she'd ever wanted with Billy?

Jack must have read her thoughts, for he shrugged her out of the red shirt, then tugged at the buttons at the throat of her flannel gown. In a matter of seconds, the material parted and Jack's lips sought out the gentle swell of her breast and the taut nipple. She arched her back, welcoming him. This couldn't be happening. Not to her. Spasms of lightning darted throughout her mind, raining through her in blinding shards of pleasure.

Doubts came crashing inside her that maybe Billy had been wrong about her after all. . . .

Jack had been with enough women to know that what was happening between himself and Holly was more than physical. A meeting of the minds, the spirits, and the unique need for oneness had overshadowed all else. Never had he wanted a woman so completely he would give everything to have her.

As he tasted the sweetness of her skin, rolled the tip of her pure breast between his tongue, he knew he would protect her at all costs. He would give up the case; he would save her. He would take her away from Deadwood, use another alias . . . He moaned and kissed the blossom-scented valley between her breasts. . . . He would give up his life of falsehoods.

The admission filled him with a sense of awe as he realized it meant he was in love with her. Jack dusted his lips to the hollow of her throat, kissing the pulse point at its base. "Damn the suspicion that haunts my mind," he breathed against her warm flesh. "I am free of it."

"What?"

Holly's winded sigh came to him, and he ignored it; instead, he grazed his nimble fingers down her arm, the inside curve of her elbow, to her delicate hand, where he entwined her exquisite fingers with his own.

"What did you mean?" she asked again, breathless.

Jack searched her unfathomable blue eyes, and it jarred him. She was disheveled with unspent passion, her lips bruised and wet. Seeing her like that ignited a downpour of fiery sensations that made him ache with need for her. "Nothing . . ." He leaned his face in to kiss her again.

Holly turned her head, and Jack's kiss met the corner of her mouth. "What you said . . ."

"It was nothing, dammit." Jack condemned his own impatience, but what he'd said had been an indiscreet admission he never should have spoken aloud. He wanted to forget it; why couldn't she?

One look at her questioning gaze and he knew she wouldn't leave it alone. What was he to say? That he'd considered her capable of murder, and now that he loved her, he was willing to forget it? It was a confrontation he wasn't ready to have; he'd only just accepted the circumstances himself. How could he explain it to her if he had no explanation for it for himself?

His endless mood had been broken, his ardor doused by a dip of cold reflection that had come from his own mouth. It cooled his veins to iron, and he bit off a raunchy curse and lifted himself off her.

"What's the matter?" she called after him as he bent down to snatch up his gun belt.

Standing, Jack slung his holster over his hips and buckled it with numb fingers. "I'm not thinking clearly," he practically yelled at her.

Holly pushed herself onto her elbows and, with embarrassment, buttoned the top of her gown together. She felt a fine sweat break out on her brow and she swallowed, almost feeling as if she would be sick. It was happening again . . . the rejection. Had she not been so emotionally distraught, she would have seen that it had nothing to do with her sexual abilities at all. But all she saw was Jack, the broad back of his long coat as he shrugged into it and the quick movement of his arms as he hastily fastened the buttons closed.

It was as if he couldn't leave soon enough. The pain tore through her like a dull blade, and it was ignorant pride that made her whimper, "I hope your suspicion has been appeased by my lacking—" She broke off, unable to continue.

Jack swung around, and she refused to drop her chin. She flipped a lock of tangled hair over her shoulder and waited for him to say something.

"You should have thrown me out after my attempts at an apology. Now it seems I have to make another before I drag my tail out that door."

Holly gasped as he reached for her, then surpassed her and stretched his hand out to the mattress to collect his stray hat. He smacked it on his tousled hair.

She couldn't find the words to say anything. It seemed as if they were both sorry, and for different reasons.

The sound of Jack's heavy boots striding on the floor broke the tension-filled air as he made it to the door. He paused, his fingers curled over the knob. Without turning around, he said, "A man should be what he seems. . . . The devil knows I've tried."

Then he was gone, and she was left with her own unfulfillment and despair. She was alone—again.

But this time the gravity of her solitude was made worse by the unthinkable.

She'd fallen in love with Jack Steele.

Perched on the splintered seat of a mud wagon was a woman who could have been dainty in bone, but her garb diminished any chance of being called feminine. She wore a shabby dark cloth coat, cheap little hat, a faded frayed skirt, and arctic overshoes. Even if the beholder looked beyond the tarnished exterior, the woman's claim to God's given speech was her ultimate undoing. A voice from leather lungs and salty vocabulary cussed up a blue streak that carried all the way down to the northeast end of Main Street.

"Of ill-said sire and dame!"

Crack! The sharp snap of a five-foot-long leather whip and its popper on the end smacked through the air. It achieved an explosive sound that awoke old echoes slumbering peacefully since a geological revolution threw White Rocks above the gulch.

"Damn yourn faces! And yourn souls, bodies and tails!" *Crack!*

"That yourn fathers be accursed and yourn mothers three times over."

Crack!

"Damn yourn sisters and brothers, aunts and uncles."

Crack!

"I'll eat 'em all fer Sunday dinner!"

Crack!

"Gee!"

Crack!

"Gee!"

And with all this, the placid team of eight oxen that towed her didn't flinch or twitter a single hair on their ears. They trudged through the street at a slow roll, chewing their cuds contentedly.

Josephine Goodnight was the first at the restaurant to step out of the kitchen and stand at the window. Not soon after, Holly set down the coffeepot at the sideboard and stood next to Mrs. Goodnight.

They stared at the spectacle, for it was always a sight to see a bullwhacker rambling into Deadwood; but there was something special about the woman who'd had more rumors spread about her than any other in the territory. And most of them had been spread by the woman herself.

"Clar the road, you bunch of boozin' bumpkins!"

"Martha Jane's back," Josephine stated with a half smile as she dropped the curtain back in place.

"And it looks like she's brought the stove," Holly commented, peering through the panes at the large crate in the bed of the long, open wagon.

"It's about time. That old thing we've been using isn't fit for kindling."

Josephine habitually wiped her hands on her apron as she crossed out the door, Holly following her.

The sun shone brightly in warming yellow, the wind from the previous day blowing away any clouds and leaving a perfect robin's-egg blue dome. Holly stepped onto the boardwalk with Josephine, who'd put her hands on her waist to greet Martha Jane Cannary.

"Calamity" Jane looked much older than her twenty-five

years, though there was a certain youthful vitality in her all-seeing blue eyes.

"Crack a day to all you folks," Martha Jane called down from her wagon. She sat with her legs stretched apart, the numerous leather ribbons woven between her fingers dangling between her heels. "Damn near chanc'd makin' it inta town with them Injins flying arrows at m'scalp. An Amerrican ain't safe. But here I am, nary a scratch on me."

"Did you bring this crate for us, Martha Jane?" Josephine asked.

"Damn if I didn't, Jo." She talked around the wad of tobacco in her mouth. "Ya owe me a ton a freight fer the contraption. Damn near topped out the scales. What the hell's in it?"

"A stove."

"Then let's get the beast unloaded. This gal's hungry nuff to et the paper menu in your pocket." A grin spread over her swarthy features. "Whar's that young miss a yourn, Jo? That buck a hers, La Fors, ain't fer behind me."

Josephine nodded over her shoulder. "She's manning the old stove, but soon as she hears Conrath come in, you can count on anything in the skillet to be burned blacker than coal. She'll be out here in a glimmer."

Holly took a step forward and looked curiously into the back of Martha Jane's wagon. It was filled to the brim with canvas bags; small mining equipment: rockers, shovels, and pans; eggs in beds of straw, and several long crates with cats meowing in them.

Holly poked her finger in the cage and ruffled the fur of a marmalade cat. "What are all the cats for, Martha Jane?"

"Oh, them. Well, seein' as how Phatty Thompson did so good with 'em, I thought I'd try m'luck at sellin' off a few. Several a the girls down to the Number Ten said they wuz interested in havin' a pet."

Holly didn't have the heart to tell Martha Jane that since Phatty's last visit, when he'd shipped in dozens of cats, there were now more cats in Deadwood than people knew what to do with. They scourged the garbage bins and scampered freely across the street, becoming targets of many a hurling beer bottle.

"They're cute." Holly smiled. "If you don't find homes for all of them, let me know."

"Youbedam, I will."

From the west end of town came the pistol-shotlike sound of a bullwhacker's popper, and a team of matching white oxen plodded through the quagmire. Holly shaded her eyes with her hands to see Conrath La Fors expertly wielding his whip. He was tall in posture and built as sturdy as a barrel; a well-worn hat capped his rich earth brown hair. His green eyes nearly matched the hazel color of Carrie's.

He was a man completely skilled at his job. With his cracker, he could flick a fly off an ox twenty or thirty feet away without disturbing the animal.

Just after Lee Street, Conrath whistled a special whistle, and soon after, the front door to the restaurant slammed open and Carrie came running out. Her skirts and bleached white petticoats flew behind her as she ran into the street, heedless of the mud squeezing around her high-top shoes and soiling her hems.

"Con!" she squealed with delight as he yanked her up on the buckboard bench with strong arms. Mindless of the spectacle they were making, Conrath wrapped his arms around her and whispered something in her ear that made her blush and laugh at the same time.

Holly bit back a pang of jealousy as she watched the young couple. She'd never once been privy to such open affection, not even when she'd been a child. She'd grown up in a household of six brothers who were as gruff in manner as her father. And her mother had never shown her only daughter a soft consideration.

Holly drew her gaze away from Carrie and Conrath, pretending interest in the frisky cats. She stroked the underside of one's chin, then lifted her eyes. She was startled to find Jack Steele staring at her.

He stood on the end of the block, three businesses down. Despite the heavy sidewalk traffic, their eyes had met amid the congestion of heads with hats.

Holly swallowed, and willed herself to look away, but the command was long in coming. For some reason, embarrassment heated her at being caught looking wistfully at

Conrath and Carrie. It made her appear to be pining away for someone . . . namely him. No matter the reason or truth, just seeing him flustered her. Something special had sprung up between them, and it was hard to cast it aside no matter what their last words to each other had been.

Wes Travis chose that moment to come whooping it up down Main Street on a flea-bitten gray gelding. Wes's wild hollers and snorting horse, its unshod hooves spraying up mud, broke the spell between her and Jack. Holly found the courage to turn away and forced her attention back to Martha Jane and Mrs. Goodnight.

"S'pose ya git yerself on down here, La Fors," Martha Jane called out to Conrath, "and rile up some extra-strong arms and git this damn stove off'n my bed." Cussing, she hopped down and kicked at the hubs of her wagon wheels where gumbo soil clogged the spokes.

Conrath gave Carrie a deep grin, then ran his fingertip along her jaw. She smiled back unabashedly as he bounced off the spring seat and landed surefootedly in the street. His long, buckskin-covered legs took large strides to reach the women.

"Afternoon, Mrs. Goodnight. And you're looking indecently pretty today." His teeth shined white as pearls against his tanned face, and he touched the tips of his fingers to his hat.

"Conrath, you're a rascal." Josephine's face colored ever so slightly with a soft flush of pink. "Don't you try sweet-talking me. It's Mr. Goodnight you need to save the charm for."

Conrath laughed good-naturedly and released the tailgate of Martha Jane's mud wagon. Cupping his hands, he yelled at a group of men departing the Red Bird across the street. "Hey, give me a hand with this."

They obliged, several hopping up into the bed while two others stood near the drawn-down rear. They began pushing the stove off the edge, but the weight was too much for the handful of men at street level to handle. Without being asked, Jack and several others—patrons from the restaurant—had come up to the wagon and pitched in.

170

Holly stood back and watched as Jack strained against the heavy crate. He used his right shoulder for most of the load, then he was forced to use both arms to help guide the carton down.

No one but Holly knew about Jack's injured arm, and Holly wanted to scream what an idiot he was. Surely the stress would cause him damage. But as he lowered the wooden crate along with the others, he hid any signs of pain he was having—if indeed he was. His only show of exertion was a fine sheen of perspiration that dampened his temple. He didn't grab at his arm, nor did he look pale.

The men from the Red Bird departed, but Jack stayed. No one seemed to notice as he stepped back to the boardwalk. Carrie and Josephine were too anxious to see the new stove.

Holly could barely concentrate on the opening of the crate as Martha Jane brought out a crowbar for Conrath. Why didn't he walk away? Why did he stand there for her to sense and be aware of? She dared not move for fear of falling. She kept her back ramrod-straight and forced herself to be interested in what went on around her. Yet all the while she kept asking herself why the only man she'd been attracted to since Billy's death was the one man who could hurt her beyond feeling.

The loud crackle of wood splintering saw the lid open, with numerous nails protruding from its underside. Holly leaned forward as Mrs. Goodnight pulled out handful after handful of curly wood shavings, digging her way through the contents of the crate. When she'd gone far enough, she withdrew her hand, letting the packing rain down in the street. A bemused expression lit her matronly face.

"This isn't my stove."

Martha Jane peeked a look and raised her brows. "Damn if it ain't. That's a bathtub."

Carrie pulled out another handful of the stuffing material. "That can't be. We ordered a stove."

Holly inched ahead to view the inside. It was a bathtub, all right. A bold, brassy tub obviously meant for a bordello. Painted on the inside of the lacquered black enamel vessel, naked ladies lounged in all sorts of suggestive poses.

"Carrie, back on away from here." Josephine bristled and waved her off.

Carrie took her time, her large hazel eyes scanning over every curvaceous woman with intent curiosity.

Holly had the decency to blush in front of Conrath, but when she looked up, she found Jack's gaze on her again, and suddenly blushing was the furthest thing from her mind. She pictured him sitting in that tub. And with her in it, too. Why the image had so quickly settled over her was beyond her comprehension. It just did.

"Well, what do I do now?" Josephine wrung her hands together. "I'm so mad, I could . . . I could cry. I've been waiting for that stove over six months."

Conrath consoled her. "First off, you don't send the tub back. Round-trip freight on it will cost you good. I'll send a wire on to Cheyenne and see what the problem was."

"Lines were down this morning, Con," Carrie told him.

"I've already sent one telegram!" Josephine complained.

"Then I reckon the only way to solve this is to go directly to Cheyenne and see what the trouble is."

"No!" Carrie cried out. "You just got into town!"

Martha Jane stood back. "I'll float ya on the freight, Jo, till ya git things settled."

"I'll go," Holly said, but no one listened.

"I just can't understand how all this happened." Josephine Goodnight peered into the crate again with tight lips. She sniffed in disgust.

"I'll go," Holly repeated.

"Con, you can't be serious about riding off for Cheyenne. You no sooner got in from Sidney, you were heading for Cheyenne. And you said you wanted to—"

"I'll go," Holly said a little louder.

Her voice stopped Carrie, and she peered at Holly. "Go where?"

"To Cheyenne."

This time Josephine, Conrath, and Martha Jane looked at Holly. "If Mrs. Goodnight will give me the time off, I'll go to Cheyenne for you and see what the problem is with the stove."

"Mrs. Dancer, you can't be serious." Then Josephine

apparently contemplated the idea. "Would you? It's a lot to ask. . . ."

"You're not asking. I'm volunteering. I've always wanted to see Cheyenne. . . ." It was partially the truth. She had wanted to see Cheyenne, but not in the way she was going. She'd wanted to see it for fun and adventure: a vacation. Now her intent centered on getting away from Deadwood. Getting away from Jack Steele. Though no one else paid any attention to his presence, and it was all she could do not to be suffocated by it.

"Can you manage the restaurant with one less waitress?" Holly asked.

"I'll help more, Mother," Carrie stepped in. "I'll work extra-hard."

Holly smiled, knowing how much it meant to Carrie to stay with Conrath. Even though the trade-off would mean additional work, she'd be with him on Sundays when the restaurant was closed.

"Well . . ." Josephine hesitated. "I guess you could, Mrs. Dancer, if you really want to. I'll cover the stage fare, of course." Then she tried to laugh at the situation. "You're a darn sight lighter in weight than that tub!"

Everyone laughed.

It was settled.

"I'll pack my things and leave on the first Concord tomorrow morning." Turning up the boardwalk, Holly nearly collided with Jack. He steadied her with strong fingers.

"Don't leave on my account," came his richly timbred voice. Spellbinding, it caressed her ear . . . words alone for her to hear.

She shuddered and slipped her lids half-closed. She'd wanted nothing more than to be in his arms again, yet not under the watchful eyes of an entire city. She couldn't allow herself to get caught up in him; not now, not ever again. Whatever she'd hoped would happen between them would not. Jack had seen to that when he'd left her room.

Holly digested his words, stiffening her resolve. "What I do is my own business and doesn't concern you."

As she backed out of his hold, her pulse wavered unsteadily. She took one last look at his handsome face, noting every fine detail about it. The fullness of his dark brows, the masculine curve of his nose, the light scar at his wonderful gray eyes . . .

Jack allowed her the freedom of staring. It was the only thing she asked for, and it gave him reason to drink in her own face as well. He'd never been more discouraged than he was to hear she was leaving. Only a few words from him could keep her here, and he knew it. Then why was he afraid to say them . . . ? "Holly, I'd like to talk to you."

"You are talking to me, Mr. Steele. Anything you have to say can be said right here. But as you pointed out, you don't owe me much of anything at all. What you do is your own affair. I don't understand why you broke into the recording office, yet I haven't asked you about it. Don't put insinuations on my actions. Now, if you'll excuse me, I have to pack."

She marched off without a backward glance, leaving Jack to feel empty. He knew she had every right to treat him the way she did. He'd done her wrong by not confiding in her.

Jack hopped off the boardwalk, bound and determined to let her go. He would concentrate on his case, pooling heavily on the new suspect he'd been observing. If he could clear Holly, then he could clear his conscience.

As Jack neared his post, a man exited a building, locking the office door behind him. Dressed in a suit, he headed toward the livery. Jack followed.

He'd been having second thoughts that the person he was after actually mined a claim. A miner might be the wrong suspect to watch. This week Jack had ridden out into the surrounding forest and checked on the claims from his list taken in the city recorder's office; only one site was operating—Holly's.

If his new theory proved valid, Steele could be closing in quite soon.

Holly left Deadwood under the lamplight rays of kerosene lanterns. The first stage pulled out at five in the morning, and despite the dark hour, the departure had begun with confusion. The road out had been choked with mule trains, ox trains, express wagons, hacks, and buggies; it was a perfect jam, and a fearful amount of profanity was breathed upon the crisp air before the entanglement got straightened out. Now, nearly fourteen hours later, it seemed a long, long time ago.

Her earlier enthusiasm over the journey had waned, wilting her jubilant spirits. As the miles rolled away under the coach wheels, the scenery became less enchanting, the cramped quarters more compressed. When breakfast had been passed by without a stop, she'd eaten what she'd packed from the restaurant—a piece of bread and strawberry jam. She'd eagerly looked forward to the lunch stop, but once it arrived, she'd wished they'd kept on going.

They had stopped at a small station, not overtly kept up. She and her traveling companions had been shown a place to refresh themselves. It consisted of a tin basin on a bench, soft soap in a side dish so strong, it could have curled the hide off a buffalo, a roller towel that had seen better days, and a more or less toothless comb detained by a rawhide string. Needless to say, Holly shied away from it, passing over the halfhearted fare—supposedly lunch—that had been set out.

As the coach lurched in the rutted road, her stomach grumbled with hunger and she promised herself she'd eat something for dinner, whether it looked edible or not. She grabbed hold of the leather tug strap and perused her fellow travelers. She shared the coach with five men and two women. The jostling and bumping had made fast acquaintances of everyone, but nearly all kept to themselves.

She recalled with a smile the list of instructions they'd been given that morning by the coach messenger, blithe and alert on his semihigh seat. They were to avoid tight boots in the cold weather; walk when the driver told them to; avoid liquor, which added to a body's freeze all the more; put up with food in the stations; spit leeward; and understand that there would be no shooting—it scared the horses—no swearing, no discussing politics and religion.

No wonder they all sat in silence.

The coach made a smooth turn, hugging the hills. Holly refused to imagine how the driver could see in the fading twilight. Recalling the competence of the horses, she felt more at ease: six red roans with neither blemish nor flaw on them, and affectionate dispositions to match their beautiful exteriors.

The team clung to another mountainous turn, the jangling of their leads methodic. Then, without warning, the brake handle clamped down to a squealing halt and Holly was nearly knocked from her calfskin seat. She groped for the tug strap, her hand sliding down the wooden paneling; her fingernail caught on a fitting of polished metal and broke. The jolt blew the hat right off her head, the long pearl-headed stickpin flying with it. A lock of her hair drooped free and tickled her nose.

After retrieving her hat, she lowered the drop-glass window, unable to tell what was the matter. They were stopped in a grove of ponderosas, the impending night blending their shadows nearly to oblivion.

She listened to the passive blows of horses and didn't figure they belonged to the stage's team. Then she heard a nasally voice, twanged with a backwoods accent and muffled, as if the owner were talking into his hands.

"Throw down your prop, mister, and put your heads up!"

Gasping in surprise, another voice broke in to correct the first. "You mulehead, it's hands up!"

"Shut your yap, Cole. You said it was my turn to say it, and I'm saying it the way I want. Heads up, hands up, it don't make no never mind."

There was a shuffling sound, then a third voice. "You said I was Cole. You're Jesse."

"Don't make no never mind who's who!"

"Throw it down, mister. I ain't got all year."

"No, we ain't got all *day.*"

"'Sat another question of my wording, Frank?"

"Frank? You said I was Jesse."

The third voice chimed in. "You both shut up. I'm in charge and I'll say what is. The Youngers and Jameses find out we're filching their names, we're apt to be skinned like dead meat, so it don't make no mind who is who! It was a stupid idea to begin with! From now on, use the one your ma gave you. That said, tell 'em what this is."

Holly bit down on her lip. Despite the obvious discord, the voices sounded as if they meant business.

The first man spoke up again, and his words confirmed Holly's worst fears. "This here's a robbery, mister, and we aim to take all your gold."

Chapter Ten

*H*olly heard the low voice of the driver. "We don't have any gold."

The coach messenger who sat up on the box with the driver shouted down, "This isn't a treasure coach. We're the Cheyenne and Black Hills Stage and Express."

There was a momentary pause, then one of the would-be road agents spoke up. "Well, it don't make no never mind to us. We know ya'll have to have some gold on ya, so we might as well relieve ya of it."

"Get on down from there and hold the team afore we blow the top of yore head off," came a smothered-sounding order from another of the bandits.

A rustling came from the cab's top as the driver and messenger scaled down the coach.

The compartment door banged open and the long barrel of a Sharps single-shot rifle nosed into the interior.

"Come on out!" Holly could not see the robber as he held himself back, though she recognized the voice as belonging to the first man who'd spoken. Her traveling companions alighted like sands in an hourglass—spilling out in competition for the single bottleneck exit with elbows jarred and knees bumping. Holly was the last to disembark.

As she did, the evening sky greeted her, its purple hues streaked with different shades of melon on the western horizon. In that light, Holly wasn't able to get a good look at the robbers, though she saw they wore triangular-shaped bandannas around their noses and mouths. From what she could discern, all three were well over fifty years of age. They stood bowlegged and lanky in frame, their denims trail-ridden, cloaked by long dusters fanning out over the tops of pointy-toed boots.

"Rally on over, folks," one of them said, waving his gun-holding hand.

"Hey, Dunk, I'll search the coach."

"Ya do that, Beans."

Holly watched as Beans climbed aboard the vacant Concord. The passengers had been herded into a spot just in front of the team of horses, and a second man nudged Holly toward them. She stood next to the driver and the other two women on the coach. They were matronly and huddled together, the slackened skin under their chins trembling.

"Now," Dunk began, standing at attention in front of them, "me and Valentine will set ya folks straight." With the tip of his pistol, he scratched at his jaw through the bandanna. "We rob coaches fer a livin', and we damn well mean business. I don't rightly take too kindly to the fact that the driver here had to point out to us we was robbin' the wrong gig."

"Well, we is," Valentine added under his breath.

"Put a plug in it, Val."

Valentine shrugged and spat out a stream of tobacco juice from under his scarf.

"We are trained professionals in what we do," Dunk continued, marching up and down, his coat flapping open to reveal his midlife paunch. "And so if ya folks know what's best fer ya, ya'll will listen to every word we say. Any questions?"

Holly looked around at the somber faces next to her. If anyone had any questions, they weren't voicing them.

"Good," Dunk said through his mask. "Now we'll commence to step two. Everything ya got of value, take it off and put it in Valentine's bag. And that includes gold teeth."

179

The coach messenger advised them it was best they complied, then proceeded to lift out his gold chronometer. The passengers followed suit, dropping their belongings into the dirty pillow slip Valentine held open to them. Valentine asked the dowager ladies if they were wearing hairpieces, shocking them into near vapors. Much to their mortification, he poked at their coiffures, then purloined an ivory cameo, pin-on silver timepiece, and pearl necklace.

Holly glanced down at her coarsely woven red Scotch plaid traveling costume with its heavy pleats. The reticule in her hands contained only a single-eagle gold piece, enough to see to her hotel accommodations; her round-trip stage fare had been paid in advance.

She had nothing of real value on her person; she wore no jewelry and had no watch.

Valentine held out the trinket-laden slip; he stared expectantly at her. She nervously untied the strings to her purse and gave him the ten-dollar coin.

Even in the waning light, she could see the pale greed in his blue eyes, the expectant expression as he waited for more to follow. "I don't have anything else."

He was more than flabbergasted by her admission. "Ya have to have something. Earbobs?"

She shook her head.

"Watch?"

She shook her head.

"Gold teeth?"

She vigorously shook her head.

"Weddin' ring?"

She swallowed. "I'm not married."

Valentine rubbed the top of his nose where the scarf crept down the bridge of it. "Say, uh, Dunk, what am I s'posed to do if she don't have anything but an eagle?"

"Huh?"

"This lady don't have nothin' else to throw in."

Dunk sauntered over, his pistol still in hand, but aimed carelessly at his toe.

"What's the problem?" he asked, positioning himself next to Valentine.

"She's busted."

Dunk turned his head to stare at Holly. She saw the whites

of his eyes disappear as he squinted to get a look at her. He craned his neck, a gesture that made her hop a step backward. "Hold still, gal, so I can see ya."

Holly tried to remain calm and rooted to the spot, but Dunk's solemn appraisal made her lick her lips.

"Dang blame it all, I cain't see a blasted thing." He combed through his coat pocket, pulling out a pair of wire-rimmed spectacles. He perched them on his nose the best he could with the hindrance of the bandanna. When he leaned forward to peer at Holly again, he almost bumped his nose against hers.

A match scratched to life against Valentine's thumbnail. "This help, Dunk?" he asked as he raised the glowing flame several inches from Holly's cheek.

Holly was able to see Dunk's eyes were a sloe black, creased at the corners from wear.

"Well, well, well," Dunk pronounced. "Why, yore about the purdiest thing I ever saw. Ya ain't got any fancy bobs to toss in?"

"No." Her voice cracked, and she wished to heaven that someone would intervene.

"Hey! Hey, Dunk! I found something!" Beans stuck his head out the boot of the coach, littering the air with letters that floated in every direction.

"What do we need mail fer?"

"No, no, it ain't that!" He frantically pointed. "It's a treasure box sure as I live and breathe!"

"No gold, huh?" Dunk snidely squawked to the driver, then ran to Beans.

"Ouch!" Valentine cried as the match in his fingers burned out and singed his skin.

"Come on over and give us a hand, Val."

Valentine left, leaving the prisoners completely un-attended . . . and apparently forgotten.

Holly chanced a glance at the driver and the coach messenger, the latter whispering in a low tone, "Best stay right here and set comfortable."

And as if the robbers could read her mind, she heard Dunk say, "Don't nobody get any ideas, 'cause we got us a fourth man in the brush over yonder with his sights on ya'll."

It wasn't long after that the three struggled to lift out the steel chest and it landed on the hard-packed earth with a loud thud.

"Somebitch! Ya got my toe, ya old coot!"

"Sorry . . ."

"Let's get on out of here," Dunk said, drawing up his sagging waistband. "Turn them six horses 'round."

Beans and Val took care of the coach as Dunk made his way toward the passengers and preached, "When ya'll get on back to Deadwood, pray tell the awful story how ya fought and shot and gave us a piece o' yore mind; when in fact, ya'll didn't have the spunk to draw a gun or open yore mouths. Now, load on up, ya sorry buzzards. 'Cept ya." He winked at Holly. "Ya'll are comin' with us."

The grassless ground underneath Holly felt like rock. She slid her eyelids open to see the hazy filter of morning light painted across the Dakota sky. The army blanket she'd been given provided little warmth, so she stayed curled up on her side. She was afraid to move, afraid to draw any attention.

It had been an interminable night, one that had seen the trio and herself—there was no fourth man—crossing over a small portion of the Black Hills. They would have put more distance between themselves and the holdup spot except that the robbers hadn't figured out a way to keep the gold chest secured.

They'd barely left the Cheyenne and Black Hills Stage when it became apparent that the strong box was far too heavy to be tied to and between Beans's and Valentine's saddles. It swayed dangerously on a hardy hemp rope that slackened and pulled when the horses trotted out of sync. Not an hour later, they'd reined up in a copse of cottonwood to calculate a different method of hauling.

Holly had been glad for the quickly called rest. Hanging on to Dunk's saddle horn had been awkward, her legs chafing where the saddlebow and fork rubbed against her thighs. Dunk seemed perfectly happy with the arrangement, taking every opportunity to tighten the hook of his arm around her midriff.

Once the entourage had stopped, they tried to improvise a way to strap the chest on Valentine's horse's back; it took three of them to lift it up to the saddle, dropping it as many times until they decided to rope it on. Just when they thought they had it, the horse cried in protest, bucking the unwelcome burden from its back. In the end, the bandits had to relent and tie the treasure chest on a short line of oakum and let it trail behind Beans's horse. It had thumped, butted, and bounced the entire ride to where they were camped now, scarring thickly barked tree trunks and up-rooting rocks, making enough noise to wake the devil himself.

Now, as the strong smell of coffee wafted over to Holly, the three road agents were clustered around the brass-trimmed trunk on their haunches. Their voices raised periodically in argument, and occasionally a hat was thrown melodramatically in the dirt, then quickly whacked back on a thinly haired head. They'd removed their masks, and Holly had been able to see that they were indeed as old as she'd first thought.

Beans got up from the group and sheepishly made his way toward Holly. She immediately closed her eyes and feigned sleep.

"Ah . . . ma'am?"

She scarcely breathed.

"Ma'am?" He took a step closer. "Hey, ma'am!"

Holly pretended he'd woken her and opened her eyes up slowly. "Yes?"

"I need one of yore hairpins."

The request completely caught her by surprise. She pushed herself to a sitting position, her every muscle aching. "A hairpin?"

"Ya got any?"

She'd only had three left after the hard ride, and those weren't doing much good. In places, lengths of hair fell down to her waist. "Yes . . ."

"Give me one. Better make that two."

Holly pulled them free and handed them to him. "What seems to be the trouble?"

Beans brightened the shade of a newly painted barn as he scrubbed his fingers across his white-stubbled chin. "We, uh . . . we fergot to take the key to the box, and we cain't commence to openin' it."

"Haven't you ever done this before?" She tried in vain to comb her hair with her fingers. That being a failure, she separated it in three strands and attempted a braid that she hoped would hold with pure suggestion.

Dunk had apparently heard her question, and he tipped his head up, answering for Beans. "Dozens of times."

"Hundreds," Valentine added. "We specialize in train robberies, though. There ain't no trains up in these here parts, so we's takin' some a the load off'n by droppin' a few coaches."

Valentine sauntered over to the other two, and they each took turns jiggling the hairpin in the lock's cylinder.

Holly warily stood up, wondering how she'd go about asking for a minute's privacy. As time wore on, she didn't think it was going to be as big a problem as she'd thought. The men had become obsessed with opening the lock. So obsessed, they paid her no notice.

She took a shy step backward, then tentatively another . . . then one more. She crept her way farther from her abductors until she reached the dense growth of outlying trees. There, she gave them one more consideration, determined to go through with her plan. Filling her lungs with a well-drawn-in breath, she turned and ran.

She'd barely gone several yards when Dunk seized hold of her waist. "Darlin', darlin', darlin', where do ya think yore goin'?" In spite of his years, he had a masculine strength she couldn't match.

Forced back to the camp, she was promptly tied to a tree, her hands drawn behind her. Her knees buckled in front of her, hugging her breasts; the skirt of her red dress bunched around her ankles. Thankfully he didn't gag her, and she told him exactly what she thought of him, borrowing a few of Jack's fine curse words.

Dunk only laughed with amusement. "I can see why ya'll aren't married, ma'am—no offense. Though yore a mighty fine lookin' woman. It's no wonder I set my craw on you right away. 'Sides yore bein' mighty fine, I was hopin' you could do some of the cookin'. All Beans is good fer is Lincoln shingles and range beans. We're all out of airtights, and I've been havin' me a hankerin' fer some twisters."

She stared disbelievingly at him. They were out of canned goods, so he wanted her to make him some doughnuts?

"Soon as we settle up the gold, we're goin' to settle up on ya." He puffed out his lean chest. "And I aim to win you fer myself."

Holly's nerve endings went numb. She'd thought they only meant to bring her along as a silly joke . . . not as anything more. Certainly not as sport . . .

Blind fear made her speak the first thing that came to mind. "I don't think any of you is smart enough to know what to do with me."

"'Sat a fact?" Valentine called as he looked above the chest and made a show of smoothing back his gray brows with a gnarled finger.

"Yes," Holly nearly choked. "If you were smart, you'd have shot that lock off, rather than poking at it with a useless hairpin!"

"Why, I'll be jiggered!" Dunk let out a holler, popped the thumb strap free of his holster, and made a fast draw. "Stand clear, everyone!"

Holly's ears hurt from the loud explosion as all hell broke loose. Dunk unloaded a succession of six shots that banged off like firecrackers. When the gray smoke finally cleared, the lock had been shot off, all right. So was the right corner and the front facing of the chest.

Beans, Valentine, and Dunk dove at it in a frenzy, prying back the lid; they dug their fists inside and took out pouch after pouch of pure gold dust.

Jack came to mind, and for once Holly was glad of his presence in her thoughts. She recalled his every feature, his laugh—when he indeed had one—his scowl, his velvety warm kisses. "Jack," she sighed, missing him more than she could have ever imagined.

Holly could only watch with total helplessness. She closed

her eyes and willed herself to think of something other than the impending disaster that lay at her feet.

Dunk, Beans, and Valentine sat back on their heels, their attention fixed on a small circle that had been marked in the earth by the end of a green twig. Inside the sphere and scattered outside it were a dozen or so colored marbles.

Beans leaned over on his knees, placed a blue shooter in front of his dirt-stained thumb, and flicked it with his fingernail. It smacked a red marble, knocking it from the circle.

"Heigh ho!" he screamed. "That gives me seven!"

Beans scooped up the pile of marbles in front of him and held them out for the other two to verify. "She's mine!" he declared exuberantly.

Holly, still firmly affixed to the tree, moaned.

It was done, and a winner had been proclaimed.

They'd spent all morning divvying up the gold, then taken a break for lunch, during which they'd offered her a piece of beef jerky and a biscuit called a hot rock. They'd given her a brief time alone to tend to her personal needs, going as far as to count out exactly sixty seconds. After the meal, they'd commenced playing a game of marbles to see who she'd ride with and who she'd . . . be with.

Holly still couldn't believe it. The only hope she regained was that they'd spent so much of the day at camp, surely the law was not far from their trail. But even that chance quickly soured when the weather swerved against her.

Just after noon, dark, threatening clouds began to gather in the west, spreading until the whole visible sky was overcast. Soon threads of lightning stitched through the black clouds hovering over the lofty, jagged mountain crests to the north and west.

Holly watched the natural display, hoping against hope it would blow over. But the magnificent flashes and subsequent rumbles played out their sequence closer and closer together, gaining momentum.

The three men were not in the least disturbed by the weather. They were insensitive to it. The game had not gone the way Dunk had wanted it to, and as Beans took his first step toward her—his prize—Dunk spun him around.

"I don't give a hoot who won that marble game!" Dunk howled above a crescendo of thunder. "She's mine. I saw her. I wanted her."

"Yeah, well, I got her now!" Beans tried to shrug off his companion's hand.

Valentine stepped in and added his own two cents. "I'll take her," he suggested with a gap-toothed grin.

In an instant all three were arguing vehemently over another game: two out of three, three out of five . . . five out of seven. . . .

Holly could only close her eyes against the defeat she felt. Her fate was going to be decided over a ridiculous game of marbles, and no matter how ludicrous, it was a degrading way to have her worth determined.

She felt a single cool droplet smack the tip of her nose, but being tied left her defenseless to brush it away.

Surely no one would come after her in the rain. And even if someone did, the bandits' tracks would be washed away, sunk into the muddy terrain of the Black Hills.

Jack Steele sat motionless in his saddle, his gloved fingers wrapped firmly through the leather reins. Large raindrops fell sparsely around him, but he was unaware of the pelts. Every muscle, his every sense, focused on one thing—the mahogany-haired woman tied up at the edge of the clearing below him.

A tic played at his jaw, and a deadly glint filled his eyes. He swallowed and licked the rain from his lips, his gaze narrowing in on the three men who stood several yards from Holly Dancer. Though their voices were raised, he couldn't discern what they were saying. But their body language spoke louder than words. It was obvious they were fighting over the woman they'd taken into their possession. That thought filled Jack with a violent rage, and only his iron will kept him from losing his good judgment.

He nudged his black-coated knees into the horse's flanks and followed the rise downward through the cover of profuse juniper.

187

Once at the base where it bordered the small encampment, Jack dismounted and tethered his animal to a low-lying branch. He crouched down on his haunches and circled the clearing until he was directly behind Holly's captors. He immediately sized up their weaponry, each man holstered with a dueling pair of Colts slung low on his hips. A Sharps rifle lay discarded by the campfire.

On closer inspection, he could see that the men were on in years, though experience had taught him age made no difference in how a man handled himself.

As the one who appeared to be the leader angrily turned, Jack was struck by a vague sense of recognition. Under the circumstances he had neither the time nor inclination to match the face to his past.

Steele unshouldered his Buntline Special and waited through several blinding flashes of lightning as they lit up the misty sky. A tremendous thunderbolt shook the earth. The clouds burst open their floodgates, letting the rain come down in a vast torrent.

It was all Jack needed.

He charged the camp like a wild man, the barrel of his lethal revolver pointed threateningly at anyone who dared reach for his own.

Beans, Dunk, and Valentine stood dumbfounded, caught unawares by the feral attack. When understanding lit on their wizened faces, they were too scared to dispute the respect demanded by the foot-long weapon.

"W-where the hell did ya come from?" Dunk stammered, raising his hands to the heavens.

"Not from where you're pointing," Jack growled dryly. "I want you to take off your gun belts nice and slow. Once they're off, rebuckle them and kick them over to me so my thumb doesn't slip across this hammer." He measured the web of his thumb over the cocking mechanism of his Colt .45.

"Holy sweet Mary," Beans cried in breathless fear, "it's him!"

Valentine and Dunk had shimmied out of their holsters and gladly kicked them toward Jack. Beans shook so, his fingers couldn't unhitch the steel buckle. "It's him," he repeated as the rain poured over the top of his hat and dripped beyond the brim in front of him.

Beans struggled and tugged, finally able to carry out the order, dropping his belt onto the ground that was fast becoming slick with mud.

Jack reached down and looped the holsters over his right shoulder. Keeping his Buntline leveled in the men's direction, he looked directly at Holly for the first time. She was gazing at him with such relief in her azure eyes, it nearly knocked the wind right out of him.

"Did they hurt you?" he called to her. The chords of his throat tightened painfully, and he flared his nostrils against the bitter ache.

"No," she answered back in a soft voice that hinted it was on the verge of splintering.

Jack grappled to pull his gaze away and focus on the trio of cowering men. He aimed his revolver directly at Beans. "Get some rope and tie your partners up."

Valentine's blue eyes grew wide, and Dunk muttered a free-flowing oath as Beans did as he was told. He fetched a piece of cord from his saddlebag and wrapped it first around Dunk's wrists, then Valentine's, twining the two together.

"Now you," Jack bade Beans, and he promptly handed Jack the coiled tail. In a matter of seconds, Beans was bound to Valentine and Dunk, their backs accordioned together.

During a quick brush-down on their pants, Jack found a hair comb, a pouch of chaw, and a small utility knife, which he quickly divested them of. Only then did he reholster his Buntline and make his way toward Holly.

With fluid, purposeful strides he closed the distance between them. He openly studied her smudged face to see if her denial of harm had been true. There was no telling what she'd suffered on the inside, but her outer appearance, no matter how disorderly, was a soothing balm to his pounding heartbeat. He'd found her.

Dammit, he'd found her.

Her eyes brimmed with unshed tears, and he nearly choked on his own. Seeing her tied up made him go mad with a fierceness to protect her. He'd never been so driven to guard another's life. Never had he come so close to losing his wits and temper that he'd almost come blasting into a crime, damning the consequences of his actions.

Jack knelt down before her and touched her cheek with the back of his wet, gloved hand. She leaned into his caress, her richly shaded pink lips parting. "You came."

The two words were spoken with such relief, their innocent impact dissolved his heart. He was not a man to show emotion; he was hard, immune to sensitivities. He was Jack Steele. But he was a man first, and those little words found root deep within, shattering his self-imposed barriers. Freedom let him breathe again. "Damn right, baby. I came."

Laying his hands on her shoulders, he cursed at the rain which had soaked through the front of her traveling costume, leaving her no protection against the elements. The bodice molded to her breasts like a wet sheet, and he longed to wrap her in something warm.

His gaze rose to meet her pale face. Her hair had lost all its pins and hung in a wet curtain about her waist. Gently he reached out and stroked back the mahogany tresses from her cheek. Her evident sense of relief was mirrored in her soft blue eyes, and she smiled up at him. He wanted to kiss her, but forced himself to wait; wait until he could crush her in his arms, explore her lips, and soothe her.

Jack dug into his pocket and pulled out a Barlow knife. He repositioned himself to the back of the tree trunk where the rope secured her hands together behind her. With a low growl, he sliced through the bind and cut her loose.

Holly drew her arms forward and rubbed at the pinkened flesh across the insides of her wrists.

Dunk gruffly called out over a clap of thunder, "What do ya'll aim to do with us?"

Jack raised himself up, then reached down to help Holly. He grasped her hands firmly in his own, taking care to be considerate of the delicacy of her cold fingers. Once standing, she wobbled on her feet, and he slipped an arm about her slender waist, helping her toward the campfire, where the embers sputtered and smoked under the dousing they were receiving from the rain.

As he paused with Holly, Steele's blazing eyes glared at Dunk. "I'm going to leave you here for the law to handle."

Beans clicked his teeth together noisily as if he'd seen an apparition in Jack. Wide-eyed, he shook his head. He kept on shaking it so fiercely that Valentine ultimately butted the back of his own head against Beans's to cease it. "Quit your twitchin', ya old coot. Ya'll've been acting tetchy from the moment he rode in on us. What in Jericho's the matter with ya?"

Beans generated a nervous laugh. "Ain't nothing wrong with me, but somethin' mighty wrong with yore memories, you ol' sidewinders. This here's that fly cop!"

Dunk slanted his black eyes expressively down on Jack, assessing him from head to toe. "Fly cop, ya say?"

"I remember him from Ogallala," Beans babbled. "I'd know 'im sure as a steer does a clover field."

Jack recognized Dunk in that instant. He knew now why the men at first looked familiar to him. Dunk Canfield, Beans McGillycuddy, and Valentine Mooneyham. It had been in Ogallala more than a year ago that he'd apprehended them on rustling charges; so much for the necktie party they'd been sentenced to.

Staring at them through hooded eyes, Jack wondered if he should attempt to take them back to Deadwood in this weather. He glanced at Holly and decided against it. Her face was etched with puzzlement. This was not the time to go into any explanations, and he didn't need a trio of over-the-hill road agents for witnesses.

"Sheriff Seth Bullock should be passing this way," he said to the trussed-up men. "He'll take you on into Deadwood for arraignment."

Jack enveloped Holly's hand in his own, bent down to pick up the Sharps, then propelled Holly away from the now dead cook fire and its acrid scent.

"What about the gold they took?"

"It's not mine; let Bullock worry about it."

The rain fell relentlessly on Holly, slicking her hair to the sides of her face. Steele bit down hard, thinking she looked vulnerable—not at all the woman who had defied the nature of women and kept on with her husband's mining claim with the grit of salt.

"Is the sheriff really coming?" Holly asked through chattering teeth.

"Yeah, Bullock should be along in a few hours. We picked up your trail several miles back, but lost sight of it. The stream you crossed over swelled up enough to wash away the tracks. Bullock went east, I went west. He'll come up short soon enough and head back this way."

"Ya can't leave us here!" Dunk cried out belligerently. "We're American citizens, and we demand our rights to the utmost of the law! Ya'll, bein' a fly cop, should know better'n anyone the rules a justice!"

Jack snarled over his shoulder, "The only justice I know for you three is in the chamber of my revolver. You want to stand trial against it?"

"Shut up, Dunk!" Valentine begged, and kicked him in the shin with the heavy heel of his mule-ear boot.

Dunk let out a wail and hopped on one foot; he staggered, losing his balance and toppling them all like a felled tree to the boggy soil.

Holly blinked her wet lashes at the heap of arms and legs as Jack tugged her forward to the outside of the clearing. He untethered his horse, slipping his fingers over the halter's bosal and turning the steel-dust gray around. Removing the circle of holsters from his shoulder, he emptied the Colts of their bullets, and the rifle of its cartridge. He flung the empty weapons as far as he could throw, storing the ammunition in his gear.

Jack ducked under the horse's head and gathered Holly up in his arms. She shivered uncontrollably, and he set her back to take off his ulster. "Put this on."

Holly did as Jack told her. The greatcoat was far too big, the hem touching the tip of her shoes, but it offered a small sense of warmth. Unable to make her numb fingers work and fasten the buttons, she hugged it around her. "W-what are you going to w-wear?"

Jack withdrew a yellow slicker from one of his saddlebags and whipped it over his head. He stood in front of her, rivulets of water running off his hat and bronzed face; he reminded her of that first time he'd come into Goodnight's Restaurant. She'd felt it then, but hadn't been able to understand it. She was electrified over this man's presence, over his overt masculinity and appearance.

There were so many things she wanted to say and to ask him, but he was turning away and hoisting himself up in the saddle. "Put your foot up in the stirrup."

Holly complied, and he tilted down and snatched her up next to him. Both her feet dangled over one side as he took up the reins in one hand and commanded the horse forward.

Pressing her cheek against his wet slicker front, she allowed Jack full control. She was too tired to wonder anymore what would happen next; she trusted Jack.

Battling the elements, they gained higher ground and traveled on a ridge of open timber without the skirt of much underbrush. To the west was a small valley dressed with bountiful quakensap, spruce, and willows.

Flash after flash, peal after peal, followed in rapid succession, a signal the storm was directly upon them. The wind rose, blowing great slanting shafts of water in their faces. Holly buried hers deeper into the slick folds of Jack's oilskin, feeling safe in his arms. He touched his rawhide finger to her chin and tilted it upward. She had no time to think as his lips met hers.

Holly tasted the sweetness of rainwater on his warm mouth as it possessed hers, filling her with immediate heat. As if she were a lost floral wilderness under months of winter snow, spring captured her, and she melted in the golden warmth he gave her, blooming in a season of gold.

The short kiss left her senses careening as she stared into the depths of his mercurial eyes. Who had she been trying to fool when she'd left Deadwood? She had been running away from herself, not Jack Steele. Everything she felt when she was with him frightened her; but it was frightening in a maddening way that made her forget all reason, all logic. She'd come to love this man and his hard-edged ways, and no well-intentioned denial could put an end to it.

Steele left one hand on the reins, freeing the other to clench her tightly to him as he steered them through the drenching rain.

They traveled a wide distance, with no signs of the storm letting up. Holly wondered if they'd be forced to weather it out under the saturated canopy of a pine. Just as she resigned herself to the possibility, the faint, distant smell of smoke caught on the breeze.

Woodsmoke.

It clung to the sodden air with a sharp tanginess the forest floor didn't emit when wet.

"Do you smell it?" Holly asked Jack over the pelting rain. She sat up straight and tried to see through the low-lying mist and haze that billowed over the rock and shrub.

"Yeah," he answered, and she detected reservation in his voice.

Jack threaded their trail between mammoth cedars, pursuing the scent. Laden branches trickled water down on them, some of the spiny boughs slapping at their arms. Soon after, a break in the fog opened to what appeared to be a deserted city.

Twenty-five to thirty log cabins clustered together in a remote part of the woods. Most doors hung open, the glass broken out of the few that had been able to afford the panes. Window curtains rippled in the wind, their hems tattered and torn by a constant beating from nature.

"Hill City," Holly murmured, having lost all sense of direction. She hadn't realized they'd come this far. "It was abandoned a couple years back. I didn't think anyone still mined around here."

Jack's eyes narrowed in on the single cabin whose rude chimney trailed out a slim curl of gray smoke.

"Should we go in? I'm sure whoever—"

"No," he cut her off, his gaze still riveted to the cabin; then he scanned the surrounding area with an eagle's keen sense of awareness.

"Why not?" Holly saw no reason to delay. She was nearly half-frozen from the cold. She squeezed the folds of Jack's coat closer together, feeling Jack automatically tighten his grip.

"Because it's late afternoon," he said in her ear.

"So? What does that have to do with anything?"

"I don't smell supper cooking."

Chapter Eleven

Stay here." The deadly calm in Jack's tone made the fine hairs on the back of Holly's neck stand on end.

Jack swung his towering height down from the saddle and handed her the reins. Clenching the rounded fingertips of his gloves between his teeth, he shucked them free and shoved them at her without taking his eyes off the shack. She watched his broad back retreat, his bare fingers splayed at the line of his hip.

Holly wiped the hair from her forehead and stared at Jack, fearing for his safety. Suddenly the bitter reality of the situation hit her—Jack could be walking into some kind of trap. Nevertheless, she remained still.

She watched him circle around the log building, then take a leap up the two steps and bust open the front door. Starting, Holly thought that if anyone was inside, the person would be getting the life scared out of him.

Holly scarcely breathed during his absence; it seemed an eternity until Jack came out, his stance slightly relaxed, but circumspect.

"No one's inside. Come on." He took up the reins and walked the horse to the forepart of the cabin. Helping her down, he ushered her inside the crude, but dry, home.

Holly quickly glanced around. The place was definitely

196

being lived in and not used by a passerby. The windows were covered by fresh flour-sack curtains. An elongated, two-planked pine table fit along one wall, stocked with canned goods. A narrow cot took up one corner, and across from it was a small table with a dry goods box as a chair. The slow-burning logs in the hearth didn't do much to dispel the chill in her bones or the soaking heaviness of her Scotch plaid dress.

"Fire's been unattended a good couple hours," Jack commented as he assessed the flames. A stubby yellow candle in a shallow dish lay atop the mantel, and Jack lit it from the box of matches beside it.

"Do you think someone was caught in the storm?"

Jack hesitated, then picked up more tinder and wood, adding them to the dying embers. "Yeah."

"Do you think he'll come back?"

Sparks rose up the flue as the dry timber cracked and popped, getting a start of golden flames. "Don't know. He's probably holed up somewhere for the night."

"Oh . . ." Holly stood in the middle of the room, her dress and Jack's ulster leaving a big puddle on the floor. "Do you suppose he'd mind if we stayed here?"

Jack hunkered down over the hearth and warmed his outstretched hands. "I don't think he's got a choice in the matter."

Holly slipped off the sodden greatcoat and walked onto the narrow threshold at the doorway. She wrung the garment out, squeezing the water over the handrail. Securing the door behind her, she shivered against the miserable weather and the clinging wetness of her bodice.

The heavy droplets persistently pounded against the tin roof, and she glanced toward the open-beamed ceiling. Several spots were peppered with tiny holes which had succumbed to the rain; she quickly forgot her chill and snatched up what few pots and pans there were to place combatively under the drips.

"Take off your dress."

The old black enamel roasting pan Holly had been holding slipped free from her fingers and clamored to the roughly planked floor. "I beg your pardon?"

"Your dress. Get it off." Jack stood up and folded his arms across his chest, his slicker hanging loosely over his frame. Small rivers ran down the folds and landed in puddles at his booted feet.

His sudden command swept the breath right from her. He stared at her as if she'd institute his wishes, no questions asked. Had it come to this? He'd rescued her and now he demanded payment?

Her blatant hesitation made him lift one corner of his mouth into a half smile. "When you're undressing for me, you'll know it."

Holly's mouth gaped open a fraction.

Jack headed toward her, and she put her hand to her collar. When he walked right past her, she trembled; whether it was from relief or disappointment, she wasn't sure. She was afraid to turn around to see what he was doing, but soon the door opened.

"I'm going to take care of my horse."

She heard him go down the steps, but he didn't close the door behind. She whirled around to shut out the cold when he suddenly appeared at the doorjamb, tossing a bundle to her. She instinctively caught it.

"You'll find a dry shirt inside. Put it on."

Then he was gone.

Holly closed the door shut, pressing her back to the rough framework. Her breasts softly rose and fell, and she could feel the blood flowing through her fingertips as she clenched them into the parcel. She melted down to numbness, closing her eyes against the heaviness of her breasts, the heat radiating through her body.

It hit her with stunning reality that she wanted Jack Steele. No matter how much she was afraid of it—of him. Her body responded to him as it never had to Billy. The impact of these feelings left her confused and dizzy. How could it be that she desired him so, when she herself was an undesirable woman?

Holly stepped away and covered her burning cheek with her hand. How long would she be haunted by Billy's prophecy? She was no woman in bed. She was as exciting as a burlap sack and just as pleasing. There was something wrong with her, for Billy had said she should have felt the things he did when he . . . when he did his husbandly duties.

The pain had haunted and tortured her for the short months of her marriage. She'd agonized over the fact that lovemaking was something she'd never be fulfilled by because she'd been born cold and unresponsive. She'd tried. She'd tried so hard with Billy, but just as she felt a tiny inkling of emotion, of elation, Billy was rolling off her saying it was her own fault she was so inept.

It had taken her a long time to come to terms with her inadequacy, and just when she thought she'd accepted it, Jack Steele came into her life. She felt more from his disarming gaze than she did when Billy had touched her.

The irony of the situation made her laugh with bitterness. The one man who had the legal right to make her his had only succeeded in destroying her self-esteem; and the one man who could rescue her from her desolation and her insecurities was the one who could hurt her the most. She knew, as she did the first time she laid eyes on Jack, he was a man who took what he wanted. And when he took it, he took it completely and unequivocally.

Jack Steele was a man who could steal her heart, and that was the one thing there was no law against him doing. She would be left to suffer out the sentence the rest of her life, long after he'd ridden out of it.

Holly sighed and pressed her lips together. Dropping the bundle to the cot, she began unfastening the front buttons of her bodice. The task was slow, the wet fabric shrinking around the tiny jet buttons.

Minutes later, she freed herself from her dress and stepped out of the wet circle around her ankles. She still had her corset to contend with, and she pulled the tapes free, wiggling out of the horsehair bustle and stays. Clad in her chemise, red flannel pantalets, stockings, and shoes, she crossed over to the crate and sat.

Removing her high-topped shoes without the aid of her buttonhook was nearly impossible. Frustration, made worse by her trying ordeal, took its toll in the form of a hot tear blinking off her lashes.

She worked fervently at the buttons, her fingers becoming

199

raw from the difficulty of her task. As each one relented, she felt a little of her reserve crumble away until she couldn't control the sobs that were shaking her shoulders.

After Jack had stabled his horse, he circled around the cabin again. The rain bit down on his face as it poured on a bleak angle. He adjusted his hat against it and took in the surrounding area.

The rain had washed away any tracks that would have given him a clue as to where the occupant of the shack had gone. The storm had been giving off enough signals to prove itself a real downpour. No one in his right mind would have gone off into it.

Jack walked around to a stand of ponderosas that overlooked a fast-moving stream curling between a group of bleached boulders. The water had swollen and flooded the embankments, taking with it the muddy edges.

He scanned the scene, looking for signs of life. He saw nothing. Only the sounds of water rushing and straining against the earth; the splatter of drops on the leaves above his head.

Turning away, he felt an uneasiness that had grown from years of experience. He doubted the miner would be joining them for supper.

He doubted the miner would be around when the storm passed over them.

All he could do now was hope that whatever trouble there'd been had washed away, much as the heavy current of the river.

Holly had scoured the entire cluttered tabletop and rude shelves for a can opener and couldn't find one. She held on to a tin of Borden's beef biscuits in one hand and a blackened cast-iron pan in the other.

The door burst open on a current, and she jumped. She wore Jack's winter shirt of unbleached muslin, and the hem twirled around her damp pantalets as she turned in place with a fright, curling her bare toes.

His saddlebags slung over his shoulder, Jack paused a moment, then sealed the door closed behind him. His gaze roamed over her in a way that was far from honorable, taking in her body in his clothes. The frank perusal jeopardized the rhythm of her pulse, and it sped to an alarming rate. She managed a friendly smile, then looked away swiftly at the sight of his scowl.

Entering the room, Jack flicked off his hat and tossed it on the hook in the wall; it landed without a hitch.

Holly gave an anxious little sneeze and stammered, "I—I can't find a can opener. I thought I'd make us something to eat."

Jack stripped out of his slicker and hung it over the dry goods box where Holly's dress was draped. "Try above the hearth."

She raised her eyes to where he directed and checked. Sure enough, a metal opener was stuck on the ridge of the narrow mantel.

As she worked to get the lid off the can, Jack took off his Wellington boots and removed the small Frontier pistol he'd kept housed down the side. He stripped off his socks, then the other two holsters strapped to his shoulder and waist; he set them on the cot next to himself. To her dismay, he slipped out of his navy blue button-down shirt. She caught glimpses of him as he drew his undershirt over his wet head; his bared skin rippled bronze under the firelight. His ribs were defined by flanks of muscle, the swell of his chest covered by a mat of curling dark hair that tapered down to his waistband.

Quietly she made a pretense of arranging the biscuits in the pan while slipping a peek at his shoulder. The wound had left him with a shiny pink scar no bigger in diameter than a thimble head.

Bringing the iron pan to the hearth, she stuck it on a front brick to warm. Only then was she faced with the issue of his dishabille—there was nothing else left to do to keep her occupied. She nervously worked her lower lip as she watched him search through his leather bags, bringing out a dry undergarment. It flowed over his broad chest, clinging to the lines and planes of his masculine physique. The gray woolen garment may well have been a second layer of skin for all the room he had in it.

Holly felt her mouth go dry watching him attend his personal needs.

Jack stared at her, his ebony hair tousled around his head. He ran his fingers through the shoulder-length strands to comb free some of the tangles and shake out any leftover moisture. "Your feet cold?" he asked, and she quickly looked down at her bare toes.

"A little . . ."

He reached in the saddlebag and produced a pair of pearl-knit socks. "Here."

Holly took them and shyly fit them over her feet, the warmth instantly enveloping her. "Thank you."

Jack left his own feet uncovered, and her eyes moved downward, noticing how his toes were finely shaped, with a small sprinkling of hair over the large one.

Holly tried to alleviate some of her tension by flipping over the browning biscuits with a fork. "You were gone a long time."

"Yeah."

"Do you think the sheriff has found those men yet?"

"Probably."

She sensed his eyes boring down on her cotton-covered back. The heat from the hearth overwhelmed her, suffusing her face with unwanted color. She told herself it was just the intense flames making her feel red-hot in the cheeks. When she faced Jack, her suspicion was confirmed by the pair of striking gray eyes directed on her. She caught her breath, more aware than ever her face was burning up.

In that instant, she thought of telling him she loved him. It was only a deep-seated fear of his amusement at her avowal that kept her silent. She searched his face, trying to reach into his thoughts. His expression was full of life, pain, and an unspoken trouble that plowed a deep crease at the middle of his smoothly arched brows.

Holly tried to smile with a tender empathy, hoping he'd unburden himself to her. She waited as Jack traced his lower lip with his tongue, then bit down on the warm-colored flesh, working it over his straight, white teeth. Swallowing tightly, he reached for his Buntline.

The upturn to Holly's lips dejectedly softened as she

observed him take out a pouch of fabric squares and lubricants. He took up a clean cloth and rubbed down his weapons. The tiny room filled with the pleasant scent of holster leather and the mustiness of the tallow Jack smoothed on the insides.

Not ready to give up, Holly sought to gently coax him into talking, absently twisting a strand of hair around her forefinger. "I'll bet there's a reward for those men you can claim." Releasing the skein, she wound it in the opposite direction. "They were menacing in their own rights . . . yet pitifully inefficient. . . ." She paused and dropped the lock over her shoulder. "Did you really know them? They seemed to know you. . . . I wonder why they called you a . . . what is it, 'fly cop'?"

Jack ceased his polishing, his hand going still inside the holster's interior. He transferred his gaze to hers; the intensity went right through her, making her flatten her palms on the front of her shirt. His pupils narrowed to glimmering black points, highlighting the spheres of his gray irises. She almost reeled backward from the magnitude of emotion in his eyes, an anguish the likes of which she'd never seen before. She gulped hard. "Jack . . . what is it? Surely whatever—"

"I knew you'd get around to asking about it."

Holly didn't fail to catch the note of sarcasm in his voice; just the same, she was bewildered, and the feeling came across in the slight raise of her eyebrows.

"A fly cop," Jack defined with a jerkiness as he rammed his Smith & Wesson back into its scabbard, "is a detective."

The air in the shack grew thick and still.

A chilling understanding swam through Holly's veins, but even as it settled and made her hands grow cold, she refused to accept it. She ignored the mocking voice inside her, telling herself it couldn't possibly be true.

"You're wondering." Jack shoved his Buntline away. "I can see it in the pretty blue of your eyes." He pointed his finger lightly at her, as if he were playing some kind of game. "Wonder no more, baby. I am."

An icy tremor twisted around her heart, and she stood motionless. She could barely breathe, the suffocating air pressing down on her lungs. She managed to whisper in a small voice, "You're scaring me."

"Good!" His yell was a blend of triumph and misery. "I've been scared from the moment I first saw you."

Holly's first instincts were to blot out his words and maybe even run from them, but she could not. She remained frozen in her own misled world that was crumbling around her. "Why didn't you tell me before?"

Jack hunched over and positioned his elbows across his knees. He sunk the webs of his fingers through his hair and looked down at the floor with a desolate slump to his wide shoulders. "I've never told anybody that mattered; how could I tell you?"

"You could have trusted me." She desperately tried not to surrender to the dull pain that spread throughout her body. He'd kept his occupation from her, scaring her into believing he was a hardened criminal when, in actuality, he was a man of law. "You could have trusted me," she repeated.

He jerked his head up, his gray eyes bright and embattled. "Don't you understand? I have no trust within me."

If he had lashed out at her, she would have fought him. Instead, his unreserved disclosure brought life back into Holly's limbs, and she was able to take a step toward him. His silence had been fueled by a reason, a reason she didn't understand but hoped he'd tell her. She could feel his misery, as she'd lived with her own, bearing her own secrets of torment. She wanted to touch him, to comfort him.

Steele flinched, as if he couldn't bear to have her sympathy. A quiet knowledge filled her, and she kept herself at arm's length. She tried to discredit his statement. "When you came to me, you trusted me."

"I did not." Jack peered at her, with his hair ruffled about his handsomely chiseled face. "Not completely."

"And do you now?"

"Christ!" Slamming his fists into the wooden frame of the cot, he bolted upright. "Don't ask me that!" He paced the room with pent-up energy.

Holly stood rigidly, with her chin angled in a level line and her spine straight. She watched him as he made numerous passes in front of her. "If you have to think about it, then you must not," she said, a trace of hurt in her tone.

"It's not that easy," he accused, coming to a direct halt in front of her and pinning her with his hooded gaze. "I've been alone for too long. I've trusted no one but myself and my instincts."

"Then why did you come to me?" she brazenly asked. Despite herself, her pained feelings shined through her question.

"Because I knew you'd take Jackson Steele in," he said with forged self-righteousness. "You'd take him in before you'd take me, that's for damn sure."

"But . . . you're Jack."

He reflected a moment, his eyes darkening nearly to black. "I'm an illusion. The real man in me is too lost for anyone to care about. Jack is of my own making, and despite his desperado image, he's more readily accepted than I ever would be."

The biscuits on the hearth sizzled dryly in the pan, scorching and leaving a pungent burnt smell to thicken the air. Quickly snatching up the pan with a folded towel, Holly dropped the skillet on a spider on the table. It was just as well they were ruined; her appetite had vanished.

The man she'd thought she was coming to know was a stranger after all. She'd discerned he was coarse, unpredictable, and even illicit. But she'd also seen a side of him that was compassionate, gentle, and caring. Now he professed to be a different man entirely. . . . "Did you do anything criminal in Texas like Sheriff Bullock said?"

"No." His finger scraped across the rough shadowing of beard across his jaw. "The agency printed up warrant posters with Jack Steele's name on them to give me a notorious past."

"Have you ever killed anybody?"

"Yes."

His voice, absolutely emotionless, frightened Holly into silence. Everything hit her at once, and her vision clouded with tears. He'd been less than honest with her; though she'd carried her own secrets, never had she invented falsehoods to elude him. "Everything you've made me believe about you has been a lie." Her voice sounded pitifully weak, even to herself.

"I've never lied to you, Holly." Jack spoke in an odd, yet genteel tone. "You saw what you wanted to see."

"I saw what you showed me," Holly confronted him, smothering a sob. "You made me believe you were a dangerous man."

Jack smiled humorlessly. "I am."

"I don't think you're half as menacing as you pretend to be."

"William Pinkerton," he disputed with a wry grin, "thinks I'm crazy. He hired a frustrated man who wanted to catch the criminals who kept falling between the cracks of the Chicago courts." With dramatic satire Jack conceded, "The lawyer who wanted to be adventurous—look where it landed him. In a two-bit mudhole town, shot up in the arm and willing to sacrifice everything for a woman. I swore I'd never become entangled again."

Holly went pale with humiliation and resentment. "You needn't worry yourself about becoming entangled with me. It requires devotion on both sides, and mine, quite simply, is expended."

"You don't mean that," Jack said quietly, walking forward and stopping to touch her. He cupped her face between his callused fingers and stroked the soft curve of her cheek.

The reservoir of her tears threatened to spill free, despite the dam she'd so carefully erected. She would not give in to his beckoning gaze. It was subtle with warmth and concession, as if he'd accepted his fate. Holly was trapped by the memory of her own emotions, the soft sensuality of his lips on hers, the unexpected awakening he caused within her body. It would be so easy to allow him to take her into his arms . . . yet still, she resisted.

There were too many things left unspoken.

Holly tried to free herself from him, but Jack slid his hands down her shoulders and held her firm. When her first tear of frustration came, she fought it. Only after the second and third did she surrender openly to the battle. At first she cried softly, then her body trembled with shuddering breaths that she was powerless to hold back.

Jack's arms circled the high slope of her back, massaging and drawing her near. She put up only a small protest, then buried her face in the sinewy swell of his chest. She yielded helplessly to the confusion of sobs that shook her. "Why did you come to Deadwood?" she cried into the soft material of his undershirt. "Does Seth Bullock know who you are?" Holly lifted her head with a resurgence of spirit and tried to break free, but Jack's grasp was unremitting. "Does that girl from the Melodeon know who you are?"

"No." Jack wove his fingers through her flowing hair and angled her face up to meet his. "Only you." He brushed his lips across her dampened eyelashes, soothing away the tears.

Holly felt the very fabric of her being unwind from the tight bolt in which she'd kept it so carefully guarded.

Jack breathed soft, persuasive kisses on her forehead, eyebrows, the rise of her cheekbones, and lastly her lips. She moaned as his mouth came over hers in a shivery, slow meeting. It was too much for her to bear that he could do this to her when she was so confused. He took all her common sense in one breath, leaving her yearning for his touch. She gave in, molding her body into the rugged contours of his chest, his taut waist and powerful thighs. Instantly she felt the hard definition of his desire next to her as he gathered her closer to him.

She wanted desperately to depend on his strength; she was tired of being strong for herself. Tired of the endless hours of bone-weary work she inflicted on herself in order to leave her too fatigued to think of her loneliness. She'd been running away from herself ever since Billy's death; and now here she was, faced with the thing she feared the very most. It was no longer a matter of his desiring her; she knew he did. She needed to overcome her feelings of inadequacy, exiling Billy's battering words. But she needed to tell Jack . . . in case her husband had been right.

She broke free of the kiss, nestling her face in the hollow of his throat. She felt his pulse there, potent and defined, yet pounding irregularly. Knowing what she must say, she felt a heightened blush stain her face. "Jack, I want to . . . but I don't want to disappoint you. . . ." She closed her eyes tightly, her ear to his chest and hearing the rhythm of his heartbeat. The drone of the rain on the tin roof filled her other ear; it was deafening as she waited for him to say something.

"What are you talking about?" Jack whispered into her hair.

Shame claimed her flesh, burning her and rendering her silent for an explanation.

"What are you talking about?" he repeated, his thumb working over the sensitive shell of her ear, her lobe, and the bone of her jaw.

She felt hot tears accumulate again, unable to blink them back. In a smothered voice that broke, she said, "I'm afraid to be with you because . . . because I couldn't bear the look of disgust in your eyes when you find me lacking as a woman."

"Christ, what did you say?" Jack's hand grazed the length of her neck, caught her chin, and turned her face to meet his. His gaze was filled with blind rage. "Who told you that?"

She was unable to confront him. "It doesn't matter."

"It goddamn does matter!" He practically shook her into submission. "Who told you that?"

Desolation was sickeningly familiar, knotting her stomach. Swallowing the sob that rose in her throat, she looked up. "My husband," she whispered, feeling the scalding tears course down her cheeks anew. "Billy."

The veins at Jack's temples became pronounced as he flared his nostrils and cursed between clenched teeth. "Bastard! The perverse bastard." He scooped her so tightly in his embrace, she could scarcely breathe. It was as if he meant to squeeze out Billy's accusations.

"I-I'm so ashamed. . . ."

Jack swore vehemently and released her. She nearly fell from the force of his deliverance, and she struggled to stay on her stockinged feet. "That's what you were talking about in the mine, only I was too blind to see it." A rawness edged his voice. "I thought . . ."

Jack dominated the room like a madman, going as far as

taking up one of the nearly full pots of rainwater and hurling it against the front door.

Holly jumped, terrified. His bare footsteps thundered to an end; he gripped her in the vise of his brawny hands. "My name is Robert. Robert Jackson Burnett. I want to hear you say it."

She quivered as his hands tightened around her. It was as if he needed to hear her say it more than anything else she'd ever said to him. "Robert," she tried in a fragile tone.

"Say it again!"

"Robert," she repeated louder.

"I want to hear you say it when I make love to you." Jack kissed her briefly—hard and swift. "We're two lost souls, you and I, and I vow to make you see who you are." Closing his eyes, he leaned his forehead onto hers, his black locks mingling with the wispy hair surrounding her face. "God, you've made me know my name again."

Jack cupped her face in his palms. "You are the most desirable woman I have ever met, and I will erase any doubts about that from your head." Jack rubbed her brows and the skin above them, stroking in tight circles as if to free the demons from her skull.

He lowered his face to kiss her, and she broke free of her misgivings. Everything inside her became awash with heat and a heady dizziness that made her reach up on tiptoe to return the pressure of his mouth. Her arms curled around his neck, and she welcomed him with newfound liberty. She trusted herself, teasing him back when he teased her with the edge of his teeth. Clinging to him, she stretched her hands over the muscles of his back, melting into him. He kissed her almost violently, as if to remove her pain. When he stroked his tongue over the fullness of her lower lip, she trembled.

Jack broke the kiss only long enough to snatch the linsey blanket from the cot and throw it on the knotted pine floor. Lowering her in his arms, he brought them to their knees, their fingers entwined. He kissed her chastely, then lifted his hand to the top button of the shirt she wore—his shirt.

Holly shivered, never having been undressed by anyone in her life. Modesty rose in faint alarm even though she wanted him to remove her clothing. "Aren't you going to blow out the candle?" Though the obscure light of the fire would be sufficient enough for him to view her nudity, she'd expected him to snuff out all other means of illumination.

"Hell no," he croaked in a husky tone. Then his gray eyes darkened. "Have you ever seen a naked man?"

It was another truth she was forced to admit, and she did so with a delayed shake of her head. "No."

"Then we'll go slow." The backs of Steele's roughened hands browsed the swell of her breasts at the top cotton ruffle of her chemise. She grew weak and heated, her nipples tightening. She made fists at her sides, and when she could stand it no more, she brought her fingers over his wrists and implored him with soft pressure to continue with the buttons. After the last pearl fastener came free of its hole, he didn't open the curtain of material. He let it stay together. "How long were you married?"

"Four months . . ."

Jack shook his head and gritted his teeth. "And the bastard tortured you slowly," he said between feather-light kisses, "not fathoming he'd already killed you."

Holly wasn't sure what Jack meant, only that the look of unmasked fury in his eyes said he possessed the power to kill a man with his wrath.

Jack stroked back her hair, tucking it gently behind her ear. "I'm going to show you the other side of torture."

His words shook her to the core.

Jack slid his hands into the drape of unbleached muslin, skimming his touch across her waist, the rounded sides of her breasts, and then her shoulders. He caught the shirt's collar and drew it slowly down her shoulders, letting it fall in a cloud of ivory at her knees. Holly's heart thundered like the storm that continued on outside. She wet her lips as Jack brought down first one strap of her chemise, then the other.

Her nipples were prominent under the thin lawn of her undergarment, showing through the fabric in light circles of nutmeg. Cupping her breasts, Jack traced his thumbs over the buds; the feminine apex between her legs throbbed with heat and she swayed toward him. He didn't give up his exquisite strokes; instead, he intensified them, alternating them with flicks of the crests of his thumbnails. The contrast was as agonizing as it was fulfilling.

It was Holly who untied the pale blue ribbon at the valley of her breasts. She felt as if she'd die if he didn't caress her naked breasts. Jack loosed the crisscrossing riband of satin, unthreading it, then peeling down the delicate material so she could shift free of it.

Tingles skittered across her skin as he stared at her with blazing eyes. "You are a beautiful woman." He swept his fingers across the fullness of her breasts, fitting them into the palms of his hands. Her heart beat against the confines of her ribs as Jack leaned forward and kissed the pale brown of her nipple. He took it into the heated cavern of his mouth, teasing it with the tip of his tongue. Sparks shot in her mind, blinding her and showering her with a fiery liquid that melted through her veins.

Holly's fingers burrowed into his long hair, locking onto the rich mane. Jack kept on with his masterful dance, sucking and enticing her to a pinnacle of raw need the likes of which she'd never in her life experienced; it was earth-shattering, it was wanton, and it was so beautifully tangible, never in her dreams could she have imagined it. Suddenly she wanted his shirt off him. She wanted him naked and next to her. Frantic and urgent, she tugged the hem of his undershirt out of his pants.

Jack bolted upright and without a word raised the ribbed collar over his tousled head. He threw the knitted shirt away and clasped her to him. Holly reveled in the coarseness of his chest hairs against the smooth fullness of her breasts and the points of her nipples, the abrasion erotic and sensual. It made her feel wicked and wanting, and with no shame at all, she reached out for the button at his waistband. Her hair fell across her cheek as she slipped her fingers into the warmth of his denims and worked free the brass rivet.

"I don't want to go slow," she heard herself telling him, surprised by her own impatience.

Jack groaned as her fingertips connected with the shape of his erection. She wasn't embarrassed by her intimate touch; in fact, it made her realize she held a certain amount of power over him. "I can't slip them off you," she breathed into the fine reddish brown strands that teased the corner of her mouth as her face leaned down. "They're too tight."

Jack leapt to his feet, shucking his Levi's free while she removed her pantalets. Though her sexual experiences with Billy had been in the dark and with her dressed in her nightgown, she'd known the slightness of his anatomy. Seeing Jack defied everything she knew about the male gender.

Jack was all rock-hard with muscle; his arms bulged with them, his flat belly was disciplined by them. He was ethereal in splendor, a perfectly formed body; big and proud, over-whelmingly beautiful to her. She held her arms open to him, and he returned to her on his knees. She traced her fingertips over the scar on his upper arm; his skin was sleek and hot, faintly damp from perspiration. Softly her lips met the mark, murmuring against it. "Does it still hurt?"

The tip of his flesh brushed her inner thighs, fiery and rigid and smooth against her skin; she caught her breath.

"No," he rasped, bending his arm around the nip of her waist. He careened them backward, cushioning her fall with his forearm.

Jack's body covered hers, joining in every dip, hollow, and curve; masculine texture melded with silky femininity, fusing in sensual currents. He ravished her lips with kisses, bruising her swollen flesh. Holly writhed beneath him, parting her thighs and feeling the length of him at her juncture. She was maddened beyond reason or sanity. This place he had taken her to was all-consuming with a swelter-ing heat that made her wilt and tremble.

"Ja—Robert." She whispered his name in a hoarse plea, the sound of it odd on her tongue. "Robert . . ."

He shoved his knee between her legs, and parted her damp curls with his thumb. She was slick with liquid heat, ready for him with every nerve of her body singing out to him.

Raising himself up, he thrust himself inside her. The meeting made Holly arch her back, realizing there was a difference between being ready for a man and not. In this moment she understood the fault of her marriage bed had not been her own, but Billy's. The revelation winged across her, left her free of doubts and inadequacy. She was a woman; she could feel.

Wrapping her legs around him, she gloved him tightly as he began to move in slow, purposeful strokes. His hardness rubbed over the sensitive bud hidden inside, awakening it, nurturing it. Holly wasn't sure how long she could stand the sweet agony. Her nipples scraped against the wiry hairs on his chest as she dug her fingernails into the cords of his buttocks. She felt herself beginning to fall into a deep eddy that left her gasping for air. Still, Jack held back.

With a strangled cry, she thrashed against him, urging him to go faster. He complied, his face contorted in passion. The turbulence of their lovemaking swirled inside her, blinding her with a molten light and taking her over the edge. She fell into a pool that drugged her every sense, rendering her senseless to everything else but the man within her. He reached into her heart and played his magic, and the butterfly was released from its prison.

Holly held on to him with fierce gasps that shook her. She felt him tense, then shudder as he reached his peak.

He collapsed, his body sweaty and spent. He didn't leave her; he stayed entwined with her body. Holly knew no words to describe what had just happened to her. Her emotions battered by the hazy aftermath of love, she felt a sated tear escape and roll down the corner of her eye. It met with his nose where he'd nuzzled his face in the curve of her neck and shoulder.

He rose enough to question her glistening eyes. "Baby, what is it?"

Chapter Twelve

I never knew."

Holly's voice was so fragile, Jack thought it would break. The blue of her eyes shone with a faraway look, yet pure in clarity like a spring pool that had been filled with melted snow. She blinked her thick brown lashes and smiled almost shyly at him.

Her modest declaration provoked a fierce longing in Jack to keep her with him always, to show her all the ways of making love. To prove to her that she was capable of loving and receiving pleasure.

He shifted to his side, keeping her within the circle of his arm. A soft sigh came from Holly as she nestled into the niche of his body, resting her cheek on his chest. Jack thought about how content he was at this very moment, closing himself off to anything but the woman he cradled next to him.

For a long time he lay there stroking his fingertips across the arch of her back, listening to the rain as it fell on the sheeted roof, and the sounds it made dripping into the strategically placed pans. A quiet peace filled him. He was no longer running from himself, from his past. It was as if he could now see the errors of his way. He could have a future if he desired it. And he did.

But first he needed to clear up the present.

Jack stretched the edge of the blanket over Holly, loosely fitting it atop her bare legs and bottom. Her fingers splayed across the triangle of hair at the rise of his ribs, and she snuggled closer. It brought a satisfied grin to Jack's face, and he tucked her head under his chin. How was it that he came to love this woman so completely when he really knew nothing about her?

Billy Dancer. He knew about that. A sorry thread to unite them, one that could unravel everything.

The idea of her being with Billy Dancer made his stomach sour. Had the man not been dead already, Jack could have gunned him down in cold blood. An irrational hunger for vengeance consumed him. But someone had beaten him to it; someone who hated Dancer enough to take his life.

Whatever Holly thought of her husband, Jack knew she could not have killed the man. There were no doubts in him anymore. But the question remained, if she hadn't, who did?

The fire popped and cracked, sending a shower of glowing red embers flying up the chimney. Holly jumped, and he quieted her with a kiss to her brow.

"How is it you came to Deadwood?" Holly asked softly without looking up. "You never answered me."

Jack had thought she'd dozed off. Her gentle voice gave way to a hushed patience, and he knew he owed her a reply; he would not go into grim detail or absolute truth. He could only tell her enough to appease her. There were other factors to consider now. Were he to involve her, her life might be endangered by the man who had murdered her husband.

"I was the right man for the job." Jack toyed with the slant of her shoulder. "Pinkerton knows I never come in short."

"Pinkerton . . . you mentioned him. You're a Pinkerton detective?" Holly absently fit her leg between his, and Jack closed his eyes with a drawn-in breath. "A private eye . . ." She lifted her chin, and he forced himself to meet her gaze. "That's why you left me an eye."

"What?" She had said it with staunch seriousness he couldn't make light of.

215

"The eye. The day you vacated my room, you left behind a piece of stationery at my desk with an eye drawn on it. Below it you wrote: 'We Never Sleep.' I hadn't an idea what you meant . . . Now I understand." Sighing, she lowered her head again.

"I didn't realize I left anything behind." Except maybe a small piece of my heart, he added to himself. Was that when he'd begun to fall in love with her?

"What kind of a case are you working on?"

Jack knew it was coming; there was no getting around it. Had he the foresight to think of a plausible answer, he might have—if only to keep her satisfied and safe. Instead, he resolved to be as honest as he could. "I'm working on some charges that could be dangerous for you if you knew about them. I can't take the chance of that." Bunching up her reddish brown hair in his hand, he rubbed his fingers through the satiny texture. "When it's all over, I'll tell you everything."

"I'm frightened for you." Holly held on to him tightly and placed a kiss on the bare skin of his shoulder.

"Don't worry about me, baby. Most people are afraid of me."

"I'm not . . . not anymore."

Jack bent his knee, playing the toes of his feet over the inside of Holly's calf. She squirmed with a laugh, as if it tickled her. The innocent motion of her hips against his thigh was an inviting temptation that he warded off with great restraint. He had to ask her a question of his own, knowing that she'd either answer or tell him to mind his own business. It had nothing to do with him being a detective; it had everything to do with him being a man.

"Why did you marry Billy Dancer?" He felt the query rumble in his chest and practically choke him.

She didn't hesitate with an answer, but the one she gave wounded him deeply. "I married Billy because I was hopelessly in love with him."

Jack forced his muscles to remain lax and not yield to the knots tugging at them. He kept stroking her hair where it fell around him in waves. Holly must have had the need to explain, for she continued without any coaxing on his part.

"I met Billy in New York."

"Is that where you're from?" he interjected. "Your accent . . . ?"

He sensed her smile. "My accent is Polish and Czechoslovakian, though I suppose East Coast, too. You westerners talk so different."

A slight smile worked Jack's lips. He wasn't a westerner by a long shot. He'd been born and raised in Chicago, the middle of the Midwest.

"My oldest brother—I have six—worked on the fishing docks and brought Billy home with him one day. When I first saw him, I thought he was the most beautiful man I'd ever seen." Her voice took on a wistful edge, and Jack knew she was picturing her husband. He was fiercely jealous of an image he could neither see nor understand.

"Billy was full of youthful enthusiasm for life. Such a contrast to my own . . ." She trailed off for a moment. "He came to supper that night with excited talk of gold fever out West. I was captivated by his stories. . . . I held on to every word. I'd never heard of something so wonderful, so different from the world I knew.

"He came three other times regaling us with more stories. He boasted of riches in the Black Hills that were to be envied by kings. By the end of the third night, he took me outside and said he was leaving for the West and would I like to come with him."

Jack bit down on his lip, his brows furrowing in a harsh line.

"Of course, I said yes, and we were married the following week. We left that afternoon for Deadwood."

Jack caressed the silky skin of her arm with his thumb, making spiral strokes. It disturbed him to visualize her as a young girl full of dreams and visions, only to have them turned into nightmares. It made him pull up his own past; in many ways, they'd both been fooled by words and promises.

"Once we settled in Deadwood," she began again, her voice wavering slightly, "I saw a different side to Billy. He lost his youth, his vitality, and became a man who . . . who was always angry with disappointment. At first I tried to comfort him, but I learned that comfort in my arms . . . was not . . ." She broke off.

Jack drew a cleansing breath into his lungs to calm himself.

"He made me feel less than whole." Holly trembled in his embrace, and he could sense there was no stopping her. She'd held back the hurt too long, and now that the barrier had been broken, the river would flow. "I wondered to myself, is this all there is to this? I came to think that maybe I'd done something wrong and . . . and when the next time happened, it was no better than the first. I asked Billy, and he said it was my fault . . . that I was my own trouble." Holly's voice cracked. "I tried . . . Billy said I tried too hard, that it wasn't worth it."

"But it is worth it," Jack said, his throat tight. Leaning up on his elbow, he cupped her chin between his fingers. "It's worth more than anything to give and know you are giving everything you have."

"I know that now." She smiled softly.

Jack stared into the depths of her azure eyes and saw for the first time a contentment that had been missing in her. Male pride made him glad he had been the one to put it there. He'd made her his, making love to her, for her, and though he'd found his own need in the act, it had all been for Holly. It shocked him to realize the feeling went beyond mere physical need. He wanted her soul, her spirit.

Holly's delicate face grew solemn, and she closed her eyes as if reliving the pain. "God forgive me, but I never cried when Billy died. I . . . I was glad he was dead." She met his stare. "Does that make me sound like a criminal?"

"Christ, no!" Jack said, knowing if it had been any other person with such a confession, he would have harried her for answers.

Holly smiled wanly and looked with pensiveness at the scar on his upper arm.

"What about your family?" he asked. The expression on her face was remote, but he continued anyway. "Why didn't you go back to New York after your husband's death?"

"You don't know my father. He had six sons and wanted

seven. I was never good enough for him to bother with. My parents run a bakery, and my mother never had time for me, nor did my father. I was shoved from one job to another, paid little more attention than a crumb on the table." Hot color clouded her blue eyes. "That's why I need to stay and mine the gold. I need to prove to myself I'm worthy of something good."

"Is that why you do it? Christ, Holly, gold is only as important as you make it."

He related to what she said. He had money; plenty of it. In a bank in Chicago were more notes than he knew what to do with. But he didn't want them. He'd found out that wealth was a ladder in life that people trudged up mercilessly. To attain its elusive top rung, they would do anything. A bitter vision rose in his mind of a dark-haired woman who had ground him under her heel until he'd seen into her game. But not before Robert Jackson Burnett had died from a broken heart. Jackson Ledgeway Steele had been exhumed from the hell Robert had made him up in, and he'd been living his life as an alias ever since.

Maybe now it was time to come home.

Jack bent down and kissed Holly's soft pink lips, running his tongue across the sweetness. "I would like to be there when the gold sprinkles down from the ceiling," he murmured against her mouth, "and covers your hair with all its glitter. Then you'll know it's nothing more than decoration and that you are worth far more."

With a quiet passion Holly returned his kiss, slipping her arms around his neck. Jack positioned himself against her milky white thighs, his desire stirred and not to be subdued. Teasing, he said, "You never took your socks off before. . . ."

A surprised gasp escaped her lips as he met the sensitive part of her womanhood with his hand. "You . . . We can do it again in one night?"

Jack bit back the laughter that threatened him. "Hell, yes. Again and again and again."

Then he kissed her deeply, fervently, as if there were a thousand nights ahead.

* * *

Clouds hung low in the sky, though they threatened no rain. Instead, the wispy softness was of the purest white, the light shapes offering holes for the sunshine to stream down.

Jack hopped off the step of the miner's cabin and stuffed his fists into his greatcoat pockets. It was cold, but the rain had left a cleanness about the earth, scenting the air with pine and dew, minerals, and uprooted worms. It seemed as if the downpour had brought spring with it; all the bare trees clustered with newly formed green buds.

Jack made a quick check on his horse, fed him, then explored the surrounding area. He'd left Holly inside to put coffee grinds to boil. Already the robust smell wafted toward him, and he wished he were back inside with her and the cozy warmth, but he couldn't do that. Not until he made one more attempt to find the miner.

Whoever lived in the old shack hadn't appeared at first light, and Jack didn't hold out hope that he would return at all. He was grateful Holly hadn't mentioned him this morning; there was no point in alarming her until he was sure.

Jack walked to the west, heading downstream. The river, when he'd checked it yesterday, had already risen to capacity; today the current churned with a deadly swiftness that collected anything in its path. The damage done by nature was massive—unearthed saplings floated helplessly atop the foaming waters that rearranged rocks big enough to be called boulders. Jack tracked the edge nearly a mile and a half until something at the water's border caught his eye.

A strip of material, blue and tattered.

He traversed the muddy ledge, noting a sluice box and mining gear at the shore as he held on to fibrous roots and stable rocks. When he'd reached the patch of blue, his suspicion was confirmed: It belonged to a man's outer coat.

The man still wore it.

The body had been hung up on a snarling knot of decayed wood. Swearing under his breath, Jack gripped on to a strong branch that twisted above his head. With all his strength, he yanked the dead man from the stream by his feet.

Jack's muscles strained as he dragged the burly miner to

the upper bank, where he deposited him on his rotund belly. Kneeling over him, Jack huffed to roll the man on his back.

A hotness closed off his windpipe. Jack jumped onto his feet, nausea warning his stomach.

The fabric of the miner's shirt where it stretched across his chest was stained a dull brown-red; and in the center protruded the broken-off shaft of a Sioux arrow. Half of his forehead and the thatch of brown hair meeting it were missing.

He'd been scalped.

Holly found an empty glass bottle that had been used for maple syrup, and on an impulse, placed a plug of crabgrass in it for a table decoration. Of course, a flower would have been better, but she was afraid to traipse off alone to find one. She'd noticed the abundance of the weed right by the side of the cabin when she'd taken care of her morning privacy.

The tabletop had been rearranged to afford more room at one end, and she'd located a much-used dishcloth to drape over it. She flattened her palms outward across it to press out the wrinkles, then set the makeshift vase on top.

Standing back, she tilted her head objectively. It would have to do. She set the table with two mismatched forks and lumpy tin cups. The coffee was ready, so she took it off the iron arm above the fire and rested it on a scorched hot pad at the side of the place settings.

For breakfast, she'd opened a can of creamed corn, mixed it with flour, molasses, and lard, and let it brown on the griddle she'd used for the beef biscuits. It may have been a sorry substitute for corn bread, but she was hungry enough to appreciate the semisweet aroma.

Everything readied, all she needed was Jack.

She busied herself with the forks again, first moving them to the right, then back to the left. She wasn't sure why she was so anxious. Maybe because of the overwhelming desire to please him. To make him as happy as he'd made her.

A dozen times this morning she'd thought to tell him of her love; a dozen times she'd stopped herself. She didn't want him thinking that she was only speaking because of the intimacy they'd shared. Yes, what he'd shown her had been wonderful, something she cherished with all her heart. But it was Jack—his strength, his smile, his loyalty—that she'd fallen in love with. She wasn't sure he was ready to understand this himself; she sensed in him a feeling of denial—that he wasn't a man worthy of her love. So she'd remained quiet. In lieu of her avowal of love, she would show him, in subtle, elusive ways, until the time was right.

Standing back, she clasped her fingers together in front of her full red skirt. She glanced down to glide her hands over the pleats that had lost their starch from being soaked. What a poor sight she was in her disorderly dress, with her hair twisted in an emergency knot and anchored by a pencil she'd found in the windowsill next to a dead horsefly.

With a heavy sigh, she sat down on the crate and crossed her ankles. The sides of her black shoes remained open, the buttons resisting all attempts at closure. Even the prong of the fork was no match against the stubbornly cut-out keyholes in the leather.

With one last sweep of her gaze, she ascertained that everything was in place.

Not a minute later, she heard Jack's boots scrape against the rickety planks that led up to the front door. Standing, she smiled and held her shoulders square.

The latch lifted with a protest, and the door swung open on the whack of Jack's knee. "Get your stuff together, we're heading out."

He didn't look at her, striding right past her to put his saddlebags to order.

Holly remained where she was, staring at the broadness of his back and the curl of black hair resting over his collar. He swung around. "It's time to go."

She couldn't help feeling hurt by his curtness; he still hadn't noticed the table setting, or her, for that matter. "What's wrong?"

"Gather anything you need to travel." Jack took in the breakfast spread and moved his eyes to meet hers. "Take what's in the pan and wrap it up." Quickly he slipped the Smith & Wesson, which he'd put on the mantel that morning, into his shoulder holster. He'd left the revolver with her, and at the time, Holly had thought he'd forgotten it. Now she could see she'd been wrong. He'd left it for her in case she'd needed it for protection.

"What happened?" Foreboding moved her into action, and she snatched up the carefully placed tablecloth, tipping over a cup in the process. The steaming corn bread burned her fingers as she crumbled it out of the pan.

Jack faced her. His eyes, the color of fine granite, caught her attention. "I found the miner. So did the Sioux."

She needn't hear more. His voice said it all.

They'd been climbing the uneven terrain steadily since noon. The rains filled streams to fast-moving, and each one they'd encountered had required Jack to seek a crossing where the water wasn't so fierce. It set them back nearly two hours. Jack cursed at the impediments to their progress; Holly was secretly glad for them.

Each mile they grew closer to Deadwood, she speculated what would happen to them. Holly knew she couldn't expect Jack to stay in one place for very long. In his profession, he was a drifting man, going where the next case would lead him. She only hoped that he felt strongly enough about her to maybe consider . . . consider what? Marriage? A home? As much as she vowed she would never make that mistake again, with Jack, she was hard-pressed to imagine anything else but spending the rest of her life with him.

But wanting that for herself was one thing. She wasn't about to pin Jack into something he didn't want. She would never trap him. She'd been trapped herself in a marriage, remembering the feeling too well.

The hooves of Jack's horse sunk into the soft earth as Jack clicked his tongue to his teeth, signaling the animal to climb a slight rise bordered by weather-grayed stumps. There, they joined the well-traveled road that led into Deadwood.

After a few minutes they came to a divide whose crest overlooked Whitewood Creek; Holly knew then they were within three miles of Deadwood Gulch. The panoramic view was something to behold, still awing her as much as it did the first time she'd seen it from Johnny Slaughter's coach. As far as she could see, the pointed tops of pines darted heavenward, looking more like a thicket of new saplings barely several feet tall, rather than the aging granddaddies they were.

She roved her gaze to take in the grade of hazardous road below them. Midpoint, a canvas-covered Conestoga hovered, minus its team. The descent to the bottom where Splittail Gulch's tributary ran was more of a difficult problem for the wagons to encounter than for horse riders. However, the approach was still something to be carefully considered, especially since she and Jack shared one horse.

At the base, the broken and twisted remains of two wagons that had been wrecked in trying to reach the bottom was a significant testimony to the danger.

To Holly, it looked as if the precipice was a straight fall, without so much as an angle to cushion the horse beneath them.

Jack allowed no play in the reins as he stood up in the stirrups to assess the situation. Holly felt herself sliding down into the bow of the saddle, and she struggled to keep a grip on the horn. As Jack returned his weight, the solid muscles of his inner thighs cupped the swell of her buttocks.

The hard feel of him made her tingle and lean into his chest as Jack slipped his arm securely about her waist. He pressed his legs up to hers where they straddled the horse, his knees covering hers. Her feet dangled without the restriction of the stirrups, and she slid her shoes back, her ankles locking around Jack's.

Breathing unsteadily, she lifted her gaze to his face, surprised to see it engraved with humor, not the seduction she felt melting through her. "You ever do this before?" he asked in a low-timbred voice that filled her ears.

Holly could only wonder what exactly he was getting at since his tone was serious, defying his bent smile. "Do what . . . ?"

"Go down this anthill," he said rakishly, "with somebody you don't mind being close to. Because, baby, you better hang on to me with everything you've got or we're going to be getting to the bottom a lot faster than I want to."

She stared up at his full lips and the raised stubble

covering his face. The sun picked up several shades of black and brown, even a few prickles of white in the growth. Holly was amazed that the mere beginnings of his beard could intrigue her. She had the strangest desire to kiss his chin and test the roughness for herself. "I'll hold on," she said, lifting the corner of her mouth into a gentle smile.

Jack dipped his head over hers and kissed her soundly on the mouth. "I'll hold on to you, too." The vibration of his lips against hers sent a shimmering warmth through her.

Jack sat up, and Holly could see he was contemplating his own method of conquering the ridge. He pressed his horse into a slow, guarded walk, but rather than aiming for the creek, he reined the animal parallel to it. He went one direction first, then made a sharp turn and changed his course to counter the one he'd just left. Unlike a wheeled vehicle, Jack was able to zigzag his way down.

Holly felt her back fit against Jack's tight chest, leaving no room to breathe as he focused his attention on steering his horse. The steep pitch caused her to lean into the hill, switching back and forth, depending on which way they headed. Holly concentrated interest on their progress, more to keep her mind off the uneven balance than anything else. Each time they crossed with the side of the road, she took notice of the trees and the marks on them where they had been girdled by ropes used to ease the wagons down.

As Jack neared the Conestoga, Holly could hear the stout voices of men as they maneuvered it downward. With a heavy rope attached to the rear axle and played out gradually from the tree around which a wrap had been taken, men on either side lowered the guide rope. The wagon, in turn, dropped several more feet until the ropes could be secured around another set of trees. The work was slow and laborious, but performed without loss or damage.

Holly watched in fascination as Jack circled around one of their line trees and proceeded to skirt the Conestoga. The men nodded in greeting, Jack returning the salute. A little self-consciously, Holly waved, wondering how often a man and woman on horseback navigated the side of Splittail Gulch.

Once at the base, Holly breathed a sigh of relief, taking note of the four black horses who waited patiently for the load to meet them. Beyond the team, sitting under the shade of a tree, were two women in ruffled calico bonnets. In a quick and perceptive sweep, they took in Holly's appearance and maintained their conversation without so much as a friendly smile.

It was a foreshadowing to the stares she would receive once they were at the outskirts of town. Holly told herself she didn't mind. After all, what was she supposed to do? It wasn't as if she planned on being taken captive and left without fresh clothing. And what was she to do about transportation? Walk while Jack rode? Defiantly she raised her chin, proud to be sitting next to Jack, no matter what kind of eyeful they were giving the bountiful traffic.

They crossed over the bridge by the sawmill, the smell of fresh-cut lumber cleansing the air, challenging the odorous sediments that clouded it farther up Main Street. The county commissioner, flanked by several officials, stood on the steps of the city hall and tipped his hat politely, though the gesture wasn't initiated with the same breeze-generating enthusiasm it usually held. Five modestly dressed women from the Ladies Relief Society stepped out of Wentworth's tearoom. Upon seeing Holly, they flocked together, speaking in low tones, their clustered hats crowned with long, black-tipped plumes of mottled brown.

"Too bad I don't have my hunting rifle with me," Jack quipped. "Pheasant season's early."

Holly resisted a smile. So he had noticed they were being scrutinized; the dry tone in his voice said he didn't care. For some reason, neither did she.

"Bullock will want to see you," Jack said, handling the horse around an open shaft directly in front of Herrmann & Treber Liquor.

"Do you think I'll have to face those men again?" She spoke with a shudder.

"I'll handle things."

Holly saw the familiar false front of Goodnight's Restaurant and felt the tension ease from her travel-weary muscles.

Jack stopped his mount and swung down out of the saddle, taking his secure warmth from her. Now that they'd reached home, Holly filled with a mixture of relief and panic. How would she part his company with so many people watching? She should have said her good-byes several miles ago. But what could she say to him? Thank you? The words seemed so cursory after what they'd shared.

Holly's joints were stiff and tired, and she would have slipped right off the saddle and landed on her bottom in the street if Jack hadn't come around to give her a hand after he'd tethered his horse. She gripped his lean fingers, meeting his gray gaze with unspoken thanks. She embedded his image in her mind: the way his ivory hat rested on his head, the turned-up collar of his long coat. His black hair waved down over his forehead, nearly into his eyes. Were she not in the middle of the street with him, she would have brushed it from his brow.

He held her hand longer than necessary, stroking his thumb into the sensitive pad of her palm. The light pressure made her pulse chase her heartbeat. She pictured being crushed in his embrace, being kissed again and again.

Now that she knew the promise, the expectation was all the sweeter. Something completely new had happened to her, capable of creating a whole new world. A world in which she forgot all her fears and felt at ease; free and magical.

The slam of the restaurant door broke through her thoughts as Josephine Goodnight ran down the boardwalk, with her apron whipping behind her. "Landsakes!" she called above the traffic. "You're all right, Mrs. Dancer!"

Josephine ran to the awning's edge, and Holly obligingly went to her, leaving Jack behind.

"You are all right, aren't you?" Mrs. Goodnight asked, looking over Holly's twisted hair and the pencil holding it. Josephine insightfully stared beyond Holly to Jack, then back at Holly. "Aren't you?" she repeated.

"I'm fine," Holly assured the woman.

"Well, when we heard you'd been shanghaied by road agents, my Lord, I about worried myself into an early grave." Tears misted in her eyes, and she wrung her hands together. "It's all my fault; I never should have let you go on the stage by yourself."

"It's not your fault, and as you can see, I'm fine. Though I didn't make it to Cheyenne to ask about the stove."

"Oh, forget the stove!" Josephine cried with a wave. "What matters is your safety. And besides, Conrath, the dear, was able to wire a friend who lives in Cheyenne to help us. The lines are operating now. And—" she paused only long enough to take in a deep breath "—not to mention I thought I'd try out that new post office, though little good that will do. It takes forever to get service. Oh! And the town's been in such an uproar while you were gone; two men discovered a wealth of gold down by Deadwood Creek. Everybody is flocking down their to stake claims. Your district of the forest has been deserted. Landsakes, I think you should sell out. I'll worry myself sick if you're out there on your own."

Holly smiled at Josephine's rambling, and was about to turn to Jack when Lee-Ash and Sheriff Bullock exited the restaurant.

"Darlin'!" Lee-Ash came to her in an easy stride, encasing her in a gruff hug, and despite herself, her throat clogged with tears. It was good to be back and know that she'd been missed.

"Mrs. Dancer," Seth greeted with sociable formality. "I'm glad to see you're safe. My men and I got in an hour ago with the three who held you up. We were just preparing to go on back out to locate you. How are you faring? Steele treat you all right?"

"Steele," Jack said, crossing his arms over his chest, "treated her just fine."

"Can't you see she's a sight?" Josephine cried with a shake of her head. "The poor thing has lived through a miserable ordeal. Let's get you inside and fill up a tub in the kitchen." She linked her arm protectively through Holly's, Lee-Ash sidling up to her other side.

"I'd like to ask you a few questions once you get settled." Seth took up the lead and guided them to the restaurant's front doors. Holly could only look helplessly over her shoulder at Jack, who remained in the bustling street next to the hitching rail with his steel-dust gray horse.

Seth Bullock hung back after the door closed behind Holly. He cocked the angle of his hat and took a step toward Jack. "I've been hearing some wild talk about you, Steele, from those three robbers locked up in my jail. Seems this wasn't the first time you've crossed trails with them."

"That right?"

"You meet me in half an hour at my office and give me your side of things."

"I was planning on it."

On a plateau some three hundred feet above Main Street, Jack crouched down low, looking over the darkened rooftops of Deadwood. The time neared one in the morning, and it was colder than a witch's pocket, but Edward McIntyre had insisted on the meeting. At least this one wasn't in the pit of hell. Though it may as well have been. Moriah, the mountaintop on which he stood, had several graves scattered on the bluff overlooking the town.

Rubbing his hands together, Jack fought the need to reach for a cheroot; knowing the light of a match would carry, he refrained.

He was early, leaving him with time to think. Since he'd told Bullock he was a Pinkerton detective and why he'd been hired by the league of miners, Jack felt a little of the pressure back off. It had been queer telling the lawman why he'd broken into the Lost Mining District, and even odder yet when the sheriff said if he needed any more documents, he'd be obliged to supply them. The sheriff stepped aside and offered what assistance he could. Normally Jack never told the local law who he was; this time things were different. He had Holly to think about. He hadn't wanted her to face those three criminals again, and cleared it with Bullock so she didn't have to.

After he and Seth had gotten things straight, Jack had immersed himself in work these past four days since returning Holly to Deadwood. In those days he'd come no closer to finding who murdered her husband, or the other four miners. He had a gut feeling that Devlin Breedlove, an assayer he'd been surveilling, was involved. Though the businessman did nothing out of the ordinary while being watched, he owned two of the mines on Jack's claim receipt list. Enough to cast him as a suspect.

Since no other murders had taken place after Jack's arrival, he had nothing new to go on.

During the four days, Steele had stayed away from Holly for reasons he told himself were for the best.

It wasn't as if he didn't want to talk to her, take her in his arms again. But things had gone beyond his control. He'd gotten too involved, and that involvement threatened his job. He couldn't think straight, he couldn't work without seeing her face in his thoughts, and more important, he couldn't figure her *out* of Billy's murder.

In his heart, he'd cleared her of her husband's murder. It was the evidence, the logic, the tangible proof, he couldn't dismiss. Just like the business man, Holly owned two of the mines that had seen owners murdered.

"Steele?" came McIntyre's heavy baritone. "Where are you?"

"Over here," Jack replied without standing up. As Edward McIntyre hunkered down beside him, Jack couldn't help making a snide comment. "You always find such good spots, McIntyre. Snake holes and graves are about my two least favorite places."

"Damn better here than in town, where people can connect us. Anyone finds out you're a detective and the case is lost."

Jack swallowed the bitter assessment.

"I would have talked to you sooner after your jail stay, but Bullock was keeping accounts on you like a dog does his bone. I didn't want to be the cat that veered in his direction." Edward sat, crossing his legs Indian style. "Amaryllis give you much trouble with the bail?" he asked vaguely, but Jack sensed the man was rather fond of the scatterbrained blonde.

"No more than any other female."

"She'll keep it quiet, Steele."

"If you believe that, I suppose I'm obligated to presume it myself."

"It's all over town you saved Mrs. Dancer from road agents."

Jack wondered where the offhand comment was leading, knowing he wasn't going to like the outcome.

"She's a good-looking woman. I reckon any man would find himself . . . caught up in her."

"What the hell are you getting at?"

"I happened upon you—" Edward hesitated "—watching her at the grocery. I would never bring it up were it not for the importance of your work here in Deadwood." Edward's words were rushed. "I can understand your wanting to see a pretty face, but don't you think burning the midnight oil and basking in the sunshine of her smile might slow things down a wee bit?" He made a gesture with his fingers to show an inch mark.

Jack replied with untapped anger. "How I work my case is up to me. I don't need uninvited opinions and assumptions to rile me up. I make a mistake and you'll all pay for it. Now, McIntyre—" Jack rocked back on his heels, not chancing to sit down on someone's dearly departed "—you didn't call me up here to talk about the women in Deadwood. Get on with it."

"Aye, I did not." Edward calmed, getting to the business at hand. "The league had a meeting, and we want to know what you've found out."

Jack delayed an answer, though he knew it was a perfectly legitimate question. Contemplation filled him; it was one thing to keep the findings on the claim receipts to himself and ponder their importance, yet another to speak them out loud. McIntyre would form his own opinion, and Jack didn't like it.

"Nothing much," Jack demurred.

"Nothing?" Clear skepticism rang in Edward's tone. "Why do you think I got you liberated from that jail so quickly? I knew you found something in the city recorder's office. Something that made you get thrown in jail. Fess up, Steele. You're being paid damn good money."

"You may have hired me, but I work for William."

McIntyre grew suddenly nervous. "I didn't mean to imply you were out for any velvet."

Jack was familiar with the term, meaning money taken on the sly without the company knowing about it. He'd never do that to William Pinkerton. Their friendship went back too far. Focusing on the handful of lights spilling into the street below him, Jack decided he owed the man an explanation, at least enough to appease him and his fellow miners that the case was being worked on with progress. "I went through the files and found out who owns the mines of the murdered men."

"That should point us to our man!" McIntyre's words turned hopefully animated. "Who is the bastard?"

Jack licked his lips. "I can't tell you anything more until I run checks on them."

"What?" McIntyre was incredulous.

Jack grew irritated. "I do things my own way. If you don't like it, fire me." For a minute, Jack wished Edward would. Never before had he wanted out of a case without seeing it through to the end. There was something about this one that had him in knots. Fear. Fear for himself, fear for what he might find out about Holly, fear that he, Jackson Ledgeway Steele, might become the instrument of ending her life.

"Can you at least tell me if there's any connection you can see?"

Jack held silent a moment. "Yeah, there's a connection, all right."

"Then follow up on it. There hasn't been a killing in over a month. Let's hope they've stopped and the bastard is biding his time."

"Right."

"I'm going home." McIntyre scoffed at the wind ruffling the ends of his red mustache. "It's a damn shame I came up here and left me a warm bed for little more information than I could read in the *Black Hills Pioneer.*"

Jack narrowed his gaze.

"I'll be contacting you soon."

"Do that."

Jack watched Edward disappear into the darkness, and he

stood, stretching out a cramp in his calf. Carefully skirting a grave marker, he lit up a cheroot, not caring who saw him. As he took his first drag, he went over the claim file receipts in his head again—making this well into the hundredth time. Out of the five claims that had been up for resale, one had been passed down to a surviving relative, two were owned by Devlin Breedlove, and the remaining two . . . he inhaled deeply, letting the smoke curl into his lungs . . . were owned by Mrs. Billy Dancer.

His stomach tightened, and he told himself it was from a lack of decent food. He'd been living on free lunches of hard-boiled eggs, cheese, and cold cuts with every purchase of nickel beer at the Gem. Perhaps it was time for him to go on over to Goodnight's and have a real meal.

At noon tomorrow, he'd do just that.

Holly bent over her garden, her hands covered with cotton gloves, and the top of her head by an oversize straw hat. The earth had been cold and hard on her skirted knees, so she'd taken out an oval rag rug to kneel on.

She poked and irrigated the moist soil around the tiny plants that were springing up seemingly overnight. The rain and the sun that had persisted recently were doing the vegetables good.

Holly scratched the tip of her nose, inadvertently smudging it with a streak of dried mud. For the dozenth time she looked up, thinking she'd heard someone approach. Each time she expected to see Jack Steele standing in front of her. A dozen times now, she'd been disappointed.

There was no one in the back alley behind Goodnight's Restaurant except for a calico cat that prowled around a full garbage crate of Josephine's.

It had been five days since she'd seen Jack. She would have thought him vanished from Deadwood had the sheriff not mentioned him at breakfast just this morning. She speared the earth with her hoe, her anger showing. Why had it hurt so much to hear that he was in town and hadn't come to see her? She had known her involvement with Jack would be one of no obligations or promises.

Still, the thought of him in the same town and his not even coming by her room, or at least the restaurant, wounded. Deeply.

She'd started out to the Gem nearly as many times as she'd looked up this morning. Each instant she closed in on the Gem Theater, her nerve faltered. To get to Jack, she'd have to go through Adley Seeks. Though if she were honest with herself, it wasn't only Adley she was afraid of confronting—it was Jack. Was the reason he'd been staying away because he'd had a change of heart toward her? Though he hadn't voiced any declaration of love, she knew—she felt—he cared for her.

Possibly Jack was giving her some time to herself, allowing her to come to terms with what happened between them. In that regard, she should be grateful. The feelings inside her were too new, too untried, and she should have given them more thought before surrendering to them.

But surrendering to Jack—Robert, she corrected—was the best thing she'd ever done in her life.

She wondered if the case he was working on was really as dangerous as he claimed. The thought of something happening to him was bone-chilling. A notion she didn't care to think on further. Whatever it was, surely Jack was the most capable man to handle it.

Holly dug up an errant weed that managed to make itself at home where it wasn't welcome. Smiling, she thought of Dewdrop. This was one day she'd welcome the nanny goat. Returning the animal to the saloon would give her a legitimate excuse to go directly to the front doors of the Gem.

A commotion of raised voices from the main street reached Holly's ears. Gunfire peppered the air like a basket of corn popping over an open fire, followed by almighty masculine hollers that would put a pack of roaring bears to shame. From the chorus of it, it was more than a handful of men, and they were going at something like savages.

Holly tugged off her gloves and rose, making a quick turn for the alley and the front thoroughfare between Bent and Deetkin's Drugstore.

Ambling dead center of the street was a gleaming private coach nearly six feet tall being drawn by a team of perfectly matched white horses. The carriage itself was overlaid with a coat of canary yellow paint and glossy varnish. Regardless of the fact it had been exposed to the elements, it was surprisingly clean, the brass fittings glinting in the beginnings of the sunshine that came over White Rocks. The vehicle's scarlet wheels took up muck and animal droppings as they rolled effortlessly through a wide-open path made especially for them.

On the side dangled a banner that looked worn for the wear with mud splatterings and frayed edges; it read:

DEADWOOD OR BE DAMNED

But it wasn't the fancy coach or its team, or even the red wheels. Its cargo had the menfolk of Deadwood in a tizzy. Sixteen scantily clad women made up in a rainbow of colorful gowns hung out of every open space the coach could provide.

They were upstairs girls. All of them. Holly stared at them as they swayed on past, their hair a range of shades from silver and gold to copper and bright orange. Some wore feathers, others sequins; some both. It was apparent by the crowd's enthusiasm that the girls would be setting up business just as their heels touched the ground.

Holly was about to go back to her gardening when one woman in particular caught her attention. She wasn't acting like the others. She didn't squeal with peels of laughter or try to seem eager to please the men. On the contrary, her aloof features, curling black hair, alabaster skin, and red lips were all she needed to take command of the assembly. She smiled serenely, seductively, Holly thought, without being obvious in her intentions. Raising a lace handkerchief, she waved it gently in the air, and the boisterous calls escalated anew.

Holly turned away and walked down the alley again, dismissing the ruckus as nothing more than everyday living for the Black Hills.

As she came upon the rear of Goodnight's, where the

screened-in porch was stationed, there, to her amazement, was Dewdrop. The goat's hind feet were on the ground, her forehooves planted firmly on the top step of the porch.

"Dew!" Holly called, placing her hands on her hips. "What are you doing up there?"

Holly almost laughed at the situation. Here she'd been thinking about the nanny, and now it appeared out of nowhere—oddly, not in her usual habitat, her garden—but rather the back entrance to the restaurant.

"What's the matter with you?" Holly crossed over to the pecan-colored animal whose white tail wiggled contentedly though she didn't look up and acknowledge Holly as she usually did.

As Holly came upon Dew, she gasped. "Dew!" she scolded, seeing exactly what the nanny was up to.

Earlier that morning, Holly had been attempting to make candy. The sugar hadn't formed the proper caramelizing, and she'd had to discard the mixture as a complete failure. The kitchen had been so cluttered, she'd placed the hot pan on the back steps to cool off.

And now Dewdrop's head was submerged in the pot, her teeth nipping at the last hardened pieces of sugar that had formed a solid mass. When the nanny did lift her bearded chin to bleat at Holly, she found her jaw locked tighter than a tom-tom.

"Dew! What have you gone and done this time?" Holly stepped closer to part the animal's lips.

Dew shook her squat-horned head and moaned, her teeth now jammed together, hopelessly latched down on the remains of crystallized sugar. "Oh, Dew. You really are stuck. . . ."

Holly ran up the short flight of stairs and swung open the screen door and fetched a ladle of water, dumping it into the empty pan. "Drink that! Or at least put your mouth in it. . . . Oh, my."

Dew protested and backed off. Holly tried to coax her forward, but she'd hear none of it. In a flash the nanny was off and running in the direction of the Gem Theater.

For a brief moment Holly considered her choices. Then,

without a thought to her appearance, she picked up her soiled brown skirts and took off in a run after Dewdrop.

The nanny had the goods on how to wind her way through the town's rearmost establishments. Holly crossed lots, darting past George Shingle's Mountain Town Wyoming Store; Langrishe's, where her path was obstructed by a broken theater seat placed haphazardly in the alley; the drugstore; the dry goods, where Dew ran temporarily out of view as she rounded a row of boxes; Wardman's Hardware; then off the curb at Wall Street. There, the nanny clopped up the boardwalk and bounded by Gus Schugard's Beer Hall, Flaherty's Barbershop, and into the waiting lap of one Adley Seeks as he reclined on his favorite bench with his cronies.

Holly stopped herself short, her hair floating in all ways about her waist; her hat danced on her shoulders, kept on by the ribbon tied around her neck. Gasping for her breath, she put her hand to her racing heart.

"Miss Holly," Adley drawled, and scratched his fingers through Dewdrop's bristling tan coat. "What the hell are you doing chasing my sugar?"

Dewdrop nuzzled Adley's hand, then frantically shook her head as if the jarring movement would free her fused jaw.

"I was trying to—" Holly began with gulps of air, but was cut short.

"What the hell? I say!" Adley demanded. "What the hell have you done to my sugar?" Poking around Dewdrop's mouth, Adley examined the yellowed teeth pressed together by an invisible glue. "I knew you hated her, Miss Holly, but hornswoggling the critter is a downright display of barnyard confetti."

"I did nothing of the sort!" Holly defended herself, absently tucking a strand of hair behind her ear. "I was trying to save her. She got into one of my—"

"Barnyard confetti, Miss Holly," Adley repeated, his slick features narrowing down on her. "And in case you're too refined to know what that means, I can explain it to you."

Throwing back her head and meeting his icy gaze straight on, Holly challenged, "I know precisely what it means, Mr.

Adley Seeks. You've been shoveling it at me since the day my husband died, and I've just about had enough of it." She drew an imaginary line under her chin that brought out a snicker from Adley's drinking partners.

Adley drew himself up to his feet and called an order to the man next to him. "Hobbs, take Dew on in and figure out something to get her teeth unhitched."

Holly knew a fleeting second of panic as Adley took a step toward her. Standing her ground, she didn't flinch when he reached into his fancy vest pocket to lift out a fat cigar. He placed it to his lips and lit up. Smoke puffed from the corners of his wide mouth while he talked. "Now, Miss Holly, I believe we need to get a few things aligned between us. Let's say we go inside and talk about it." He opened his arm, a gesture that invited her into the crook of it.

"I should say not," she declined with enough starch to stand a shirt on its tails.

"You come on in and watch the show, relax a little while." Ignoring her refusal, he chomped down on the tight roll of tobacco. "I consider that's your problem, Miss Holly. You're too damn high-strung."

Swill Barrel Bedford and Homer Cudney snorted their amusement and shuffled across the bench with their heads bent together in a whisper.

Holly became increasingly uneasy under Adley's scrutiny, wondering if someone would come to her aid if things got out of hand.

"You missed quite an exhibition, Miss Holly," Adley bragged. "Me and the boys hired on some new business girls fresh in today, and they gave us a little strut on the balcony." Adley pointed with his cigar above his head to the long balcony that spanned the second floor. "They did a little striptease up there, and half a Deadwood's in the Gem to see what's under them eastern corsets."

Holly was sure if he spoke the truth, Sheriff Bullock would have had him arrested.

Adley came closer, and had she not been so attuned to him, she would have realized Swill Barrel and Homer were up to something.

"I can let you have the nicest view in the house, Miss Holly, on account I like you. Show's packin' them in, and I have one special seat left."

Holly kept her back ramrod-straight.

"And it's right on my lap!" Adley hooted with laughter, then swiveled on his boot heels to resume his spot on the half-log bench seat.

He'd no sooner rested his buttocks on it when he lunged up with a grimace contorting his face. In a yelp, he cried, "What the hell?!"

His drinking partners broke out in uproarious laughter and pointed to a knothole that had a deadly needle sticking from it.

As he rubbed at his hind end over the expensive wool material of his trousers, the corner of his left eye twitched. "You mangy sonsabitches!" he yelled, pitching the Havana, his face turning redder than a summer beet. "I'm going to assassinate every living one of you!"

Adley lowered his head and stampeded them with the stamina of a bull. They all hightailed it off the bench and scrambled into the Gem Theater.

With wide eyes, Holly stared after them, suppressing her own trace of laughter. She'd seen Adley play that trick on many an unsuspecting greenhorn, and she was glad to see he now got a sample of his own humor.

From inside the Gem, she could hear the crunch of chairs tipping and tables breaking into splinters. Curious, Holly stepped up to the entrance doors, which were partially open. She stood within the boundaries, slipping in unnoticed and leaning against the red flock-papered wall.

All around her were men: miners, gamblers, merchants, cowboys, and even a few city administrators. The "girls" grouped together and egged the brawl on as it picked up speed and involved more and more zealous participants.

A smack on Homer's cheek sounded like a whack to a slab of meat, and Holly shuddered watching Homer grow starry-eyed. Shards of glass rained down behind the bar, and Holly took in the plate glass mirrors and rows of shelves on which the various-hued liquor bottles were arranged.

Amid the chaos, she took in every detail of the notorious Gem, from the richly cut crystal chandeliers and velvet-curtained boxes, right down to the carved back stage with its fringed gold draperies and the handsome floral carpet that covered the entire floor.

A beer mug whizzed past her ear, and she ducked, realizing she stood at the landing of one of the two stairways that led to the second-floor apartments. She latched hold of the balustrade and inched her way up the first few stairs.

It hadn't been her intention to seek Jack out under these circumstances, but since she was here . . . She smiled lightly, disregarding her plain brown dress and the soiled white apron around her waist. It was rather amusing at that.

She quickly slipped up to the second floor and dashed out of view to the long hallway that ran in both directions. She chose the left wing, having no idea which room Jack was in—or, she thought suddenly, if he occupied it at all. The latter thought sobered her, and she considered backing down from her impetuous search. Then she shrugged, walking on tiptoe and pausing at a door now and then.

Most times she heard the grunts and merriment of the guests and the new "employees." Holly prayed that her decision to continue on was the right one and Jack wasn't behind one of those closed doors.

When she reached the end of the hall, she heard his richly baritone voice. Her elation at finding him got the best of her, and had she not been so anxious, she would have known that if he was talking, he was not alone.

About to knock, she noticed the door slightly ajar. Taking the chance that he'd be glad to see her, she dismissed knocking, not wanting to alert anyone who might happen to peek a head out of a doorway to see who was in the hall.

Holly gently touched her fingertips to the door and pushed inward. "Jack . . ."

She moved under the jamb, then the smile on her lips froze with her heartbeat.

Jack stood in the center of the room, the bronze of his naked chest sleek in the daylight that filtered in the tiny area. In his muscular arms snuggled a beautiful woman with curling raven hair. Despite her numbness, Holly identified the woman as the one from the stage that afternoon.

A strained half minute later, Holly found her voice. "I-I'm sorry," she mumbled, feeling heat rush to her cheeks, proclaiming her naïveté. How could she have thought . . . ? She couldn't move, and yet everything inside her was tumbling down. The shock deflated any feeling she may have had, though mortification made her see she'd wrongly assumed he'd be happy to see her.

Jack didn't speak any hasty apologies or even back the woman from his arms. It cut her to the quick, and her gaze met Jack's; his smoky gray eyes glazed with pain. She could only wonder if it was with the pain of being caught in an embarrassing situation. Had she not been so distraught, she would have noticed he was an unwilling partner in the embrace.

"Who are you?" the woman asked, her flawless emerald eyes sizing Holly up. Holly couldn't help but follow the woman's assessment, seeing for herself her disorderly hair as it hung to her waist, the ruffled knot of ribbons at her throat, right down to the muddied toes of her shoes.

"I'm a friend. . . ." she whispered, trying not to look at Jack; but compromise led her eyes to the woman. Her elegant, tight-fitting ruby and black satin dress made Holly feel all the more disorderly.

Jack cursed under his breath, the first attempt he'd made since Holly entered. In a tight voice, he suggested, "I think you'd better leave."

The dark-haired woman looked up at him, pressing her palm to his bare skin. Holly felt that touch with her heart.

"Which one of us, darling?" the woman asked.

Holly gave him no chance to interpret his words. "It's all right . . . I'm leaving. I'm sorry to have . . . bothered you."

"Wait a minute, honey." The woman's sultry tone invited Holly to stay, and she found herself immobile. "I can see you're wondering who I am, but you don't have the bad manners to ask, and he doesn't have the good sense to introduce us."

She batted her lengthy lashes up at Jack and gave him the opportunity to do the introductions. When he groaned and shoved her away, she clung on to his arms, keeping herself next to him. Wetting her red lips with the tip of her tongue, she sighed, "I'm Robert's wife."

Chapter Thirteen

*H*olly felt as if the floor had fallen out from underneath her. "Jack's wife?" she echoed blankly.

Belatedly it dawned on her the woman had called Jack by his real name. The only word she had registered was "wife." Stunned beyond words, her mind burned with the memory of being in his arms; someone had taken that place—her place. A wife. She couldn't bear the thought, not without breaking down, and she was on the verge of it. Tears blinded her eyes, and she fled with a choking cry.

"Holly—" Jack spoke her name.

She barely heard it; she'd already turned and run from the room. She tore down the stairs, pounding the steps. Indifferent to the fracas still blazing, she stumbled out the double doors of the Gem Theater and didn't look back.

Jack shoved Vanessa Burnett away, a feat he'd been too senseless to do earlier. His breath seared his throat as he smothered his shock in a heavy gulp. With a shaking hand, he ran his fingers through his hair as his wife laughed; the bubbling lilt infected his rage, pushing him to the edge of control.

Grabbing hold of one of the bed's tall wooden corner posts, Vanessa swung around. "My, my, but I do think the girl was disgraced. Don't tell me, darling, you didn't mention me?"

"Shut up, Vanessa," Jack warned, the veins in his hands becoming prominent as he bunched them to hard fists.

"Oh, I wouldn't go on talking to me like that, Robert." She stopped her swaying. "Or what did she call you? Jack? Is that your name now?" Vanessa pushed free of the post and fluffed up the black ruffle at the ample swell of her creamy breasts revealed by the exceedingly low cut of the gown.

Jack pounded his fist into the post Vanessa had just vacated. The wood crunched under the thrust of his blow, a long crack splintering its way through the thin, circular column. Better the bed than Vanessa's skull; with a tight lead, Jack kept himself in check—jerking away from Vanessa so as not to wring her ivory neck. Once again he raked his fingers through his hair, rumpling the strands. Christ, if it had done any good, he would have gone after Holly. But the dazed look in her eyes had warned him she needed time to reconcile the scene she'd been subjected to. Hell, he needed his own time to accept Vanessa's appearance.

Vanessa had only been in his room for several minutes prior to Holly's arrival. It had been a halting surprise—to say the least—to see Vanessa at the door when he'd opened it. He'd felt the blood drain from his face, a mirror of that same sensation in Vanessa's beautifully made-up features. After the initial jolt, she'd sashayed into his room and amusingly explained she was in Deadwood with a singing troupe. She'd been told by one of the established girls a good-looking man with dark hair, and a personality to match, occupied the room—who never had taken up with a single one of them. Always one for a challenge, Vanessa had gone directly to the mysterious man to see if she could change his mind about some company. Little had she expected to see the object of their gossip was her own husband—ex-husband, Jack had reminded her. Vanessa had merely laughed at the absurdity of the situation and cozied up into his arms. Then Holly came in.

"What happened to the papers?" Jack ripped the words out impatiently, towering beside her, yet refusing to be caught up in her appearance, which she'd so expertly primped in her favor. There was a time when he would have taken her into his arms and kissed every inch of her; now she repulsed him.

"I don't know." Vanessa blinked her green eyes once and feigned total ignorance.

"Dammit, Nessa, don't lie to me." Jack glowered at her. "I left them with my lawyer. All you had to do was get Boyce to give them to you for your signature."

"Boyce never gave them to me."

"You're lying. He's my brother; no matter how bad the blood between us, he wanted you free."

Vanessa frowned prettily. "Boyce always did favor me."

Jack snorted. *"Favor,"* he spit out with leaden sarcasm. "Such a courteous word from a whore."

The heated slap caught his cheek off guard. His flesh stung, but he didn't bring his hand up to soothe it. He wanted to feel the sting. He wanted to remember how much pain he'd already endured under her spell.

The day he'd found his wife in bed with his brother, he'd seen through Vanessa's artful game. Never content to be just a wife, she'd always wanted more—and he only had so much of himself to give. She'd wished to be a singer; he'd seen to it she had lessons. She'd desired to sing for an audience; he'd filled his home with influential guests. She'd wanted to sing in a public theater with an assembly of paying gentlemen; he'd put his foot down. She called him a fool and said she'd do it anyway. Then he'd seen her for what she really was. She had a penchant to perform for men, and wasn't satisfied with anything less. The day he'd found her with Boyce had been the final stand.

After leaving his estate, he'd gone directly to his law office and seen to it that his colleague, Lawrence Merrick, had papers drawn up for a petition of divorce. The laws in Chicago were lenient, some easterners even traveling to the city for divorces. Jack had thought he'd have no trouble in securing what seemed to be an ideal solution for both of them.

He'd left Chicago with his signature on a document assuring his freedom from marital obligations; he rode for Pinkerton with no strings of his former life to bind him.

He'd even left his practice to Lawrence, determined to see the other aspect of criminal law without the confines of a courtroom. It had all seemed so simple. So logical.

What had gone wrong?

"Don't tell me we aren't divorced." His tone was critical. "You had to have signed the papers." He damned himself for never following through with the suit in his brief and far-between letters to Merrick; he'd only assumed Vanessa was just as eager as he to be rid of the union.

"I signed nothing." She gave him a syrupy smile and an arch of her delicate brows.

Jack felt his palms moisten, resisting with every fiber inside him not to reach out and thrash her within an inch of her life. He didn't want to believe her. She'd lied so many times in the past. Surely she was lying now. She had to be. "I'm going to wire Chicago and check your story, Nessa." His voice, surprisingly calm, contradicted the turmoil running through his blood.

"Please do," she said, bouncing down on the spread of his bed; her narrow skirt tumbled above her ankles. She teased him with a show of netted stockings and fancy black kid slippers with low heels. "While you're waiting for an answer, why don't we take up where we left off?"

She made an enticing picture in her alluring pose, but he'd long ago stopped being responsive to it; now he was immune to the sheen of her carefully arranged black curls and bewitching green eyes. They'd been overtaken by hair the color of coppery brown and eyes that reminded him of clear, mountainous skies.

"I want you out of here." Jack snatched up his shirt, quickly fit it over his shoulders, and fastened the buttons.

Vanessa made no move.

"You'd be wise to heed my orders," he advised in a deadly stillness.

Vanessa rose and nonchalantly pushed her skirt down. "My, my, darling. If I didn't know any better, I'd say you preferred—"

His fingers twisted around her wrist, and she cried out with a startled wince. "Don't say it or you'll find you have no voice to *sing* with."

Shaken, though doing her best to hide it, Vanessa left him alone, clicking the door closed behind her.

Jack braced himself at the door's edge, slipping the lock into place. Closing his eyes, he heard Vanessa's soft laughter flowing down the hall. His stomach cramped against the sickness threatening it.

Holly prayed she wouldn't run into anyone she knew. She wanted nothing more than to dash up the stairs to her room and seek a refuge where she could unleash her tears.

Fate was not on her side.

"Hello, Mrs. Dancer." Carrie Goodnight stood on the back porch filling the loam bucket with vegetable peels and food scraps. "It looks like the rain's been generous to your garden, don't you think?"

Holly had entirely forgotten about the garden and the small sense of accomplishment the sprouting plants had given her. It all seemed so trivial now.

Carrie's easy comment required an answer, and Holly willed the moisture that bordered her eyes not to slip free.

"Y-yes, it has." In spite of herself, her voice fractured, but Carrie didn't seem to notice.

"I've finally persuaded Conrath to take me to Langrishe's tonight. He thinks it's as illegitimate as all the others, but I told him it's a tony theater that even Father confesses to have taken in a time or two—with Mother." Carrie took up a pail of dirty dishwater and said, "Why don't you come with us? It would be great fun." She came down the short steps and tossed the water into the muddy back way.

Holly forced an expression of polite decline on her face. "I really don't think I can."

"Of course you can." Carrie paused a few feet from Holly. "Why, Mrs. Dancer, you look like you're going to cry."

"No . . . no I'm not," Holly denied, but even as she was repudiating it, tears slowly found their way down her cheeks.

Dropping the empty pail, Carrie immediately encircled Holly in her arms and guided them to the stairs that she had wanted desperately to climb only minutes ago.

Holly couldn't seem to stop crying. She hated tears and

had never been one to indulge in their shedding. Tears were nonsense, and she'd prided herself on being stronger than that. But everything hit her at once. It had all been a dream. Jack, his love, what she'd felt in his arms. False. All of it from the very beginning. He'd been a facade, the product of her own longing, her own need to live down her past.

"I seem to be falling apart," Holly sniffed into her sleeve, wetting the brown poplin. "I never cry . . . you know that."

Carrie looked up at her and smiled knowingly. "It's that Mr. Steele, isn't it? He's the one that's making you distressed."

Holly hiccuped with puzzlement. "How . . . ?"

"I saw him leaving your room once. Don't worry, I never told my mother. She wouldn't have understood about matters of the heart for people as young as us." Scooting closer to Holly, Carrie snuggled her arm about her waist. "I could tell right off that you liked him."

Holly raised her hands to her cheeks, for surely they were flushed a deep scarlet. "How did you know? I wasn't even sure myself."

"Oh, I can tell." A smug smile sprung up on Carrie's lips. "It was much the same way for Con and me. The first time I saw him I felt as if I was coming down with flu. I was all flustered and hot and feeling as if I swallowed a dozen butterflies."

Holly wordlessly looked at her.

"There's nothing wrong with loving a man that totes side irons for a living—if that's what's bothering you. He could hang up his guns."

"It's not that simple, Carrie." Holly sighed, wishing it were. In a voice barely audible, she said, "He's married."

"Oh, dear." Carrie cast her gaze down at the tips of her shoes. "Oh, dear," she repeated in a solemn tone.

"There's nothing I can do about it. I can only hope he'll leave Deadwood soon and I can forget about him."

Carrie lifted her chin, her hazel eyes determined. "Then you've got to start forgetting about him now. You'll come with Conrath and me tonight. No argument."

Holly feebly gave her one anyway. "I really wouldn't be much company. I—"

"No argument," Carrie stubbornly repeated.

Holly dabbed her tearstained face with the hem of her apron. Taking a quivering breath, she weighed her choices. One being the solitude of her room and her memories. The other, a night out. It was best to try and get her mind off things. "All right, Carrie."

"Wonderful." Carrie stood and nodded, her honey blond hair wisping across her brow. "You meet us down in the restaurant at eight o'clock just when Mother's closing up."

"All right."

Carrie trudged toward the porch again.

"Carrie," Holly called out, and the young girl glanced over her shoulder. "Thank you." Holly found a fragile smile.

Carrie broke into a grin, turned, then went inside.

At five minutes after eight o'clock, Holly strolled down the street with Conrath La Fors and Carrie Goodnight on their way to Langrishe's Theatre. The tepid night air played on Holly's face, a slightly soothing balm to her nerves. As they passed Devlin Breedlove's assay shop, the brown-haired man was just stepping out. Dressed in evening attire of bottle green tailcoat and white tie, he locked his door.

Devlin tipped his top hat. "Good evening, ladies. Mr. La Fors, I believe it is?"

Conrath extended his hand, and the men exchanged a formal greeting.

"We're off to the Langrishe's Variety Theatre, Mr. Breedlove," Carrie jubilantly supplied.

Breedlove, smoothing the lapels of his resplendent coat with stained fingernails, remarked, "As it so happens, I am on my way to that very same establishment."

Holly helplessly glanced at Carrie, hoping against common sense that the younger girl would oppose basic good manners and decline to invite Devlin Breedlove along.

With a shrug of her shoulders, Carrie ignored Holly's look and smiled her brightest. "Mr. Breedlove, would you like to join us?"

"Why how very gracious of you," Devlin accepted. "I'd be honored." Holly's heart sunk below her rib cage. To suffer the evening with Devlin Breedlove, especially in her present low spirits, would make for a long, long night.

Devlin took up a place next to Holly, conveniently brushing her arm with his own; his touch angered her more than usual. The fact that he would take such liberties without permission demeaned her respectability. She kept her arm pressed close to her waist as the four of them entered the entertainment house.

For Holly, the rest of the evening poured by as slow as molasses on a cold day. She barely concentrated on the singers and musicians. Not even the house-roaring fiasco between Mrs. R. O. Adams—the postmaster's wife—and Mr. J. Langrishe himself over a certain pair of opera glasses lightened the heaviness in her heart.

It seemed Mrs. Adams, wanting to be modish, brought in a pair of fancy opera glasses with which to view the show. Langrishe's being as small as it was, a person could be half-blind and still see the acts with perfect clarity. An old prospector, by way of poking fun at the woman, returned with a two-foot piece of one-by-six lumber with two beer bottles stuck through holes in it. He peered through this device at the performance, annoying Mrs. Adams profusely. Langrishe had to stop the sketch in a convulse of laughter, saying he'd never seen anyone look through the bottom of a bottle from the outside.

In the end, even Mrs. Adams cracked a smile. Everyone in the audience did. Except Holly. All of her attention focused on Devlin and the casual way he kept bumping her knee with his, or scrubbing his elbow against hers. She ended up leaning so close to Carrie that she practically sat on her friend's lap.

When at last the entertainment finished, Holly let her shoulders slump with relief and they all milled out of the building and into the cool night air.

Holly had taken a closely crocheted shawl with her, but she could see now that it wasn't enough. The bare skin at her dropped neckline was cold as she wrapped the knitted garment closer about her.

"I can see Mrs. Dancer safely home if you two would like to go on," Devlin offered.

With her eyes, Holly beseeched Conrath to disapprove of Devlin's request, but he was so entranced by Carrie, he never noticed Holly's silent request. Carrie, in contrast, took in every detail, and as she assented to Breedlove's request, gave Holly a look that said, "Get on with your life." Granted that's what she needed to do, but she wasn't interested in executing the plan with Breedlove.

The two couples parted ways, and Holly thanked heaven it was only a quick walk to her apartment. Devlin kept his right hand in his coat pocket, but the other he slipped under her elbow. Holly abided the contact, knowing she would be home soon.

Once in front of Goodnight's Restaurant, Holly told Devlin she could cross the alley herself.

"I wouldn't dream of it."

Bleakly she allowed him to guide her through the narrow passage and to the bottom of her stairs.

She put her hand to the banister and turned, not wanting him to go any farther with her, not allowing him to. "Thank you," she murmured.

"The pleasure was all mine." He came uncomfortably close and she pulled back, trying to be obvious without being rude. "I have to confess, my running into you tonight was no accident."

"Oh?" Holly felt for one of the steps with her heel and took it, hoping to put some distance between them. Too late she noticed it made her the same height as Breedlove, and they met eye to eye.

"Yes, you see," he offhandedly explained, "I was in the restaurant for a late lunch when I heard Miss Goodnight mention you were going to the theater. I made it a point to be leaving my office when you were passing by."

Holly kept quiet. Any other woman would have been flattered. But she wasn't interested in Devlin Breedlove. She was interested in . . . But that didn't matter anymore.

"You see," Devlin began, "I decided to let you be alone for a while. That's why I stopped calling on you for a time. But when I realized the mistake of my honorable intentions, I decided to pick up the pursuit again. You know, Mrs.

Dancer, Deadwood is not a place for a widowed woman. You would be wise to marry again."

Holly stared at him, her throat dry with forthcoming dread.

"I was thinking that a union joining the two of us would solve all our problems."

What problems did Breedlove have? Holly fleetingly wondered while recovering from his proposal. "Mr. Breedlove, I'm honored, really. But I must turn you down. I cannot marry anyone." And as she spoke the last words, she traitorously thought of Jack.

The sugar in Devlin's voice suddenly turned bittersweet as he countered, "I have been very patient with you. Very patient indeed. But even I have my limits." Then, without warning, he bracketed her head in his hands and kissed her solidly on the lips.

Startled, Holly opened her mouth and Devlin took advantage of the moment, darting his tongue inside her. The ends of his brown mustache pricked the soft skin around her upper lip as he ground his mouth over hers. The kiss ended as quickly as it began, and Holly was left standing there, outraged.

Had she the wits of an unclouded mind, she would have struck him.

"Good evening, Mrs. Dancer." Devlin nodded respectfully despite the liberty he'd just taken with her. "Let this be a warning to you that my patience has now been dwindled."

With that, he walked away.

Holly escaped up the steps and drew out her key from her purse. Shaking, she fumbled with it in the lock, and it dropped to the landing. As she groped for it in the dark on her knees, the key fell over the edge and landed on the ground below. She turned to go down and retrieve it when a figure stepped out from the shadows at the base of the steps.

Jack Steele strode into the muted light that escaped from the edges of a drawn window shade at the Bent and Deetkin's Drugstore; he held up the key to her. It gleamed like a priceless gem.

"You looking for this?" he asked.

Jack took the stairs two at a time, and once at the landing, swept Holly's outstretched hand away. He fit the silver key in the lock and pushed the door in. Treading inside, he waited for her to join him. She hesitated, then slipped past him, and he closed out the outside world.

Slapping the key on the washstand, Jack shed his long, black greatcoat, resolving not to lose hold of the reasons he'd come to her. "What were you doing with Breedlove tonight?"

"Your interrogation has no validity here, Lawman Steele, or whatever your name is." Holly's voice came to him in the semidarkness of the curtained room. He could barely make Holly out as she yanked off her shawl and tossed it to the bed.

Jack doubled his arms over his chest and stared at her while she turned up the stem on the glass lamp. Once the glowing light from the wick brightened and reflected off the four walls, he could see her perfectly. And she was perfect in her black lace and crimson-rose velvet dress as she flitted around the room, setting her purse down.

As was the style, the skirt pulled tightly over her hips, outlining her trim figure. The curve of her lower back was decorated by a waterfall of pleats and lace ruffles in ebony. His gaze slipped to the swell of her breasts and the dress's décolletage, demurely scooped and adorned with a fragile web of elegant lace. The gathered satin sleeves billowed off her shoulders like rich clouds, a tiny cluster of pink roses anchored in each center. The flowers were adorned with green sprigs and other feminine embellishments he had neither the desire nor patience to figure out. The rich color of her gown, its soft, yet vibrant hue, complemented her flawless porcelain skin like nothing to compare.

Never had he seen her more lovely, and the thought of her troubling over it for Breedlove and not himself sent a fiery shaft of jealousy piercing through him. The man's name burned in him, and only the firm bridle he kept on his temper had kept him from going after the assayer.

"I want to talk to you," Jack began, trusting his voice not to show his emotions.

"There is nothing more to say between us." Holly put a hand to her hair, and he was distracted. She'd swept up her mahogany tresses in a dance of curls, with delicate bows anchored here and there to match the rose and black of her dress.

Jack's muscles bunched up in heated knots, and he couldn't control the fantasies that played in his mind. He thought to pluck the pink bows, watching the curls come tumbling down. He saw her naked and yielding in his arms. The subtle and female curves of her body, the high firmness of her breasts as they lay bare for his view. He'd make love to her, over and over. . . .

"Stand over there." Holly's frazzled voice caught him unawares; he hadn't realized he'd been stalking her. Damn him for his wretched thoughts; he resembled a hungry wolf, and she the recoiling animal trying to break free of his snare. He'd come here with the purpose of explaining things to her, not securing his reputation as a lecher. But seeing her with Breedlove, seeing her so enticing, all objectives ceased and he could only think of holding her.

"All right," he muttered coarsely, his own voice betraying him, heavy and thick, crammed with desire. He willed himself to sit down on the edge of the old chest she kept next to the wall. "I came here because I wanted you to know the truth."

Holly's delicate brows rose, and even to Jack, his words sounded cheap.

Jack met the azure of her eyes. "I know you think that everything I've symbolized has been a lie. But it hasn't. My not telling you my real identity was not a lie, it was an omission of the truth."

Holly's bosom rose and fell with the softness of her breath as she coolly pointed out, "As your wife was a convenient omission?"

There was an embittered challenge in her words, and he knew he warranted every grain of it.

"She's not my wife," Jack said quietly. With a stark, tight-lipped smile, he had no choice adding, "At least I don't think so."

"Oh?" More skepticism.

"We were married—in Chicago. But when I left, I had

papers of divorce drawn up. All she had to do was sign them. I think she did, but she's lying about it. I don't know why."

"I see." Holly folded her hands in front of her, meshing her fingers together. "Are you finished now?"

"No, goddammit, I'm not." Jack rose in one fluid motion and commandeered the center of the room. "You must think I'm a son of a bitch, and I won't deny I have been that in my life. But with you, I've been as honest as I can be."

"Then you expect too much from me and too little from yourself. You asked me to understand about your alias, and I did. You asked me to trust your silence when it came to your job, and I did. But a . . . a wife." She lowered her lashes. "How could you do that to me?"

Raw guilt flooded him as her forlorn whisper reached his ears. "I don't believe her," he said woodenly.

"You have to believe her until you can prove otherwise. So, please," she implored him, "leave me alone." Holly slid onto the bed in a defeated motion.

"No. I won't let you give up on us when I've only just begun to hope." For the first time, he saw his future with a woman; enjoying a woman for the pure fascination of female companionship. Not only was there a physical element in his attraction toward Holly, there was a joining of lost souls; together, they stood a chance against their pasts.

Jack sunk down onto the bed next to her. "I can't leave you alone." Her blue eyes sparkled with tears, and he felt as if he'd been kicked in the stomach. He'd hurt her, he knew. But an existence without her . . . He couldn't leave her alone. "God help me," he choked, "I can't. I love you too much."

Holly's breath caught and she squeezed her lids closed; two crystal droplets fell off her long lashes. "You can't love me . . . you love her. You're married to her."

Jack took Holly's shoulders in his hands and willed her to look at him. She did so with unveiled anguish that tore him apart. "I don't love her," he insisted in measured words. "I—there was a time, yes, but no more. That part of my life is over and finished."

"Why is she here?"

"Hell, I don't know!" Jack drew Holly's face closer to his, her sweet breath caressing his jaw. "I don't know," he resigned in a groan. "She came in with the working girls Seeks hired. She's a singer . . . of sorts."

"What do you mean?" Holly bit her lip.

"Christ, I don't want to talk about it, about her."

She stared at him, her chin held high. A dare filled her expression for him to continue, and like a fool, he blurted out, "What do you want? For me to say it? She's a pagan, a hedonistic woman who no doubt slept with the city of Chicago before she slept with my brother." His laugh held a discerning edge. "She's probably notching out half of Deadwood at this very moment.

"I'm sorry!" Jerking his hands away, he put them to his temple. "I'm sorry. Do you think it makes me feel like any kind of man to hurt you so?" His entire body ached with a pain so dull, he hadn't taken into account until now that it had been with him all the years since leaving Chicago. He was beginning to understand the depth of his scars; for the first time, he confronted them. The mark inside him hadn't faded like the scar on his arm; it had festered and built until there was no more denying the pain of his failed marriage. He'd always thought it had been his fault in some way; he understood now, he'd done everything he could to make Vanessa happy. She just wasn't happy with him—with any one man.

Why had it taken him so long to see it, to allow himself to come to terms with it? He damned himself for breaking in front of Holly.

Steele felt Holly's fingertips weigh lightly on his shoulder, and he faced her, so overwhelmed with love for this woman, he could barely breathe.

"You ask so much," she said softly. "How can I keep understanding when I understand nothing at all? I want to stay angry with you. I should be showing you the door." She paused, a far-off look in the clear blue of her eyes. "I wish we had known each other in a different place. A place where there were no shadows to haunt us, nothing to come between

256

us." Sighing, she trembled with a lowering of her fringed eyelashes. "If I had any sense at all, I'd know we were on a perilous road."

She raised her gaze to confront his. "What can we do?" Her question was so soft and so sweet, he shook.

She was giving him a chance—one that he was too much of a bastard to give to her when it had come to Breedlove . . . and even Billy Dancer. How could he deserve this woman?

He would die trying.

A surge of longing filled him, making it hard for him to gather his thoughts. "I sent a telegram to Chicago. Half the message made it out—the lines were severed. I think it's enough for my lawyer, Lawrence Merrick, to distinguish. I don't know how long it'll take for a reply."

"Then we'll wait."

The words fell through him in a glittering wave, and he took her into his arms. His heart pulsed through each nerve of his body. "I know what the answer will be." He kissed the corner of her mouth. "I'm free, and yet I'm more bound to you than I've been to a woman in my life."

"Robert . . ." She spoke his name in a melting cry. "I'm afraid I love you too much."

The endearment flooded his every emotion, tearing down his self-imposed walls and filling him with a tenderness he hadn't known existed inside him. He kissed her again. Long and possessively. His lips blended with hers, and she responded, pressing into the hardness of his mouth. The tips of her fingers dragged across the taut strain of shirt material stretching over his back; the light and tantalizing touch drove him to the brink of madness. He felt himself tightening against the closure of his pants.

"I want to know everything about you," she breathed against his lips, drawing her hands over his shoulders and pulling him closer. "Everything." She kissed the line of his jaw, his cheek, and the scar that ran below his eye. "How did this happen?"

Jack moaned under the feathery caresses she gave him. It was all he could do to think up the incident that had left him scarred. "It . . . happened one night when I sat with my back to the door. A fight broke out on the street, and the men burst in through the glass window behind me. I got cut."

He felt her smile brush his lashes. "Is that why you wouldn't sit where I told you to the first day you came into the restaurant?"

"Yes," he raggedly replied.

"And your . . . scowl." She pulled back long enough to mark it with her fingers. "Why do you scowl so much?"

His answer wedged in his throat. "Because I'm unhappy."

"Still?"

"No." Then he lifted one corner of his mouth, but the furthest thing from his mind was smiling. He raged with pleasure and want from being in her arms. The touch of her skin was soft as flower petals; the fragrant scent of her hair and the way it teased her shoulders made him yearn to drag the pins out of it to watch it flow down her back. He'd be tugging out the decorative bows she'd so proficiently arranged were it not for her intimate questions. "Do you intend to interrogate me all night?"

"Were I to, you'd have it coming." She sat back, and the silky rustle of her petticoats filled the air, making him imagine the slender shape of her legs underneath. A tendril of reddish brown hair curled over her brow, and she absently brushed it aside. She hesitated, as if choosing her next words carefully. "I think you should know about Devlin Breedlove and me."

Jack's heartbeat skipped. Any other time, he would have wanted to listen to what she had to say about the assayer. Now he tightened his body against the suspicion that overpowered him in a consuming fire of resentment. Could what she'd tell him make him deny his heart? He had no power to stop her from explaining.

"Devlin Breedlove means nothing to me. He assays my ore, that's all. What you saw—" she swallowed "—was him taking liberties he had no invitation to take."

That was all she said. Her confession was nothing more than an innocent declaration. Damn him for even thinking it would be anything else. Again, he'd betrayed her in the

258

silent misgivings of his mind. He vowed it would be the last time.

Jack crushed her to him in a fierce embrace. The power of it startled Holly, and she slightly resisted him with confusion clouding her face.

"What is it?" Her eyes were wondering and contemplative. "Did I say something wrong?"

"No, baby. You said everything right. It's me who's wrong. Wrong about everything. There are things about my past, about why I'm here." Drawing her tighter to him, he inhaled the scent of her hair into his lungs—orange blossoms. They nearly killed him with a combination of fear and desire. "I don't want to lose you."

"You can tell me." She traced her hand along his jaw and fit her thumb over his chin. "You can tell me," she murmured, and kissed him.

Jack lost all reason. He kissed her back with every emotion he knew and some that had been lost in the deepest part of himself. He gave his spirit to her, completely and without reserve.

Holly gasped and circled his neck with her arms, bringing him closer. They fell backward to the bed, all thoughts of talk forgotten. The only thing that mattered was being in each other's arms, of loving each other. There was no time for slow seduction; Jack felt Holly's impatience matching his own. As deftly as he could, he reached around the back of her gown and slipped each satin-covered button free. It was a long task, made longer by the position they were in. But he refused to stop kissing her. He needed to feel her mouth on his, discovering him.

She parted her lips, and he tasted the inside of her sweetness with the edge of his tongue. Her hands roved up the curves of his shoulders, then met at his throat, where she fumbled with the row of buttons that ran down his shirtfront.

It was a clumsy ordeal, each of them struggling without breaking the kiss, but at the same time, the tugging and urgency aroused already inflamed passions.

Jack heard the material of his shirt tear as she pulled it off him as far as she could; then she'd come to the obstacle of his shoulder holster. He laughed deeply and grumbled lovingly against her mouth while he unbuckled the belt, along with his waist holster. "You're an alley cat."

"Don't tease me," she said in an uneven breath.

"Never."

Jack slipped the top of her beautiful dress off the silky slopes of her shoulders, the fabric coming away in a sensuous swish of liquid black and crimson-rose. She wore a corset cover of plain white lawn. Looking down, he traced the curve of her trembling breasts and captured the ribbon of the chemise in his fingers, untying it.

Holly watched him with a radiant expression flushing her face. He rose, keeping his knees on either side of her hips where the dress had bunched around her waist. Skillfully he drew out the undergarment's hem and brought it over her head. As he tossed it over the side of the bed, it floated down in a gossamer mist. Her breasts strained against the bottom edge of her whalebone stays, and the portrait could not have been more enticing had she been nude. He cupped each perfect mound in his hands, stroking and teasing the nipples beneath the satin of her corset.

Holly moaned and grabbed for his undershirt. Ducking his head, he gave her access to slip it free of his body. She did with a hard pull, then threw the heavy woolen garment in the air. Her hands reached up to his bare chest, her palms trembling over the patch of hair between his flat nipples. He shivered like a youth, feeling himself throbbing hotly.

Jack bent down, put his hand behind her head, and swiftly kissed her. With his free hand, he jerked the gown from her. It gave way with a crisp whisper. Looping his fingers into the band of her petticoat and bustle tie, he ripped them free.

Patience was no longer a virtue. It was a hindrance.

Holly grabbed for the fastener of his denim trousers, the brass fitting snugly in place. A low whimper of frustration tore through her. Jack nudged her hand away and easily popped them free. The freedom made him turn to fire as he slipped from the tight confines of his pants. He knew he couldn't wait; he wanted her too much.

This time it would be need that brought them together.

In a quick and rending motion, he freed her legs from the feminine obstruction of her pantalets. Holly arched her back, and without undressing her further, he pushed the length of himself inside her velvet warmth. She was ready for him, curling her legs around his and matching each stroke he set.

There was no time for exploration, no sweet words or caresses. They came together in a fitful frenzy, worshiping each other utterly without restraint.

No matter how difficult, Jack held back for Holly; he met her hips in perfect rhythm. It was heaven and hell at the same time, heating him, then the moisture of his perspiration chilling across his skin. A bolt of lightning spasmed through him, leaving him on the border of release. With an iron will, he fought it; fought it until he heard Holly cry in fulfillment, until he felt her shudder beneath him.

Bunching the comforter in his fingers, he thrust one last time, an explosive and jolting lunge. Sheened in sweat and the perfume of Holly's own body, Jack splayed his fingers across her back, keeping her to him; they lay together poised in a fine thread of exhaustion, completion, and fulfillment.

In this web, they drifted off to a light slumber, Jack still inside her, his boots on his feet.

At first, Holly didn't know what woke her up. Then the gunfire down on Main Street sounded again. She paid it no regard, snuggling up to Jack's warmth as he lay next to her. He slept soundly, ensconced under the warmth of her comforters. They'd made love one more time, slowly and gently, then slipped under the sheets to sleep. Holly was nude, never having slept so. It felt wickedly delightful.

She knew she risked heartache by being with him; but it was a risk she was willing to take. She could no more send him away than she could deny being in love with him. It had always been there in the back of her mind, from the first time she saw him, but she'd been afraid to voice it. Afraid to get hurt. She understood now that the chance of being hurt was not enough to stand in the way.

She believed him about his wife. Though as much as they

both did, a belief wasn't strong enough to exempt the truth. Were he still married . . . It all hinged on the reply he would receive from Chicago.

The lantern burned in hazy brightness on her desk, where she'd left it turned up. She smiled, thinking of when she never wanted to sleep with the light off. Now, with Jack here, she wished it extinguished. She wanted to feel the darkness around her knowing she was safe because Jack was with her.

Quietly she slipped from the bed, it straining with the loss of her weight. She glanced down, hoping she hadn't disturbed Jack. He lay on his back, his breathing even. He was so beautiful to her, she ached from loving him. The sinewy expanse of his bare chest, the dark mat of hair, contrasted against the whiteness of her sheets. There would be a way, she told herself. Now that he had been honest with her.

Holly rose, sweeping her hair over her shoulder. Putting her hands to her earlobes, she went to remove her Chinese jade earrings. One was missing. A quick glance at the bed told her she'd have to wait until tomorrow to look for it; most likely it was hidden in the folds of a sheet.

Once at the desk, she leaned forward and cupped her fingers to blow out the lantern. She caught a glimpse of Jack's coat where he'd strewn it on the washstand. Left there the rest of the night, it would wrinkle. She moved to pick it up to hang it by the door when a small leather book fell free of the pocket.

Holly collected it and went to replace it when the pages fell open in her hand. She could see by the scribbles and notations, it had something to do with his detective work. She should have closed it and put it away, but something caught her eye and she brought it toward the light.

There in Jack's bold script was her name—recording her events from the day he'd ridden into Deadwood. A sickening feeling washed over her, and the ink blurred under her gaze as she shivered. Numb, she read on. When she came to a page that listed her name and Devlin Breedlove's, her mouth went dry.

He'd drawn a list of the claims she owned, and those Devlin apparently owned. Four altogether, with a fifth labeled "unclaimed." On the next page, the claims were listed again; this time after each one . . . a description of . . . of . . . a death was entered. Billy's name boldly stood out. *William Dancer—shot in the back on August 7, 1876.*

A heated prickle washed over her body, her fingertips growing so numb, she could barely hold on to the book. Her head ached with a sharp throb that stemmed from her jagged heartbeat.

The bed creaked.

Holly looked sharply up to Jack, who'd moved to his side, one arm curving over the pillow. Pulse pounding, she quietly lowered the book and closed it, setting it on her desk.

Mindless, she opened her clothes cupboard and picked out a floral flannel robe, drawing it over her body. Walking to the bed, she sat on its edge and forced her quaking heartbeat to still. Her stomach in knots, she kept swallowing down the vortex that swirled and pulled at it.

It took every ounce of willpower to wake him with a soft voice. Holly nudged Jack's chest, giving no thought to the bronze skin she'd so recently admired.

A slow and sensual smile etched his lips as he roused. He tried to lean over and kiss her, but she jerked back as if she'd been burned.

With a stiff back, she said tonelessly, "I want to know what you're investigating, and then I want you to get dressed."

Chapter Fourteen

A lock of black hair tumbled over Jack's forehead as he raised himself up on his elbow. "What are you talking about?"

"I think I'm the one that should be asking questions." Holly stood and tried to remain composed, battling the rising light-headedness that assaulted her. The memory of the day she'd first met him filtered into place; by the notes in his book, it was no accident he'd come to the restaurant. How could she not have seen this coming?

Her throat went raw with unexpressed shouts of condemnation as she hastened to say, "I never pressed you to tell me about the case you were working on. I trusted you and tried to respect your occupation. But I can see now, I was wrong. Horribly wrong."

Jack shifted and sat up, swinging his bare legs over the side of the bed. Absently he brought the covers to his lap, and they fell effortlessly over his corded thighs. Watching him, it was hard for Holly to deny that even now he affected her. Nevertheless, she knew that she had to remain detached or she would suffer for it.

"What is it?" His voice sounded thick with sleep, though she sensed he knew exactly what she was talking about.

Holly couldn't help taking up the tiny leather book and

throwing it across the rumpled coverlet. "I think that explains some of it."

Jack made no move to retrieve the notebook. He stared at it for a brief second, then returned his gray gaze to Holly. With a heart she forced to be cold and unfeeling, she waited for his words of vindication. They never came. In a clear and resonant voice, he stated without ceremony, "I've been hired to find out who's been killing the miners for their ore claims."

His bluntness startled her; she had expected him to tell her, once again, that for her own protection she need not know. She battled back the thought that maybe there was a good reason he'd kept it from her. "I see," she said, keeping a frosty edge to her words. "And why did you write my name in there?"

"Because I'm investigating Billy Dancer's murder."

Her dizziness grew, and she braced her fingers on the desk's ledge to combat it. Billy . . . Jack was here because of Billy's murder. All the time she'd agonized over it and wondered who could have done it, Jack was the person who might have been able to answer her questions.

A whirling tide swept through Holly's body. She took in slow and steadying breaths, raising her eyes to Jack's face. "What kind of a man are you? You made me . . . love you."

Jack's face shadowed with deep-set lines; his scowl had returned. "I should have told you everything after our relationship changed."

Pushing away from the cherrywood writing table, Holly relied on her dignity. "Nothing has changed. We never had a relationship. Everything has to do with finding the man who killed my husband. As his widow, I should have been the first person you confided in. I could have helped. Instead, you kept on about my welfare, not wanting to see me hurt. I'm not a frail woman. No, this was something you should have told me long ago, unless . . ." The suffocating tension inside her built anew, and she felt the meter of her pulse decline to a deadly slowness. "Unless you thought me involved."

Jack's lethal silence slapped her with his answer.

"You did . . . didn't you? You think I killed my husband." As she swayed against the blinding anger upsetting her stomach, shock yielded to resentment. "Damn you."

"At first." Anguish dulled his expression as Jack ran his hand across the stubble on his chin. "My every instinct told me you weren't involved, but each time I came up with something more to tie you in with the murders."

"Like what?!" She twisted the tie on her robe, wrapping it around her finger until it whitened with lack of circulation. Releasing the knot, she shoved the tie aside. "Like what?"

Jack agonized over his words. "Like your admission of wanting Billy dead."

Too stunned, Holly could not move. "I told you that in a moment of weakness, and you knew I didn't really mean it."

"I know." Jack's gravelly voice faltered. "You wanted him dead because of the mental abuse he put you through. I don't blame you."

"You had no right to keep this from me." She paced the room, treading over the carpet until her wayward thoughts dominated her steps. "Was part of the job making love to me?"

"Holly—"

"I told you things . . . personal things." Visions of their intimacy flooded her—whispered talk of her marital life that she'd never shared with anyone before.

"And they'll remain safeguarded in my heart." Jack ascended from the bed completely nude. His body rippled darkly with lean muscle, void of any unwanted flesh; his skin gleamed in golden hues under the kerosene light. Without any embarrassment over his nakedness, he slid into his underwear and denims, agilely fastening the closure. "Holly, what we shared is still here."

"The relationship you keep talking about has been built on a foundation of lies. You can't expect it to withstand the thrashing it's just been given."

Jack came to her; furious, she crossed her arms and pointedly looked away. "Don't, please." He stopped where he was, and she could feel him surrounding her with his presence; she could smell him, the unique scent his alone—

balmy hair soap, leather, and even a rugged freshness that came from the woods. She raised her eyes to find him watching her, his brows set in a straight line. "What else is there? Tell me, or ask me, so I can defend myself."

When he said nothing, she reproached, "Don't stand on formalities now. There is something else, isn't there?"

"How many claims do you own?" His facial expression strained.

"Two. But you knew that." Something clicked in her mind. All too quickly it came to her, and she began to recognize Jack's reasons for wanting to know. "I own two. The first was mine and Billy's. The second I bought from the widow whose husband had been killed a month before Billy. She didn't have any money to return to her relatives back East. Since she and I shared a common tragedy, I gave her what I could for it. I'd forgotten I had it. The claim is dormant. I don't have the time to keep it operating." Hands trembling as she grasped them to her collar, she said, "I can only imagine what you thought when you found that out."

"Holly, I don't suspect you."

"But you did," she hurled at him. "You did! That alone is proof enough there's a thread of doubt in you when it comes to my integrity."

Jack took a long step forward and gathered her into his arms. She wanted desperately to be comforted, and she allowed herself to blend into his warmth and solace; her cheek met with the hot skin of his chest, the crisp hairs that played in the shallow valley. Jack's fingers splayed the flannel covering on her back, stroking and rubbing . . . soothing away the stress. Then she tensed, the man consoling her was the one who made consolation necessary. Breaking free, she nipped her lower lip with her teeth, fighting the tingling sensation that coursed throughout her body. "I can't, Jack. I can't. I don't know what to think anymore."

Backing off, Steele reached down for his discarded shirts. He deftly fit them over his head and tucked the tails into his trousers. "All right, Holly. I'll give you time." Scooping up his hat and guns, he replaced them. "But not too much.

When I told you it was for your own protection I didn't want you knowing what I was investigating, I meant it. Someone did take a shot at you in the restaurant that day."

Holly caught him taking up the leather notebook and tucking it into his pants pocket, while not particularly regarding his speculation as anything more than a voicing of his opinion. She kept her fingers locked in the folds of her robe, not daring to let them be free; free to help him with his ulster, free to touch him again. She would not surrender to the confusion embroiled within her.

Jack drew up his greatcoat and fit it over the hard length of his shoulders, leaving the front open to curtain his strapping frame. He opened the door, and a chilling draft tumbled inside the room, curling around Holly's bare ankles and feet. "No matter what you think of me, know that I love you." Grasping the knob, he paused. "I'll be back." The door closed behind him.

Holly remained where she was, the coldness settling everywhere around her. Stumbling to the bed, she crawled into the sheets and tugged them around her chin. Out of habit, she checked the time on the watch that hung from her headboard. Two o'clock. Many long hours until dawn.

She couldn't stop shivering. The comfort she should have felt over Jack's parting should have been enough to blanket her in warmth, to make her see clearly; but sadly, the blanket was threadbare and alleviated nothing. It only added to her misery, reminding her she used it as a substitute for Jack.

What would she do now?

Goodnight's Restaurant smelled delicious, heady with the aromas of just-baked buttermilk biscuits, bacon strips, and fresh-ground coffee. Holly moved proficiently to the dining room's sideboard and scooped the coffeepot to refill a patron's cup with the hot brew. She scurried past Earl Graves's usual table and noticed he didn't occupy it, but rather a downtrodden-appearing stranger who'd happened in for an inexpensive breakfast.

"Darlin' while you're holdin' that pot, I'm in need of a spot more." Lee-Ash leaned forward in his customary chair by the window and gazed across the street. "Earl's late today," he remarked absently, a pipe between his teeth, the ashes smudging the chest of his miner's togs.

Holly met Lee-Ash's cup with the pot's spout and fleetingly glanced outside, too. The numerous hauling wagons and even the morning Concord on the thoroughfare didn't allow her to see much, but she intuitively looked for the brown suede pinnacle and the turkey feather with its buff-colored tip pierced through it. Amid the sea of high and low crowns, Earl's wasn't to be found.

"I'm sure he'll be around shortly," Holly said, much to alleviate her own misgivings as well as Lee-Ash's. "He's not likely to miss out on a good meal before going out to work his mine."

"That's for true," Lee-Ash mused. "He ain't a man to kick up the dust of a new day without stompin' a mug of coffee."

The front doors opened and Sheriff Seth Bullock came in, followed by two deputies who took up seats in the corner. Trailing them was Jack Steele.

Holly's heartbeat cartwheeled to quickening. She had known that she'd cross paths with Jack Steele, she just didn't expect it to be so soon. Her every sensible inclination said to disregard him, to look right through him; but telling herself that and putting the plan into motion were two entirely different things.

She lost miserably.

Jack appeared not to have slept all night—what was left of it after he'd departed her apartment. His long hair overlapped his collar, as if he needed a haircut but was too busy to be inconvenienced over it. The strands, black and sleek, softly waved over the breadth of his broad shoulders. She knew how firm and compelling those taut muscles could be, and she felt herself blush at the recollection.

She could only speculate why he was here, and whether he was with the sheriff. The latter didn't seem probable. She had to act accordingly, keeping up her pretense as an attentive waitress, not letting Jack unsettle her.

"Good morning, Sheriff. Deputies." Holly found her voice and rounded up three mugs, setting them down on the table the two men occupied. She didn't dare address Steele, though despite her every effort to dismiss him, she was excruciatingly aware he kept vigil by the door—as if he knew something . . . something to do with the sheriff's presence.

With a sickening feeling, she tried to discount the possibilities that had brought the men to the restaurant. "You're in here early today." Her voice sounded foreign to her ears, drawn and taut, dreading Seth's reply.

"I was on a sunrise call and it seemed obligatory I come in here afterward."

She began to shake, her mind a crazy mixture of trepidation and hope. As the two sensations clashed within, fear took the upper hand. Somebody else had been murdered; she could tell it from the sheriff's expression, his voice.

"Earl Graves was found facedown in Whitewood Creek this morning. Appears he was killed several hours before dawn."

Holly knew she went white. Her hold on the coffeepot jeopardized, she managed to raise it to the tabletop; the enamel bottom scorched the linen tablecloth, but she paid it no mind—no one did.

"Earl?" Lee-Ash mouthed, his face aging beyond his years. "Ol' Earl got it. Durn it to hell and back." Lee-Ash knuckled his eyes, having a hard time fighting back his emotions. The two men had been friends for several years. He respectfully slipped off his three-starred forage cap.

"Do you have any idea who did it?" Holly asked the question of Seth, but her entire body concentration fastened on Jack. This was the reason he was here. If anyone would know anything, he would.

"Not yet." Bullock's solemn mood held. "But maybe you can help me, seeing how you deal with a lot of womenfolk in Deadwood." Seth dug into his coat pocket and produced a small Oriental earring, intricately carved in jade. "I found this at the site."

Holly felt faint as blackness inked across her focus of the tiny earbob. She knew her composure was under attack and fast being defeated. With a negative shake of her head, she wrenched her fingers around the coffeepot's handle. "If you gentlemen will excuse me, I'm needed in the kitchen."

* * *

Holly had been in the kitchen but a few minutes when Jack came through the revolving door from the dining area. She stood in the corner at the dry sink attacking a side of bacon with a lethal knife and didn't look up, knowing it was him; feeling it was him. Despondent, she paid no caution to the blade and would have sliced a cut in her finger were it not for Jack taking the knife from her hand.

She let him, looking up to see Josephine Goodnight and Carrie watching the transaction with preoccupation.

Jack tipped his hat to the ladies. "If you don't mind, I need to talk with Mrs. Dancer."

Holly made no resistance. His sure fingers guided her by the crook of her arm and outside to the screened-in porch. Taking the steps, he led them to the alleyway and the plot of her garden. Once there, he freed her and waited for her to say something.

She did not.

What could she say? Her life turmoiled on a storm of fate, and she could only wonder when Jack would figure out it was her earring, if he hadn't already. He had seen them on her last night. Turning away, she stared at the cold ground, searching over and over in her mind for a plausible explanation as to why her earring had been left behind. There was none. Even the time frame was right; she could have been there.

Stretched to the limit, her nerves frayed like a ball of yarn being clawed at endlessly by a cat. "What is this, Mr. Steele? Did you bring me out here because you wanted to question me?" She knew she was blindly and unjustly ranting, but she couldn't stop herself.

"No." He spoke quietly, deeply. "I'm worried about you."

Her every sense wanted to believe him, wanted to give in to his arms and tell him her side of things. Yet he'd already thought her capable of murder; this would only add to the rift between them. No matter how she disavowed it, she wanted Jack to trust her, to love her. Just as she wanted to love him. How could she when she wasn't able to prove herself innocent? It may not be her earring after all. Her thoughts turned to her room . . . her bed. Though she'd made it up this morning and hadn't found the Oriental piece in the sheets, she hadn't paid it too much attention. It could be on the floor . . . it could be . . .

"Holly." Jack brought his hands to her shoulders. "You're trembling and pale. Christ, this is killing you."

"I . . . It's not." She had to get to her room. "I'm upset over Earl. It's understandable," she snapped, but not really meaning to be short with him.

"You have to know how all this affects you. You own two of the mines, Holly." His face darkened, his brows slashing downward in a grim line. "Whoever's behind this wants you dead, too. This is too dangerous for you to be careless. Damn, that's how I got my arm shot by that idiot Deerhorn."

Her chin shot up, her lips quivering. There was no doubting him this time; if it was her earring, someone was trying to see her hung. If it wasn't, it was a cruel twist of fortune. One way or another, she had to find out. On her own and without Jack.

"I have to go." She broke free of him and started up the restaurant's back steps, her hand resting on the railing. "Don't think I don't appreciate your concern. I'll be careful."

Holly moved into the warm kitchen, its soothing cooking smells wafting over her. The first chance she got, she'd take every inch of her room apart. It had to be there; if not . . . if not, she'd retrace her every step back to Langrishe's Theatre.

She would be careful. From now on, she'd carry Billy's .22-caliber Smith & Wesson with her.

Holly brought the folds of her fur-trimmed woolen cloak together as she walked into the lower section of Deadwood, labeled Chinatown. It twisted along with shabby little shops that plied great quantities of beautiful Oriental silks, embroidery, eggshell china, sandalwood, teak, and ivory.

The pockmarked streets flowed with fingers of smelly water, and the boardwalks were in greater disrepair than those on the south end of Main Street. The Chinese population was secluded and considered to be on their own, and any problems that arose from bad sewage and street maintenance were strictly their problem.

As dismal luck had it, she caught the tail end of a funeral procession. All around her the ground was strewn with hundreds of slips of paper punched full of holes. The Chinese believed the devil had to crawl through each hole before it could reach the soul of the deceased, and by that time the body would have been buried. Such superstition didn't mean much to Holly, but she was respectful enough not to step on any of the pieces of paper just the same.

The smell of rice whiskey drifted strongly across the air as she passed a liquor parlor. Rounding the corner, she walked into the first shop on the left. Upon entering the whitewashed dwelling, she was immediately overcome by the scents of incense and opium above the cloying mist of heavy starch.

Poppy Sing Tsue hovered over a long board, an iron braced in her hands as she swept it over a shirt.

"Missy Dancer, how you are?" she asked, a bright smile on her oval face. Though she was painted and wearing mascara in a way no decent American would understand, the effect on her was charming. Her ebony hair was built in a high pyramid with ornamental pins and combs in shades of red.

"I'm fine," Holly answered, and met the woman at the ironing board. Though the outside air was cool and any warmth the indoors offered inviting, the heat in the small laundry was practically unbearable. In one corner a seasoned black cast-iron stove served to continuously heat the two irons Poppy Sing Tsue rotated. Already fine beads of perspiration had broken out on Holly's brow, but Poppy Sing seemed unaffected.

"You come for pickup?" Poppy Sing asked, swiping methodically at the white dress shirt, putting an exact crease on the sleeve.

"Yes . . . and no," Holly said slowly. She'd spent the better part of yesterday afternoon scouring her room for her earring; retracing her steps to Langrishe's had turned up nothing. It was not to be found. She kept telling herself she'd lost the earring legitimately and just couldn't find it; maybe the one the sheriff had was a copy someone else had purchased. That glimmer of hope had sent her to Chinatown. "I wanted to ask you about the earrings you gave me. Remember several months back? You said your son made them. They were like this." Holly loosened the drawstrings on her dimity purse, working around the tiny gun concealed at the bottom to finger her remaining jade earring. She lifted it and showed Poppy Sing.

"Yes, yes. I remember." Poppy Sing nodded without losing her pacing over the board. She easily switched irons and worked on the collar in one smooth stroke. "Pretty on you, missy."

"I was wondering, does your son make these for any stores in Deadwood?"

Poppy Sing finished the shirt and folded it lickety-split, wrapping it in brown paper and tying it with string. "No, no. He do just for Chinese shop."

"Which one?"

"It down on lower Main. Call Lee Wong's." From the wicker basket of clothes at Poppy Sing's sandaled feet, she snatched up a scarlet taffeta petticoat that obviously belonged to one of the saloon girls. "Why you ask, Missy Dancer?"

"I wanted to buy another pair . . . for my . . . mother."

"You no ever talk about mother. She right as rain?"

"Oh . . . she's fine." Holly choked on the lie. She hadn't spoken to her mother since the day she and Billy had gotten married.

"You come with me first. Have tea. Then I tell you where Lee Wong's."

Holly wanted to decline, but the look on Poppy Sing's face said it was useless to say no. She followed the woman into a back room fragrant with sandalwood and Chinese punk. Holly sipped her tea and politely took a small candied lime when offered.

When she could stay no longer, Holly stood and thanked her hostess, who then told her where Lee Wong's was located.

Holly left the laundry shop with a brown package under her arm—her own petticoat and shifts and the sheets that had been stained by Jack's blood—and headed in the direction Poppy Sing had pointed her.

A light March wind had swept down into the gulch, taking with it the numerous pieces of paper. They swirled around her ankles like dry white leaves and tumbled down the boardwalks and across the streets, sticking in the many mucky holes. From a distance came the slow beats of drums where the funeral was being held at the outskirts of town.

Ashes flitted on the air current, Holly blinking back their stinging bite. Most of Chinatown was involved in the laundry business. Evidence of this were the numerous lines and twines strung from building to building clothes-pinned with all sorts of garments.

Holly found Lee Wong's, its roof of white sheeting, without any problems and pressed open the front doors. The shop was small but humble. Upon first inspection, the merchandise seemed to be a vast collection of perfumes, the combination of odors almost too thick for such a cramped room; there were trinkets and baubles of Chinese origin. And in one alcove, a sort of apothecary of herbal treatments and a brass scale on which to weigh them.

A bell tinkled above her head, the melodious note rousing a short man who scurried from the back to greet her in a stooped bow.

"Af'ernoon, m'm." His broken English made it sound as if he'd called her "mom" rather than "ma'am." She cordially smiled at him, immediately liking his friendly manner and wide grin.

"Good afternoon. Poppy Sing Tsue sent me. She said you sell these." She held out the earring for his inspection.

He nodded vigorously and turned to the case in front of him, pulling out a black velvet tray strewn with various forms of jewelry. Holly immediately saw two other pairs of earrings exactly like her own.

"Has anyone else come and bought these?" she ventured. "Any Americans?"

Lee Wong shook his silk-capped head negatively, and her spirits were dashed.

"You like?" Lee asked. "Very goo' price."

"I like," she said ruefully.

275

Another customer entered the shop. Holly looked up and saw the back of a woman exquisitely dressed in forest green velvet as she closed the door. When she turned, she recognized Vanessa Burnett immediately, and from the look on her face, Vanessa remembered Holly.

Holly assessed the woman, screening the jealousy that spurned her. Admittedly she was flawlessly beautiful. Her complexion, light as cream, was protected by a smart felt hat that angled saucily over her temple and tied under her chin with a wide green ribbon to match her gown. A perfect upsweep of lustrous black hair framed her face, which beheld an air of inquisitiveness as she swept her gaze over Holly.

Holly suddenly felt very plain in her serviceable pelisse and navy serge dress. They were no comparison to Vanessa's stylish dress, cut notably tight at her slender waist and hips. Great fantails of frills and lace spread out at the back and onto the floor. The ends were muddied, but somehow it didn't degrade the costume in the slightest.

Vanessa raised a fine brow. "You're in love with him, aren't you?"

The frank question startled Holly enough to make her jump slightly, and she directed her gaze to the woman's face. Vanessa gave her no chance to respond.

"Don't bother denying it. I can see the look in your eyes. I know, I had it three years ago." Vanessa strolled over to Holly, who remained quiet, silently appraising her competition. Whether she was Jack's wife or not, he'd once been in love with her, and it was a wounding mirror to confront. "Robert is an easy man to fall in love with. He's powerfully wealthy. You didn't know that?"

Holly felt betrayed by her own look of surprise.

"He was a lawyer in Chicago. One of the best, they said. We went to lavish parties with all of the elite. Mayors, governors. Robert's father was a lawyer, too. He still was, last I heard. And of course, there's Boyce. But that's another matter."

Holly glanced to Lee Wong, who had watched the entire one-sided conversation with a wide grin on his beaming face. Holly doubted he followed much of the discourse, but remained good-natured for propriety's sake.

Facing Vanessa, Holly drew in her breath and squared her shoulders. "Are you really still married to him? He said he divorced you."

"He would say that." Vanessa raised a vial of clove perfume and, in a dainty motion, whisked it below her nose. "Yes, I'm afraid we are. But even if we weren't, it would do you no good. Robert will never marry again. The institution doesn't suit him."

"It would if he was married to the right woman." Holly spit out the words in cold sarcasm.

Vanessa chimed with laughter and replaced the vial on the counter. "My, my, darling, but you do have backbone, after all. I was beginning to wonder."

"I think you're being unfair to him—"

"Unfair?" She raised her curving brows. "I've never been unfair to Robert. I gave him plenty of warning what my intentions were. Can I help it if he didn't listen?"

"You could tell him the truth now, instead of torturing him."

"Robert wouldn't know the truth if it came up and bit him on the behind."

The thorn pricked Holly, and she couldn't find the words to retort. She'd had her own dealings with Jack and his ideas on truth; suddenly she felt very insecure. "If you'll excuse me," Holly said, and skirted past Vanessa.

"I've won, you know," Vanessa called after her.

Holly froze at the door and placed her hand on the knob. "You haven't won anything, for you see, I have his heart, and that's worth more than you've ever had." With her chin high at a dignified angle, she departed Lee Wong's shop without a backward glance.

The late afternoon sky hovered low in bands of muted purple and blue, casting in shadow and outlining the weathered buildings of Chinatown. Holly's footfalls were precise and briskly orchestrated, in contradiction to her emotions, which raged beyond her control. She had never been jealous, and the emotion threatened her entire composure. It had required all her internal reserve to keep from shaking Vanessa Burnett until her teeth rattled; the woman had to be lying.

Holly could see now some of Jack's frustration. The woman was infuriating . . . and too pretty for Holly's comfort. How could Jack find her attractive after being married to Vanessa?

The unfamiliar odors of Chinese suppers cooking in woks made Holly's stomach more upset than it already was. Tangy ginger, pork, and soy permeated the street from restaurants cubbied between businesses, their fronts broomed clean of dirt.

Weariness enveloped her as she tried to concentrate. She'd come too far not to have been any closer to finding her earring. Once again, she went over the events that night, from the moment she'd put them on to when she'd found one was missing. Each time, her mind had stumbled when she came to Devlin Breedlove. Try as she might, she couldn't rid the image of his kissing her. He'd hurt her by the brutal assault his hands made on her face to pull her closer. His fingers had . . . Holly faltered in her steps, pausing only long enough to gain back her momentum.

Devlin's fingers had grasped the side of her face, curling over her neck, his thumbs stroking her earlobes. Devlin . . . Devlin could have taken her earring off, and being as upset as she'd been, she hadn't figured it out until now.

Jack—she had to get to Jack and tell him.

Practically running, Holly had only made it half a block when a masculine voice halted her. "Mrs. Dancer, I'd like to talk to you about your ore samples. I think you'll be encouraged."

Heart racing and nearly out of breath, Holly looked up to see Devlin Breedlove standing under the open doorway of his assay office. His features were animated, and for a moment, she believed she'd made a mistake about him. . . .

"Mr. Breedlove." She put a hand to her collar. "I . . . can we please schedule a meeting at another time?"

"I really don't think so." He stepped onto the boardwalk and grabbed hold of her elbow, the paper package in her hands slipping down. The pressure he applied was enough to cause her to wince and look up helplessly to see if the scene was being witnessed.

"Mr. Breedlove, please, you're hurting my arm."

He'd managed to half pull, half shove her into the assay office. "That's not all that's going to be hurt if you don't shut up and come in here."

His tone took on a vicious edge as he slammed the door closed, tugged the shade down, and with a chilling click, turned the key in the lock.

Chapter Fifteen

*D*evlin shoved Holly through the divider curtains and into his laboratory. His fingers pinching her elbow, he steered her in the direction of the long counter cluttered with bottles and jars. Though she'd always been fascinated by Devlin's concoctions, at the moment, the chemicals smelled deadly to her. She gagged. Ignoring her stifled cry of distress, he pushed, slapping her back against the counter's edge.

Holly grabbed hold of her arm where Devlin had bruised it and rubbed at her skin through the thickness of her cloak. The package in her hands fell free, and she bent to pick it up.

She caught the shape of his boot heel as Devlin used it to smash the paper wrapper and grind it on her freshly laundered underpinnings; then he kicked the parcel aside.

"Don't bother, Mrs. Dancer. You won't be needing them."

She straightened. Her first thought was to reach into her purse and pull out her pistol. She tried to think what Jack would do; he would be cautious. He'd play Devlin as long as he could, then catch him unaware. To draw out the Smith & Wesson would be foolish. She'd wait, then get to it; and if need be, she'd fire.

"What do you want?" A ridiculous question, but the first one that popped into her head.

"What I want, Mrs. Dancer," Devlin stated, running his fingers down a glass beaker and drumming its bottom with his dirty fingernails, "is something I gave you many opportunities to give me. Now I'm afraid I've run out of options. I'm taking it."

Holly swallowed her fear; he sounded insidiously collected. His calm demeanor challenged her enough to confront him with less apprehension than she felt. "You killed Billy, didn't you?"

Breedlove warmly laughed, and with a smile that could still be rated as handsome. "My dear Mrs. Dancer, I really don't think that's a proper subject for conversation."

"You did it, I know it."

Devlin came forward and crashed the beaker to the floor. Holly sidled away as the glass shattered all around her feet and crunched under her shoes. Her heartbeat thumped wildly against her ribs as she reluctantly awaited his answer.

Devlin stared pointedly at her with the coolness of spring water. "I did."

The two words were uttered without a single note of remorse, callous and calculated.

"You're not going to get away with this." Though as she said it, she expected his reply.

"I already have."

Breedlove stepped to a tall stool, rested his foot on it, and flicked a speck of lint from the hem of his trousers; the material was spotted and discolored from bleach and tea. She thought of the gun once again, but was unable to make a move as he'd lifted his head to her.

"Why?" was all Holly could ask. The nightmare she'd been living without proof or tangible cause stared directly at her face, and she needed to know at last what had been the driving force behind Billy's murder, since surely the claim wasn't worth such a deed.

Devlin leaned his weight onto the stool's red-cushioned seat. "I don't see any harm in telling you, since it will remain our secret. I owned a handful of claims—dry diggings, actually—and came to discover that though they were far apart in location, they were connected to the same vein. I kept coming up with the same combinations of minerals in my extractions. I found out there were a string of claims on this southern vein, your husband's included. When I offered to buy him and the others out, they didn't see it my way. So you see, I had to dispose of them."

As she listened, a chilling perception crept over her skin, causing gooseflesh to rise.

"The first few victims were easy. I made them look like accidents. Billy Dancer, on the other hand, was more defensive and put up a fight, so I shot him and made it look like a robbery."

Holly trembled so, she had to hold on to the counter for support, overcome with the picture of Billy's lifeless body at the funeral parlor. The man standing here was responsible for it, for her endless nights of haunting dreams.

"It's a pity I missed you at the restaurant. We wouldn't have to be going through all this now."

Holly's senses adjusted to calm clarity.

"I wasn't able to carry it off at such a confined range. I couldn't risk making my identity known."

"It *was* you . . . Jack was right about the shots being meant for me."

"Jack Steele?" Devlin's face contorted to an ugly twist. "The man was in here this morning asking me questions."

Holly's pulse tripped at the mention of Jack. "Jack was here?" Had he been able to put the pieces together?

"There's something not right about that gunslick. Said he was interested in the assay process on some ore samples he took out." Breedlove had a far-off look in his eyes, then snapped out of it with a shake. "No matter."

Drawing on every reliable and stable nerve she possessed, Holly slipped her hand secretly into the circled closure of her purse. "How did you get my earring?"

"Give me some credit for being a man."

Breedlove pushed away from the chair, and Holly froze, trying her best to conceal her reticule in the wrap of her pelisse.

"It was a stroke of genius on my part. I killed Earl Graves in a sloppy manner to make it look much like a woman had done it. Leaving your earring there should have been enough to direct Bullock to you, though he's too slow to catch on for my tastes. I can't wait for him to figure it out."

"What are you going to do?"

"Now, Mrs. Dancer, we have to part ways. I had tried to make a clean offer to you, but like the others, you held on. I even tried to scare you into leaving by climbing down into your claim, going as far as planting that arrow." In his ranting, Holly lost some understanding of his tirade.

"What arrow?"

"You know which arrow!" he accused. "But no, you held on. Well, there is no holding on when it comes to gold. And I want yours."

Holly's hand shook as she felt for the trigger and hooked her forefinger around its steely coldness. He talked in riddles, and as much as she wanted to shoot him, she was afraid; afraid to face the sight of blood on a man again. But if she didn't at least scare him, she would be at his mercy. She bit down on her lips to keep them from quivering, pulled the .22 free of her purse, and leveled it at Devlin Breedlove. "I don't want to have to shoot you, but I will." She could only hope she sounded like she meant it. "Let me go."

Devlin wasn't cowed in the least. "I didn't expect this of you, Mrs. Dancer. You're much too respectable to have to resort to this sort of thing. Come now, give me the gun." He stretched out his hand.

"No." Elevating the firearm to a more imposing angle, she pulled on her courage. "I won't."

"Then you're a fool!"

Devlin lunged at her, and she squeezed the trigger. The hammer came down with a snap, but the cartridge failed to explode. With sickening horror, she saw Devlin had wedged his thumb in front of the hammer, obstructing the firing pin from connecting with the bullet. As she yanked the pistol free of his skin, he let out a yell when the trigger mechanism's point left him with a puncture. Blood came fast, and in thick droplets that splattered the front of his suit coat and the floor.

"Damn you!" he sobbed, and seized a rag, clutching it over his fist.

Holly caught her balance, but Devlin lunged at her, grabbing her wrist and wrenching the gun from her hand. As he pitched the weapon into the corner, he circled his arm around her waist, squeezing so hard, his fingers cut into her ribs. She coughed in reaction, struggling to wrestle her way out of his grip.

"I'll let you leave," he wheezed in her ear. "Actually, we'll both leave."

"Where are we going?" she cried, laboring to breathe without it hurting her chest.

"That, Mrs. Dancer, you'll have to wait to find out."

Tom Deerhorn nuzzled the column of Amaryllis's swan-like neck with his nose. He lay in bed with her, their naked bodies flushed and cushioned by the dozens of violet throw pillows. "Sweet harmony, but you smell so good, I can't hardly keep from flying full-staff every time I take a whiff of you. I've done had my morning proud all gol'damn day."

Tiny snickers peeled from Amaryllis. "I declare, Thomas G. Deerhorn, ya'll are one of the sweetest versifiers I ever heard. This little ol' gal gets an incorrigible itch with all that highfalutin talk." She teased him with her fingers.

Planting a whopping kiss on her lips, Deerhorn broke his mouth free with a loud smack. "Sweetheart, sweetheart, sweetheart. You are going to see me flat out dead we keep up this hyar pace."

They'd been ensconced in Amaryllis's room behind the Melodeon since Amaryllis had gone back to the jail and bailed him out. The tiny crib was strewn with turned-over Century jugs, candy boxes with the chocolate papers tossed in as many directions as there are compass points, and bottles of spicy perfume with the stoppers missing.

"Befer we start up again, sweet pet," Deerhorn said while taking nose-rippling sniffs of Amaryllis's wrists and the soft skin that molded her breasts, "this boy's got to shake the dew off the lily."

Amaryllis sat up in bed, her striking white hair tumbling around her shoulders. "Ya'll just did that not more than an hour ago."

"Didn't know you was keeping track." Deerhorn slipped into his faded red long johns and pulled on his gray socks, his left one having a hole in the big toe.

"I'm not." Her pout, swollen from kisses, begged to differ with him. "I just miss you, is all."

"I'll be back afer them sheets are cold, sweet thing."

Fluffing her hair and shaking her breasts, Amaryllis reached down for her chocolate box that she kept on the stand beside her bed. It was empty. Frowning, she licked her red lips. "Ya'll be a darling and go on over to Fuddle's Emporium and get me a new box of these here."

"Damn, you really need those?" Deerhorn plopped his hat on his sun-bleached hair, his brown eyes taking in the box of brown wrappers minus the candies. "I don't want to go out in the cold further than I have to. Just puttin' on my duds to keep from freezing my duff off." He shoved his feet into his boots, the spurs jingling as he crossed over to the door.

"Now, if that don't beat all," Amaryllis called out to him. "Ya'll said you love me and won't go and fetch me any more chocolate. I swan, it makes me think I should have taken up those other bucks when I'd a had the chance."

Deerhorn's face blazed hotly as he glared at the object of his delight, her naked body a tempting and ripe sight: her breasts like mounds of whipping cream with two red cherries in the center . . . her legs lush and white as pearls. "What kind is it you like?"

"Miss Dixie's with the soft middle. Don't you go get any of them caramels. They stick to my teeth." She lay back with a satisfied smile.

Deerhorn muttered under his breath, calling himself every kind of love-sick rooster. Grumbling, he reached for his coat and yanked it hard from the nail on the wall. It rent with a shrill tearing sound, and he cussed up a blue streak. "Hell and high water, ding bust it! Golblast! What'll I wear now?" Disgusted, he took out a plug of tobacco and slipped it between his lower lip and teeth, then he threw the useless coat across the room.

"Ya'll put on that fur coat of mine. Mind you be careful with it."

Deerhorn fixed his gaze on the ball of dyed-red fur heaped on the floor in front of the furnace. With a grimace, he fetched it and stuck his arms in the sleeves. It came to his bony knees, hemming his long johns and boot tops. "Cripes. I'm not going to Fuddle's like this."

"Oh pooh, old man Fuddle is near to closing. There won't be a soul in the place. Go on now. Ya'll have unfinished business with me." She shooed him with her wrist. "I'll be right here pining for ya'll, so hurry up."

Tom felt himself rise to the occasion at the prospect, then he lifted the latch and crossed out into the frigid night. The back alleyway to the Melodeon was deserted, so he took care of nature's business, then found his direction to Fuddle's Emporium.

On that route, behind the assayer's office, an odd sight caught his eye. A tall man stepped out, with a woman in front of him. Deerhorn wouldn't have paid them too much mind except there was something vaguely familiar about the way the woman held herself, the way she wore her hair. She walked with a strained gait, as if she was being forced. Sure enough, the man nudged her and she nearly stumbled.

Instinctively Tom reached for his twin carved ivory-handled Colts. To his dismay, he gripped thin air. "Damn . . ." He was light.

Inching back into the shadows, he watched as they approached. Once they were under the light of a street glass, Tom stiffened. He knew now where he'd seen the woman. In the jail. She was that lady friend of Jack Steele's.

It wasn't until they passed over the sidewalk and toward the livery that Deerhorn saw the gleam of a gun.

"Son of a bitch," he hissed, then kicked up his heels in search of Jackson Ledgeway Steele.

The kerosene light in the Red Bird was just high enough to interfere with Jack's mental drawing. The knifed-up table-top intruded on the map he kept trying to draw in his mind. He sat in the rear, the smoke-filled saloon carrying on with its business with no regard for him at all. Not that he wanted attention.

The rolling dice of chuck-a-luck brought hollers that didn't affect him as he called for Angel to bring a fresh candle to his table. She was back in a matter of minutes, setting it on the center and lighting it. She waited expectantly, as if he'd ask her to join him. When he didn't, she shrugged off with a sigh.

Jack finished the last of the whiskey in the Early Times bottle, then ripped the label off. Turning it over, he made use of the back for drawing paper. He positioned several dots and started to connect them by means of lines. Then he added ridges and other markings.

True to his word, Bullock had gotten him access to the Lost Mining District's city recorder office again. There, he'd searched the hundreds of files, looking for names, clues, anything. He'd come across one name over a dozen times: Devlin Breedlove. Charting it all out, he felt a sinking feeling wash over him as he began to put the pieces together. The claims were all there, marked and in line with the one vein they had in common—a southern link to the Homestake.

Breedlove owned nearly all of them that landed on the trail leading to—

Jack's concentration was distracted as cheers and whoops from the local patrons filled the saloon.

Tom Deerhorn self-consciously snuck over to the bar and stood up on the brass railing to get a better view of the crowded room over the sea of hats.

"Say there, cowboy, you taking up the occupation?" A miner and his cronies lounged at the bar with mugs of beer.

"Hell no." Deerhorn held on to the bar's oak ledge. "I wouldn't go getting your hopes up, girls," he mocked the man and his group of friends.

"Whooee!" the miners laughed. "You got any guns under that red critter that's likely to scare us off?"

"What Thomas G. Deerhorn's got under this hyar—" he searched the room again, then seeing Jack, hopped down "—is God's given gun and what all the ladies are after."

Tom elbowed his way through the crowd, disregarding the pats on his back and the whistles over his exposed legs.

"Steele! Jack Steele!"

Jack lifted his gaze, his eyes widening a fraction as he took in Deerhorn's costume. "What the hell happened to you?"

"Never mind about me," Tom said with a seriousness Jack took for what it was worth. "I seen that fine lady friend

287

of yours leaving the assayer's office in front of the barrel of a gun."

Jack's pulse stumbled as he bolted out of his chair so quickly, it toppled. "When was this?"

"Not more than thirty minutes ago."

Jack had gotten halfway through the front door when Deerhorn caught up to him. "What do you want me to do? I can get my shootin' irons and meet you—"

Jack called over his shoulder and in a voice layered with held-in-check emotions, ordered, "I want you to round up Sheriff Bullock and send him over to the assayer's."

Deerhorn stopped dead in his tracks. "We don't need the law in on this. This is work fer gun experts like ourselves."

Jack turned on his heels and grabbed Deerhorn by the fur collar. "I am the law." He shoved his Pinkerton identification up Deerhorn's nose, then left Deerhorn standing in the middle of the street, his face as buttery as dough.

He'd swallowed his chaw.

It took Tom Deerhorn a second to get his wind back, and when he did, he ran like the dickens to the sheriff's office, the ends of Amaryllis's fancy red coat floating over his knobby knees.

Holly knew with stunning clarity where Devlin Breedlove was taking her; she couldn't understand why. They'd saddled up horses from Wes Travis's livery, Breedlove fetching Jubilee for her.

That had been some time ago, and now they made their way through the woods—he was taking her to her claim. For what reasons, she couldn't think of at the moment. Her judgment was gone, her perception blurred. She'd thought Breedlove to be a friend—of sorts.

Once they came into the vague clearing that marked the beginning of Dancer's Destiny, he slowed down his pace and loosened his hold on her reins. His horse snorted and blew as he dismounted and came around to force her down.

"What are we doing here?" she managed to ask.

Breedlove didn't allow her an answer, merely tightened his fingers around her upper arm again and hastily tethered the animals.

It was nearly pitch-black outside, and though she knew the perimeters of her claim, even she had a hard time distinguishing them.

Devlin steered her toward the shaft's opening, his footsteps sound and steady. Then he took out a small piece of oilcloth that had been folded in his breast pocket and plucked up a match. As he struck it with his thumb, a fuzzy yellow flame appeared, casting his face in a muted pallor.

Grabbing her arm, he pushed her to the claim's entrance and handed her a match. "Go down and light the first candle."

Holly thought for a long second, weighing out the odds of running. Breedlove being city-soft, the chances of outrunning him could possibly be in her favor. But could she outrun his gun? She glared at him and decided to go down. She feared the gun and knew she would have a better chance in the tunnel. She was familiar with the mine, and Breedlove wasn't. She knew each curve and drift, and if any opportunity came to run away from him, she would have the advantage over him.

Slowly she grabbed hold of the rope ladder she kept at the mouth and made her descent.

Devlin Breedlove followed her down once the candle had been lit. She went through the motions of lighting each on their way, resolving to bring him as deep into the interior as possible. That way she'd have more lead space when she'd extinguish them one by one and escape into the darkness of the drifts.

Once at the end of the tunnel, Holly brightened the last candle and stuck it back in its holder. She waited for Breedlove to do something, to say something, but he was so mesmerized by the shaft's walls, he appeared to be in a trance.

He unfastened what she'd thought had been his belt, only to see that on the side of it was a small leather pouch. He dug into the contents and began removing small instruments. At first she thought they looked like physician's tools, then realized they were the numerous utensils he kept at his laboratory.

Holly pressed her back to the edge of the shaft and sidled

closer to the exit. Breedlove picked at the walls, scraping off tiny bits of rock and sand. He rubbed it between his fingers and caressed it, then brought it to his nose and smelled it.

She inched closer to the mouth of the claim, Devlin seemingly unaware of her. She kept her eyes fastened to him and slowly moved away.

"No!"

His voice startled her, its baritone echoing down the damp channels and ending in a chorus of voices that came back to sting at her ears. She stopped and stared at him.

"No! It cannot be. I was so sure once I was here that it would be as I suspected. It has to run along the same line. . . . I know it spiders through this mountain! Plague it all, to come so far and be deceived? I did it all for this. *I* salted the claim of those two miners on Deadwood Creek to keep everyone away from here. From this!"

Holly seized the moment of his madness and made a dash for the exit. She'd run as far as the first candle in the narrow drift and just snuffed it out when he raked her hips and plunged her toward the floor. She hit the ground with a thump, biting back the dirt, her hands scraped by the tiny rocks underneath her.

She let out a wounded cry in the dark, its echo sifting through the blackness as she was dragged back the way she'd come.

"I didn't say you could go yet. When the time comes, your soul will make it out."

His chilling words froze the blood in her veins.

He meant to kill her.

Chapter Sixteen

At the end of the claim, Devlin thrust Holly next to the wall. A shooting dart speared its way up her spine where her back connected with the rough-hewn walls. Small trickles of earth sifted down to cover her head with particles of sediment.

Devlin leaned on the wall across from her and examined the sides of the tunnel with a haunted gaze. "I thought you too unskilled to take the right samples to me. But it's here . . . I know it. Dancer had it."

Holly, too shaken to manage a reply, could only lick the dryness from her lips and blink the dust from her lashes.

"Where does that other winze lead to?" Devlin asked suddenly, his voice booming through the chamber. "The one we passed."

"Nowhere," Holly whispered. "It stops just a few yards in."

"That must be it then!" He brought his hand to his mouth and absently ran his fingers over his brown mustache. "The fool turned the wrong direction. . . . It would make sense that what you've been giving me is worthless. The samples he brought me months ago were filled with promise of color."

"If you want the claim, I'll give it to you."

"You take me for a bigger fool than Dancer if you think I'd allow that." Devlin scanned the ceiling, then the surrounding area. "No. I don't think you'll need to give me anything. I'll have it regardless." Kneeling down, he sorted through the equipment she kept in the mine. He passed over shovels, picks, and a cold lantern, then snatched up her metal canister of black powder.

"What are you going to do with that?" she croaked, but knowing exactly what he planned to do.

"I'm afraid there's going to be a little accident. You weren't very careful, you see, and come morning when you are nowhere to be found, they'll come searching for you—only to discover you've been killed in a cave-in. Alas, Mrs. Dancer, this is where we part ways."

Holly scrambled to her feet, intent on running at all costs.

Yet once again, he slammed her flat with a short, vicious tackle to the tunnel floor. Flailing and thrashing her legs, she fought him with her every ounce of strength. Between kicks, she screamed, hoping for the remotest of possibility she would be heard.

Breedlove fought back, and she vaguely fathomed she was doing some good, for he had a hard time subduing her. For a minute she thought she could get away from him. His hands let go of her middle after she connected with his lower abdomen. Struggling to her knees, she balled the skirt of her dress out of her way. She'd barely taken a single step when she collided with a solid chest.

She shrieked, not knowing which way to go. Strong arms came down around her shoulders and pulled her toward an equally strong chest. She twisted away, wanting to flee, but as she did, something clicked in the recesses of her mind.

Jack.

Jack held her.

The feel of his muscles, the play of his hands across her back, and even the smell of him alerted her to his presence. Had he not held her, she surely would have fallen.

His chest rumbled as he spoke to another man who'd gone around him. "He's in there."

Seth Bullock, his Springfield revolver poised on Devlin Breedlove, stepped into the low light and ordered the assayer to his feet.

Devlin slowly rose, his hair tumbling over his brow. "This is all a mistake," he said, trying his best to make light of the situation.

"It is a mistake," the sheriff reiterated. "And you made it." He took out his handcuffs and shackled them to Breedlove's wrists.

Jack's fingers brushed Holly's cheek. "Are you all right?"

"Yes . . . I think so." Her neck ached and she rested her cheek on his chest. "Now that you're here. Oh, Jack, he was going to kill me."

Steele cradled her head tightly, pressing his lips into her hair. "It's over." Raising her chin, he brought his warm mouth to hers and kissed her.

Holly awoke in her room, though not enough to will her eyelids open. She felt the heat of a fire which had been stoked in her heater and the soft comfort of her bed encasing her. She'd been dressed in her nightgown, and all around her, she heard muffled voices. When she was able, she discerned them as belonging to Josephine and Carrie Goodnight. Then there was a baritone that she didn't quite recognize. Dozing off for a minute, she became conscious of it belonging to Conrath La Fors.

"My lands," Josephine cried. "She's waking up."

When Holly flitted her lashes, Josephine Goodnight's face came into view, with lines of worry across it. "Oh, you gave us all a fright. When the sheriff knocked on the door to come fetch me, I about left in my robe, Mrs. Dancer."

Carrie loomed over the bed, as well as Conrath, his arm absently around her waist.

"How did I get here?" Holly found her throat sore and her words soft as snow.

"Mr. Steele brought you," Josephine supplied, then looked over her shoulder briefly. "There is a lot of good in that man that I'm ashamed I didn't see before. He's a lawman, you know. A Pinkerton detective." She said it with pride.

"Where is he?" Holly managed, feeling more tired than she had in her entire life.

"Where I should be," came Jack's voice from the proximity of her desk. Holly heard his Wellingtons over the wooden floorboards as he came to stand next to the bed.

Feebly Holly smiled at him. There were a hundred different things she wanted to tell him; though of them all, there were only three small words that really meant anything.

Josephine waved her hands. "I don't think you should distress yourself, Mrs. Dancer. I've got a crock of vegetable soup on in the kitchen. I'll be bringing it up. It's just the thing you need; that and a good night's rest." She stood and shooed Carrie and Conrath away. "Everybody out and let Mrs. Dancer have some peace and quiet."

Carrie held back and knelt beside the iron headboard. She looked into Holly's face, her hazel eyes soft and sparkling. She whispered in a low tone that only Holly could hear. "Anything worth having is worth fighting for. Mr. Steele has been here the whole time. He loves you awfully, Mrs. Dancer."

Tears crept into Holly's eyes and she blinked them back. "Thank you, Carrie."

Carrie rose and departed with Conrath. Mrs. Goodnight swished Jack from the room, bringing up the rear of the group.

Defenseless to do anything about Jack's leaving, Holly could only watch him go.

The door hadn't even closed when she heard Carrie calling out she'd left her shawl, and would Mr. Steele be a gentleman and get it for her. Carrie disregarded all her mother's protests that she leave it for now; soon after, the footfalls faded away.

Except for one.

Jack filled the doorway. Handsome as no man she'd ever seen before, he strode to her, a hesitant smile on his lips. He'd taken off his hat, his ulster hanging open with a show of guns underneath. "How do you really feel?"

"Foolish." She struggled to sit up, but the dull throbbing in her head wouldn't allow it. "I should have told you I lost my earring the morning Earl died. But I was afraid you wouldn't believe me."

Jack sat down on the bed's edge and smoothed her hair.

His fingers felt warm and hard against her forehead, and she shivered from the tiny sparks working through her body. "I would have believed you."

"I know that." Holly smiled softly at him.

A heartbeat passed and then they both spoke at the same time, Jack shrugging off with a slight laugh to let her speak. "What were you going to say?"

"I was going to ask you how you found me."

Jack picked up a strand of her hair and caressed it between his fingers. "Tom Deerhorn. The crazy cowboy that keeps getting in my way." Jack smiled lopsidedly, as if remembering the past escapades. "For once, he did good. He got me out of the Red Bird and told me he saw you with Breedlove. I sent for the sheriff and met him in Breedlove's office."

"You told the sheriff about your real identity . . . and the Goodnights. Why?"

"I told Bullock the day we got back into Deadwood." Dropping the lock, he smoothed it behind her ear. His touch made her skin tingle, and she felt a warm blush color her cheeks. "I couldn't risk the chance of something happening to you. For the first time, I went against Pinkerton's system of one man on the job. I had to bring in another lawman."

"When Earl died . . . you were with the sheriff."

"Yeah. He called me out with him."

"And the earring . . . Did you know I had a pair like that?"

"I did."

"Then why . . . ?"

"Why didn't I ask you about them?"

She nodded, her head pounding with the slow traces of a strong headache.

"Because I knew it couldn't be yours. The horse tracks left at Whitewood Creek didn't belong to your horse. Yours picks up a crooked track."

Holly tried to smile. "I guess I should be glad for that."

Jack brought his fingers over her lips. "When I saw the blood in Breedlove's office, I lost control. Seth Bullock almost had to haul off and hit me."

"What happened to Devlin?"

"He's in the jail. Don't worry about it. There's nothing else that's going to happen now. He'll be standing trial."

As much as Holly loved him, and he loved her, she knew that there was still a barrier between them. "I saw your . . . I saw her . . . this afternoon. In Chinatown." Holly hesitated with the question that tormented her. "Oh, Jack, do you really think she's lying?"

Jack's hesitation was just as misplaced as hers. "I would swear it." Stroking her cheek, he said, "I still haven't been able to get an answer from my lawyer. The telegraph office isn't my favorite establishment."

"It's only been open for three months. I guess it's understandable they have trouble, but it's hard to take." Holly sighed. "I think she needs a good smack so she'll fess up."

Jack threw his head back, and deep, rumbling laughter filled his chest. "Baby, I didn't know you had a mean streak in you."

"I'm getting one."

Holly was afraid to ask him what came next. Were he still married to Vanessa, it would be the end . . . unless he still wanted to proceed with a divorce, which could take a long time. Though as dismal as that was, the other answer was just as frightening. Were he free of Vanessa, what would happen between them? Jack had made no mention of marriage, and even she wasn't sure about it. There were so many things to consider . . . so many things different between them. She could only hope love would be enough.

For now, it was.

For now, all that mattered was Jack as he kissed her gently on the lips.

The crowded interior of the Melodeon overflowed with swarthy men armed in rough costumes to take in the evening show. Candles in tin sconces anchored on the walls burned dim. Lamps smoked in the drafts from windows let down to renew the air in the cramped room. The last games of keno played out, the large wheel flapping to a stop and a number being called out. Someone yelled, "Keno!" while others muttered oaths.

A handful of gents started clapping in unison, their gazes directed toward the footlighted stage. Its long curtain was down, cascaded in velvet ripples of gold. A banjo picked out a tune; minstrelsy and ballad singing took up in the corner. Soon after, Adley Seeks, decked out in the finest of selections from the local haberdashery, cut his way through the host. "All promenade to the bar and make room for the ladies!"

The long polished bar was immediately invaded by zealous patrons who took their drinks back to their appropriate seats, and some not so appropriate, as more than one bout of fisticuffs broke out over who would tenant the front row. When at last the final punch was delivered, the room calmed enough to let the entertainment get under way.

Holly eased around the front doors, nearly disguised in her long pelisse with its hood turned up over her head. She positioned herself at an available space in the rear, amazed at the oversight on everyone's part in failing to observe that she was a female, and obviously not one of the upstairs girls. When the stage ropes creaked, hoisting the massive curtain upward, she could see why she'd been overlooked.

There on the wide stage stood a dozen of Adley's new eastern girls, made-up with pots of cosmetics. Posed in dead center, Vanessa Burnett wore a heavy black satin gown with a wide skirt that swept the floor, finished with a lavish double ruffle. The little basque was tightly fitted, very low in the neck, and had short, puffed sleeves. But it was not the cut or tight fit that made it distinctive. Rich embroidery in the figures and symbols of cattle brands, interspersed with shining silver roses, covered the entire gown; the appliqués twinkled in resplendent shades of red, blue, green, and purple.

It was clear from all the hoopla and catcalls, each of the local ranchers who'd ridden riotously into Deadwood was finding his own brand on that gown. Even cattlemen looking for a little diversion when coming into town from miles away could find their stamp.

How Vanessa had managed that in the short time she'd been in Deadwood, Holly could only speculate.

The roars and hollers were nearly deafening, and the girls had been standing there for a strong ten minutes before it even got quiet enough for Adley to commence with the proceedings.

The crowd went crazy as the girls did a risqué dance and showed a lot of legs in fishnet stockings. Vanessa more or less paraded around them all, swishing a little of this, shaking a little of that. In all the time the rusty piano music cranked out, her lips remained fixed in an artful smile of ruby red.

Jealousy consumed Holly. The woman was undeniably beautiful. Her figure was lush and shapely; her black hair curled in small waves, fanning above her brow in a seductive swirl.

By the dance's end, the place fairly burst at the seams. Holly was shoved against the wall as even the working girls from the Melodeon, Bella Union, and Wide West Saloon had come on in to see the show.

Then the noise level dropped to an amazingly low volume; enough so that when someone coughed, half a dozen revolvers whipped out and trained on the man, warning him to keep his explosive noise at bay.

Even Holly anticipated what was to follow as Adley made a big to-do over the extinguishing of nearly all the footlights except the middle three. The candlelight reflected off Vanessa's gown, spangling the crowd in shimmering drops of blinding white each time she moved.

Wedged in the corner, the piano, violin, and even a clarinet struck up a lilting melody, and Vanessa began to sing; she had a lovely voice, deep and throaty. She cast a spell over everyone in the house.

The song ended, and Holly thought the saloon would come down around them with the applause being so loud. Vanessa elegantly curtsied, her face animated as if she lived for the feeling of praise. She strolled from the stage and exited, the whistles and calls growing higher for an encore. To their delight, she gave them several.

When the evening concluded, Vanessa's cheeks were flushed rose from the enthusiastic fanfare. Leaving the stage for the last time, she was circled by a group of men, young and old, thin and heavy, who waited at the edge of the platform. She bantered with them all.

One man, strikingly handsome, rested his elbows at the rail. Vanessa sidled closer to him, dipped and bent, expertly showing off the best features of her body. She flirted brazenly with him, laughing and brushing up against him.

Holly stared, suddenly not caring to confront the woman at all. She'd come to the Gem to demand Vanessa tell her the truth about her marriage. And now it didn't matter.

It wouldn't matter in a thousand years if Vanessa was still married to Jack. She didn't love him. It was so obvious, it was sickening. She had no intentions of being with Jack, now or ever. She'd left him in Chicago, much as he'd left her. It was there the marriage had dissolved; whether legal or not, it was no more.

With a faint smile of her own, Holly left the Gem with all its subtle lights and laughter. She left behind the past, confident for the first time that there would be a future.

Jack exited the sheriff's office with the proper documents to send to William Pinkerton. He'd met one last time with Edward McIntyre and Seth Bullock, both men extending handshakes. Officially he had nothing to bind him to Deadwood.

Except Holly Dancer.

As he made his way toward the center of town, it struck him that the night air had held on to some of the day's warmth. The evening wasn't nearly as cold as it had been. Seasons were changing; he was changing with them. Jack wondered where his next case would take him. Under normal circumstances, he'd be anxious to get on with something new; now none of the anticipation filled him.

It never occurred to him that one day he may want to leave detective work. He'd run headlong into it without much thought to anything else. Though through the years, it had become a part of him. A complex part which he hadn't understood until now meant quite a bit to him. There was a satisfaction he felt when a case ended, much as one would feel upon completing an intricate puzzle.

Things had gone beyond his expectations. He was now

considering marriage. Wrong, there was no considering it. He wanted to marry Holly. But what kind of life could he offer her without giving up his own livelihood? It seemed a selfish reflection, but one that he couldn't disregard altogether without being unfair to them both. The life of a detective was more suitable for a single man.

Jack came to the corner of Main and Lee, where he crossed over to the Red Bird. He'd left the Gem several days ago, not wanting to confront Vanessa again, not trusting himself to confront her. Halfway to the other side, Holly ran to meet up with him.

Breathless, she practically jumped into his arms and buried her face in his collar.

"Baby," he rasped, his own breath snatched away, but not from any exertion. "I'm glad to see you, too, but do you know what time it is?"

She laughed and kissed him on the mouth. "Way after midnight. I don't care."

Jack fit her more closely to him. "I care. It isn't safe for a woman like you at this hour."

"Jack, I went to the Gem and I saw her. She doesn't love you; I don't think she ever did." She sighed in his embrace. "I love you, and nothing else matters."

"You saw Vanessa?"

"Yes. I was going to talk to her, but I changed my mind. It doesn't matter now."

The words tore through Jack, and he knew she was right. Everything would have to fall into place. He wanted nothing more than to take her away and make love to her. To show her how much he needed her.

While Jack was thinking of the respectable reasons not to take her to her room, James Halley, the telegraph official, barreled down the street. The wind from the force of his run caught the brim of his visor and snatched it from the top of his head.

"Mr. Steele! Glad I saw you before going down to the Red Bird." He tried to get hold of his breath. "Got that telegram from Chicago you've been waiting for. Came in just five minutes ago." Handing Jack the half-folded piece of paper, James mopped at his brow with his jacket cuff.

Jack released Holly to take the paper, his throat going dry as a brittle leaf. "Thanks."

"You bet," Halley huffed. "You said it was important." He nodded to Holly. "'Evening, Mrs. Dancer." He stood there awkwardly a moment, as if waiting for Jack to open the message and comprehend its meaning. When no move was made to do that, he said, "Well, I'll see you folks off. 'Evening."

Jack looked down at the snowy paper in his hand, realizing his fingers shook. Glancing at Holly, he saw his own worry mirrored in her azure eyes.

Holly rested her cheek on Jack's bare chest and snuggled into the warm crook of his arm. She felt more complete, more content, in the last few minutes than any time in her life.

They'd made love with surprising urgency and a swiftness Jack had apologized for; but she had been just as eager. Though there had been no foreplay that led up to the interlude, Holly had been completely fulfilled.

As she lay listening to the thrum of Jack's heart, she smiled, not thinking about anything but the moment.

Jack played his fingers across the skin of her back, massaging her spine and sending shivers of pleasure through her.

"I think," Holly said, "I'd like to stay this way forever."

Jack smiled. "Yeah. Damn nice way." He grew thoughtful. "You know, all these years, I never felt married. Now I know it was because I wasn't."

Holly glanced to the opened telegraph that rested on the desktop. When they'd opened it, it had simply stated:

DIVORCE OFFICIAL ON SEPTEMBER 17, 1873

Sighing, Jack cradled her closer. "I know I'm a sorry substitute for a husband, but I'd like to marry you."

Holly propped herself up on her elbow and stared into his gray eyes. "Would you really want to marry me, Jack?"

"Hell yes." He kissed her soundly. "Hell yes."

She spoke on his lips. "Is your job always dangerous?"

"Mostly. Christ, maybe I should give it up."

"You won't," she told him softly. "You can't. Whether you like it or not, you are a part of Jackson Steele."

He held her strong and hard, kissing her again. "Do you know that it's going to be difficult for you? At times, you'll be deprived of my company, and you'll have to shut your eyes to the fact that sometimes I have to associate with all kinds of women to solve a case."

"As long as you don't touch them."

"I don't have any reason to."

She toyed with the dark wedge of hair on his bare chest. "You haven't said yes yet." His eyes were deep and penetrating, filled with longing.

"Yes. You knew it would be yes." She kissed him and teased his lower lip with her teeth. "What are you thinking of?"

His voice resounded within his chest against her breasts. "Whatever it is, I'm still thinking it."

Then he rolled her over and pressed her into the mattress, his body covering hers.

A week later, Holly and Jack were married by Reverend L. P. Norcross in a quiet ceremony in a carpenter's shop across from Boughton and Berry's Sawmill. The borrowed shop was acting as the Congregational Church of Deadwood until one could be built, the air pungent with fresh-cut wood and sweet-smelling sap. The gathering was small, consisting of the Goodnight family, Conrath La Fors, Lee-Ash Malmer, and Sheriff Bullock, as well as Tom Deerhorn.

It was, after all, Deerhorn who'd played a part in Holly's rescue.

When they were pronounced husband and wife, congratulations flowed. The newlyweds stepped several businesses down to have their wedding portrait taken at Monsieur Andre's, a new-to-Deadwood photographer.

Folding his arms over his chest and feeling the most damned proud a man could, Jack watched as Andre stationed his wife in front of a curtain.

Holly looked radiant in her gown of black lace with floral rose accents. She'd pulled her hair on top of her head in a loose twist, ornamenting it with a sprig of tiny white flowers and a single ribbon to match the splendid crimson color of her dress. New pearl earrings dangled from her earlobes, a wedding gift from him.

"Monsieur, now you."

Jack moved toward them, looking down intently at Holly.

Holly felt herself involuntarily tremble, gazing at the handsome picture her husband made, with his dark hair combed back, a black suit about his broad shoulders, and the soft cut of his robin's-egg blue shirt. She warmed as the Frenchman eased her into the crook of Jack's arm and took long minutes positioning them to face the camera.

"I am ready. Make me zee how in love you are, monsieur." Andre removed the brass cap and pulled a black slide from the rear of his camera.

Muscles cramped in Jack's neck from the awkward position he'd been made to hold, and in that instant, he moved. He didn't want to tell Andre how much he loved his wife, he wanted to tell Holly.

"The hell with it," Jack mumbled, and broke his stance to fit Holly intimately into his arms. He lifted her chin with his finger, her hand coming up to meet his. She gazed at him with a reflection of love so strong, it made him override every moment in his life as insignificant until now. "I love you, Holly."

Then he kissed her; softly, lovingly.

"Mon dieu!" Andre cried, tapping his left foot and capping the lens. He swiftly pushed the slide into the plate case. "You should not have moved! Zis is horrible. You might have blurred the photograph. I will have to take it over."

"I don't want to take it again." Jack brushed his lips across Holly's, admiring the blush to her cheeks, the fullness of her mouth. "I want this one. Blurred or not."

"But, monsieur—"

"I don't care if it doesn't look right—it felt right." Jack clasped Holly's hand in his, stroking the gold band on her wedding finger. "We'll be back for it. Later. Much later. Quite possibly tomorrow."

Holly and Jack advanced to Goodnight's Restaurant for a

wedding supper and the cake—baked in the new Perry and Co. stove, which had arrived a few days before.

Holly kept peeking glances at Jack as he stood on the other side of the dining room dressed in his elegant black suit. He conversed with Seth Bullock, and she wondered if they discussed Jack's next assignment. It would be in Arizona. The prospect excited her; it would be a grand adventure, her life with Jack.

Lee-Ash came to her and kissed her cheek, his full gray mustache tickling her skin. "Well, darlin', I reckon this is it. I cain't say I'm happy about seeing you go."

Holly fought back tears, telling herself she would not cry. "I will miss you, Lee-Ash, more than you know. You were my special friend . . . my only friend." Despite her resolve, a tear slipped free. "I want to give you something, and I'll have no argument about it. I already gave my one claim to Carrie—the one I bought from the widow a while back. Carrie and Conrath are going to be married, and it would be a hopeful wedding present—maybe settle Conrath down." Holly stared at Lee-Ash's ruddy face, observing his hollow cheekbones. He looked years older to her; too old to be working alone. "I'm giving you Dancer's Destiny."

He made a bit of a protest, and she silenced him with a well-meant frown. "I told you, I won't have any arguments. I want you to have it. Maybe there is gold in it, after all. Devlin—" she said the name with a slight pause "—seemed to think so, though I can't honestly say I trust his mind. I couldn't think of selling it. . . . I worked too hard."

Lee-Ash's eyes brimmed with moisture, and he yanked out his handkerchief and blew his nose. "I swear, if this don't beat all. You've gone and ruined me to blubberin'." Grabbing her in a big bear hug, he crushed her to him. "You better write or I'll be one ornery old cuss."

"I will," she said into his sleeve. "There's one more thing. Do you think that if you happen to see Mr. Deerhorn and he's in need, could you offer him work in the claim?"

Straightening with a sniff, Lee-Ash lifted his gaze to Tom Deerhorn, who stood next to the sideboard, cleaning his fingernails with a pocket knife. "Durn, it would have to be him who spied you that night. All right, darlin', I'm not saying I like it, but if the need be, I reckon I'll ask him."

"Thank you, Lee-Ash. You be careful. With the talk of a Sioux uprising, I'll be worried about you."

Jack came up to them and put his arm around Holly. She melted next to him, resisting the urge to rest her cheek on his chest.

"Son, I hear of one durn thing you ain't doin' right by my Holly, you can bet I'll come callin' after you."

"You don't have to worry about it, old man. I love her."

Holly felt a heat warm her insides, much as if she'd taken a sip of the finest brandy. It swirled in a soothing liquid, covering her until her heart sang.

Jack loved her.

And she loved him.

The talk around her filtered through her mind, but without much meaning as she was preoccupied with her own thoughts. She smiled to herself thinking of the days to come, thinking of the mountains and the valleys they would cross. Spring had come with all its glory and seasoned the hillsides with wildflowers in warm colors: yellow, orange, and bronze.

Gold no longer came in the form of ore or dust; the value changed. It was now a season that she could follow and admire, cherish and love, all her days long.

Epilogue

"*F*ine woman that Mrs. Steele," Tom Deerhorn accoladed. "Damn fine. She really said to take me into hiring out this hyar gold mine, huh?"

Lee-Ash led the way through Dancer's Destiny with a glowing lantern that reflected off the tunnel's damp sides. "Yep, she did, bless her foolhardy heart. So don't go give me call to kick your behind. Only reason I'm takin' you on at all is 'cause my own claim is buried under from a durn cave-in." Lee-Ash ground out a few choice oaths. "Take me months to brace it up again."

"You know, much as I appreciate this hyar offer you made me, I still think my talents are being flat wasted. I'm a damn better gunman and card player."

Deerhorn stepped on Lee-Ash's heel, and Lee-Ash swung around with a warning. "Watch where you're going."

"Sorry. You know, my sugar, she won't speak to me unless I bring in some money. She's damn mad at me since I bought this hyar with all my winnings." Deerhorn fondled the two-foot-long watch chain with gold nuggets the size of chestnuts that looped out of his flannel pocket. "Said fer me to take it back to the jewelers. No, sir. Not this boy. I don't care if she is my wife." He stepped on Lee-Ash's heel again.

"Watch it!"

"Sorry," Deerhorn muttered, and wiped his nose with the sleeve of his shirt.

"Why don't you use a handkerchief?" Lee-Ash glowered at him.

"Damn near don't need one when I got this hyar." He swiped at his sleeve again.

Grumbling, Lee-Ash made a move forward when Deerhorn locked his hand on his shoulder. "What's that down yonder?"

Tom pointed at the original length of tunnel Billy Dancer had cut into, before stopping it after several yards. It had been abandoned to continue in an eastern direction; Lee-Ash kept a storage reserve of a few dynamite sticks there, so they'd be out of his way. One lay only four feet from the opening.

"It's an old winze," Lee-Ash commented, then shrugged free of Deerhorn.

"Yeah . . . ?" Lingering back in the semidarkness, Deerhorn stuck a crooked cigarette on his lips. He fingered a match and scratched it with his thumbnail. Raising the flame to his smoke, he lit it, then flicked the match into the winze with a shrug.

A loud concussion rocked the earth, the force of it sweeping Tom right off his feet, landing him square on the behind. His ears rang much as a cluster of church bells on a Sunday morning. He wheezed and coughed, sputtering like a coffeepot on an open flame.

Boot tips turned up and legs spread out in front of him, Tom spied the light of Lee-Ash's lantern as the old man ran toward him. "What in durn tarnation were you thinkin'?! You fool idiot! You were likely to blow us to our maker's afore our time!"

He could see the old-timer's mouth moving, but nothing came out—or at least he didn't hear anything. The light came over Deerhorn, and he thought better of asking Lee-Ash for a hand up. He looked down at his clothing; blotched with black, he was smoked up like a ham. Thank the good Lord, his watch chain hadn't a mark on it. "What the deuce happened?" he yelled, over the incessant buzz in his head. He rubbed at his face, feeling a fine grit across it.

"What happened?! You put a match to a stick of explosives, you lame cuss." Lee-Ash stepped into the abandoned drift to assess the damaged walls still crumbling down in a fine trickle, then he threw down his forage cap. "I knew this weren't no good idea!" Suddenly bits of the ceiling sifted down on Lee-Ash's head. Pieces of quartz with traces of gold broke off from an outcrop of a rich vein.

Under the light, the dust sparkled and shimmered like fine sequins, settling over Lee-Ash's shoulders. It salted the floor and painted a picture of majesty.

Lee-Ash's fingers shook as he lifted the lantern to poke at the ledge above his head. Chunks of glassy, milky white quartz held fine threads and plates of gold embedded in the rock. "Gold." He said it so softly, it merely mouthed from his lips silently in slow motion. "Gold. Gold. Gold."

Deerhorn bugged his brown eyes and tripped up next to Lee-Ash. "What are you saying? What are you saying?!"

"Gold!"

"Gold? You said gold?!"

Lee-Ash was laughing hysterically and grabbed hold of Deerhorn's hands, jumping them both up and down. "It's gold! We're rich!"

"Gold?!" Deerhorn youthfully giggled, his knees nearly buckling. Digging his fingers into the sifting walls, he bunched his hands into fists. "You mean it's mine, too?"

"Son, were you not such an incompetent mule, we wouldn't have struck it. Wait till we write Holly and tell her!"

"Gold!" Deerhorn screamed, barely hearing himself. "Amaryllis, sugar, ya'll are going to have as many chocolates as your lily white body can stuff into a fancy dress! It's gold!"

It was what Devlin Breedlove had killed for; what inspired Billy Dancer to come West for; and what Holly had dreamed of.

It was, indeed, the missing link to the Homestake Mine.

Author's Note

In creating this work of fiction, I tried to be as accurate as possible; however, for the sake of the story, I took some creative liberties.

Adley Seeks was a character of my own invention based upon two men: Johnny the Oyster, who worked for Nuttall and Mann's No. Ten, and Johnny Burns, the real box herder for the Gem Theater. Dewdrop, the goat, was a figment of my own imagination.

I moved a few buildings here and there; Crumbs of Comfort Along the Crack in the Wall was really a lunch counter in between the Bella Union and No. Ten.

Sam Bass, the man responsible for Johnny Slaughter's murder, was wounded in an ambush in Texas; he died the following day, July 21, 1878, on his twenty-seventh birthday.

Martha Jane Cannary did indeed work for a time as a waitress after Wild Bill Hickok's death in the No. Ten on August 2, 1876. The cliff on which Jack Steele and Edward McIntyre stood was a grave site, but not incorporated to Mount Moriah Cemetery until 1895. Wild Bill's body was exhumed from the city in 1878 and laid to rest there.

Martha Jane died on August 1, 1903, and was buried next to him.

Pinkerton's National Detective Agency was founded in 1850 by Allan Pinkerton, left to Robert and William Pinkerton, whose sons continued the organization as a model for a new federal agency—the FBI.

The U.S. Supreme Court decreed the Black Hills illegally taken from the Indians, and it approved a $122.5 million settlement. Spurning this award, many Sioux are demonstrating for the return of their sacred Paha-Sapa.

The Homestake Mine, between 1877 and 1901, yielded George Hearst $4 million in gold and silver. Any link between the Homestake and Dancer's Destiny was purely wishful thinking on my part.

My special thanks to Kathleen Sage, a colleague whose friendship and intellect were instrumental in shaping this endeavor into a novel. And to Kat Martin, who read like mad so I wouldn't miss my deadline. Also, thanks to my parents, Frank and Gloria Wysocki, for their keen eyes.

It's always nice to hear from my readers. Your comments are invaluable to me. If you have a minute, drop me a note. A self-addressed, stamped envelope would be helpful.

Stef Ann Holm
P.O. Box 1564
Simi Valley, CA 93062

A Captivating New Novel of Passion and Pride in the
Bestselling Tradition of *A Knight In Shining Armor*

JUDE DEVERAUX

ETERNITY

The saga of the Montgomery family continues in
the stunning new novel from the *New York Times*
bestselling author Jude Deveraux.

Carrie Montgomery had never had to fight for
anything—until she met the most wonderful, most
exasperating man. Savor the romance and
adventure as they discover if their love can last for
all ETERNITY.

Available in Paperback from Pocket Star Books

POCKET
STAR
BOOKS

470-01